GIA'S FOLLY
THE CHOSEN CHAMPION
BOOK 1

SECOND EDITION
By: Edmund E. Umstot Jr.

INTRODUCTION
Zindar

In all the universe, there are hundreds of billions of stars. There is what seems to be an infinite number of planets soaring around these stars, yet in the entire universe there are only thirteen stars that has produced a single planet each to inhabit humanoids. Of all the species of creatures ever created, only these humanoids have ever looked up into the sky and wondered, have ever thought of what was out there, ever thought that maybe they were not alone. Only the humanoids ever really cared that they might have cousins out beyond the stars. Of the thirteen planets, only seven have been created that are the home to humans, the very beings that have been created in the images of the gods. Or maybe, actually they are the god's own offspring? Sometimes, one can only sit back and wonder! They certainly often act as though they are! Then one must remember it is this strange and unique species that are pawns in the god's games. It is this species that the balance of light and darkness, order and chaos, good and evil, has been given to maintain. It is to this species that the entire universe is watching for its ultimate survival.
May the GODS have mercy on us all!

From the chronicles of Massy Thorn, High Priestess to
Holy GIA, The Mother of Creation
and Friend of the CHOSEN

In the Universe, also called the Prime Material Plane, one of the largest of known stars positioned at the very center of creation, possesses the tiniest planet of humanoid habitation. It is in this galaxy of stars that the gods were born. It is here that Gia first opened her eyes, spread her arms wide, and first uttered the phrase "I AM!"

Or so it is said!

Gia, the only true creation of the entity we call The Father of Manifestation, was created out of nothing and when she said, I AM, all of creation began in one cosmic explosion. Thus, the mother was born!

It is in this galaxy that Zindar was made, and on this planet, the smallest of worlds, that the Garden of Pan was born. It has been called by many names in the worlds of humanoid habitation. The Humans have had the most different of religions, and amongst them the most different ideas of creation. They have called Pan by so many different names that even the gods, themselves, have often times become confused. It is here that Pan was awakened, the living Garden, the hub of all life, the beginning of creation, and still the home of The Mother Goddess, Gia.

Also, known by many different names, amongst the humanoids, the mother of Creation has been watching, manipulating, and controlling, since the dawn of time. The Mother has been watching her little experiments, with the open joy of a proud parent. The other gods seem incapable of the amusements that Gia has with her creations. The other Gods seem to view the humanoids, with so much disdain.

The chess pieces, little else, in the games of life. Of course, the gods themselves are really nothing more than pieces in the game that Gia has been playing, with herself. And, on the fateful day that the mother of all the gods, realized that she was not the omnipresent being she thought, that they all thought, one of those gods stepped aside and evil was brought to the worlds.

Hear the story, oh mortals. Hear and understand, just how close to utter oblivion we all became:

The beauty of the Garden spreads for miles, but today there is much discontent. Kutulu Lucifer and Jeasuas were once again watching their game pieces play out a battle they had created.

Kutulu was bored! His creation of a universe, he called Hell was a near failure. The ugliness was almost more than he could stand to look upon. He was so sure that he could do whatever the mother could, and seeing the near failures at creating that his siblings had done, he decided to show them how to do it.

After all he was the first born, the brightest and most beautiful of the Ancient Ones. His creation of the planet Hades was perfect. Yet, when he attempted to create another universe, it ended up becoming a hideous pursuit of imperfections.

Kutulu Lucifer sent six of his nine Archangels to the different levels of Hell in order to stabilize it. The Universe was still acting with unknown chaotic randomness, and the six immediately became deformed. Tiamat grew six new heads; Molech became a monster of such ugliness that he went insane and nearly destroyed the

4

level of Hell where he had arrived. Forcas, once a beautiful angel of glorious imagery, found himself with the lower torso of a great serpent. Asmodeus grew goat legs with cloven hooves and a tail suddenly sprouted from his backside looking as that of a pony. Mammon grew bloated with hideous pockmarks all over his skin.

The worst of the changes had come to Baalzebub. Once the second most powerful Archangel, as well as one of the most beautiful, his head became that of a fly. His sudden multitude of eyes appeared multifaceted; his ears shriveled to form into antennae. His hair became thorny with hard tufts, and the mouth of jagged teeth that would never close, creating a visage so horrible to look at, even most of the other angels would turn away.

The three Archangels that were busy doing something else; were lucky in not being sent. They were the only three of Kutulu Lucifer's angels left that still possessed their father's beauty: Samael, Belial, and Nebiros.

Jeasuas offered to help stabilize the created universe, but Kutulu was reluctant to accept. After all, Jeasuas had to turn to Gia for help when all the angels sent to Heaven, the universe that the second born son had made. The first ones to arrive there had sprouted wings, and gained an aura that glowed eternally and too bright to look upon.

Gia had forbidden the two creations, but of course, boys being what they are, the two eldest were constantly in competition with each other and chose to ignore the request.

When Jeasuas went to the mother and admitted what they had done, asking forgiveness, Gia was persuaded to help and show the godling what he had done wrong.
Kutulu was upset, because Gia would not help him. Of course, he refused to admit that anything had been done wrong, and Gia was not the type of mother that would forgive without first having been asked for it.

The discontent between the brothers grew afterwards. Jeasuas did not hold anything over his brother, but Kutulu Lucifer could not understand how every time the two would do something, Gia seemed more inclined towards forgiving Jeasuas. After all, Kutulu Lucifer was the eldest, but in terms of creation, they were nearly identical. Kutulu was the brightest and most beautiful; yet, even the other Ancient Ones seemed to follow Jeasuas more than Kutulu. The elder brother's ego could not allow him to understand!

5

"This is nothing!" Kutulu Lucifer suddenly said.

"What now?" Jeasuas sighed.

"Day after day, your humans beat my makatiels, or my giants beat your humans. Let's try something different. Spice things up a bit!"

"Tread wary, brother! We are still not fully out of trouble from the last idea, you had!"

"What are you worried over? She'll not hold anything against you! I'll take the blame, like always. You will be coddled and loved, like the butt sucking worm you always act, in her presence!" The added insult towards Jeasuas is what started the downfall of humanity.

The wager was made and the exile was finale. Gia, after it was over, sent all Greater Angels and younger out of the Garden, never to return again. The angels were sent to Heaven or Hell; the mortal humanoids were scattered throughout the universe to the thirteen worlds created for their existence. The wager was one of love verses lust. The original sin was Kutulu Lucifer forcing emotions onto the gods, themselves. Gia's mistake was not seeing the outcome, beforehand.

****

Lilith watched as Adamunith worked with the lion. She had tried to tell him that the big cat would not be able to be tamed. Adamunith had been charmed into thinking he could train it, by Evelith, the silver angel created by Isis. Lilith did not really mind, but she did have other things on her mind. There were a hundred different places she would rather be with her favorite man, and a hundred different things she would rather be doing with him, as well!

Adamunith appeared not to notice. So, intent on the great cat, he did not even see the seductive poses Lilith was making towards him. Normally, he could not refuse his golden angel anything, once she put her mind to wanting. Yet, this time Lilith could not even gain his attention.

"What is it about Evelith that makes him forget me?" Lilith questioned, not for the first time. "After all, she is a small silver, not as pretty, certainly not as vigorous. Can my lover, be so threatened by my superiority? He is a Golden Angel, just like me, after all!"

6

So deep in thought, she did not notice that Samael and Evelith were walking towards where the couple was playing with the cats. Holding hands, they had been conspiring. When they reached the break in the forest, Samael moved to Lilith and Evelith towards Adamunith.

So sure, was Jeasuas, that neither of his Golden Angels could be seduced away from the other, he willingly played the game, Kutulu had suggested. Jeasuas did not notice the attraction the little silver angel had already gained from the oldest living human. What surprised both Ancient Ones was how fast he yielded to Evelith's charms. The biggest surprise was the reaction of Lilith when she saw!

Of course, the first-born Angel of Kutulu Lucifer was not without his own charms, and Lilith was fascinated by the power of Samael. But she did not love him, not like she did her Adamunith.

Samael and Evelith watched the couple for a few minutes; Evelith was giddy watching the man she was already in love; lust with, doing exactly as she had asked. He was working with the lion!

Samael watched the poses of Lilith, as she attempted to garner her lover's attentions. He saw the near perfect form in her movements, yet also, saw the flaws in her auras. Lilith could be seduced by power. He turned to look upon the young lady beside him and smiled.

Evelith had been a rare find. An angel of very little psychic strength, she was pretty, with her golden braids that fell across her shoulder to fall down the front all the way to her naval. Her bright green eyes held an innocence, and the way she was watching Adamunith, Samael was sure, the young silver was passionately attracted to the man. She did not possess the unearthly beauty of Lilith, but Samael was sure the innocent attractiveness would inspire the man more than Lilith's flawless features would.

Jeasuas had made the female Golden Angel too perfect. With the subtle emotions that Kutulu Lucifer had instilled in her, she was a bomb waiting to go off. Lilith moved the Archangel deep inside, and when Samael stepped towards her, feeling his own lustful urges rise, he knew he could win.

The two meter tall Golden Angel looked up and smiled. She had seen Samael before, and always thought him handsome. He closely resembled the Ancient One, Kutulu Lucifer, in looks but held a spark of the darker emotions that none of the other angels seemed to have. A dangerous spark that all the other females seemed to be attracted to, as well!

Lilith stood to her full height, her long bluish black hair, flowing loose down her back to below her buttocks. Her sparkling black eyes radiating questioningly at the man before her, as the nearly perfect woman took a deep breath to bring her racing heart under control.

"What do you want, Samael? I won't be as easily seduced as the other women in the Garden!" She stated calmly, matter of fact. Outwardly she appeared nonplussed, unmoved. Inwardly, she was feeling his charms, feeling the lustful risings; Lilith was feeling her frustrations from Adamunith's earlier rejections.

"Ah, my dear sweet Lilith. Why are you sitting here alone? Someone of your rare perfections and power should be commanding a hundred men to your bidding. Maybe even a thousand!"

She was so sure she could resist the Archangel that she continued to stare into his eyes.

"Sure, have pretty eyes!" She thought, mumbling aloud. Samael smiled.

"Yes, you do!" He answered. Lilith was startled; she did not realize she had spoken her thoughts aloud. "Lilith, you and I should be together. I could make you even greater. I could convince my father to make you even better than your own creator did. Think on it, Lilith! I have Kutulu Lucifer's ear, he would do it for me. And, I would do it, for you!"

Lilith turned to look at her one true love. Adamunith should be concerned at the Archangel's advances. He should be rising up away from the lion to come to her rescue. Adamunith should be saying something, but he wasn't.

Lilith's eyes widened at what she saw. She felt something inside her stir and when Samael touched her, the jealousy rushed through, with a force, no human had ever felt before. Let alone, any angel!

Evelith had moved over to where the man attempted to urge the great cat to lie down. Created by Isis in her own image, Kutulu Lucifer had chosen Evelith for this bet, because he knew the man was already captivated by the Silver Angel. Evelith's imperfect movements complimented the innocent look she carried.

8

When Samael found the nearly perfect state of her mind, he corrupted it with a full instilling of Lust. A lust that would not be sated, until she had what she wanted. And, Evelith's wants, was a man that claimed he belonged to Lilith!

Evelith leaned across the back of the lion and nuzzled its mane. She looked up at the man watching and slowly opened and closed her bright green eyes. When she smiled, her lips opened wide exposing the bright whiteness of her teeth.

"Would you like something to eat?" She asked holding out the piece of fruit. Then thinking herself feeling somewhat more brazen than normal, she followed with Samael's suggestion.

"Or perhaps, you would rather a taste of my lips?" She softly spoke as the blush moved into her cheeks and down her neck. Once again, she slowly batted her eyes.

Adamunith was startled. About to take the fruit, he stopped as his hand was reaching for the pomegranate. He had wondered about Evelith before, but always thought her more of a little sister idolizing her big brother. Now, the woman was attempting to seduce him, and not being near as perfected in it as Lilith, her more forward suggestions, had him off guard. He turned to look at his mate and saw her being entertained by Samael, of all people!

"Evelith, if I accept both offers," he finally began, when she moved off the cat to stand before him. "You must understand that it would never lead to me leaving Lilith!" He finished.

Evelith took the fruit and bit down into it, allowing the juices to spill down her throat and across her breasts. Something else, Samael suggested. The redness of the seeds stained her lips, making them bright, and when she smiled once again, Adamunith moved to her.

Lilith watched as Evelith reached to embrace the Golden Angel and saw the arousal on her lover. Stunned she quickly forgot about the beautiful Archangel standing before her, and could only think about the betrayal.

Samael touched her forehead and opened up the psychic channel within Lilith, adding even more jealousy into her already growing angry mind.

Lashing out, Lilith sent a lightning bolt directly towards the couple. Only Adamunith opening his eyes at that very moment gave him enough warning to fall back to the ground, pulling Evelith onto him.

The flash went sailing across over where the two had been standing and instead, hit directly into the lion, slaying it where it stood. Killing the lion brought the attention of Gia to the game, as well as that of all the Ancient Ones.

When the eight gods appeared, seeing the scene laid out upon the clearing, they wondered what was happening. Evelith lying on top of Adamunith, and Lilith was being embraced by Samael. Only Kutulu Lucifer and Jeasuas knew the full circumstances, but both were too stunned by the actions to properly react.

Gia was incensed. She had forbidden any harm to happen to those animals in her Garden. If Kutulu Lucifer and Jeasuas wanted to harm their game pieces, that was their business, but her creations were to be left alone!

Samael became the first Archangel forbidden Pan, as he was cast out to the lowest level of Hell! Only his own sense of strength and the power of his will kept him from becoming deformed like the other six Archangels. Still, he was slightly transformed. He grew horns, wings, and his skin and eyes changed to a golden color as well.

The three smaller angels she stripped their immortality. Ripping the angelic essences from them, Adamunith, Lilith, and Evelith all became less than even the silver angel had once been.

Pushing Evelith off him, Adamunith moved to bow before the Mother Goddess.

"Grandmother, forgive me! I was weak and fell to the charms of a beautiful seductress. I am of deep sorrow for what I have caused Lilith to do. Forgive us, please!" He begged. Gia smiled, but remained silent. Turning away, she disappeared.

Lilith stood, stunned at her power being stripped away. Evelith sat on the ground crying, having lost not only her angelic immortality, now she could see she had possibly lost even Adamunith from her wanton lustful ways.

When Lilith moved to her creator, Jeasuas was still silent.

"Father, are you going to allow her to do this to me? Your most perfect creation?" She asked; no remorse over what she had done entered her tone.

"Lilith, my child, are you not even sorry for what you did? Look at those other two. They at least pretend remorse!" Jeasuas asked his former Golden Angel.

"I did nothing wrong, father! What was done was an accident. It should be Evelith the whore, whom is dead. Not the lion!" Lilith answered. Jeasuas shook his head and turned away.

Seeing the look on the woman's face, at her father's rejection, Kutulu smiled. He knew he could use this to his advantage.

Adamunith was shocked by the offhanded comment of his lover.

"Lilith, you can't possibly believe in what you said?"

"Believe what, Adamunith? I saw your actions. I saw how she made you feel!"

Kutulu Lucifer moved and put an arm over Lilith's shoulders.

"You need not fear reprisals. And, child, if you come with me, I'll make you even more than you were. Come!"

Seeing the hurt in Adamunith's face, did nothing to soften her heart. Instead, it hardened, until she could only think on what the Ancient One had said. The promise of power!

"You will make me even greater? How is that?" Kutulu smiled at her comment. Lilith turned back to Adamunith.

"You want that lesser creature, my former love; then take her! I will be better off without you!" Lilith turned taking Kutulu Lucifer's hand, and the two disappeared.

When Gia announced that no more would the Garden be used in the game, Lilith could not be found.

The Mother Goddess created thirteen gateways, commanding all the humanoids to leave. They dispersed to the worlds, the dwarves walking through eleven of the gateways. The gnomes picking twelve, and the elves ten. The mermen picked six of the gateways to go through and the trolls picked only four. The makatiels and goblins scattered through all thirteen, and the ogres and giants picked eight.

The humans began to enter all thirteen, like the makatiels, but at the last moment, Jeasuas forbid them one of the Gateways. Kutulu's Hades was forbidden, but still several dozen had walked through before the Ancient One could stop them. After several hundred of each race had walked through Terra's gate, he closed off the door, to that world, as well.

All the remaining silver and golden angels were swept up and placed on the worlds called Hevan and Brommelta. It was when he noticed one of his Golden Angels missing that the real troubles began.

"What has happened to Lilith?" He asked all the other Ancient Ones. He had seen Adamunith and Evelith enter Terra's gateway, together. He thought that strange, now he really became concerned over the missing female. Lilith really was his most beautiful creation. Jeasuas had made her in the image of his beloved sister, Selene, as a tribute to the Ancient One that never seemed to manifest the proper emotions that he had attempted to instill.

"Kutulu, only you could hide Lilith from me! Where is she?"

"Fear not, brother! I don't hide her, she came willingly, and I have claimed her for my own. She is safe and will never be harmed!" Kutulu, The Prince of Light, answered.

The argument ensued and soon Gia had had enough. As the fight over Lilith's soul became heated, Gabriel, the Archangel of War of Jeasuas, took up arms against Nebiros, the Angel of Destruction of Kutulu. The two Ancient One's appeared not to notice, so caught up in their own quarrel.

"Children stop!" Gia announced. "Is it so difficult to see, Jeasuas, that your brother has gained her through his charms? She is, after all, the one that caused the exile!"

"That's a part of his doing as well, Mother!" Jeasuas answered.

"Still, her actions! She is not deserving of Heaven, my son. And already is not the beautiful spirit she once was. Hell has claims on her!"

Jeasuas still believed that any spirit could be saved and left to plan his next move. Smiling, Kutulu Lucifer bowed to Gia and left for Hell, knowing he had won this game! The seed had been planted! The angels all could feel the tension between the brothers and this time Kutulu did not leave without altering things!

The only true sin in Gia's eyes is the sin that is not forgiven. Kutulu Lucifer still had not asked forgiveness for his creation of Hell. Not liking the unstable dimension touching hers, not to mention the still slight instability of Heaven on the other side of her perfect universe, Gia created the Astral plane as a buffer.

Extending it from the center of Pan outward, it became a cushion. Protecting the universe from any new creations, her children could come up with. She then removed Pan from the sight of Zindar, insuring none that was not of true angelic spirit, would ever see it again.

Never would her sons' game be played on her island continent. No more would any act of violence be allowed. She thought, that day!

Moving through her forest, Gia pointed at the mightiest of her oak trees. Each time she touched one; it became filled with her spirit.

You thousand will be my guardians! Even my children, The Ancient Ones, will have to bow to you might. Treants, you will be called, and protectors of Pan you are named. Guardians against violence, I bid thee!"

Thus did Pan disappear from the known world of Zindar, and the battle of Heaven and Hell began.

CHAPTER 1
Lilith's charms, Gabriel's fury

No one expected Jeasuas to take vengeance against Kutulu Lucifer. They knew the forgiveness in his heart and soul would not allow it. All the Ancient Ones watched as the second born walked away, a tear falling down his cheek.

"She chose Kutulu Lucifer's instability over Heaven's beauty?" He mumbled as he slowly shook his head.

The Archangel Gabriel felt his father's frustration and tried to entreat Michael's help.

All of Jeasuas' Archangels and no matter how their creator and father felt at the loss of the Golden Angel, the betrayal by Kutulu Lucifer stealing one of the Ancient One's souls, forgiveness was first and foremost in the Lamb of Creation's spirit. And, the Archangel Michael was the most like his father. He attempted to entreat Gabriel from his pursuit, but to no avail.

That Gia had sent the lesser of the angels from Pan, forbidden from ever returning, mattered little to the Archangels. It was the sin of stealing a soul that bothered them the most.

Lilith went freely with Kutulu, having succumbed to the promise of Power. Isis smiled watching her near perfect creation, Evelith, leaving with her elder brother's own Adamunith. The Golden angel was believed to have picked the silver angel over his original mate. It mattered little that Adamunith had no choice. He lost Lilith the moment he succumbed to his weakness.

Lilith had too much of Selene in her, and vengeance was the strength of her motivation. Lilith promised to return, and Evelith would regret that day!

Selene felt the pain of Jeasuas over his loss. The third born Ancient One knew her brother would never retaliate. But she knew the mother's actions would also, be harsh if she herself did.

Her own Archangels felt their mother's frustrations and moved to act. Four of Selene's seven Archangels were more vengeance minded and Inanna led the charge. Approaching Gabriel, she convinced him, the only way to make their creators' happy, again, would be to get the former Golden Angel, back.

Gabriel agreed and Aleandral, another of Jeasuas' Archangels, was also easily convinced. No matter how hard Michael and Diancecht plead and begged, the two strongest Archangels of Jeasuas were joining the four warriors of Selene in returning Lilith's soul back to where it belonged.

The "War of the Gods" was about to begin, and nothing short of a miracle could stop it.

****

When Kutulu Lucifer arrived at his planet Hades, he smiled down upon the mortal Lilith. She looked upon the Ancient One with wonder, seeing the Prince of Light in a new way. He was beautiful and strong. Powerful enough to face down his own mother, The Eternal Goddess Gia!

His abilities rivaled her own creator, and Kutulu Lucifer did not hide behind the false sense of gentleness, like Jeasuas did. There was no softness to his features, only a raw blinding beauty that made the woman stir, like she had never before.

His promise of Power inspired her, but his beauty moved her. Lilith began attempting to seduce the first-born creation, with all the lust and drive that she possessed.

Amused, Kutulu watched and stood as Lilith's charms began to even stir his own lusts. Belial and Nebiros watched as the woman Samael had first been commanded to charm, now, turned her attentions towards their creator.

"Why have the child when the father is so much more?" She once answered all the other Archangels attempts to gain her attentions. So flawless in her beauty, so perfect in her greed, Lilith quickly became the target of all Hell's Lusts.

When Gabriel led the Archangels into Hades, Kutulu screamed at being interrupted. Bothered as he was by their arrival, he was just about to accept Lilith's charms, when the six arrived.

The scream opened a channel between the two universes and the "Gateway to Hell" sprang into being. Out rushed all seven of the Archangels from Hell to join with their two brothers to fight against the six invaders. Lucifer lifted Lilith into his arms and disappeared.

Gabriel, Aleandral, Inanna, and Marduk were the most powerful warriors ever created. The strongest of all Archangels, but against all nine of Lucifer's, even with the help of Nuada and Frigga, they found themselves out matched.

When Nuada was sent to Pan for aid, Asmodeus and Tiamat followed. Thus, did the "War of the Gods" become a part of Pan, and the first blood of the Ancients, did spill.

****

Lilith embraced her new lover, and when they entered into Hell, she was changed. Not as drastically as those first arrivals to this plane. Her beauty was not harmed, as it had been with the others.

It would appear that when Kutulu created the "Gate," uniting his universe with that of Gia's Prime Material Plane, stability, of a sort, was made. Hell would now become a livable place for all of Kutulu Lucifer's Angels.

The Ancient One opened a small wound in his chest and ordered Lilith to drink. Without hesitation, she knew her angelic power would be returned. She also, suspected, even more would come, as well.

With the lust given her by Samael, the psionic strength given her by Jeasuas, and the greed of her natural voracious self, she devoured Lucifer's blood. As her power grew, bat-like wings formed on her back along her shoulder blades, and her eyes added a golden glow to the black, the long bluish black hair hiding the tiny horns that were just above her forehead.

Kutulu cried out in ecstasy as Lilith continued to take from him all he had to offer. A mortal no longer, Lilith was not even the Golden Angel, she had once been. When the newest and most powerful Greater Angel fell away from her latest lover, she bore him the first of the many children she would bare the Lord of Hell.

From her womb, flew the beautiful demons that would become known as the seducers of men. The golden angels of stunning beauty and ultimate chaos, called the succubus. The only demons to possess a soul.

It was from the incubus and succubus that the demon lords would come!

****

For ten thousand years the battle of the angels created a chaos that none would remain unchanged from. Heaven and Hell erupted in a chaotic climax that shook even the Prime Material Plane, Gia's universe!

Left alone from the gods' interference, though, the mortals of the thirteen planets of humanoids began to make their own way. Gia, frustrated at her first signs of failure, watched the Ancient Ones vie for power in their game as it continued to move from the use of mortals and lesser spirits to the use of the immortal angels. Once again, she turned away to seek out her own worlds, in her own universe.

Seeing the humanoids in need of immortal guidance, she began spreading her word. Using her own Archangels, she taught the stories to the mortals and watched them grow.

Removed from the "War" raging all around her garden, she sat and watched happily the mortals striving for life in their new worlds. The Treants protected the Garden, but not the rest of the immortal continents, and the spread of the fighting became such that it spilled upon even the continent of Pan.

The angels could not enter her Garden, with violence on their minds, and it was not until the first drop of Ancient One's blood was spilled, that the mother finally took notice.

The last two thousand years of the "War" was joined by the Ancient Ones, themselves. They had never participated in the game, themselves, but when Phaleg was first struck behind by Belial and Baalzebub, he turned to slay the two without a thought what it would mean.

All his seven Archangels rushed in, as well as all seven of Minerva's. Soon, it was easier to find those that were not involved, so few of the angels refrained.

Jeasuas and Selene remained in the Garden, away from the fray. With them, Jeasuas had his Archangels; Michael, Abellius, Diancecht, Illmatar, and Surya. Selene only kept the Archangels; Enlil, Ishtar, and Brigitt out of the War.

Merylon was forced into the war, when Minerva asked his aide in creating her a shield. Only his youngest Archangel, Oghma, did not stray from the Garden.

When Isis went to Phaleg's aide for making him some supple armor, the Archangels, Nephthys and Tefnut went with her for protection. That left her with only five of her Archangels to remain out of the war; Bast, Aphrodite, Freya, Balder, and Ki.

After two millennium, Gia had enough and called for a halt. She gathered her children to her and made her proclamation.

It was that very day that the Gods all began to wonder. It was that day, that Gia thought,

"Maybe I should simply start over."

The Angels had been at war with each other. Then of a sudden it stopped. All the Angels moved away quickly at the realization the "War of the Gods" was over. Gia had simply raised her arms and when they were lowered, all death ceased at that moment. Of course, there had only been one death in the Mother's Gardens, before. There had never been this type of violence before, either.

The war of the gods, themselves, had been going on for a little more than two millennium and when Gia had raised her voice, the Ancient Ones failed to listen. They listened now, though. They were forced to listen, now.

"I said STOP!" She had never yelled before. That the angels themselves had partaken in the hostilities was itself a little disturbing, but when the Ancient Ones, began fighting amongst themselves, The Goddess had had all she could take. When the gods' own blood flowed in Pan, Gia put an end to it.

For ten thousand years, the gods had never seen Gia in such a state of anger; not since the exile of the humanoids and Lesser Angels, from the Garden. The seven Ancient Ones, gods of the universe, beings beyond the comprehensions of the mortals and immortals alike, had actually shed blood, becoming little more than the humanoids they had always used as pawns.

The argument had started mildly, as was the normal. Usually, just a manipulation here, a tuck there, and then watch as the humans, dwarves, elves, gnomes, and all the other humanoids, would play out their game, and in the end, no one ever lost, no one ever won. This had been the way, for all of eternity. Before there were the humanoids, there were the spirits, before the spirits, the angels. Always, the gods had used others for their game.

The sibling gods, though, called the Ancient Ones, by the angels, were no longer using the mortals. The dissension between them was caused by the first-born. By the brightest and most beautiful of all of Gia's creations, Kutulu Lucifer, the Prince of Light, The Creator of Evil, later to be called the Father of Lies.

The Ancient One looked at his siblings with so much hatred, so much loathing, emotions he had created in the humanoids for the game, and now, he seemed to be infected, becoming his very own creations.

He acted human! The sacrilege against their mother, was more than the other six could take. Their own angels, feeling the emotions rage through their creators, went after each other, and the war of the gods was begun. For now, though, Gia had put a stop to it.

"No more will violence be allowed in my home!" She yelled. "I warned you all before, of this!" Watching the Ancient Ones, as they eyed each other, suspicions ran through each of them. Mistrust, another of the base emotions that were beyond the gods, or had been until now, was running their minds at the moment. They could not understand the feelings they were having, and could not know that their mother had just realized her own mistake.

The seven were still arguing, though. That the war had stopped was only momentary, and Gia knew the problem that she faced. No longer believing herself omnipresent, she was shaking with fury. Of course, the living Garden of Pan was shaking as well, being one with their mother. Those Angels that were called the Archangels, those that still lived, and those that were reborn were moving to their own gods.

"Thy voice is most contemptible, brother!" Minerva, Queen of Combat, called the wisest of all gods, said, as she looked at the older one's contorted face. "Surely thou are't sorry for thine actions?"

"Mother got what she deserved. I am only sorry that it took me so long in seeing it!" Kutulu Lucifer jeered. "We can do anything she can, and probably do it better!" he spit out with disgust.

"You will, brother, take that back, or we shall become only six!" Phaleg, youngest among the seven, Master of the duel, called the Prince of War, The Blade Dancer, stepped forward, towards Kutulu as the trees themselves, begin to move.

19

"STOP THIS, I said!" The voice was loud, the grounds shook, the living Garden of Pan, rumbled as the life in it felt the frustration in its Goddess. The very Garden was ready to attack the Ancient Ones.

"There will be no violence in my home, I say. This is not a suggestion, it is A COMMANDMENT!"

"Mother," Isis, Queen of Love and Beauty, almost as beautiful as Gia, herself, a near perfect physical creation of the Mother Goddess, lacking the control of her new test with emotions, stepped forward, between her brothers.

"Can not you see how this has happened? Can you not do anything about this contemptible situation?"

The others stirred in agreement as Kutulu Lucifer looked on. He only smiled, knowing that once given, emotions cannot so easily be taken away. He did not want them removed. The exhilaration he felt, at the moment, was new, and he would fight against its removal, even against the mother, if necessary.

"Mother, his sin is contemptible. Surely, he should be punished. Certainly, the sin he has committed will not go untouched!" Isis finished.

"The sin was done to me, my children, and it is my decision to make, on how to enact justice. Not Yours! The time has begun, and the universe trembles, just as before today, the death of the gods is now most assuredly at hand!"

They all moved, involuntarily, at her words, stunned into silence. They cannot die, they know they can't. No matter what Phaleg threatened, none of the Ancient Ones can die. Only Gia could remove them.

"Gia, your words make no sense. Explain how this can happen!" Merylon, known simply as The Sorcerer, Natures Wizard, The Creator of Magic, calmly asked.

"My dear son, you more than any, know that even though our spirits may go on through eternity, if the mortals do not believe, then we simply cease to exist. Titania is the perfect example. No gods, no belief, and no us.

"Terra is on its way to become another. How many on that planet no longer believe in any god? There are some that even worship a mock version of Lucifer there, as an evil spirit. And, forget that I even exist, let alone five of you. How many

20

believe that I am a man, and that I am so vengeful as to have once destroyed the planet? Think, children, what about on Haven?

"Only one of you is known. How many more planets are losing touch? Here on Zindar, our home planet, my greatest creation after you seven. There are those that no longer remember me. Not with the humans, anyway." Gia only shook her head before continuing. "Those that do remember no longer practice their faith correctly. Hear me now, and hear the truth of the end!"

Kutulu Lucifer moved closer to the group, having been standing away from any of the trees. The Treants, living trees, allow no violence in Pan, and even the Ancient Ones were subject to their discipline. Phaleg, still staring at him with war on his mind, moved away, to stand opposite him, in the circle of the eight. The others showed equal discomfort, but refrained from so obvious a show.

"For two thousand years the "War of the Gods" has been allowed to progress. For even longer, has this conflict been going on! I say it is over, now! No more, will I allow the children of Heaven and Hell to fight your battles! You have made the humans, for your little game, let them once again, be the pawns of your own destruction's. Since you have chosen to fight for so long amongst yourselves, that is all I will give you.

"Two thousand years, the humans will have, in which to produce a champion for each of you. Seek them out among the seven worlds. Seek them out and bring them here. The war will no longer be fought by you. I will have no more wars between the universes. The angels are almost gone, because of the atrocities you all have committed in the need of sport. Even you, Jeasuas, my most faithful to my teachings, have partaken in this damning destructive uselessness. I will have no more of it!"

She watched each of the seven, their reactions to her words. To move, only, on their legs, rocking back and forth on the balls of their feet. Their thoughts racing, feeling the anger that was in their mother.

The gods could feel the anger at them all, rising within. They knew without any outward sign, without any vocal tone, that their mother, Gia, is almost beyond rage! They do not need a show, to feel it in her being. They are a part of her, after all, and this is the first time that they have felt the moment of uncertainty emanate out from Gia.

21

"There will only be one champion from each of you. Only one chance and in the end, the winner will decide if order, or chaos, or balance will reign on these worlds. I catch any sight of any of you entering the battles yourselves, and I will interfere. You will not like my interference. Am I understood?"

Her last statement shook the Ancient Ones to their very cores. That the mother would threaten her own children, her first born, with so much callousness, was more than they could stand, so new to emotions, they felt their legs shake with an uncertainty.

"How can you eliminate us?" Kutulu asked. "To kill one will eliminate all of us. If you undo your creations, won't it undo the universe as well? This will not only destroy all your precious creations, but could destroy you, as well, Mother! I challenge your threat as idleness, Gia. I challenge you!"

"If you challenge me, Kutulu Lucifer, then I simply need undo all and start over. I have so obviously failed, by the looks of You! I will feel sorrow, certainly, but I am infinite, my son. I can start again, without any of the mistakes, as I have made with you seven!"

"Mother, you are a fool to believe this will end it. I transcend your creation; and if you unmake the universe, my own universe will be all that remains. I am your equal, and will soon be your better.

"Remember, this is your proclamation, and once said, cannot be unsaid. I will accept your little game, Gia. I will be the victor, and the universes will be mine!" Smiling, Kutulu Lucifer disappeared. The others standing open mouthed, could not believe all they had heard. Visibly shaking of fear, a new emotion in them as well, they looked from one another and then back to the Mother Goddess, Gia.

Isis, Queen of Love and Beauty, the vainest of the Ancient Ones, laughed as the tension rose to a boil. She was filled with mirth at her brother's statement, and openly showed of disdain for it.

"He is Gia's equal? Is he mad?" Catching herself together, at the look from the mother, she quickly added,

"Mother, certainly you know that he will not honor the terms. He may very well, possess a human and simply call him his champion. Every angel, every monstrosity he has ever created will be thrown into the game. He will open the doors

22

of Hell, to send them at our champions. Certainly, we cannot be held to so strict of rules when he will not follow them, himself?"

"Then I suggest you make sure your champions are really champions. Use that which I gave you, something called intellect and wisdom! Make ones that will be able to win, no matter the odds against them. Semi-mortal angels, comes to mind!" she paused.

"But I say this again, mark my words my offspring, regardless how your brother plays the game, I will not have you turn it into another free for all.

"No more than one champion each, and only from among the humans. None of my mortal children are to be touched. And, Jeasuas, I want none of your Archangels involved. None of any of you had better use one of your current Arch or even Greater Angels. They are the cause of that whole blood bath, before. AM I UNDERSTOOD?"

They all agreed. None knew what to say to Gia, after that. They moved off to prepare. Only two thousand Zindarian years, that seemed awfully short a time to mold and create a life that could stand up to Kutulu Lucifer's Hell. And, for the universe to rest in the balance, all seemed most daunting, indeed.

The six Ancient Ones looked at one another, and stopped at the end of Pan. Jeasuas, Lamb of Creation; Selene, Princess of Healing and of Vengeance; Minerva, Queen of Combat and Goddess of Wisdom; Merylon, The Sorcerer; Isis, Queen of Love and Beauty; and Phaleg, Prince of War. They all wondered at the game and the rules laid before them.

They nodded to each other, agreeing on a time and spot to meet. They only have nineteen hundred ninety-nine years to find or make their champions, and then an intense year to train them. Merylon agreed to use his own world as the perfect place for the training.

"It cannot be invaded by Kutulu. And, time and space are easily manipulated there. That will give us more than one year to work with these humans, if needed."

"It is settled, then. We shall meet there in two millennium." Jeasuas stated and they all then, disappeared.

Hecartae, youngest of the Mother's Archangels, the first dryad, appeared to Gia, wrapping her wings around the goddess.

"Mother are you all, right? You won't really undo all of us, will you?"

"I will do what I have too, my pretty little fairy."
"What about the love you have given us? You would destroy us all, as well?"

Gia looked down upon her youngest of the Archangels and sighed.

"I will do what I have to do. Chaos without order cannot be allowed. Just as order without chaos cannot!"

"What did Kutulu Lucifer do, Mother? To cause such distress in you and between you and your first born?"

"Never you mind, daughter. Never mind!"

The Ancient Ones scattered to the far reaches of the universe, seeking that which was to become the ultimate game of chance. They all sought to manipulate the mother's commands, knowing that one would more than just manipulate it. They sought the perfect choices, until it occurred to them to simply create the perfect champions. They would make the most physically perfect creatures of human birth ever created. At least, all but two had chosen that route.

Phaleg never considered making someone; instead, he found one and trained him to a higher level. Selene had chosen a more direct route. Seducing Jeasuas, she allowed two eggs to be created. Perfect twins from which to work with.

Handing one to Jeasuas, she then placed her own egg into a human female, she watched, as it was reborn through several lifetimes, becoming more knowledgeable, yet, more hidden. Her creation would be more than just a man, but should possess fewer thoughts for power. Instead of manipulating the creation, she chose to manipulate the life around her spirit son.

The seven planets to still possess humans, from which to choose from, were Zindar, Terra, Titania, Haven, Muridian, Brommelta, and Launam. The war would be fought on Zindar, and most of the others chose to go outside of this planet for their creations.

Only one stayed, within the home world, the Ancient One called Merylon. He knew that his brother and sister were conspiring to make a duo, and thought, better for him, to stay home. Pick one that will aid the two. Someone that would know the planet, and know where to find the resources which would be needed.

The others chose different routes, but all had the same goal. All wanted to insure victory, for themselves.

CHAPTER 2
The Chosen Seven

When Lilith refused to lay with Samael, Kutulu Lucifer was at first amused. Yet, when he realized she really was not going to do it, he became incensed. Many times, he had had to punish the woman for her insolence.

Lilith was always disobeying an order from him, and often times would openly oppose him in front of the others. After many millenniums of it, Lucifer had finally endured enough.

"Either produce offspring with all the Archangels, or else!" The Ancient One ordered.

"Else what? You may rule my heart, my God, but you do not rule my actions." Lilith responded.

In his rage, Kutulu Lucifer proclaimed her Molech's consort. For one hundred years the most hideous of the Archangels, the most unstable and insanity driven, would enjoy her pleasures. Lilith cringed at the thought of the beast taking her.

"You will regret this!" She spoke, as Kutulu laughed waving his arm. Lilith was banished to the sixth level of Hell, the level that was pure chaos and the most demonic filled.

In his insane rampage, when he first arrived, Molech had destroyed most of the level. Now, it only appeared to be rock, lava, and smoke filled.

When Lilith arrived, she felt the ugliness of the land and the despair permeating the air around her. She made several attempts to leave, but somehow, Kutulu Lucifer had cut off her ability. She was stuck on this level, yet, she still thought that for the next century she could easily avoid the Archangel.

When the demons moved on her, she quickly realized the need for shelter. Mindless and single minded; demons are a lesser spirit created out of the vilest of souls. Only good for one purpose, the destruction of whatever they were sent to do, they were an uncontrolled mass that recognized nothing, but strength!

Lilith struck out with her power and fought. After more than a year had gone by, without much more than a few days of reprieve, she finally yielded and presented herself to Molech's palace.

She spent the next fifty years with a slave collar around her neck, chained to the bed. Molech had tried to be nice to the woman, but an angel that would defy a god, would certainly be uncontrolled by the weakest of the Archangels!

As powerful as he was, Lilith tried to resist sleeping with him for as long as she could, when she first arrived. Finally, the ugly Archangel had enough of her putting him off. Overwhelming her with the aid of several lesser angels, he managed to collar her and allowed for her to be raped and beaten by every fiend that followed him.

When Molech himself, took her, Lilith was a beaten woman, and did not resist. Instead, she spent the remainder of the imprisonment, plotting!

Plotting vengeance on Molech, plotting vengeance on Kutulu, plotting vengeance on every Archangel that Molech would give her too. Most of all, Lilith was plotting vengeance on Evelith, the small weak silver angel that had been the cause of all these problems, in the first place! Lilith would have her revenge!

****

Kutulu Lucifer watched the half-makatielan half-human priestess and smiled. He thought this woman should even be able to survive the mating. He had tried pure humans, but found them to be too fragile. Those few that did survive, could not handle the pregnancy, and then the even fewer that managed to take the baby to full term did not survive the birth.

"How can I have enough shells that will look identical, if no woman can survive more than once?" He had thought until he began looking at the non-humans. He did not care that Gia had ordered only humans to be used, and it never occurred to him, to use a surrogate father, instead of mating himself. Or, if it did, he discounted it as more enjoyable, his way!

He sought the giants, and quickly discounted them. Although, superior in strength and size, they were a low intelligent creature, prone to too many fears and superstitions. Ogres were too greedy, and could be bought off, he thought!

Besides, the sheer ugliness to the creature, not even Kutulu Lucifer could bring himself to mate with an ogress.

Goblins were too small and would never survive the delivery, any better than the humans did. He settled for the makatiels.

Human size, though of tougher stock. They were sociopaths, but that would not matter. At least, the females could sustain a little brutality and did tend to be smarter than the males of that race.

That they had ugly pig snouts and ears mattered little, at least they were human bodied. He searched till he found the perfect one. Picking a half-makatiel, the human blood in her would stimulate the psychic channels and make the female even stronger than normal. And, thus, Kutulu Lucifer's child would be even greater!

Placing a hand to the woman's back of the head, he pulled her hair roughly, as she looked up into his eyes, smiling. Gruldarash stood over 208 cm, the tallest and strongest female makatiel ever to be born. Lucifer shifted to take the form of a large half-makatielan male, as he felt the most powerful sorceress in makatielian society, attempt to probe his mind.

When he shut off her ability to use sorcery, he caused every nerve in her body to feel a pain of intense agony. He then changed it to pure pleasure, causing her agonizing eruptions of pleasure after so much pain. He then began to alternate, pain then pleasure, and then back to pain. After tormenting the half-makatiel female for over an hour, he finally released her.

"Now, woman, you are ready to bare me the coming savior!" Kutulu whispered. A screech in her ear that nearly blew out her eardrum.

"I serve you, always, my God! I await your touch eagerly!" She gasped, filled with excited fervor.

Nine times in nine years, Kutulu Lucifer came to the female, each time producing a single male baby that was quickly whisked away by a waiting devil. Normally, makatiels produced litters of four to six offspring, but each of those nine; only a single solitary male child was born, alive. The rest were still born, looking as though they were strangled, clawed, or otherwise beaten to death within the womb.

The nine near godlike offspring, are embedded with a strong psychic awareness. They are physically strong, fast, and all nearer to human appearance, than that of makatielian. Gruldarash smiled at the beauty of each birth and watched with happy eagerness, when each half-makatiel baby was taken to Kutulu's Palace in the world of Hades, where the Gateway connected Hell with Zindar's southernmost continent, also; called Haden.

There they grew, in a stasis chamber, void of existence, except a magical slumber. Only one was left to grow, with an awareness. Only one was to become the Chosen Champion of Kutulu Lucifer!

At the age of fifteen, reaching adulthood, the half-makatiel, Martinith, first born of the nine, stepped into the *Gateway of Hell*, and found himself on Zindar, in the city of Havendale, on the continent called Haden. He proclaimed himself the Chosen of Lucifer, and was crowned King and High Command over all the forces in Hell, as well as, the non-humans and monsters that lived on this world.

Only Haden's non-humans and humans honored the title, of course, but Martinith still maintained the claim.
Given immunity to non-magical weapons, as well as, most magical attacks, Martinith ruled with an iron fist, over all that was the continent. His eight younger brothers, all identical twins to himself, remained in their comas, yet, still continued to grow.

Kutulu Lucifer had explained to him that facing six Chosen of those other, "lesser gods," he would most likely die until he learned to face combined forces. By having the extra shells to install his spirit into, it would create a guaranteed immortality.

As long as the spirit is not trapped or destroyed with a shell's death, Martinith can be reborn, without losing his memories.

Lilith was finally freed from her own exile. But, when told to come back to Kutulu Lucifer's palace, she refused.

"You want me, Kutulu, then you will apologize for your rashness in sending me away." She had told him. He was still upset that during her century of imprisonment, she had managed to refrain from baring any children for the Archangels.

"You will learn, Lilith! I am your God, and you answer to me, not the other way around! You have defied me, for the last time. No wonder, your own father no longer wanted you!"

When she attempted to leave, she found that she was unable. Damned to spend her existence in Hell, Lilith would never gain her revenge against the one woman, she really wanted.

What upset her the most was that no other devil lord, demon lord, nor Archangel would allow her sanctuary. She would be condemned to stay with Molech. She had the choice, Kutulu Lucifer advised her.

"You will live in subjugation to me, Lilith, or else to Molech! Those are your only choices, I allow you."

Her vengeance thwarted against Evelith and Adamunith, she sought for a way to get back at all the Archangels and their God. For centuries, the most powerful Greater Angel, and most beautiful of Hell's denizens, plotted and manipulated.

Creating chaos within the nine levels of the Plane of Hell, as Kutulu Lucifer continued to watch and participate in the "Game of the Gods." He pretended not to notice, Lilith's actions. He pretended not to see what his former favorite angel was doing, and allowed the chaos to continue.

After all, she was only making his Archangels stronger and more useful to his own uses.

When Gia announced the end of the war between the Ancient Ones, Lilith saw her chance. No longer would Lucifer be able to tie her only to the Hell's Plane.

His Chosen Champion would eventually summon her, and then she would be free. She waited and watched.

She watched as the seven Chosen Champions of the seven Ancient Ones were created. Two in particular caught her attention. Selene's child was put through a gauntlet of lives. Each a difficult test of unlucky events. When Selene's boy was in his thirty-first life, Lilith could see the power being carefully hidden deep within him.

"He will be the one to face, Kutulu's Martinith!" Lilith thought. She could see the careful manipulation Selene had done. And, Jeasuas, as well, with his own. It was as if, Adamunith and Lilith were being remade.

Ten millennium after the exile, found Jeasuas and Selene were attempting to recreate the past. Lilith smiled!

"You may be giving her my power, father," Lilith spat sarcastically; "but, you failed in recreating my beauty!"

When five years of unchallenged rule had Martinith looking into the mirror. The twenty-year-old half-makatiel, smiled when told the other Chosen had arrived. The "War of the Chosen" had begun!

Martinith summoned Samael and all the other Archangels and Greater Angels. Even though the Archangel wanted nothing more than to slay the 212 cm tall, 125 kg heavily muscled, gray skinned half-makatiel, he obeyed grudgingly, when Martinith commanded him to send out Greater Angels after the Chosen of Selene, Jeasuas, and Merylon.

"Tell the Chosen that I am present, and await them the day they all die."

When Samael advised him that he was being foolish, Martinith attacked the Archangel and, Samael teleported to the other side of the room. Knowing that Martinith's word was law, as far as Lucifer was concerned, Samael had no option, but to comply.

The Chosen Child of Lucifer had commanded, and out of his mouth "speaks the word of God!"

****

Jeasuas watched the girl grow and suffer. This was the thirtieth time her spirit had been reintroduced. Thirty-one lives would have to be enough. Time was running out, and he thought this the one would work.

"It will have too! Even Selene had agreed to his plan. If all goes well, this girl will be the one to awaken his sister's champion."

In all the previous lives the twins had been close. Friends or family, they had always been together. This last life, they had been separated their entire life and

Jeasuas could not understand what Selene had been doing with her half of the twins. He was too old, and had been on Zindar twice during his life. Jeasuas wondered Selene's manipulation.

"I just hope I am right in this." He remembered telling Selene. She agreed that he must be, but an awful lot depended on the timing. If not, then all hope will have to fall upon the other four. It was, for sure that the others would be going for pure power, and pure strength. Only Selene and Jeasuas were to bring in less than perfect humans. But, the second born among the Ancient Ones knew his mother. And, he knew her tricks.

Sheryl, what a nice name, Jeasuas thought, and he smiled at the girl's strength under such duress, as she had had to endure in this life. Her only flaw would be how young she was. Selene almost, mistakenly, went too old, with her champion, for this young girl. But, now was the time to take her. She would not last another few years. He stopped time, stepped out of the shadows, and walked in, a glow of soft white light surrounding him. The aura of light was, obscuring his features. He appeared as a god, to the young beaten abused woman, and she shook not of fear, but of exhilaration at finally being freed from this life.

Sheryl Mattingly-Ling was born in South Vietnam to a Chinese woman and an American Soldier. Her mother was born in south China, and raised in North Vietnam. Sheryl's grandparents tried to flee to the south when the war started. They were killed along with three of their children. Shao Ling, was the oldest, almost seventeen, when her parents were killed. Only she and her youngest brother of eight, made it to South Vietnam, alive.

When the Americans came, Sheryl's mother had gotten a job at the local army post cleaning laundry for the soldiers. That was when Corporal Jonathan Mattingly met the young woman and fell in love. Only nineteen years old, very tall, with dark hair and dark eyes, when Shao Ling met him, she saw a way to a better life.

She allowed the man to buy her things and to set her and her brother up in an apartment close to the American's military post. Sheryl was born a year later, in 1964, on the day of the Christian holiday; December 25.

For three years he had tried to get permission to marry the woman, but it continued to be denied. When the soldier was sent home, Sheryl was only three, the Corporal was not allowed to take his daughter nor her mother.

When her mother died, two years later of some sickness that made her cough all the time, Sheryl, remembered being told it was tuberculosis and would be common but not common to die from it. Sheryl found herself sent to an orphanage for Vietnamese born to American GIs. That only lasted a few months and then began her long life of bouncing from orphanage to orphanage.

Never staying more than two years in any one place, she grew to live a life of hardship, and never making friends, for fear of losing them all over again.

When she was twelve, she met a man that offered to take her to a whole new world, and she went with him. But he ended up wanting to do things to her she did not think right. In a city called Shigatse, in the country of Tibet, she ran away from the man, and ended up in one of the monasteries.

Sheryl learned a lot during the next nine years. She became one of only two women to be considered a trained priest. There were only three women in the monastery at the time, yet, things were going well. She had finally found happiness with the monks, and found love with all the people and a true sense of belonging. Of course, nothing good can last forever. She did not realize, at the time, that she had been put on this world to suffer.

The Chinese government sent soldiers to destroy some of the monasteries, still making the attempts at subjugating the country into their own society. It was a brutal effort, and, her home was one of the unlucky ones, that did not survive. Many of the monks escaped, and while the group she was with, were all walking a few days later, a squad of soldiers caught them and killed all, but her and another of the females.

They were taken to the soldier's camp and turned over to the men for entertainment. Both girls, only twenty-one and nineteen years of age respectively, were stripped nude and chained by the neck, inside a tent.

There, they were beaten, tortured, and raped. Li, the nineteen-year-old, did not survive long, and on the fifth day, in the morning, was found dead.
Sheryl prayed every day. She prayed while the soldiers were having their way with her. She prayed to Buddha for strength while she was being beaten, and she prayed to Buddha for deliverance after she would be tortured.

Most of all, she prayed for death! But, to no avail it would seem to her, she still lived. Nearly starved, only given one glass of water a day, she could not understand how she could continue to live, but still refused to take her own life.

On the night of her salvation, she was left lying, after several of the soldiers had used her and left her bleeding in many areas. The soft glowing light, that entered the tent, where she was curled up in the dirt, was almost comforting. It was on the seventh day of her capture, that the light appeared to her, and, lying naked on the ground, collar around her neck with a chain connecting her to the tent's center post, she thought that they had returned for more. Her heart hardened in that moment. She felt all her training against violence, wash away. She would fight them, until they either left her alone, or hopefully, she thought, would end her life.

The light spoke to her, softly, lovingly, bathing her in warmth, washing the pain and filth away. He spoke with a soft male's voice and told her she was needed for a far greater purpose than to die for unholy reasons at the hands of unholy men. The voice calmly told her she would find peace in her heart, again, in time, and even that she would find true love and faith in a man, as well.

Sheryl could not believe that last part, but she would accept anything at this point, just to be away from where she was.

The voice calmly told her she would serve as the new dove to his plan. She would be the dragon in a land that needed a warrior. He introduced himself finally as Jeasuas, so close a name to the God of the Occidental world, and when the light faded, standing before her was a beautiful man, dark almost mahogany colored skin, shoulder length dark brown hair, clean shaven, and wearing a robe of light mauve, that seemed to glisten with glitter when he moved. He had a white aura that shone so brightly it almost seemed silvery golden in color; with piercing dark brown eyes and a tenor voice that was like a song.

So melodious when he spoke, she could believe him to be a god. Deep resonant and filled with so much compassion, one could only be relaxed when in his presence. Touching her bindings, he caused the chains to fall away without even opening. She was covered in a robe of soft linen, and all her wounds were suddenly washed away, physical and mental.

She was in awe of him, and thought he must be Siddhartha, The Buddha come to take her to Heaven. He only chuckled, smiling with a warm loving smile, he claimed that he was once known by that name, but now, on another world, he was called by the name he had been given by his mother, Holy Gia. His true name, he had said.

34

The most important thing he told to her was, she would be his prophet. He had need of her, and she felt blessed and happy that she could be needed, by anyone!

When Sheryl arrived at Launam, the place of their training, the 168 cm tall, 55 kg, black haired beauty, introduced herself as Sheera Lu Che. A name she had taken from a book she once read. A new name for a new life.

Only one of the other five could speak any language she could understand, a man, an elder, middle aged from the country of the United States. Sheera looked at the man, and thought, simply, he had pretty eyes. She became especially amused when a woman, with pointed ears and pale almost white skin, walked up to that man and tried to kiss him. She remembered laughing, on that first day, at the man's blush.

****

Selene stepped into the room, looking mirthfully at James Carl Tigara. The man was sitting in his chair, and did not even move, when she appeared seemingly out of the shadows. He was deep into his drink, and seeing the beautiful woman in front of him, he only smiled, and slightly raised his glass, as if in salute.

Selene, The Healer and Goddess of Vengeance, hoped she had not miscalculated. Hers and Jeasuas' children were supposed to find each other, to awaken each other. But this man was very far, indeed, from the loving warrior he would need to be. He would certainly make an excellent tool for vengeance, but only if he could learn the rest.

Standing tall, over seven feet in height, black hair to just past her shoulders, wavy and worn loose. Selene wore a light almost sky-blue gown that buttoned up the front to just below her neck. Medium build by the day's standards, she had a Middle Eastern look to her, but the eyes were light blue, and too rounded for one of that part of the world. Her dress was of a style that more appeared to be Celtic early twelfth century.

Her skin was a perfect absent of any blemishes, and she seemed to be only about mid-twenties in age, except for the eyes. The dark brown eyes, which glowed and spoke of many years more than the rest of her.

And the aura, that surrounded her! A white that shined almost bright enough to be silvery golden in colors. The glow of it, made him sit up, thinking he had

35

too much to drink on his last day of freedom. James turned off the television, and looked up at her.

Was that an uncertain smile he was detecting? She leaned down and touched his forehead, with her long thin fingers, so delicate, that the strong jab she gave could not have come from such a person. James Carl Tigara relived his life.

The day of his birth, it was snowing. Not all that strange, except that in Louisiana, on Christmas Day, it is rare. The street signs were frost covered, and power was out at all the intersections. The year was 1964, and the van his father, Carlos Juan Tigara, was driving, skid out of control. His mother, Jaffe Naomi, deep in labor pains, could only hold on, as the van was hit from the side by a large truck

James' father was instantly killed, by the impact, and his mother was thrown from the vehicle only to deliver James Carl, on the side of the road. Delivered by a police officer, in a snowstorm, to a now dead woman. Somehow, the baby was alive, and the ambulance arrived just in time so he could avoid the worse of the weather. James entered the world at 9:37 pm, on Christmas Day, the night of 1964.

James was turned over to his paternal grandparents, ten days later, in Baton Rouge, Louisiana. Father, a first generation Mexican American and mother, a Caucasian American, James would experience the first touch of prejudice, when he would never even meet his maternal grandparents. Having disowned their only daughter because of marrying a poor Mexican man, it would be twenty years before James would even meet one of his cousins, from his mother's side of the family.

His maternal family, were a wealthy Jewish family and they could not understand why their daughter could possibly want to marry into a poor Mexican Catholic family. Juan Tigara, Carlos Juan's father, was an immigrant, hardworking, and always gave everything to his family. James' grandmother, Maria, was a well-liked woman in the community, always doing for others, and always putting the church first in her life.

They never seemed to have any money, but there was always food on the table, clothes on their back, and James was always surrounded by a house full of people and more importantly, love. James grew up happy, knowing love, compassion, and charity.

When his grandfather moved the family down to the city of New Orleans, James Carl was just beginning the sixth grade, and he attended the Catholic school there. When he graduated from St. Mary's High School with honors, number one in his class, he received a scholarship in science to LSU; his grandparents were the proudest people in the world.

A hard worker growing up, James was taught the need for always doing his best, and it went into all facets in his life. From his studies, to his sports, to his jobs, James was taught to, always try to do one's best.

James was not only involved with high achievement in academics, but he also was a two-time state all-around champion in gymnastics, yet, as he made his way through school, he spent no time outside the family, or outside his work.

Whether it was his studies, his gymnastics, or his favorite hobby, working as a black smith down at the local livery, all his time was spent at being the best in those things. That carried on into college, and when he graduated three years

later with a degree in biology, James found himself a twenty-one-year-old man with no real-life experiences.

After two more years, James received his Master's degree in education, and was on the way to the Olympic qualifying tournament. An accident ended his gymnastics career, when the train he was in, derailed, and James Carl, the only survivor; receiving only a broken leg and an unexplained week-long coma.

After a few months of laying around feeling sorry for himself, he signed up for a Tai Kwon Do class to help with his rehabilitation, and there he met Darlene.

She was twenty-six years old, one of the instructors, and the most beautiful person James had ever seen. She also closely matched the woman he had dreamed of while in his coma. A woman not of this world, and one not entirely human. Darlene could almost be a human relative of this dream female.

But, at twenty-three, never having been on a date, never having spent more than five minutes talking to a woman other than his grandmother or a cousin, James was too shy to let his intentions known.

So, he attended every class he could, just to be around the young woman, and between his work at the stables, where he was considered an artist with the metal, and his martial arts, where he really never got along, except for his natural ability and strength due to his gymnastics, James seemed to be living a happy, if imaginary life.

After two years he was forced to back off on the Tai Kwon Do, when he chose to go back to school for his doctorate. Cutting down from five nights per week to just two nights, Darlene noticed that her most ardent admirer was suddenly not as interested as before and inquired to him.

As he nervously explained that he was going back to school, she seemed excited for him and urged James to go out with her to celebrate. At twenty-five years old, James Carl had his first date with a being of the opposite gender; the woman of his fantasies, and he felt all in the world could not be more perfect.

Their love bloomed and for the next two years they dated, until two weeks before their wedding, she was diagnosed with a brain tumor. Postponing the wedding, Darlene did not survive the surgery.

Then James was faced with his second loss in his short twenty-seven years of life, when his grandparents died that same year, only a week apart from each other.

James went into a depression, quitting martial arts, quitting school, and quitting on life in general. Going to and from his work, only, he seemed not to really be in any place emotionally, and his one friend, Buddy Darnell, the old man down at the stables, began to worry. Then, she came into the livery.

On a warm spring day, a tall olive dark skinned, sparkling blue eyed, large full mouthed, twenty-year-old woman, wearing tight jeans and a blouse that barely covered her full high bosom, walked into the stables. Speaking no English, and no one at the stables able to understand Greek, it was James that managed to break the language barrier.

He could not only speak Spanish, but French and a little Portuguese, as well. She could speak a little French and was fluent in Portuguese, so James was able to ascertain that she was only in the country for a few weeks and wanted to ride, and after a few minutes, the woman was off on a horse. When she returned after several hours, she told James that she wanted to "dine on him," and with the shocked look James gave her, she only laughed, but insisted on his going out with her.

At the urging of the other men at the stables, he accepted and left to enjoy a great love affair over the next six years. At twenty-seven, James was still a virgin, still very innocent, in many ways, and Diane was not the best of teachers in the ways of love, but they traveled, and he learned what it was like to be around a domineering, brutish woman, that had more money than any young lady should have.

A plane crash on take-off, left James in a coma, once again, the only survivor, his love dead and a few weeks later, when he woke, he had a very bitter taste in his mouth for anything to do with love between man and woman. A curse on him, he would tell people. Those that love him, and that he loves in return, will die!

He did dream about the non-human woman from another world, once again while in his coma, and this time the added war that was a part of his dream and the love affair with this beautiful sorceress only added to the mystery of the dream. He died in his dream saving the woman's life just as he awakened from the coma.

He returned to school, got his doctorate in biochemistry, and started teaching, at one of the local High Schools, where many years later, his life would take on another catastrophic turn.

The screams coming from one of his fellow teacher's rooms, long after school had been over for the day, had him moving down the hall at a run.

When James entered Mrs. Monroe's room, he found a student, a seventeen-year-old boy, holding a knife on the young newly married woman. Her clothes had been cut open down the front, and the terrified woman was backed up against the far wall.

Without thought, James grabbed the boy, and when he felt the six-inch blade enter his abdomen, he threw the boy backwards without thinking. The ripping of the knife as it tore from his stomach, causing substantial bleeding, and the boy fell, striking his head on a desk.

By the time the police and ambulance arrived, there was no hope in saving the boy, and James was given very little chance of surviving as well. He had lost too much blood.

When he was released from the hospital after only a two-day miraculous stay, he was promptly served with arrest papers being charged with the boy's death. In court, James Carl pled guilty to involuntary manslaughter and was told he would spend a year in prison. He was given a week to get his things in order and it was on the last night of his freedom that the Ancient One, a Goddess named Selene came to him.

As her hand pulled away from James, his mind was cleared of the fog from the alcohol. He stood up, and when she told him his fate, he agreed to come, but how could he do what she stated he must do, as a forty-eight-year-old man, only five feet seven inches tall, overweight, and out of shape? Selene's only answer was a wistful laugh and a hearty,

"Hard work, James Carl. The same things you have been motivated by your whole life!"

When he arrived to meet the others, he was the oldest, by far, the shortest, and seemingly, the only one that could not make it up a hill without falling down out of breath. He would have to work hard, indeed!

Merylon rarely left Zindar, except to frequent his own dimensional planet of Launam. And it was here, on this, the smallest of planets, Zindar, that he would make his champion. He would even get it right the first try, without the need for several reincarnations of the spirits, the others were manipulating. Selene's poor soul was in his thirty-first, and Jeasuas' was in her thirty-first as well. And Minerva, well, that was a catastrophe waiting to happen. How could any man be expected to survive over one hundred incarnations and still be sane? Not to mention, Isis' one hundred fifty attempts!

Merylon laughed at those others, and continued forming the spirit. After searching the centuries, he found the perfect one. Just five centuries prior to the time of the war's beginning, she would not need much reclamation.

That it would be a woman, Merylon only wondered, but somehow when he created the soul, it had too many feminine attributes to be a proper man.

Besides, knowing that his brother, Jeasuas was aiding Selene to create the One Champion. This child would need to aid Selene's and therefore, a woman it would be.

The small addition of lust, will hold the woman after Selene's child, and it is one of Merylon's favorites among the many facets of love. The Ancient One chuckled as he embedded a part of his spirit into the unborn child, still forming in the womb of the elven woman.

The South Marshlands, a dreary place with many bogs, hilly swamplands, and many mines of shallow depth. The lord of these lands had won them in a duel with the prince. When the Lord Rustan d'Venta came to these lands, he spent the next several years until, spending more time fighting monsters, clearing bog worms, finally induced insanity and the lord killed off his entire family, leaving only his one young son left alive. The boy, thirteen at the time was named Rustan the second, ran off into the swamps, fleeing his mad father, he was befriended by the swamp gnomes.

They showed him the secrets of the bog, and after five years, the boy, now an eighteen-year-old man, returned to slay his father and claim the title and lands, for himself. Determined to lift the curse of his family name, Rustan II found in the hills, a way to safely mine the precious metals buried there. What he found that was valuable to the wizards, was a gas that had no name, and no real way to control nor contain it.

The byproduct of the death in the marsh, this gas could be used to keep lanterns burning for longer and with more heat than the fish oil, currently used. Its only problem was the volatile nature of it, and the containing of the strange product. Wizards found other uses for it, as well as ways to contain it safely. They named the strange gas, methanine, and Rustan II became a very wealthy man.

Friend to the non-humans, he hired dwarves to build his castle, and with the gnomes, mined the magical metal called mythral, as well as diamonds and platinum, and the gas methane. One day, a large rock the size of a medium house was found in the swamp, and with the extraction, the adamemnite was found to be even more magical in nature, than mythral, and it was sold off as well, making Rustan II the wealthiest man in the empire.

For several decades the d'Venta family would be the most influential and the wealthiest of all the lords outside the royal family. Some said that the d'Venta's even had more money than the royalty, but that was never proven due to the taxes that would have been levied.

When Stellen d'Venta was born, an arrangement was made with the elves, that he would marry the Princess, Listella ip Rediar, grandniece to the king of all the continent's elves. This was one of Merylon's manipulations, as he saw the perfect vassal for his champion to be born in. That he was subverting Mother Gia's commandment to leave the non-humans out of it, he only shrugged.

When Stellen was in his late twenties, Burlga d'Venta was born. Second child, her older brother already fourteen years of age, the age their father had married, had the boy been fully human.

Her mother died from Burlga's birth. A miscalculation of Merylon had made Burlga too magically powerful while still in the womb and the pain during birth, the

41

baby lashed out with an internal psychic energy jolt, which although, not powerful in a baby, it had hit the internal organs, causing the woman to die, just two days later. Stellen would never recover from the shock, and rightfully blamed his daughter, sending her to be raised by an aunt.

her brother to a school of war, Burlga's aunt sent her to the wizard's guild to be trained. When she was fifteen, about eight in human terms of growth, Burlga had already reached master wizard, phenomenally, and was more powerful in any spell she could cast, then any in the school.

When Burlga returned home, a year later, she found her brother dead, her father deep within his insanity, and her life about to become a living hell. An invasion from the rival lords had begun to conquer her family lands, and only her great powers turned the enemy back. With the war over quickly, and the woman's strength proven, not only did the d'Venta's have monetary power, but now they had magical as well, the only next step was royalty. Her father decided he wanted to be king.

Killing off all the heirs to the crown, one by one, he managed to keep all his doings from Burlga. It was when he turned to the elimination of the throne, that she became suspicious. When the King became sickly, poison was blamed.

And, the natural suspect was the second most powerful family, the d'Venta's, especially when in his often states of insane ranting, he would talk about how he would eliminate the King.

And, since, the Lord's daughter, a powerful wizardress, had just returned home only one year prior, poison would be simple child's play for the Phenom young wizardress. When the King died of methane poisoning, of course the d'Venta were accused, and the war began. With the entire kingdom, united against them, even Burlga's great strength was severely tested.

Stellen d'Venta was slain to an assassin's bolt, and the entire continent began an elimination of the powerful wizardress. At age twenty-two, only the size of a normal 13-year-old human, she could foresee the end.

Magically creating a room deep in the earth, under the castle, she moved all her family's most valuable assets. Then she took all the coin and gems and jewelry there as well, along with several hundred kilograms of mythral, and platinum. After the entire treasury was emptied, transferred to her magically created room, she set wards of protection and non-detection around it, and sat to accept her fate.

For the first time, she prayed. Not to any deity in particular. To all of them! Naming all the known gods and goddesses, Burlga sat and waited, until he came.

A bright white light, surrounding an aged male, entered her sealed chamber. Knowing the wards were still in place, that this man had managed to enter without setting them off, meant that he was beyond a simple wizard. That he possessed the most glorious aura she had ever seen, could only mean that he was a god.

At least that is what she thought. The elderly man with long graying beard and hair, the flowing robes of purple and amber silks, focused into her sight, as his aura dimmed.

Merylon offered her life. Life and the chance to clear the curse of her name, and save the universe. She eagerly accepted, without thought.

Knowing she was too young, Merylon put the girl child to sleep. When Burlga woke, two decades later, she looked in the mirror seeing a beautiful woman of over forty, half elven, approximately twenty in human terms. Standing five feet ten inches tall, almost a perfect slender one hundred ten pounds in weight, with platinum silver hair, sky blue eyes, and a full round figure of an adult. She smiled, almost a grin, as she pushed her breasts up, in an attempt at creating more cleavage.

When she arrived in Launam, she noticed the others. Most were her apparent age. Maybe not as pretty, the other two women certainly were exotic looking.

And the men were as diverse as they could be. A huge man, little more than a boy, a Nubian with the baring of a king, and a middle-aged man, about her true age, appearing to be from Selenia, The North West Continent.

Overweight, out of shape, pampered as though he was a merchant, and almost a half hand shorter. But he had the dreamiest eyes that she had ever seen. They would seem to change color, when he would move.

"Hmm, this might not be so bad, after all. It might be fun, getting the old man into fighting shape!" She thought to herself, feeling an urge come upon her; she did not know why, but she had to have this man.

Burlga marched over to the middle-aged human, and attempted to give him the most passionate kiss, until he pushed her away, chuckling exclaiming in a language none could understand! Smiling, Burlga winked, saying,

"I'll have you yet, old man!" The others only stared at her audacity! Not, yet, understanding what it was she had said, as well.

****

As he kneeled before the statue, his head in a whirl, Odyseus Zenobe Brell, knew his life was over. Only, eighteen summers old and he was about to lose his life. All, because he couldn't control himself.

"What in the name of Heaven, caused me to act the fool?" He thought. "I be the nephew to the Queen, son of Priestess Helena Zenobe, Highest of all positions in the church of Athensoria. Dedicated to the Goddess Nike, Goddess of Victory. One thinks to hast known better!"

Odyseus was born to Helena Zenobe on a hot summer night, eighteen summers ago. His arrival was much heralded for two reasons. His mother, as sister to the Queen and High Priestess was not allowed to marry. Her responsibility to Athensoria, largest of kingdoms, in all of the world of Muridian, was to produce hearty sons and daughters for the wars. A world at war, for over twenty-five hundred years, Athensoria was the premier for all the other kingdoms to compare themselves.

Odyseus was the largest baby born in historical memory. And, the second reason for the news of his birth was that Helena Zenobe somehow was impregnated by the famed General, Lord Troy Brell, whom had been dead for over a year. The High Priestess Helena would never lie, so somehow, this monster of a baby had been conceived by the wraith of a dead man. Odyseus lived his short life with that stigma from all who knew the story, and most did know it.

All of Odyseus' brothers and sisters were warriors, and there were eight of them, he being the youngest of nine. They were all better with the spear and the short sword, quicker and more suited for the battle. Odyseus had grown so fast and so strong, that his dexterity could not keep up.

Like most preteens that grow beyond the 190 cm mark before even reaching man hood, he was clumsy and slow. The one thing that he had that no other person in all of Athensoria, let alone Muridian, was a strength that was unequaled. It would seem that he was much blessed by the Goddess, and some day when he finally grew into his size, he would make the most fearsome of warriors.

Even when he was twelve, he was stronger than most adult men, and by the time he reached eighteen, he could lift twice that of any man, and more than three

44

times the average. With still five summers to go of growth, who knew where he would end up. At a height of 209 cm, and weighing over 125 kg, Odyseus was an imposing boy, entering into the university, only one year earlier. Not a great warrior, yet; he excelled in his studies, and especially in the areas of battle tactics.

He was quickly being noted for his ability at coming up with new battle strategies. All the instructors at the university lauded him with acclaims and citations every time he would present a new tactic that when tried in the war, would work.

None failed, and even those that didn't work the way he thought they would, kept the losses under the acceptable limits. Less than a year in university and he had already been cited six times.

Still shy of the age to command a legion, by four summers, he kept to his studies and eagerly awaited his coming of age. But jealousy and envy were passing through his siblings and cousins. Odyseus' own brothers were allowing their envy, turn to hatred and on this very fateful day, their hatred would spawn into an evil that would lay Odyseus on the head block for a royal beheading.

Earlier, that afternoon, Odyseus had been walking through the palace gardens, something he often did, for the relaxation it gave. All five of his brothers and two of his male cousins, jumped him, near the cherry trees. Thinking back to that moment, he had almost defended himself, but his cousins, the royal princes, were a part of it. And striking any member of the royal line, carries a very stiff penalty, so he just stood there and allowed the smaller, yet, older men, all to beat on him.

That is, he stood still until the Royal Princess, heir to the crown, stepped from behind a tree and began taunting him for being a coward. She had called him a sheep to be sheared on Slaughter Day. Hearing that, Odyseus, control already on the verge of dissipating, his eyes swollen shut from the beating he was taking, with the taunts added from the only woman he respected besides his mother, he finally gave in to the anger.

Not being able to see more than blurs, he struck out. His fists falling like the hammers of a blacksmith to the anvil, swinging wildly, each time one fist or the other met flesh, he could hear with satisfaction, the crunching of bones, the exhaustion of breath in his seven oppressors.

When the Princess Deana, his royal cousin, yelled, "Stop, Odyseus. Stop there. Dost thou not know what they are doing?" He quickly realized the trouble that was about to come his way.

Clearing his eyes, as best he could, his vision slowly coming into focus, he noticed the seven men laying on the ground, only five moving, in an attempt to clear of the raging bull that was Odyseus. He had not only killed one of his brothers, but Odyseus had broken the neck of the eldest son of the Queen, punishable by beheading, no matter the circumstances.

Seeing the horror in his cousin's eyes, the tears falling down her cheeks, Odyseus ran. He ran for what seemed hours, and when late after dark, found him stumbling the streets near the Temples, he fell into the Temple of Athena, Goddess of Wisdom.

In hopes of gaining some answers from the priests or priestesses there, to his problem, he unfortunately found the temple empty. The sanctuary held the six-meter-tall statue of the goddess, and Odyseus fell before it. At only eighteen years, not even a man, yet, he was too young to die such a dishonorable death, he begged the Goddess to have mercy on him and to give him advice.

The statue moved, then. A hand, large and hard landed on his head, gently. He looked up to see the statue looking down at him, and immediately fell to kiss its feet. Athena herself was coming to grant his request.

"Thy kiss is much appreciated, but I would rather thou face me, rather than that poor semblance of stonework." The voice was strong and commanding. And, coming from behind him. Standing, Odyseus turned, expecting to see the queen and her guards, but instead, the woman that met him in the eye, as tall as he, if not taller, and very beautiful. Broad shoulders, holding a spear and shield in arms well-muscled, that rippled of long use of the weapons, a robe of gray and white, with a single gold belt holding it tight on a narrow waist. Her bosom was full, and the cleavage sticking through the robe, kept drawing his eyes, before he would blush and return to looking at her deep blue eyes and her long dark hair. The sandaled feet below long muscular legs stretching down below the robe, which stopped high above the knees.

She had a soft white aura surrounding her that made her appear the Goddess she was and when Odyseus finally got his wits back, he knelt to bow.

"Hail, Holy Athena, I praise thy name for coming to such a lowly servant."

"Hardly lowly that, Odyseus! I went to great troubles getting the right mix into thy mother when you were conceived. Dost, thou know how hard it is to get a dead corpse cleaned up enough to mate with someone?"

She was the most beautiful person he had ever seen, and when Minerva, as she called herself, explained her need, he readily agreed.

When Odyseus arrived to Launam, he quickly saw that he was the youngest amongst the group, and the largest. These would be his companions against evil, he had no doubt. But, which one of them would be his new commander? He would have to wait and see!

****

Warned that carrying a child for so long, would cause unheard of side effects. Especially, since it was being magically postponed. But Breana Bin was sure, being the third most powerful wizardress in the world of Haven, she could avoid any bad side effects. When that mystical tall women came to her in a dream and told her that her child should be born in "The Year of Life", she knew she had to make the pregnancy go for twenty-two months.

The seventy eighth century was to be the most powerful, and her child would be born on the first day of the year.

Purana Bin Gage, almost killed her mother, at birth. Only Breana's great magic sustained her life when the baby was born. Every twelve years the best of the wizards are born. The Year of Life is known to produce the best and strongest, and this time was no exception. Born with the ability to talk, Purana, could cast her first spell by the age of two. But, that was the least of the defects that were to happen.

The baby born was twelve centimeters longer than normal. And four kilograms heavier. The midwife swore, that before she could swat the baby, Purana twisted up so she could grab the woman's hand in order to try and stop her. Her eyes glowed as if to attempt a spell, when her strength would prove to be insufficient to stop the bottom from being stung.

Jayn Del Gage, the father was put to the question for producing a demonic child, and even though he had barely enough skill at spell casting, all suddenly thought he must be trying to hide his talents.

Breana, seeing the treatment her mate was getting, kept quiet of her dream, and the visit from the goddess, and allowed her mate to be killed for demonic interference. There were plenty of suitable males in the world, any way! She knew that her daughter was to become a blessing, and nothing would interfere with her growth.

That Purana was powerful, was explained away as, only because the Lor and Bin lines, her mother's families, were powerful wizard's having sent over forty to the council of magic in just the past two centuries. Eventually, everyone forgot the happenings on the day of her birth and attributed her great power to her name, Bin Gage.

Purana grew up with very little interaction with any other people. Her studies in the schools were spent mostly with private tutors. She spent most of her time with adults that she was consistently told were her inferiors, and she hardly ever spent any time with those of her own age. She was spoiled, pampered, and as was quickly proven, completely without any love in her life. Purana was never shown love, nor did she ever give it.

By age eighteen, Purana had only half the remembered spells that most her age would have, due to her impatience and arrogance, but those she did have were by far and away the most powerful ever cast, and done with more strength than any had ever cast, as well! She was too much in a hurry, to ever really want to study properly. And never learned the more subtle of spells, but the destructive types, almost came too easy to her.

Then there was the mysterious beauty, she possessed. Darker skinned than most on her tiny planet of Haven, she had a dark olive tone, that seemed to radiate with a glow all its own. Her fiery red hair, and bright blue eyes. No one could explain the shade of her hair, nor the light color of her eyes.

There were no blue eyes in all of the world. It was as if she was an outer worlder, with the demonic or angelic beginnings, as they all thought at her birth! Standing over 176 cm tall, with a weight of 55 kg, she was only average height, yet, she was slender, yet hour glass figured, and possessed an almost perfectly flawless face. But, the exotic beauty about her would prove to be a distraction, one that would cost her much in her training and in her life.

In her nineteenth year, not even legal mating age yet; Purana killed her mother in a duel to take a seat on the council. After seven more challenges all ending in kills, the council had had enough. Voting in a new law, making it illegal to kill a council member in a duel, the vote was passed easily, by a count of 168 to 1. Purana's vote, of course, being the only descent.

The year of her twenty fourth celebration, had her being challenged by a lesser member of the council. The result was predictable, but even though she was

48

sure she refrained from using death magic on the man, he died, just after the duel was done. She was arrested and convicted, and sent to an anti-magic holding cell awaiting the beheading.

It was while in that cell, that Purana would receive a visit from someone that should not have been able to get into the cell.

The beautiful woman standing with an aura of pure white, wearing only a gossamer gown of see through blue silks, she was even more beautiful than Purana. The movement of this goddess, was perfect, as were her features. Long black hair, almost a blue tint when light would touch it. The hair flowed down past her knees in the back.

Light coffee colored skin, with a long-pointed nose that turned up, just enough to accent the high cheek bones. Bright blue eyes, round with just a touch of a point in the ends of the sockets, and crystal-clear whites around the blue. Her mouth was full, as was the bosom pushing out of the gown. Narrow waist, and full hips. Long muscular legs, accented by gold anklets, and bare feet with perfectly groomed and painted toe nails.

The woman looked so perfect, that even Purana had to admit she was the most stunningly beautiful woman to ever live.

Introducing herself as Isis, goddess of Love and beauty, the goddess claimed to have made Purana almost too perfect. It would seem, though, she lacked love, but that would come. Purana would have the next few years to find love, somehow!

When Purana arrived at Launam, she immediately noticed that this was going to be a long year. The men were nothing, and of the other two women, well, only one possessed anything close to real talent.

"I will have to be that much more, then, if we are to win." She thought to herself. "And those two that are not even nobles had better learn real quick as to who their betters are! Or else, I will teach them a real lesson on power!" Isis, hearing her creation's thoughts, only shook her head.

After one hundred forty-two tries, this was her last chance. Hopefully, this girl would learn patience, and somehow learn to care for others. Shaking her head, Isis joined the other Ancient Ones.

****

Phaleg had just about given up when during the FOURTH ERA on Titania, largest of all the humanoid planets he saw a potential. Youngest of the Ancient Ones, he was the straightest foreword, and it never occurred to him to actually create a champion, like his siblings were doing. So, when Quen Dem Lurin was approached to follow the Prince of the Duel, Phaleg had a lot riding on the answer. Fortunately, Quen agreed to come.

Born in Quartense, the largest of continents, Quen was the fifth born son to the emperor. A duke when he would obtain adult hood and ready to take over, he was one of the sons left out of the royal education, for the throne.

Since there was virtually no chance, he would ever become emperor, and the royal family never fought in the wars, Quen left to join the army under an assumed name.

As a child he would watch the guards practice with their swords, and would pick up a stick and try to emulate them. They thought it cute and would teach him. By the time he was thirteen, he had joined the military and rose through the ranks quickly. By his sixteenth cycle, he had rose through the levels of swordsmanship that he was already considered that of a master swordsman. And, with his Naming Day coming up, he would be able to join the officer's study.

Imagine the looks when young Quen Dem Lurin was named and the marshals had found out who his real parentage was. Only seventeen cycles old, a true master of the swords, enough to raise eye brows in wonder and even more surprisingly, he was already better than any man within twenty cycles of his age. Some thought Quen better than "The Right Arm, Protector of the Realm." Though, that was only whispered, as that man was supposed to be the best of the best.

In the next few years Quen would never lose a duel, and continued to work and study, until he had been acclaimed the greatest duelist ever. On his twenty second cycle, his father died, and when the call for challenges to become the new Right Arm, went out, everyone expected him to answer the challenges. But Quen had other ideas. When his eldest of brothers, the new Emperor, called him to the palace, Quen arrived to find that he was in trouble for not coming to the challenges.

"I don't like you, your majesty! As my eldest brother, you cared little for me, why should I want to live a life of boredom, for you, now?"

The outrage at the way, Quen spoke to the emperor, almost landed him in prison. If it would not have been for the fact that he was already a major in the army of duelists, and an acclaimed hero of the dueling wars, Quen would have been imprisoned immediately. Instead, his brother simply smiled, and exclaimed.

"I care little for your whining, Quen Dem Lurin. I care little for your feelings or lack of them. You have been summoned, and you will answer the call. And, as punishment for your attitude, you will duel against Quartern, another with a poor manner to him."

Quartern was the third born brother, and the only one that Quen really ever cared for. The two were equal in strength, with his older brother a little quicker. But, none had Quen's skill in the blades. Standing 192 cm tall, Quen was only average height, and his thin 90 kg, made him fast and graceful, just not like his brother. When they faced off, Quartern started with a blitz of swings, short and precise, and Quen quickly realized that this was going to be a duel to the death. It was ended a few moments later, with Quartern dead at his feet, blood filling the Court Yard, Quen calmly stoically, turned to the emperor, and threw his sword to the ground.

"Slay me now, brother. I will never bow to you for what you made me do, this day!"
Sitting in the dungeons, when the man stepped seemingly through the wall, a white aura surrounding him, a tall man with strong muscles, and an even stronger look, Quen simply smiled. Knowing there were no such things as gods, Quen thought this man must be an assassin.

The surprise showed on his face when a sword was tossed his way and the challenge was issued. After less than a minute, Quen was disarmed, and humiliated by his first loss, ever in a duel. And to have it over so quickly, to imagine the best sword fighter in all the world, could be so easily defeated.

"I will make you almost as good as I, young Quen. And, with the power I will give you, you will be king, if you come with me. What say you?"

"You will teach me the way of the blades? I say that is all the enticement you need, Lord Phaleg. The other offers are just icing on the cake! Let us leave."

When Quen arrived at Launam, he was surprised that none of the others possessed any real skill with the sword. Excepting of course, that small female with the strange slanted narrow eyes. But she danced too much, and could easily be overcome, in a close quartered fight. If, that is one could get past her quickness.

He was looking forward to learning with these other five. To see how they would help him become the champion to defeat the vilest of enemies.

Being dark brown skinned, much darker, even than the pretty redhead and the short older man, Quen had dark brown almost black hair, and light brown eyes. Looking at the others, only the large barbarian boy, was taller.

Phaleg looked on at the other champions, and thought he had made a good choice. His was a true warrior, unlike the others, and he had done it without the use of manipulation. Still, he remained silent that he had not thought of creating the perfect fighting machine, like his siblings had. But, why had Jeasuas and Selene created such flaws, he wondered? The two most powerful Ancient Ones had created less than perfect champions!

CHAPTER 3
Coming Together

In those first days that the five humans and one half-elf were gathered together, there was hardly any time that was not occupied in study. Be it hard training with the swords or other weapons of their choice, or the studying of the various prophesies, the cramming of book knowledge, the physical training of exercise, or the constant pressures of casting spells through the use of sorcery, the six champions, as they were told they would be, would fall into their beds each night with an exhaustion that none of them had ever known before.

On that first day, they eyed each other. Other than the one initial contact when the half-elf female, Burlga, had attempted to kiss the Terran, James Carl, they mostly remained apart. Only Sheera and JC seemed to understand each other. Sheera's English was limited at best, and her French was even worse. JC, with his command of several languages, never did learn to speak any of the Asian languages, so he could not understand any of her more common tongues.

Jeasuas finally stepped forward on the second day and touched each of the six on their foreheads, implanting not only an awareness in their psychic abilities, but also a "tongues spell" on each. Now, the six would not only be able to understand each other, but as it was explained, they would be able to speak, read, write, and know any known language to include that of the Heavens and the Hells.

"Welcome to Launam!" Merylon began. "This is one of the thirteen worlds to have humanoids and only one of seven to have humans. Of course, none of you need concern yourselves with that. You won't meet any of the other planetary inhabitants during your training."

"What my brother is slowly getting at, is for one year, give or take, thine all will be learning what needs be learned. Learning and hopefully becoming friends and companions!" Minerva took up the conversation.

Learn, they did!

There were four buildings that suddenly appeared, rising from the ground, with one smaller one in the middle of a triangular setup of three large ones. One belonged to the teachings of Jeasuas and Selene, one belonged to the athletics of Minerva and Phaleg, and the third to the studies of Merylon and Isis.

The smaller, fourth building that appeared, was a three-room single-story dorm style house that became their home. Three large rooms, two bedrooms with three beds each, and the third central room; a kitchen/dining area, with sitting room. The outhouse was attached to the back side, and all noticed that there never seemed to be the normal rancid odor, associated with such facilities.

For the first month, the Chosen Champions had no choices. They were told they would attend every class, every day, and learn everything taught during those first four weeks.

Only one of the six attacked each day with a fervor, and one other soon became just as lustful towards the education, yet, she had begun only in appearances for the other one's attention. The classes consisted of The History of Zindar, learning the ways of psychic healing, disciplines of sorcery, mental protections and attacks, swords, and battle craft, and finally, the study of demons and devils. All were taught the different types of Hell Spawn, and each of their weaknesses.

As well, each of the Chosen was presented with copies of their patron Ancient One's prophesies. Alas, it was not ordered they all be read, so therefore only one of the champions managed to read them all.

Something unexpected, was that JC, the eldest of the six, was actually attempting the learn beyond the "tongues" spell, and learn the language of the Ancient Ones. As well as pick up the different ones of the other champions.

The learning of the swords was fun, Sheera thought, but she could not imagine herself ever really needing it. It was not until the third week of study, that she finally understood. After reading her patron's book of prophesy, she came to the realization that she was going to become more than just a prophet. She would become a warrior against Hell. The fear that gripped her, went unstopped, until the half-elf, Burlga, and the other Terran, JC, explained she would not be alone in this.

If not for her two newest friends, Sheera would have given up, that first month. She knew, she would be thankful to those two, and that nothing would get in the way of a friendship; nothing, at least, except for possibly love!

Quen thought, that the biggest waste of time, was to learn sorcery. All he needed to do was get close enough to stick his sword in. Nothing in the universe, could stand before him and his blade. He calmly, unemotionally stood during the sorcery classes, watching the others work at meager casting, that he was sure, he could avoid.

Of the six, one had the most problems during that first month. The size of a small horse, Odyseus, had the mind of an early teenager. Not only that he was not finished growing, and, like most teenagers that had grown so fast, his coordination was askew. But, most of all it was his childlike speech that even the "tongues" spell could not counter act. It had most questioning Minerva's thoughts on bringing the boy.

Burlga also had similar problems. Being put to sleep for so long, she never matured out of her teenage mentality. Having the lustful nature given to her by Merylon, she lacked the maturity of a grown woman to handle the nuances of it. She also, was so intent on making JC see her as a woman, that her particular disturbing use of slang obscenities and openly throwing herself at him, became a problem between the two. But, she learned to control her words, and she also, quickly learned the behavior of an adult. Excluding the more subtle ways of seducing the man she intended on making hers.

Odyseus learned to enjoy after that first month. Most of the others would make fun of his speech, even under the "tongues spell" it sounded different than the others. But, two of the others never teased him. Those two from the world called, Terra. They seemed to genuinely act as if they wanted to help him. Not as agile, not as graceful, Odyseus seemed to need the help, in everything. All the others were adults. He was just a teenage boy, not yet fully grown even.

He was sure glad that JC was there. The man was a true friend to help him all the time. JC would shake his head, when Odyseus would get into one of his klutz modes.

"When you are done growing, son, you won't even remember this time of your life. Fear not, it only lasts a while! And, all growing boys go through it!" Odyseus would take stock in the old man's confidence, and continue to try harder. Minerva would smile, seeing the elder man turning her boy into a good young adult. She wondered,

"A wonderful thing, Selene coming up with such an idea for an elder priest!"

Burlga laughed at the big barbarian. He was such a klutz, and such a little boy. It was hard to imagine, The Ancient One, Minerva, could have brought such a person. But, he was a good boy, and besides, JC seemed to like him. Of course, JC seemed to like all of the "kids", as he was always calling everyone. When Burlga had tried to interest him, he had laughed, saying he could never be interested in someone so young. Burlga knew there was something else, though, he was not saying, something she saw in his eyes, a sadness whenever he spoke of love.

As she eyed the others, she could only shake her head at the two, supposed rulers. Quen and Purana, were alleged royalty, and, they were the most difficult of the group to tolerate.

"Except when JC would get bloody stubborn. Then he makes those two-look amicable." Burlga would think!

Purana hated the idea of studying the use of a blade.

"Who would need such a thing? Well, maybe those peasants would. And, of course, Quen! He had absolutely no use for magic, so he said! Too bad his skin is so dark, colored. He is the only true royal among the group. He is the only logical choice for me to pick when time to mate."

But, the thought of having such a dark offspring, would go against all her beliefs. "Maybe the big boy would work. He is the nephew of a queen, if he is to be believed. Of course, he needs to learn to keep his mouth shut. His childish speech, grates on the nerves." Purana was constantly thinking.

The group gathered in their classes, and soon, it became apparent to all where the strengths and weaknesses lay. They had been blessed with the ability of "tongues", a spell of great power that was usually only short lived when cast by a simple priest or wizard. The Ancient Ones made it a permanent spell, that second day of their arrival.

One man, among the three women and three men, gathered together, was the least arrogant, yet the most stubborn, and the most difficult to understand. Not impressed with noble separation, he would never defer to the "superiors" of the group.

Already, he had put himself aside, emotionally, to be the leader, and most of the others did not like it.

Odyseus could see the man as a father. He acted the part, especially with Burlga and the boy. That he was the eldest, was without question. Yet, his

56

insufferable attitude of wanting to be alone, after the classes, made each of the others think something was wrong with the man. Even older that Burlga, the half-elf, by more than six years. And, more than twice that of any of the others. That he worked hardest went unquestioned, though!

"He needs to work harder," Quen thought. "He was not a noble, had no pure upbringing, and it was suggested he was the least talented among the six."

But he still would insinuate his feelings on a subject and seemed to expect the others to agree with him. When they wouldn't, he would just smile, with a strange all-knowing smile that he seemed to possess, and shake his head. In the end, things seemed to always go his way, and though, he would never gloat, never give the "I told you so", the others expected; still, his calm almost priestly ways would grate on a lot of the youngsters' nerves.

When Quen and Purana would discuss the effects of the older commoner, they could only shake their heads. The two most arrogant of the six, were also, the two most difficult for everyone to get along with. Odyseus seemed the most perplexed by it.

"We be equals, in the Holy eyes of the Gods!" He would wisely say. Of course, that would just get him laughed at by the two supposed royalty.

Purana's answer to the large boy was always similar.

"Those other three, are so far beneath us, that one can only imagine why their Gods picked them. At least the elf can use magic, but those two Terran's haven't a clue what is real and what isn't! We are nobles and should stay apart from them!"

Burlga would laugh, at Quen and Purana. Being of noble birth, herself, she certainly had the upbringing, and JC reminded her the most of her masters, back at school. His insufferable calm when they were learning things, his often use, of too many questions, attempting to guide, without actually telling them what to do.

Whenever talk of leadership would take place, which was at least once a day, if Quen or Purana had their way, the six would argue. JC thought they should remain the way things were, all equal, with an equal vote. The others would bristle. A clear leader needed to be chosen among them, and it should be one of the nobles, Quen and Purana would both say.

The six Ancient Ones, would just sit back, and watch the arguments between the young mortals, and then watch as the older one would calmly effortlessly settle the disagreements without any seeming knowledge, he was doing it. A master at manipulation, the one that called himself JC, the forty-eight-year-old human from Terra, would simply point out both sides of the debates, the good and bad of both, and hint which way, he was leaning towards, and the others would all appear to eventually follow.

Yet, later, they would complain at having done what the "old man" said to do, yet, once again. To the Ancient Ones, they found this amusing, and would continue to watch on in silence.

These mortals were from different worlds, different times, and yet, each of the six had one thing in common. They all had trouble in their former lives, which they had left behind, and a future open to new beginnings of a destiny that they all were striving for. A destiny that would shape the entire universe that would settle an ages old dispute. A destiny that all thought some of them would have to die to achieve. Something that only one of the six was ready and willing to accept.

Quen could not understand why any would have to die. They were going to be the most powerful people in the known world, whatever world that would be, and they were being expected to die? Phaleg advised him, to not take the prophesies too literally. Dying could mean many things. Death could simply be a change from the old to that of the new.

In a sense, they had already died for their former lives. Quen chose to look at it that way, and would argue the point, among them.

Merylon had warned Burlga, not to read too much into the prophesies. Not all of them would die, for if they all did, the universe would die with them. Burlga would argue that point, and only JC and Quen were ready to agree. Yet, still, JC maintained that he himself, would most likely die, no matter what happened to the others. He would continually tell the half-elf,

"You just make sure that you and Odyseus are the last remaining. He will be the One Chosen Champion, and you will be his guard. If not him, then Quen! I will sacrifice everything to insure the universe's victory." Burlga would shiver at his comments, thinking only, what kind of man, is so willing to give up life for people he does not know, and a universe that has treated him so bad?

But she was more than glad to know that he felt relaxed enough, to confide in her, that much. He never seemed to want to talk outside of classes very much!

Knowing that all the prophesies spoke of death and blood, only made Sheera wonder. How could they die, if they were to insure victory over the evil? There had to be something in what Quen was saying! Death was only change. That JC kept insisting that he would perish, either was a guess on his part, or his patron, Selene, had told him. That he was so willing, gave her a sense of pride towards him.

"So willing, so able, and no fear in doing it!"

They were supposed to be coming a team, but as Quen would often announce, how would a team be maintained if they were going to be spread out on six different continents? They would have to learn to be alone, fight alone, and win alone! And, Purana would add that she did not want to depend on anyone else for her survival.

Quen was the best with blades, Odyseus was the physically strongest, so strong that even when JC, and his great constitution, would get hit by his swinging club, the smaller man would go down. Purana and Burlga were both wizardresses and extremely talented sorceresses, able to cast three or more spells at a time. Both were very beautiful women and would make good arbitrators.

Purana easily the most physically perfect human ever created, if she could only learn a little compassion, could charm anyone, without the use of magic. Quen once said of her,

"What she could not en-spell with sorcery, she could simply smile and the most adamant assassin would melt at her feet!" Everyone agreed, if begrudgingly.

Sheera was filled with an amazing balance and dexterity. She was so quick, that even Phaleg would miss, at times, when trying to hit her. She was able to almost walk-up walls, with her amazing balance, and what she lacked in physical strength, she more than made up for in mental capabilities. And, she was so calm, so filled with inner peace, especially when around others that they all wondered what made up such a person.

She never showed any jealousies or envy, but then neither did JC; it must be a Terran trait, the other's thought. Sheera never said a negative comment about another. She never lost her temper, no matter how frustrated she would become, and could even rival Quen for appearing emotionless, when called for.

She was the easiest of them to get along with, and even though, they all knew she was firmly in JC's camp for group leader, they would invite her, still, to their meetings, even when JC was not.

And then there was the "old man" in the group. JC, an ex-athlete and professor, he had a discipline of learning. He could break down or dispel any spell, given enough time and study. He rarely stopped practicing until he no longer failed at something; and he continued to push himself, long after the others would leave, to the point of exhaustion, and then would push on even more.

Ignoring pain was easy, he once told them, ignoring failure at anything was impossible. He was shorter than all of them except for Sheera, nearly as broad across the shoulders as Odyseus, though not as strong, but nearly so. He was easily more so than the other four. He was as quick as Purana, and had nearly the balance of Sheera. He was an anomaly that the others didn't know how to consider.

The younger of the group had never mentioned the physical changes in him. He was the only one to have changed in the way he looked. Having aged backwards by more than twenty years, in physical characteristics, he had become almost handsome, to the women's way of thinking. To the men, he had become less of a liability, and more of someone they could depend on.

None of them would openly oppose a suggestion he would make, but most of them would try and find fault in everything he would say. They all were unwillingly following him, and they were becoming frustrated by it.

Never taking offense when he was bettered by the others, in something, JC would only try harder, study what he did wrong, or what they did right, and then try to figure a way to counter or duplicate their actions. He usually succeeded, given time, and willingly gave the information to them.

Sheera took note, one day after a couple months had gone by. JC was no longer the out of shape, middle aged Occidental. He was now, a handsome, if not tall, man still appearing to be middle aged in the face, but with the tone and muscular body of a man in his prime of late twenties.

He still had those pretty eyes, and with the slight gray at his temples, and a confidence he was acquiring, he was becoming a very nice man to be around.

She wondered often,

"Is this the man that Jeasuas had been talking about? Is this the one I will find love in?"

Burlga continued to watch the old man, and was the first to notice his changes. Sheera had missed it, until the two young ladies were talking about it over tea, one evening.

Aging backwards in body and in strength, he was becoming a very powerful presence, even if he acted as though he did not notice.

That man was changing. In just ten weeks he had become younger looking, stronger, now, even exceeding Quen, much to the prince's chagrin. And, what amazed Quen the most, JC was becoming more assured of himself. JC was beginning to act as though he really was an equal to all the nobles.

That he still seemed as though he could only do things barely what the others could do, or maybe even a little less, he was at the least, no longer the liability, that all of them thought, in the beginning.

None of the six knew what to expect from the others, only that they would somehow have to learn trust. They all knew, of course, what the future held, but not the outcome, and not how to obtain it. Worse of all, was that most of them disagreed with each other on the final end to these destinies. And then, they could not agree on which of them would become to be known as The One Chosen Champion! The single individual that all the prophesies spoke of as *"he who would face the final battle."* They could not even agree on if all six would be present at the final battle or if only one of them would live to see that day.

They would argue daily throughout the weeks and months, at what or how to bring about this final battle. The Ancient Ones would just watch silently, answer questions where appropriate, or remain in silence if they did not know an answer nor wanted to reveal it. The most frustrating to all but JC, was when they would answer a question with "what do you think" or "how would you do it".

Being an instructor, he knew the tactic. "Learn through self-awareness." The younger ones, would get angry, not realizing some of the things they were learning were even a first for the Ancient Ones.

In the end, though, it was JC's ability to talk that would make the others listen. They may not agree, but even those that openly opposed him, did so with a respect that any would give to any elder. JC was becoming the "father" of the group, and his open affection for them often times would bewilder them.

Sheera found it amazing that the man could be so easy going while at the same time so sure he would be one of those dying in the end. She gave the outward appearance, but he seemed to really be that way. He would never turn down one of the five that would come to him for help. That is, except for Purana when she needed help for her "monthly cycle." Yet, no matter how many times he had helped the others when they would come to him, if he volunteered to help, he was shunned.

He learned after a few months that he would watch, but began to ignore their problems until asked for. In a lot of ways, they were like teenager's, he realized and JC learned to start treating them like he did his students.

The "Father" was becoming a Priest, something he insisted they all were supposed to be in their respective churches.

Dreams would play on most of them, at night. It seemed most of them had horrors needing rid of. But JC never wanted to discuss his nightmares. He would only laugh and exclaim,

"My good dreams are anyone else nightmares. Let's leave it at that!" If he survived in his dreams he felt them good ones. More than most, though, he died in his dreams, brutally and bloodily. That statement bothered Burlga the most about the man.

She was finding within her, more than just lust towards this strange short stocky man, and yet, he would not talk much about himself, nor his dreams. Only speak of nightmares as though they were common place. At least hers were not so fatalistic, nor were they so often, if he spoke the truth of it.

Unlike, the others, JC had lived a peaceful and joyful life, growing up when and where he did. It was not until that last moment, the one act of true violence, that he had even known what it felt like. And, like a couple of the others, he had not even believed in half of what he now accepted to be truth.

Before this, a simple high school chemistry and biology teacher, JC, would have thought this a fantasy in the twenty first century of the world called Terra. He shuddered as that fateful day replayed over and over in his dreams.

Quen did not understand the problems, the others were having with dreams. He rarely would dream, and when he did it was usually of winning some great duel, or taking some beautiful woman, like Purana or Sheera to bed. He did have a dream about Burlga once, but she being of mixed blood, he would never even consider something so, "evil."

His mother had warned him, on the rare occasions, that she had bothered to speak with him, insuring he understood that mating with the other races was sinful, and filthy.

"Never sleep with a commoner, and never with a lesser nonhuman creature, they carry diseases." She had said.

Besides, the way that Burlga acted like some high-born prostitute, there was no way her claim to nobility could be valid all too valid.

"It is the only one really good thing, that JC has shown, sense enough to leave that harlot alone!" He would say.

Burlga was so sure that her problems with enticing the man, was JC's problems in his dreams, bringing up his past. She could not listen to when he would slip and actually talk about something going on with him. Sheera heard, though. She heard the fear in his dreams, she heard the fear for everyone else, yet, not for himself. Sheera, wondered,

"How could he be so fearful for others, especially those that have treated him so badly, and yet, be so ready to fall, so that they, we could survive?"

Sheera most enjoyed the early mornings, when she could get up and join him in one of his runs, or convince him to work through the "forms" with her. His "kata" was so hard, so undisciplined, yet, he seemed to be learning her style with ease, and would often laugh, when he would fall or make a mistake. The rare times that she would get to see him laugh.

Odyseus would get up early, each day to find JC already out running, or doing that stretching dance, he called kata. Only that pretty little girl, named Sheera, seemed to understand it and would often be out doing it with him. Odyseus had tried it, but he would usually end up falling on his face, and even though JC would patiently tell him, it just takes practice, the laughs and harassment the young man would receive from the others, caused Odyseus to quit trying. He was just too clumsy, for it, any ways! JC seemed a little upset at first, by him quitting, but he finally shrugged, saying only,

"At least you tried! That's more than a couple of them!" JC never showed anger for long.

Burlga worked with Sheera in private for the first few weeks. At night, when JC would go off and be by himself, reading or walking. It seemed every evening, the old man would disappear for an hour or so, insisting he have some "down time," as he called it. Burlga convinced Sheera to teach her the forms, those two were doing every morning, and soon, she felt confident enough to join them in their morning rituals. Sometimes, she would smile, when she would be there early enough to be first with JC, alone.

Burlga and JC, it seemed, both needed the least amount of sleep among the group. That the man rarely slept more than four hours, was a wonder, but the others seemed to need close to eight, and she was happy that she could get time to be alone with the man. He seemed more open in the early morning, before anyone else arrived.

The first to rise, each day, the last to go to bed, JC kept himself emotionally apart from the others, except the rare occasions he would console someone that had gotten hurt. Working harder, until anything he did was done to his own particular perfection.

He seemed to have a more difficult time with sorcery than the women, but was better at grasping it then the other two men, always trying to figure out how or why a spell worked. He did have a talent for healing, though, and could even heal someone, using empathy, that would aid the victim, avoiding the shock that could kill a person that would be too injured for normal magical healings.

But he was warned about using too much of himself to save another. It could mean death for him. And, they were taught, never try and heal the dead. One might not be able to come back from the spirit world, themselves.

Raising of the dead required the healer to go into the spirit world and find the soul of the dead person, to bring it back to the corpse. The longer the person was dead, the further away from the present world they would be.

Coming back, would be difficult for the healer, themselves, let alone, being able to bring back the corpse's spirit. Necromancy was another story, but it was considered a sin, as well as evil, to create zombies, and other undead.

Why they were even mentioned was anyone's guess, but JC assumed, being taught how to do something was a good way to know what to avoid doing.

In the end, only three of the six, even bothered with the lessons on healing, and the other three would only shake their heads with scorn.

"Why learn to heal, if we are going to be destroying? I certainly don't plan on helping any of the Hell Spawn, we face!" Purana would answer.

Quen could not understand why they all were spending so much time learning to heal. What need of healing, if they were going to be warriors? He certainly wasn't planning on healing any of the demons he would slay.

All that was really needed from sorcery was the protections that it offered. And that was about all that he would successfully perform with the magic. But even Purana was impressed by the concentration he could perform the protections. No matter how hard they would try, once Quen got a mental shield in place, he could hold it with seemingly no effort, even while dueling.

JC suspected that it was because Quen and Odyseus were unable to heal effectively that they didn't want to learn, and Purana cared little for anyone else, to bother learning how to heal. She was a force of pure destruction,

"She and Quen would make a good team, JC would think to himself, often. "Put them out front and let them loose. Iron shields so that the rest of us could take out the trash."

JC was not a slow person, as the others thought, but the methodical scientist in him was always looking for the reason behind everything. The others would show impatience with the older man, thinking him dim or slow witted. They could not imagine so many questions over some things that seemed so simple.

The younger champions did not understand the need for JC to study everything so much, unless he really was that dumb; they thought. JC had learned that sorcery was not limited to power, but to the strength of one's own mind. The limits in sorcery, were caused by the limits of one's imagination.

The others did not notice, that he had held back, during their year together. JC had become concerned that to hold so much power in one person could be a negative influence on the personality. He worried about his own pride, more than what the others might have thought!

He would experiment with emulating Burlga on a number of occasions, creating two or three spells at a time. But, where the half elven woman could create the images of several different spells at once, JC would not do it effectively. Sheera often wondered, if the man was pretending to be the way he was, or if he really did only have brief signs at being more than he had shown them.

"He is not so weak as you all seem to think!" She remembered telling the others, one evening, when the five younger ones were sitting around talking.

They all laughed at her comment, thinking it just because she "loved" him. They didn't understand, she did love him, just not like they all thought. It seemed that all the other four thought about was "who is the leader and who should sleep with whom!"

JC thought physical abilities would be the handiest and worked harder in those areas. He was not the strongest, even after his body seemed to age backwards to the point where JC was physically just a late twenties man, again. He was not the quickest, nor the most graceful, nor did he seem the most prolific sorcerer.

But he worked the hardest, and he was not the weakest in any of those things, either. He may not be able to successfully cast two or three spells at once, on a consistent basis, but when he did cast one, it rarely failed.

He was not the best sword fighter, but with practice blades he could out last the other two men, and eventually wear them down. His great ability to tolerate pain, made it easy for him to take a few shots from the others, and eventually he could get to them when they tired. Something that he rarely felt!

After getting himself back into athletic shape, JC's great constitution allowed for him to not only tolerate pain and exhaustion, but also, he was able to go on less sleep, less food, and he never seemed to feel the effects of the changing anomalies within the world of Launam.

He was not the smartest, but he was the most methodical, and his constant studying of something, allowed him to often times find ways to break a spell, that the others would miss. He admired Burlga and Purana's ability to memorize something with one look. JC often thought how easy things would be, if he did not have to study so hard to learn.

Towards the end of that year, the Ancient Ones were beginning to doubt if their champions would be ready. They were no closer to being a team, than the first weeks, and only one amongst them seemed to have any desire to continue to learn, or even push himself.

Jeasuas and Selene would always smile, and seemed to sit back, watching the others. Purana noticed. The other Ancient Ones, knew that their two siblings had collaborated on the project. And, Merylon, even seemed to go along with it.

His creation, although not a pure human, being half elven, was a perfect distraction that seemed thrown into the mix. JC, was garnering a lot of attention from both, Jeasuas' and Merylon's creations, and even Odyseus, Minerva's creation, would defer to Selene's, when it came right down to it. Except during the monthly mating urges, when Purana would attempt to reconcile those emotions.

She had easily taken, Quen and Odyseus, but on the one time she attempted to interest the older man, JC had easily and diplomatically turned her aside, without seemingly any effort.

"I could never sleep with you, without having love, Purana. And, we do not love each other, yet!" Purana was so nonplussed at being turned down, that she couldn't even manage a reaction.

She loves him? He was a lesser man, a commoner, a peasant. She would never love him. He would never be anything more than a common gigolo to her!

Never in her life, had a man turned her down! Even those, on her home world, that were stupid enough to promise themselves to just one woman, as if any woman could truly be happy with one man, yet, even those men, were easily swayed by her exotic unworldly beauty. Yet, JC wasn't!

That man, a mere peasant, not as strong, not as quick, not as good looking, and much too short, had the nerve to tell her no! More importantly, actually mean it!

Quen had laughed at her on that day. It seemed to him, that if any of the women could win JC's heart, it would be the other Terran. Sheera was more subtle than the other two girls, and more in tune with the way the old man thought. Quen thought that JC was actually telling the truth, when he said that he would only bed a woman he loved. Such a strange custom, but Sheera and Burlga both had actually applauded the man for it.

Too bad, he was more in love with his patron Ancient One, than with the girls. JC could almost have his choice of the women, now, that he had become more battle ready, Quen thought to himself.

For ten months the six strangers had been learning and practicing under the tutelage of the Ancient Ones, to prepare for the final conflict between the forces of good and those of evil. Jeasuas was the most dynamic speaker of the demigods, and he was also the most serene and the calmest. He was the quickest to forgive any mistakes made by the mortal children.

JC enjoyed listening to his lessons, even if he was not the patron's own creation. Although, as Sheera pointed out, Jeasuas did seem to pay more attention to the man, than he did to the other four.
"JC, my own Ancient One watches you as much as he does me. Just like yours does, it would seem, they are both interested more in our design than in the others. What do you think on that?" Sheera had said one afternoon. JC pretended not to notice. Saying only,

"Who knows the machinations of the minds of such powerful beings?"

On a day when Jeasuas was teaching the creation story again, JC was the only one that was aptly listening. Writhing in pain, for an earlier accident, he sat listening to the Lamb of Creation, knowing where this story was going. Of the six Ancient Ones, JC was sure that only Jeasuas would reveal the way to defeat Kutulu Lucifer's hoard, but as of yet, hadn't. All he taught was compassion, love, charity, and forgiveness.

He was the only one, though, to teach other prophesies besides his own. And JC found the stories of Gia and of Kutulu Lucifer's equally enlightening.

"In the beginning all was nothing..." Jeasuas spoke. "And from The Creator's outstretched hands sprang the seven Ancient Ones; Kutulu Lucifer, Jeasuas, Selene, Merylon, Minerva, Isis, and Phaleg."

It was explained that all seven have been known by many names and that even now, on the seven worlds inhabited by humans, they were known differently. On Terra, they were known as myths, on Brommelta, and Titania, simply heroes that had come to live briefly ages ago. Titania, did not even believe in Gia or any creating God.

Only on Zindar, Launam, Muridian, and Haven, were they known as gods or demigods. That is except for Jeasuas and Lucifer on Terra. They were ancient enemies, children of the one creating God, all the others considered simple bedtime stories out of lore.

Zindar was the smallest of the seven human inhabited planets, and was the home of Gia, the creator of Pan, to Sheera and JC, the Garden of Eden. It would be on Zindar, that the final battle would be fought. Or, what they hoped to be the final battle. JC, still, listened with apt attention and paid particular attentiveness to the details of his own beliefs.

That morning, JC had really shown his one strongest talent over all the others. They knew that he possessed a very high tolerance for pain. They all knew that he seemed able to shrug off any annoyance whenever a spell of his would back fire, or he would fall, or take a hit, while practicing with the swords. What they didn't know was the extent of his great constitution.

JC had been levitating, when his concentration was interrupted. Falling over twenty-five meters, when he hit the ground hard, he just laid there. Sheera came running to see he was all right, and, stood back in shock as he slowly rolled over and struggled to stand. No broken bones, miraculously, he did sustain a great deal of bruising, though. As he refused any healing, he limped away, not wanting the others to see the pain, he knew, he could not keep from his face.

Even Purana looked on with amazement and concern, briefly, JC noted, and she hated him, as far as he could tell. The fact that he got up, was enough to amaze the "kids", as he often referred to them, but then to just walk away without any healing, even if it was a limp, made his credibility raise in the warriors' eyes, and wonderment in the women's.

Except for Sheera. He saw the hurt in her, when he pushed her hand away, and was a little abrupt in how he said he was fine. JC felt bad about that, but they all thought he was the liability of the group, and to admit that he was really hurt, would only have proven it to them. As he limped away, to enter the building where Jeasuas reviewed the prophesies, he sat down gingerly, and laid his head to the table.

"You must allow others to help you, sometimes, James Carl." Jeasuas said just before the others that bothered with his classes arrived.

The conversation was ended at that moment, as quickly as it had begun!

Sheera and Burlga seemed to be at odds, when they entered the class room. They were two of those that would always attend the studies by Jeasuas. It occurred to the other three, Odyseus, Quen, and Purana that those two girls always attended any class that JC did. What they could not understand, was how absolutely oblivious JC seemed to be, not noticing how much those two were throwing themselves at him.

Of course, how could he see it? He acted as if he was not interested in women, and often made rather scathing remarks about committal love.

Something had happened to him, Purana thought that made him keep any advance at arm's length. And, Burlga seemed intent on beating the beautiful, non-loving, man using, woman, at finding out what it was that was stopping him from accepting any of them as anything other than "kids".

He did like the "kids" though, just as he always had liked young adults. He was filled with compassion and sorrow anytime one of them would get injured or when they would hurt themselves from a spell backfiring. Just as much as he showed pride in them anytime, they did something that none of the others had done. Or did it better, or first.

They did not seem to act as if they liked him, very much, but then what young person does like an elder, that often times, acts the part. They tolerated him, and allowed a grudging respect for how hard "the old man" worked and tried at things. They also, respected his tolerance for pain. No matter how much he was hurt, he still would quickly recover.

"It's all in the mind, pain is an illusion." He would tell them.

On that day that JC had fallen, he pushed Sheera away, and limped off into the building that was their class room. Burlga went to help the man, clearly seeing he was in pain, but Sheera stopped her. An argument had ensued. The two were always fighting verbally over the old man.

Both seemed to be falling in love with him, and yet, he always acted as though, he didn't notice. Sheera was not as forward as Burlga, but, in her own ways, she was even more insistent. And, he was not the only one that had changed. Sheera was changing, as well.

Burlga had noticed it almost from the first month of their arrival. That being a part non-human made Quen and Purana treat her with some disdain, even though Burlga was just as much a part of noble bloodlines as them, Sheera though, accepted her from the start. She had even laughed that first day, when Burlga had tried to kiss the old man, before even knowing his name.

But, after a little more than a month had gone by, the two were beginning to have a competition on who would gain the man's affections first. A friendly one, but, a competition, none the less!

JC would usually just laugh when the half-elf would make one of her comments, concerning what she would like to do with him. But he did not laugh any less, when Sheera would subtly come on, to him. He always, had some nice let down, never was mean, but he would simply refuse to see that they were not teasing him.

Burlga laughed, when he said something about a curse keeping him from having a woman, but now after all these months she was beginning to see that he really did believe in it, and it was not, just some excuse that he had come up with for turning her down. Sheera wondered what that curse, he believed in, could be, and the two women would discuss it often, trying to figure what he meant by it. They both thought the man was joking, at first, now, after all these months, knew he was not!

Purana was the most beautiful person to have been born in Haven. For some reason, however, the old man did not seem to notice. That would keep her from gaining any edge at becoming the group's leader. That was her only true goal with this group. Even though she was the most powerful, and the only one to rightfully lead; those other two "twits", as she often called them, and even more times than not, Odyseus would follow his advice.

That is Odyseus would, when Purana was not sleeping with him. He was a pretty boy, and good for satisfying her female urges when the cycle hit. Too bad, he was so young, though. Not a real man, yet, but given time, might make a good donor for breeding. That is what she had told him, once. He quickly found out that she was not joking, as he had thought. She let him know on no uncertain circumstances, that he was just a play toy. Odyseus decided, he could live with that!

Quen, would be good, as well, but he was too much the warrior. Purana needed real energy; not that spent in just a few minutes, as much as those few minutes were intense. No, Quen would not do either. Too bad the old man was too short. Not at all what she liked. It didn't matter anyway, because he didn't even look her way more than to say "good job" or else, "it would work better, if...." Like she needed any praise or help from him.

But, those other two girls were good sorcerers, and could be even great, if they would get their heads out of his pants for once. Especially Burlga. She was at least as powerful a wizardress, as Purana, and an accomplished illusionist. And sorcery seemed to come to her as easily as it did Purana, as well. Why she would work with the sword as much as she did, could only be because she was trying to catch the old man's eye.

Of course, Sheera would work with the weapons. But she also did something she called "Kung Fu", which was an unarmed fighting style that JC also seemed to know a little of. They had brought that from their world, and Phaleg and Minerva, both knew it as well. Trying to teach them all the forms, had turned out to be a waste of time. Why would any of them need swords, let alone, unarmed fighting, if they could just blast the spawns from Hell out of existence. Study the sorcery and that was all that would be needed, Purana thought.

Burlga and Sheera were always working out together, with the "forms" as she called it, and "kata", as JC called it. He was very good at picking up, what Sheera would teach them, and the things that Phaleg and Minerva added, as well. And, Burlga was not going to allow, Sheera to use that as a way to spend more time with the man.

So, Burlga attended the martial art classes, and although she did not get really that good at them, she did have fun learning, even if she would not admit it, to anyone. Besides, JC was quick with a congratulatory comment, when she would get something difficult right.

"And, it is a good way to get his hands put on me!" Burlga had told Purana once!

It was the lack of a group leader that got to the two nobles, the most. They could handle anything that the others did, if only someone would step forward and take charge. Someone, other than JC, that is! Quen had tried, but too many of the others were against that idea.

If only JC was a noble born, he would be the natural leader in the group. Purana wanted the leadership, but she was too impetuous, and had a total lack of respect for anyone but herself. None of the others would ever allow her to tell them what to do. Odyseus was great at talking battle strategies, and he showed amazing wisdom for someone with such a short life. He was too young, though, and too insecure to lead, or to make others follow. How could a leader be found, if no one would even admit to seeing something so plain? Of course, Quen did not ever consider either Sheera nor Burlga.

Quen, thought about his choice of leaders, if it wouldn't be himself, of course. He would be the natural choice, but he thought that convincing the women would be an impossibility. Sheera was too much attached to JC, though he seemed not to notice. And, Burlga was becoming quite cryptic about the man. Saying often times that she thought he was already the leader.

"Who knew where Burlga's head was at. One moment she seemed ready to rape the old man, and the next she was flirting with Odyseus or even with me." Quen thought she was just having problems with being without a man, something he could understand, all women needed to be protected, and she would find one soon enough when they went on to their separate destinations.

But why JC did not seem interested, even in Purana, was a complete mystery. Of course, the way he was doted on by the goddess Selene, it was no wonder he was not interested, in the girls.
"Why would he, when he could have a real woman?" Quen thought. "But, then again, why would a supposed Goddess be so attentive to a mere man?"

Quen did not understand the whole situation there, and decided it was not worth worrying over. Right now, he thought that somehow, he would have to convince the old man to support his bid for leader. That way, Sheera and Burlga would go along with it, and maybe even Odyseus, if he could keep his pants on around Purana.

She was very attractive, he had to admit, but she was so against using weapons, that she was not worthy of Quen's attention. She would only be good to

73

bed every now and then, and maybe have around for distance fighting. Keep her in the back, where all non-combatants belonged.

Odyseus was confused. Nothing new around these people, he had to admit. They were so small, yet, so sure of themselves. All seemed to be taking to the idea that they would be world leaders, as if it were natural to them. Even though, JC denied it, he had that natural leadership qualities that would surely make him become a good king on his continent.

JC kept trying to convince Odyseus that he would be The One Chosen Champion that would face Kutulu Lucifer's champion, but the over-sized young man, could not understand why he would say such a thing.

Never having more than average skill in fighting, he was more of a designer of war, than a participant. That he was stronger than anyone, was only because of his size. He was OK, with a spear, and better than average with his club, but he never really felt that he was getting the hang of the sword. And as far as sorcery went, he could not even heal a cut, let alone anything major.

Minerva claimed it was a block in his confidence, but he could not figure out how to break it. At least JC had helped him enough to make mental shields.

JC was so good at that. He reminded Odyseus of his professors back at university. Patient, never scolding, only correcting. Never yelling, only pointing out when something could have been done better.

"And, he is the first to say how proud he is of me, when I do learn something new!" Odyseus said to himself. "He sure is a funny man, though. He has all the women chasing after him, and he has not acted as if he even cared about it. And, not only that, he always is talking to himself, out loud!"

But, Odyseus admired the old man. Older than his mother, and yet he still worked harder than any of them. And, he seemed to possess the courage of a god.

"I could never have taken that fall, like he did, and just walk away. Well, he did limp a little, he he, but still, he did so on his own accord."

Odyseus knew that he would never be the leader. It would probably be JC, even if he did not want it, unless, Quen got it!

74

Purana wouldn't. She was great to bed with, but too fickle! The whole time they would be rolling around in the blankets, she would be condemning the others over something they did, or something she perceived them having done.

"You'd think she was jealous over Sheera and Burlga, if not for the way she treated the old man. That, and the way she talked about how much she hated him." Odyseus thought to himself.

After Jeasuas' class, everyday, the three, Burlga, Sheera, and JC attended Selene's. That was another bit of debate between the six. Three were becoming better than good healers, two were unable to, and Purana thought it a waste of time.

"If there are injured, that is what the temples are for. If we are injured, none will survive to help us, anyway!" She would say.

JC kept insisting that the six would be High Priests of their religions, and that they would have to show charity and compassion for the mortals.

"Otherwise, how can you expect to lead, if the mortals don't respect you?" JC would say.

And, as such, they would need to foster trust and caring from the mortals that they would be serving. That last part made the others cringe. Even Burlga would bristle over the idea that they, the most powerful people in the world, would have to serve the mortals.

JC tried to explain that as leaders in a war against Hell, they would be serving the forces of good. That meant serving the mortals, as good leaders. But the metaphor seemed to be too foreign for the four noble born Immortals. Only Sheera grasped the idea, since she was raised in the monastery and taught to serve the people, anyway.

"The lessor's will know their place, and serve us!" Purana would demand.

"You are a fool, Purana, to think kings or queens will bow to you, simply because you demand it!" Burlga answered.

"They either bow, or are no longer kings!" Purana smiled, the look of false pride in her face.

75

When Minerva spoke up, all six heads turned to face her.

"Thy names will surely inspire fear, children. But dost thou really want to inspire hatred in those that thou wisheth to lead? Maybe even more so, than the enemy thy truly will be there to fight!"

JC, Sheera, and Odyseus simply shook their heads in agreement. The others thoughtfully only nodded. Purana, though, spoke up.

"Fear, respect, hatred. It matters not, as long as they follow my orders! We are there for a purpose, not to coddle the lessors among the world!"
"We are not there to subjugate them either, child!" JC interjected.

"You will learn humility, young one." Selene spoke. "You all will, or you will perish!"

CHAPTER 4
Bitter taste of victory

"The day of coming when six humans from afar will arrive together.
To face the Lord of Hell, in their hands are the universes salvation.
Apart from the others, will one set himself. For all of Zindar will blood be
shed.
For the universe will his blood and tears be shed for the life of all!"

From the prophesies of the Order of Brigitte

The months passed, at least that is what they thought. Time was very different here in the training ground. Merylon, Prince of Sorcery, let it slip once that they were in a dimensional world he called somewhere outside of the rules of time and space.

Things were different here, as far as space and time were concerned. They could run for hours and never move more than a few meters from their starting point. Or they could take a step and be miles away. With time, things were equally, different. Sometimes it would take hours to complete a simple lesson, and yet the sun would look like it had barely moved, or just the opposite could take place. Do something that took moments to complete, and find the whole day gone.

So, when it was explained to them that they were now immortals, and that they were nearly ready to leave, they wondered just how long they had been in this place.

One year they had been told, but to each, it seemed a different amount of time. Quen thought just a few months, but he rarely participated in any of the philosophical classes. And very few of the sorcery ones, as well.

Odyseus and Purana thought it had been maybe eight months. She calculated it by the number of times she had been with Odyseus and Quen, answering her monthly cycle urges. To the other three, they nodded at the year, or maybe thought it had been more. They of course attended every class offered, and JC did even more work on top of that, on his own.

The six new comers were advised that any wounds received by any member of the hoard of Kutulu Lucifer would heal in less than a day. And, that any draining of their sorcery would recover even faster, in just a few hours. They would only heal naturally, though, when the wound or injury would come through normal means, or by mortal weapons.

But, to the six with their accelerated constitutions, healing would still be faster over the course of a normal person's natural healing. Unlike the enemy, the creation of Kutulu Lucifer, whom would require a magical weapon to hit or harm; they would still be subject to the normal weapons. They were told that facing Kutulu's creation would be like facing one of his dark angels.

That was another reason that JC and Sheera deemed it so important to learn how to heal. After all, how could they be at the final battle, if killed so easily along the way, by falling off a horse, or taking an accidental stab from a fellow soldier in close battle? Burlga simply had a lust for knowledge, as well as her lust for a certain older human! When the other three could not be convinced, JC just stated,

"Well, maybe you three will be the soldiers, and Burlga, Sheera, and I will be the doctors!" They all laughed at that statement.

The most important character trait that Sheera seemed to admire in JC was that he would never gloat when he would better someone.

What she saw in the man that was making her find love in him, was a man that had great determination with less natural talent, a quiet confidence that was never flaunted, and a willingness to always help others, no matter what he may be doing at the moment. He had a genuine compassion and charity for others, and continued to care no matter how he was treated in return.

What she saw that upset her the most, was a man she had come to love unconditionally, that only treated her as a daughter to be fawned over and not seeing her as a woman. The distance that JC maintained from all three women, was the most perplexing to her. She could never get him to open up about that part of his past, and that made her the most frustrated.

He had only said once that he was cursed with whoever loved him and he loved back would die. But JC was really becoming the priest among the group, Sheera would inwardly exclaim, and she wanted so much to be his priestess!

The one thing that amazed all of the Immortals about JC, was the way that he refused to call any of the Ancient Ones, gods. He never treated them as such, never bowed to them, nor gave them any more respect than one would give to elders. He often called them by their names, when addressing them, and did it with such confidence, that the demigods even allowed it, without reacting negatively.

Let one of the others show that kind of disrespect to their patrons, and they were severely scorned. It must be an elder thing, the "kids" thought. Except that he never called Selene anything except "mother".

When Odyseus had tried to call Minerva "mother", the goddess only laughed, and told him,

"I am no mother. Thou dost not need to be like your elder, just be thy self." JC chuckled as well, patting the big man on the back, saying that Holy Minerva was only telling him that he was more than a child, and not to take it personal.

Odyseus, remembered that conversation, as he did anytime that JC would make him feel better about things. He remembered puffing with pride over the compliment the old man gave him.

The most appalling thing that JC had figured out how to do, in all the other's minds, was the transferring of energies. They were not taught that; he had figured it out on his own. They were taught how to bond with each other in order to create a more powerful spell, but the idea of transferring one's own psychic energy to another, was too terrifying a thought for the others to grasp.

He had tried to tell them that when healing a person that was next to death, the natural way was to use the victim's own energies to heal themselves. But that would kill a person in such dire condition. By transferring his own energy, he could heal the person empathically, without causing any shock to the victim. Burlga and Purana thought that madness.

"What if you drained yourself doing that, and then were needed in another attack? Where would you be then?" Burlga asked him. JC only laughed saying,

"That is why we were taught how to use the swords."

Quen would just tell the others,

"JC is an old man and a priest, after all. Let the healers take care of the sick, and let the soldiers take care of the war." But everyone knew that JC was becoming every bit the warrior as the other two men.

Merylon had warned Burlga about JC's way of healing. He told her that she should not even be able to do it.

"Only those of his line, would be able to handle that kind of shock." Merylon was not telling them the whole truth. By empathically healing, like JC was, he was taking the pain of the wound into himself. His own constitution could handle it, but let the others try with a very serious wound, and it could very well kill them.

Burlga decided to warn Sheera, and the two immediately began feigning that they were unable to learn it. In the end, it was believed that only he had that talent. And, the feigning soon became reality, since sorcery is simply what is believed can happen, with enough energy use.

Since, all were very strong psychically, Burlga knew that Quen's and Odyseus' blocks against strong spells, was the disbelief within themselves.

She had vowed that she would break those blocks, somehow, someday!

When the last day of the training year arrived, the Ancient Ones looked upon their chosen six, with some trepidation.

"We should call ourselves, The Chosen!" Purana announced after the group was trying to come up with a name for themselves. The others had mentioned other names and Purana was sure whatever the "old man" said, would end up the one they would go with. He had been the only one not to say anything, as of yet, that morning.

Purana was surprised when he broke through the arguing of the others, with a simple comment.

"That is what we are called in four of the seven prophesies." They all turned to look at him, with surprised expressions on them.

He had been so quiet, listening to the children argue, that when he finally did speak, they were stunned into silence.

"What did you say, old man?" Purana asked.

"Simply stating fact, child." JC answered, an amused expression to his face.

"The Chosen, hmm?" Quen simply stated.

"Are you saying you actually agree with me?" Purana looked at JC, a look that said it to all.

"We always agree with you, when you speak sense or truth, Purana. And, yes, if you think or like the name, I will go along with it. I'll go along with any you all choose!" JC sighed.

The name was taken and The Chosen presented themselves to the Ancient Ones.

Each of the Chosen had finished learning what could be taught. They had each became greater in their specialized areas, and each learned the minimum of what would be needed in the upcoming war.

Of the six Ancient Ones, only Jeasuas and Selene watched the group without any show of fear on their visages. Merylon, although, filled with some trepidation, still managed a smile.

Only JC, Sheera, and Burlga had learned or at least participated in everything they could be taught, this year. The Ancient Ones hoped that would be enough. "The day of coming when six humans from afar will arrive together.

The day finally arrived, and Merylon clapped his hands once, sending the six away in a flash of light.

When they opened their eyes, The Chosen were standing on a hillside, a beautiful spring day, with a light breeze cutting the sun's heat. The bright light-colored blue of the sun, stood large on the lower end of the horizon, indicating it was morning.

They realized as well, that the gravity was weaker and the air thicker than it was for the past year in Launam. As the six looked around, the green meadow of the short grassy hill, Odyseus pointed up slope, excitingly stating the obvious.

"Prepare for battle, here they come!"

The wave of Hell Spawn seemed too large to face, and the six stood fixed, staring at the gripping horror of well over a thousand disfigured forms, ugly atrocities, and some with a small semblance of humanity, all rambling forward down the hill, toward The Chosen.

Grappling with the fear inside them at seeing for the first time, the hordes of Kutulu, they seemed unable to move. A fear that JC d'Badger was the first to overcome.

"Purana, Burlga, fire and ice. We need to whittle them down before they are all upon us!"

Both snapped out of their fear caused trances, and Purana sent a flash of ice to cover the first five hundred or so demons coming down the hill. Quickly followed was a sheet of searing flames emitting from Burlga's outstretched hands. Spell after spell was sent forth from the group, and the numbers sank to the enemy's hoard. The masses were still great, though as they continued to close on the Immortals.

Seemingly, the endless mass that topped the hill added what seemed to be more and more of the monsters as more and more were destroyed.

All the sorcerers sent waves of energy up the slope. Fire, lightning, ice, earthquakes, tornadoes, and acid. It seemed that all the elements of nature were cast at the oncoming army, rushing down the slope. When the battle closed, making the drawing of weapons necessary, there were still over a hundred of the thousands of Hell Spawn, still standing; still moving in on them! What followed then, was pure chaos.

"The Chosen" went to work. Spinning, weaving, ducking, the flash of sunlight on blades that had been made by the Ancient Ones, powered to hit through anything. The blades sparkled, creating a show of lights, if any would have been around to watch. As the demons began dropping, the separation among the six became greater.

Forgetting the team work, there became six individuals fighting on that hillside. None to cover each other's backs, only JC seemed concerned by it.

Sheera attempted to stay close to JC, thinking he would be the secret to her survival, and she to his.

But, the wave of the enemy was pushing her away. She could still see him off to the left, but he was being swarmed under by the hoard.

With each death he rendered, JC could feel a disgust in the back of his mind, as his adrenaline rushed to grip the front of his thoughts. He moved with a grace of a warrior, something he had not shown ever having before, over the past year. It was as if something embedded in his mind was reminding him of battles past that he had learned.

Instinct took over with both of the former Terrans as their battle-hardened minds of past lives moved them on within the battle. War was to be their new lives, and both seemed to be sickened by it.

Raising his club in one hand, and his sword in the other, Odyseus found within him, a skill he did not think he possessed. Both weapons, gifted by Holy Minerva, were made with sorcery, able to hit anything, to include The Ancient Ones, themselves. Odyseus, with his great strength, and the new skill of over a year of practice, began to slay the Hell Spawn, the demons, devils, and monsters!

When she could, Burlga would watch the men. JC and Quen were amazing. Not at all like the "old man" had been during the year of training. She could remember seeing flashes of it, but nothing like he was doing now. And Quen?

"Well, he is just being Quen. Amazing, confident, a machine with his saber." she thought.

As she cast three and four spells at a time, still not having drawn her sword, her natural instincts leading her to use the magic that was a part of her blood. She could see Odyseus, using both sword and club, even though, he was not as good with the sword, he still was slicing through the demons in one blow, or crushing them into the ground with his club. He really did have the strength of a god, and this battle was proving it.

Sheera was even more amazing than all of them. Using her small curved sword in one hand, she was still casting one or two spells while severing with her "wakisashi." Her quickness, making it near impossible to follow the blade as it moved.

Burlga, could see the wave of Hell Spawn extend up and over the hill, there must be hundreds still coming. Even though the four of them had cast spells that killed off the first ones to reach them, now that they were so close, only direct spells could be used.

Feeling the thrill of battle lust running through her, Burlga stopped watching the others and finally decided to do it her best friend's way. Casting three or four spells, while chopping or jabbing with her own short sword, she began to have even better results than before. That is until she was suddenly hit from behind.

Purana drew her long dagger, given to her by Isis. She could feel the power of sorcery in it, and when the Ancient Ones had given each of their charges, weapons, they were all told that they would possess the only means to hit the higher beings within the rankings of Hell. Purana could also tell that directing her sorceries through her dagger, seemed to make the spells even stronger than they already were.

As the spawn came upon her in a rush, she began sending lightning, acid, and pure energy into the hoard. She could see Burlga using devastating magiks, both sorcery and wizardry, and the explosions the other was creating seemed to be working. Purana, was crushing and disintegrating with more subtlety, but the effects were the same.

Then she saw something really amazing. JC was out-fighting them all. Somehow, he was doing what none of the others could, actually keeping the spawn at bay.

The momentary distraction, at seeing the man, cost her the victory. Purana was swarmed under.

Far off to his right, JC saw Sheera go down under a rush of demonic flesh, and at the same time he lost awareness and sight of Purana as well. He could still hear Odyseus' battle cries, and knew where Quen was by the screams of demonic beings meeting the man's blade. He had long since lost awareness of Burlga at all, but thought he could see where she must be with the emanations of sorcery and the explosions of power.

Quen was feeling the thrill of a master duel. Not really a duel, there were too many, and he knew this must be an illusion. There was no way, the Ancient Ones would put them down in front of so many, when they were just starting in this war.

His sword moved up, down, in, and out. His sweeps and chops were moving as if of their own accord. With emotionless calm, Quen, Blade Danced, as Phaleg

84

called it, and did it with perfection. He could see the others, only JC doing what he always seemed to hide when he thought nobody would notice.

Quen knew he was better than he had showed to the others. He had practiced with the man, enough, to know that JC was holding back, for some reason. But, not now! Not when it really mattered. Quen could almost admire the man, if only, he was not a commoner!

Something overtook JC, the moment he saw Sheera go down, though. Not a fear of dying, no, what he suddenly felt was a fear for his friends. His companions were all in trouble, and he no longer thought about what could happen or what the danger was to him. He suddenly went into an instinctive whirl within his mind, the feelings of a father fighting for his children, suddenly took hold.

He somehow, turned his sorcery in on himself, and became a whirlwind of destruction. Accepting the new instincts taught him this past year, and the opening of a mind to a world of violence he had always tried to avoid, JC became an unconscious battle machine.

Cutting a path, Hell's children fell before him, a gap between fleeing bodies began opening up and JC moved in the direction where he had thought he saw Sheera fall. Lightning and energy bolts sailed from his free hand, as the sword hand sliced, cut, and chopped, with his new katana.

When his adrenaline finally ebbed, he stood alone. Blood covered, pain searing through cuts and lacerations on his legs and arms, his back shredded, as well, by claws that had somehow managed to reach him. He was not breathing hard, surprisingly though, at least, not as hard as he thought he should be.

Purana lay in a heap, barely conscious, she opened her eyes, the pain in her was something she had never felt before. With disgust, she could see the man, still standing, seemingly the only one. And, he got sick! Purana felt a loss of the last bit of respect for him, as she watched the man, clearly, winning a great victory, none of the younger Chosen had been able to stand, and yet, he got sick, over a few deserving deaths!

"What a very disgustingly weak old man! What kind of small person have you created, Holy Selene?" She whispered.

When she watched as he transferred his remaining energies into Sheera, to heal her, Purana became even more disgusted, knowing that he would certainly be the first to fall, amongst them.

"Giving of himself, like that, for a twit, like her, will certainly get him killed. And, maybe us all! I will have to make sure, that none of us, depend on him! They will listen to me, now!"

Purana watched silently, not able to move without feeling the pain, until finally, Isis arrived to heal her, Selene and Jeasuas, speaking with their charges, both of the weakest of the Chosen, getting sick after the battle. Purana thought that only confirmed her thoughts about commoners.

"They are the lesser amongst us!"

The burns under his skin, from the poisons left behind by demonic claws, felt like fire was raging in JC's nerves. He looked around at the carnage, while he calmly performed his breathing exercises to aid him in eliminating the perceived pains.

He searched for the others, as his stomach began to tighten, the sense of bile rising in his throat, and JC realized that not one of the other Chosen was anywhere in sight. Piles and stacks of demons were everywhere, but JC could not see any of his partners on this hill. He began to move, when the urge to empty his stomach over took him.

He noticed the sun and realized that this battle had not even lasted for more than a quarter hour. Surveying the carnage, he had thought he must have fought for hours, he felt nausea still within him, as he fought to keep the vomit down. Killing, it would seem, did not agree with his sensibilities, regardless the enemy.

More than thirty-five hundred demons were beginning to smoke and disintegrate. JC surveyed the carnage wrought, and finally gave into the bile. After clearing his mouth, he just barely perceived on his outer awareness, the subtle shake of a demonic corpse, which brought him standing immediately reaching within to cast a spell.

He let the fireball, die out, when he saw a small human hand, holding a small sword, called a wakisashi, poke through the debris. He knew that to be Sheera's blade, and recognized the hand holding it.

Rushing to the debris, JC began lifting the demon body parts away. He found renewed strength as the adrenaline surged once again, through him. He finally freed the young woman from her bloody grave and saw she was not moving!

JC declined delving for injuries and laid a hand to her chest, over the woman's heart. He poured a lot of his last remaining energies into healing Sheera; finally, her eyes opened. She moved to stand and when JC tried to help, his legs were too weak to stay up, he was pulled to the ground, beside the woman. Crawling to his knees, shaking involuntarily, not having the physical strength left to do much more, he had virtually no psychic strength to will himself up. He rested on all fours, as Sheera gained her feet.

Looking around, seeing what was left of the destruction, as the last of the demons disappeared to a gust of wind, leaving the odor of brimstone thick in their nostrils, her eyes went wide as she realized that she and JC were the only ones still moving. Her lips trembled, as she looked down at the man that had just healed her, a sorrowful smile not quite touching her lips.

"I thank you, Sir JC! Why am I not surprised to find you still the one standing when none of the rest of us, managed it?" She softly exclaimed, an attempt at levity failing.

Instead of sounding a joke, as she meant it, her trembling and tightening stomach, made it sound to JC, like she was scolding him. Her next statement was cut off, as she fell to her knees and began to retch, her own sensibilities suddenly affected.

JC moved to her, holding her hair, back away from her face, as he fought the convulsions that wanted to renew in his own stomach.

"It will pass, children." Selene calmly stated, as she appeared over the sick couple. A worried look passed her expression. Another person appeared next to her, and Jeasuas added.

"I would hope that you two never lose this feeling towards death. But that too will be overcome, I fear. Even that which is necessary, should not leave you cold and hard! Remember this, our children!"

"Are the others..." JC choked out. Before he could finish, though Selene finished.

"They still live, my son! Though, they are not in as good a shape as you two are."

Jeasuas exclaimed, next,

"James Carl, what you did was very admirable, young man, if but very foolish! Expending the last of your energy into healing was not a good way to insure survival. Do be more careful in the future! I would not want to feel the pain of loss that my dear sweet Sheryl would go through, if you were not there for her. You are supposed to show the wisdom of an elder priest, after all!"

Selene sighed and calmly stated,

"They still live, brother. They all live, and now on Zindar, they find themselves newly blooded!"

As the other four Ancient Ones arrived to raise up their charges off the battle field, JC stood with Sheera. Her eyes, tear filled, as the wetness flowed down her cheeks, emulating the watered eyes of her patron, Jeasuas.

Selene reached out a hand to JC, which he took in his own blood-stained hand, and sent a little energy into him. He found his wounds healed and the vigor added to his waning psychic strength. He also felt the love of a mother being poured into him, knowing the pride she had in her creation.

When she took Sheera's hand, doing the same thing, she felt much the same as she realized, both of the God's were as much her parents as were they JC's. She suddenly knew, she was the man's twin, not intended to be his mate.

A momentary sadness gripped her, but, a renewed love adorned that was even deeper than before. She was already and had always been, connected to the man.

At the moment that some of the blood was being wiped away by Selene, a rumble was felt deep in the ground and then a searing bright blinding light over took the twelve people, The Chosen and Ancient Ones, alike.

When their vision finally cleared, focus slowly returned, they found themselves standing with each of their Ancient Ones behind their respective Chosen, each with a hand upon their own Chosen's shoulder.

88

They were facing an impossibly beautiful lady, even more so than Isis, wearing what looked to be vines and flowers woven into a dress that flowed down her long legs to touch the ground.

The tall lady appeared to be of middle age, long honey blond hair that seemed to change colors as she moved, curls waved the full length, down her back to below her knees. She had gold pupiless eyes that seemed to gleam when she talked, and a mischievous twinkle in those dreamy eyes, added to the mystery that this woman pervaded.

She had absolutely no aura, and her olive-colored skin, even blended in spots where the flower veined gown met causing the illusion of the gown actually being a part of her full-figured body.

Standing over nine feet tall, she was stately, graceful of movements, and absolutely godly.

What they all noticed was how in awe, even the Ancient Ones, themselves seemed to be before this woman, and JC quickly deduced this to be the Mother Goddess, herself, Gia!

Burlga immediately dropped to a knee, never taking her eyes off the spectacular sight, mumbling a prayer to the Mother Goddess, who only smiled at the young half elf.

The other five Chosen followed suit, to include JC, who even lowered his eyes.

With a grandmotherly soft voice, filled with love and greeting, the woman started towards the humans, and spoke with a musical tone.

"Rise, my children. You honor me with the respect I command." As they all six roses, JC noticed even Purana seemed in awe of this woman, and knew there was hope for her, after all.

Gia began after they were once again standing.

"So, these are the ones that I will depend upon for my world's salvation?" Her voice was soft yet carried, commanding yet comfort emanated from it.

"My children, I thank you for the next seven years of your life!" The mischievous twinkle hit her right eye, and the tilted smile hinted that she was not expecting all of them, if any, to last the entire seven years.

Walking to one end of the line, she started, placing a long-pointed finger under the chin and slightly lifting the proud head back of Odyseus.

"Odyseus Zenobe Brell, now called simply Odyseus d'Brell, Minerva has brought thee to me to protect the continent of Lemuria. Strength personified, you will have need of it all, and more! Fear little of the future, child. Fear the present, instead!"

Stepping next in line, to the woman that was Merylon's charge, she rested a hand on the young woman's shoulder.

"Burlga d'Venta, Lady of the Marshlands. I am not surprised by the power of your sorcery. But much has changed in the Continent called Brautania, since you were last there. This is not your world any longer, child.

"And, it will take more than just sorcery to tame. I hope Merylon has insured some skill other than this beautiful face! Or perhaps some arbitration skill has been learned from your male intended? HMMM?" She chuckled as Burlga knowingly blushed, if but slightly.

"Ahh, Purana Bin Gage!" The Goddess' next subject. Holding Purana's hand, she brought it in to her chest. She squeezed lightly Purana's hand.

"Isis picked you for Atlantia. You will find it much different than the world you come from. Your beauty and sorcery will be used in equal amounts, child. Try and learn a little compassion for the little people. Much luck to thee, my daughter!"

As the Goddess grabbed the next Chosen One's arms, she almost sighed.

"So hard, so calculating. Quen Dem Lurin, you have all the skill and stoniness of thine own Phaleg in you. As, I'm sure, the Continent, Funtaland, will be tamed by you. But child; heed my prayers for thee! Find love and learn compassion! You will need the non-humans for your victories!"

Stepping back into his patron, Quen was startled, unsure what to make of the Goddess' command. His face quickly returned, though, to the emotionless outward calm of the soldier that he was.

Placing a hand on Sheera's cheek, the Goddess looked deep into the young lady's eyes. A smile just touching Gia's own eyes.

"Sheryl Ling Mattingly, now called Sheera Lu Che, the North East Continent, Katiketa, is yours. Not so unlike the place of your birth, there will find it hard if not impossible to tame.

"That Jeasuas picked a woman, no matter how capable, only makes your job that much harder. And, makes me wonder what, my son, is up to!" She added, after a slight pause, her eyes moving to her own son standing behind. An almost smile came to Jeasuas' face as he returned the Goddess' smile.

Coming to the end of the line, she cupped JC's face in both her hands, lifting so she could stare down into his eyes. The Goddess looked intently, all the way into his soul. A nonplussed unreadable expression filled her eyes.

"James Carl Tigara! What a name there has taken for this task. JC d'Badger! The self-appointed father of the group is not so old anymore, though. Yet, still, you are ever the priest, teacher, and parent, my child.

"My son, you have chosen quite the appropriate name for yourself, but you will not be alone for long, I think.

"The North West Continent, Selenia, is yours! Yet, I do not see you ruling, as the others seek to do. Selene has made you because of what is in your heart, I see. I see you willing to sacrifice yourself for others, young child, not so willing to bring unto the death that will be needed. Do remember, there are those that love you and can be trusted with your own heart. Hmm, perhaps...."

She smiled turning away, to walk a few paces to the front of the group. JC wanted her to finish her statement, but the squeeze on his shoulder where Selene still rested her hand, stopped him from inquiring.

The Mother Goddess Gia turned to once again face the six, and waved her hands, spreading them to take in all the lands.

"Welcome to Zindar, all of you! Of course, I thank you for coming, as well. The prophesies speak of seven years for the War of Darkness. And, my children, I assure you the universe quivers in anticipation that you six shall not fail!" The twinkle crossed her eyes once again, before she continued.

"Good luck, children, and may the Heavens find favor in your actions. Save me, save Zindar, and too will thee save your home worlds and all the universe as well! In case your patrons have not told you, there is a cost of failure. I will eliminate the known universes and start over. Something to think on, I suspect!"

In the moment of a blink, she was gone, as were the Ancient Ones, as well!

"That was the Creator?" Someone mumbled after a moment of stunned silence from the six.

"That was Gia," JC whispered. "In my world we call her Mother Nature! A myth to most!"

The Chosen all looked at each other in awed silence as they noticed in front of each of them, hung a gateway, suspended a foot in the air, one for each to their new homes. As Quen moved towards his, Odyseus quickly followed towards his own.

Hugging the man fiercely, she softly kissed his cheeks and then a light touch of her lips to his. One a sister would give.

"I could have fallen in love with you, my dream samurai! Now I love you, deeply. I will miss you until I see you, again, soon." She leapt through her gateway, as it closed behind her a yelp was heard issuing through.

"Oh, damn it all to hell!" A very Terran phrase, spoken in perfect English. A language JC had not herd spoken for over a year.

CHAPTER 5
From the frying pan into the fire

Quickly stepping through his own gateway, JC looked the area over to memorize it, and opened a new gateway, thinking about what he saw in Sheera's. It formed perfectly, to his surprise, as he jumped through willing it to stay open.

He was a little over forty yards away from the battle, to his horror, Sheera was fighting with a large devil, standing over ten feet tall, and eight smaller ones, standing about six and a half feet each. She was fighting for her very life dancing between jabs and slices of talons and whipping tails. Her great dexterity and superior speed being tested to its limits.

The dark rust color skinned devil with a leathery look to it, had bat-like wings and talons for fingers on two long arms. The head was large, almost gorilla in appearance, with large pointed ears, ram like horns protruding out it's temple areas, and fangs in place of teeth.

Its overly large eyes were black tear drop shaped, with the points coming together at its large ogreish nose. The only hair on its entire body was the scraggly short beard covering cheeks and chin, the long tail ending into a point, like that of an arrow head.

The eight smaller devils each looked like a smaller sized version of the larger one, except they had shorter arms with longer talons. All were surrounding the young woman, with *wakisashi* flashing, legs kicking, *Tanto* in her off hand, slicing. In all directions, she seemed a blur, as JC reacted.

Thinking of a quick energy blast, JC sent four bolts out from his single extended hand, willing each to hit a separate devil. He then began to run. All four hit and one of the smaller devils dropped to the ground, and two of the three others that were hit, turned to see him moving in.

He stopped and duplicated the spell, aiming for the other four smaller ones that were omitted in the first spell. Again, he saw one drop to the ground and this time all six of the smaller devils, began moving in his direction to meet his charge.

Still more than eighteen yards from Sheera, he was suddenly met by all six of the smaller devils as they teleported. Startled by their sudden appearance around him, JC ran head long into one, and took a rake across the back from another. Spinning to bounce off the one he smashed into, he swung his katana in an arc, slicing off one head, and an other's arm.

Sheera, now only facing only one devil, although the largest, used her superior speed to gain an advantage over it. The devil teleported, but instead of appearing behind the woman, it was surprised to find that Sheera had already spun to meet its new position, having anticipated the change. An arm was lost, in its strategy, and it began to scream in pain, as Sheera concentrated on a psychic mind crush into the injured devil.

JC, spun, avoiding renewed attacks as the five remaining devils seemed confused by the man's superior strength. The one that was knocked down from JC's head long crash, began to rise, as the Immortal swung down on its head, cleaving it down the center.

His back swing removed a leg from another and his ducking roll avoided two armed taloned fingers from hitting his head.

Sheera began pressing the larger devil as it backed away, slowly, as the effort to fight off her mental attack took much of its concentration. JC saw a dimensional door opening behind the large devil, as he removed the head of another of his opponents and he concentrated on a wall of air, blocking the doorway.

His attention momentarily removed from his own battle, he was knocked aside, but still managed to hold onto his spell. As the larger devil met with a wall, he did not expect to be present, Sheera thrust her wakisashi into its back, and twisted the blade as she pulled it free. Her next swing removed the devil's head, as she turned to see JC still facing two of the smaller devils, that were still standing.

Before she could cast a spell, though, he eliminated them in one long swing as his blade cleaved the head of one to follow through into the chest of the other, slicing deep into the heart.

As the devil's head rolled down to stop at her foot, Sheera looked down and was immediately filled with nausea, as she dropped to her knees to vomit. JC moved over to her, fighting his own urge to purge, and reached down to lay a hand on her back.

"A fine pair of heroes, we are." He sarcastically joked. "Every time we are victorious, we retch!"

Sheera gathered herself, a strained chuckle ebbing through, clenched teeth.

"Told you I'd see you soon. You didn't expect it to be this way though, I'll Bet? I could think of a better greeting for you, than for me to vomit on you twice in one morning, after you save my life on both occasions!"

"As long as you're purging yourself, it means you live. I would not want the alternative!" He answered.

After helping the young woman to her feet, JC created water above her head and helped to wipe her off of the blood and bile from her face and hair.

"Heck of a day, you have started, Sheera. That was Amaymyon, one of the Greater Angels of Kutulu Lucifer. You've already killed one of the Hell Lords! And, we now know for certain that Kutulu is going to be using them on us, just as Merylon thought he might!" The pride in his voice, belied the concern on his face.

Sheera blushed at his pride in her, and noticed the injuries in him, for the first time. Seeing the damage, he had taken just for her, she reached to heal him, and he stopped her.

"It doesn't hurt, really all that much. They'll heal up quickly, anyway!" He spoke. He watched as the nine devils began to smoke and dissipated, only to be blown away by a magical breeze that came up out of nowhere. The devil's own doorway was slowly closing and JC removed his wall of air, to see the dimensional door snap closed.

He turned and noticed his own gateway still open. He was surprised by that, and Sheera even exclaimed that it was supposed to be impossible for one to be held like that.

"I just willed it, and it doesn't seem to have taken very much energy to do it, either!" He answered. As they walked towards it, Sheera laced her left arm through his right, holding his hand tightly.

"Well, I suppose if you are going to be all right now?" He started, "I had better get a move on, before it does close." JC calmly finished, followed with a sigh.
He really did not want to leave, and he could tell that the young lady Immortal did not want him to, either.

"Allow me to fix your shirt, at the least." she stated as she reached out with her sorcery to begin attaching the cloth and the laces, causing them to become whole.

"If you won't allow me to heal you, I can at the least clean you off as you did me." Water began to flow down his head and the blood disappeared on him as he smiled.

He moved to pick at a green stone he saw laying on the ground, and Sheera let his hand go. It was Jade, raw and about two inches in diameter across one end.

"James?" She asked using his Terran name for the first time in months. "Why did you take such names as JC and d'Badger?" Quietly, not for the first time, she had asked that question of his name. "It is such a solitary creature, and you are too much into caring about people to be so solitary."

"I have been alone for over sixteen years, my dear friend. And a badger will fight to the death against even bears, in order to protect what is his." He stopped and held the jade in his palm as he concentrated, willing into the stone energies to reshape it.

"Does that mean, you consider me to be yours?" She said, as she also, watched him placing a piece of his spirit into the stone, now, a perfectly round ball less than one-half inch in diameter. She could see an outline of continents in the form of those on Terra, take place.

He continued to cast into the tiny stone ball, and took in a piece of her spirit as well to channel into it. She could almost feel the ecstatic pleasure as he drew from her when she noticed JC then surround the both of them with a protective shield against minor psychic attacks, and direct it into the stone. Taking a gold coin from his pouch, he directed even more energy into it, reshaping the coin into a necklace and wrapping it into, though, and around the stone.

She watched, in amazement at the sorcery she did not think him capable of, and only shook her head, thinking,

"Of course, he can do this. He would never have let us think he as strong as anyone else. He was always just a little behind us, purposefully, to protect our own pride!" She smiled as she watched his artistic use of the power, they had been given.

"My real name, Sheryl..." JC used her given Terran name as he looped the necklace over her head, still holding the gold encircled jade pendant in his right hand. "Is James Carl Tigara!" He was still channeling sorcery into the pendant when he said his name. She knew that would be the key to activating the magic he put into it.

When he slowly set the pendant against her skin, on her chest just above the slight cleavage showing above her blouse, she felt the energy surge through her. Radiating outward, from the stone, sending a momentary tingle throughout her upper body. Sheera shivered at the brief arousal felt in her bosom, and she blushed again, in front of the man, who still seemed to not notice.

He instead, continued to stare into her eyes, as he released his hold on the sorcery. Taking both her hands into his, JC cupped them between, and calmly finished.

"There is power in knowing my name. This token of our love, I give to you, my young lady, knowing that if you should ever need me, just call, and I will show up. Make sure the pendant is touching a part of you, though."

JC kissed her hands, and as he turned to his gateway, he stopped as he straddled between the rift. He looked back to Sheera.

"Remember, my dear Sheera, there is power in knowing the real name of someone." And as an afterthought, still watching her as he let his gateway slowly shrink, he called out.

"I do yet, and always will, love you, as well!"

****

Lilith shook her head in disgust at seeing the Chosen in action. She had teleported across the world till she finally found James Carl and Sheryl fighting together. She could not believe, only one Greater Angel and eight lessors were sent after these two.

"The two most powerful of the Chosen, and Martinith sends such a minor attack. He is insane and will most likely get all of us killed. Perhaps, I can use him, and guide him? At least, then, I can have a chance of survival!"

She continued to react to her amazement over the idiocy of the attack. Such a waste, this was.

"At least it was only Amaymyon! Too bad it was not Molech that was sent!"

****

The female immortal watched as his gateway closed. Remembering what she had told him, earlier, less than an hour ago, Sheera was stunned, as a single tear dropping down each of her cheeks.

Had he said what she thought she had heard? How, could he now, tell her that he loved her? Did he really know how she truly felt about him?

"It's just too damn bad, that you love me as a daughter or even a sister as we are. Do you know our beginnings as Selene has awakened in me? Too bad you do not see me as a woman for you to hold, you idiot man!" She voiced out to the air around her.

Of course, with Selene's touch, Sheera now knew she and JC were twins, both children of the gods, Jeasuas and Selene. He had to know, as well, she thought.

Then it hit her, the thought that if they might be deities, as well.

"Our parents are brother and sister, yet they mate. But, now knowing the truth of our spirits, does that change how I should feel about him?" she spoke aloud.

Turning and walking away from the sun's direction, Sheera did not even wipe the free-falling tears from her face.

It really did not matter how she felt, she would miss him, and would look forward to the day they see each other again. Three months now, seems a very long time away!

Her pace was steady, long strides for her legs, she appeared to be walking with a purpose, her mind wandered.

No longer the shy peaceful monk, she had spent nine years becoming, this last year of training under the six gods, called The Ancient Ones, Sheera Lu Che was now an adult version of the young girl living on the streets. She was a powerful

98

version of that girl, but she was only slightly aware of the road ahead, and the life she would be living.

A new life, a new direction, and with it, new adventures!

Her walk was purposeful, as Sheera headed opposite the rising sun. Not nearly to its zenith, yet, only an hour on this planet and already she had vanquished one devil lord, and been responsible for the destruction of several hundred, maybe thousand other minor spawns of Hell.

"Is this really what my life has become?" she mumbled.

Sheera, child of the mountains, father a tall Caucasian born soldier from a country in what was known as the western hemisphere on her birth planet and her mother born in the eastern hemisphere. Sheera, not her real name, she was born Sheryl Ling. Her path found her through many perils most she could no longer even recall.

A mental block, her old teachers had once told her, one that did not need to be opened if she did not want. Yet, when Selene took her hands, a part of her spirit had raced throughout the young lady's own spirit.

Sheera had been awakened and suddenly knew. Knew everything, about her past, and about all of her thirty previous lives, as well.

When Jeasuas had appeared, softly, lovingly, bathing her in his warmth, washing the pain and filth away. He told her she was needed for a far greater purpose than to die for unholy reasons, at the hands of unholy men.

The Ancient One's voice calmly told her she would find love in her new destiny. Well, she had at that. She still wondered though, if that was what Holy Jeasuas had meant.

"To fall in love with a man that would view me as a daughter or sister? What kind of curse have I fallen into to deserve such a fate? JC was the one that always spoke of curses, now, I am starting to believe!" She thought, as she walked on, a chuckle escaping her mouth.

Spending a year under the tutelage of the six demi-gods, Sheera had learned a whole new side of herself. Being raised to avoid violence except as a last resort and then only in defense, these six Ancient Ones were so different.

Her patron believed in her teachings, though. He had only taught peace, charity, and compassion, this past year. Yet, he had told her that she was expected to learn the other ways as well. Here was the stickler, the others taught violence! And, she was to be the "Golden Dragon!" Dragons were violent, weren't they?

True, her violence would only be against evil, but violence never the less. What she now knew to be her spiritual mother was known as a goddess of vengeance. How could such a contradiction be faced? To become the "Golden Dragon", as her patron's prophesies stated, she would be a woman of both, compassion and destruction!

And, then there was JC. A man that she could love! A man that she did love! Jeasuas was right about that! She knew him to be a priestly man, one of study and one of never-ending learning. He was her other half in this world. She a warrior of peace, and he a warrior of love.

Now, she would have to wait three whole months to see him again. But, would things change? He still could have only said it because he knew she needed to hear it. But he had given her this gift. Holding it in her hand she could feel the power radiating off of the small gold wrapped jade.

She could feel his power, his spirit within it, and she held onto it, wanting to feel his comfort and confidence, as she walked into the unknown. Sheera Lu Che would succeed if only for the two most important men in her life; Jeasuas, her patron, and for JC d'Badger!

Moving up the hill, she topped the rise and looked down into a valley. Below, she saw a large town. Her first destination, obviously, and now she would start her life. She stared down at the tiny city. The sun held towards the setting side of noon. She had been walking for about 5 hours, she figured.

Still not moving on, she squatted down instead, moving her wakisashi out of the way so she could comfortably contemplate her next move.

She would have to find the Temple and introduce herself as the promised prophet, finally come. But, how would the priests and priestesses take to a woman wearing a weapon, claiming to be a warrior/sorceress to the God of Peace. She laughed aloud at that thought. Hell, Spawn aside, it would be a very difficult thing to convince an entire continent that they would have to prepare for a war against an

100

enemy that she was expected to face. One that most would not even be able to touch, let alone harm.

The first step was always the most difficult one to make. It was the only step that is made of one's own volition. One of the only steps that a person truly has the choice in avoiding. Finally deciding to get this first and most difficult step out of the way, she stood and began walking down the long hill to her destiny!

Sheera looked at the largest building in the Village. The twenty-four demons she had vanquished on the way, were minor annoyances, and the several people she had been able to heal were, becoming so Her small army of locals that was now following her as if she was the "Messiah" or something was beginning to grate against her sensibilities.

She had to keep telling herself that she was a High Priestess, and that she was the promised one. She was a "Messiah", of sorts!

Ping Te Village was a large town, really, a tiny city, and the Sho Gun that ruled would be very powerful, indeed. That the Sho Gun's village streets were infected with so many Hells Spawn, hinted as to why this was where she had been placed to start her quest.

The town was made up of many single storied houses, some little more than huts, and many larger two storied buildings that were advertised as businesses by the signs posted on their doors. The business district she had just walked through, was the most infected so far, and the score of devils she had vanquished, were only about a third of what she had seen. The ones that got away would have to be dealt with, and she could only imagine the Hell Spawn that was commanding these creatures. She hoped it was not the Sho Gun.

Making her way to the Temple of Jeasuas, Sheera was moving, on the directions of her following. They would back off whenever a demon or devil appeared, but quickly swarm back behind when she would eliminate it, oft times with but a wave of her arm and a thought of psychic energy.

Sheera was becoming annoyed and the more she did, the less effort to her motions. She was looking more and more like a near goddess to the people, but she was too uneasy to see it.

Walking to the door, Sheera removed her sandals, and laid her back pack on them, then she slid the door aside and entered. It was a four storied bamboo and teak made construction, each story made with an inward bowed roof, and the level atop slightly smaller in dimensions than the lower. The very top level was but 5 meters across square, and topped by a high pointed bowing roof that clearly held a large bell attached to a rope hanging down into the Temple.

The bell was easily a full meter and a half, at its base, and about 2 meters tall. It would make a good strong resonance that could probably be heard far out into the valley.

The Temple when she entered was a single large room with many pillows arranged in no particular pattern around the floor. Most were occupied by men, with a couple women sitting cross-legged as well. Bowing to the statue in the middle of the Temple's sanctuary, she walked to the alter.

"I am Sheera Lu Che, chosen by our Holy Master to come unto you. I seek the High Patriarch, and wish to share words of wisdom with him." All watched her, most with disdain when their eyes would fall on her wakisashi, hanging down across her back, but no one moved.

An ancient man finally came down the stairs a few minutes later, and motioned her over to him.

"You have committed sacrilege bringing..." he pointed towards her weapon, "that thing into our Holy house. Why have you done this young lady?"

"This was a gift, from the Master, Holy Jeasuas himself, venerable one. I go nowhere without it. You were expecting me, were you not? Or at least expecting someone like me? I can only assume so, since none of you are out there, protecting the people! Especially with all the power I see emanating from the clergy of this Temple. You must have been expecting I would come to your rescues!" She finished.

His calm look reminded her of her teachers growing up in the monasteries of Tibet. Sheera was probably a lot younger, than he expected, at only 22 years old, she would be little more than a child to this man. She also stood a couple centimeters taller than him; she was sure, she probably was not at all what he expected the one of prophesies to be.

102

Sheera returned his calm, and held her hands in front low keeping her head slightly bowed in an honored position. The Venerable Priest watched her for any movement that would betray who she claimed.

"You say that was a gift, then I can assume it will only be used to clean the world of the monsters sent by Hell?" Sheera only nodded, and carefully avoided touching the weapon.

"As I said, it was a gift and cannot ever be used on Zindar's people. As priests to Holy Jeasuas, we are lambs of the world, not the lions that feed upon it."

"Yet, you claim to be the dragon, so therefore you shall feed upon the lions that abuse the lambs." he countered.

Sheera smiled and nodded before answering.

"I am the Golden Dragon that is mentioned in the prophesies, yes, but as a follower of Holy Jeasuas, our father, I am to temper my manner with the loving peace he has taught. I am truly only here with five others to free the world of the spawn of Hell and their Champion, the ruler of Haden.

"I really am here to be the steward of the people, human and non-human, alike."

Her answer satisfied the Patriarch and, he bid her follow him, as he turned to climb the stairs. They came to the second level where rooms were partitioned off and he led her to one at the far end from the stairs.

Several hours later, Sheera left the Temple with a writ signed by the Patriarch. The man still was not too sure what she would be able to do, but Sheera had been seen taking care of the people as well as eliminating the Hell Spawn. She could certainly do better than the Sho Gun's warriors had done!

Out in front, she noticed that there were still several of the followers hanging around. Even so late after sun set, they still fell in to follow behind her, as she walked away.

The stars were bright, and the moon was so large, that one could almost seemingly touch it. The brightness made it easy for her to navigate the streets. She knew she should be tired, but sleep was the last thing on her mind, so she walked instead.

"The most Holy Jeasuas has asked that forgiveness and compassion be given all who should seek it," she started. As she walked, she preached.

Never a good speaker she did not stay on any one point long. She answered the zealous questions with equal zeal. Only giving a little more than the answer. She mostly just spoke about the things she could remember of her patron's teaching.

As she would come to a person in need, she would heal what she could, and then move on. Never accepting money for what she was doing, she moved through the large town, until finally she came to the exit.

She had been given directions to the Sho Gun's estates, and was told that it would take about two weeks walking. There were a few villages along the way, and she could help to build her reputation as she went. That had been the Patriarch's idea.

"That you are female, will be your biggest hindrance. I wonder why The Holy Master would send a woman, to act as the Golden Dragon?" he had stated.

Sheera, felt good by the time, several more demons were destroyed, and as she left town, the people stopped a way outside and offered her well wishes and a speedy return.

Some even gave her food to carry, which, she accepted. She was a little embarrassed by herself; that she didn't stop and purchase anything. Next village she would not make that mistake.

****

As Burlga stepped through her gateway she looked back at JC's intense study of his own gateway. She wondered at him sometimes.

"Bloody Hell," she mumbled, "I wonder at him all the time!"

An enigma, is what he is, she thought to herself.

For a year she had watched him change. He did not even seem to notice the changes in him, or at least he did not acknowledge the transformations he had made.

104

He went from being an overweight aging merchant to seemingly becoming a man of power. An incredible specimen of human flesh. Not a pretty boy like Odyseus, but a real man, able to show feelings, a quiet confidence without boasting, a natural charisma that tried to like everyone and find good in everything.

"I all but threw myself at him like some Blue Market Whore, and he never bloody flinched! What the others must think of my actions? Well, nothing to do about that now! Of course, who cares what the Bloody Hell the others think! He still didn't even grab me, like I wanted, on that last kiss!" She finished as she looked at her location, not recognizing anything around her.

The plains extended in all directions, for miles it seemed. Desolate, the ground looked as though it had not seen rain in months, the vegetation brown and yellow, crunched under her steps. She wondered.

It was the most fertile continent in the world, when she lived here before. The only break in forests and grassy plains should be the marsh lands and the cities, of course. Even the small mountain ranges were filled with trees, forests, and soft lush undergrowth. This was definitely not her home anymore!

"He did have nice soft lips, though!" she once again allowed JC to dominate her thoughts.

Her index and middle finger touched across her lips as she smiled.

"Bet he would be a good kisser, if he would have kissed back." She stared off still thinking about the man.
    "Well, I guess I'll need to just go home and start from there." Talking aloud to herself she laughed.

Everyone uses to give JC such fits over talking to himself. He was always mumbling to himself, berating himself over his mistakes. The other five had finally broken him of the habit, to himself, such a bad habit, and now, here she was doing it herself.

"Have to get him out of my mind! Think of someone else, like Quen! Now there's another man! Better looking, faster with the swords, a true noble born!"
    But, thinking of him, Burlga wrinkled her nose, making a disgusted face. Quen, she realized, only cared about himself, void of any endearing emotions, that and wanting to be the hero that beats Lucifer's champion to a pulp in the final battle.

how things could have changed so in the five hundred years since she was brought forth. The entire South West Continent, Brautania, never had such an arid

Then again, they all wanted to be that person. She laughed at that thought, though. They all wanted to be that person, except JC.

Anyone with half a brain knows that JC has it right. It's going to take the combined efforts of them all, and whoever gets the lucky blow in that will fall the Ancient One's champion, will be the "One Champion" that the prophesies mentioned.

"Besides, there are so many different prophesies, and only JC bothered to read them all, which one of them is going to be right? Of course, in JC's way of thinking, they all could be. If interpreted a certain way, they supposedly say the same things."

"What a waste," Burlga thought. "This last year, THAT MAN, the others, everything! Purana is easily the most intelligent of all of us, yet, she refused to read the prophesies.

"Quen, the best fighter with the blades she has ever seen, yet, he refused to listen to anything anyone else would tell him. He even would only give some of the Ancient One's teachings just idle attention.

"Odyseus, the strongest, but he's just a boy. He may be of an age to be a man, but mentally he's little more than a preteen, in her world. This world, only hundreds of years ago!" She reminded herself.

"And, Sheera and JC are from a world where there is no such thing as sorcery or magic of any kind. Simple sleight of hand tricks, is what they would often speak of. She could not even imagine a world like that. And, then they spoke of wars being fought with machines, instead of the sweat of men, yet men still dying? Something she could not fathom in the least.

What she could understand the least, was JC's whole attitude at life.

"The way he was treated by all the "kids", as he called us. Hehe," she could only giggle at that image. "No matter how he was snubbed, no matter the way Purana would ignore his suggestions, he still always smiled that little wry way in which his mouth would barely move, his smile not quite touching his eyes. That wise way he would look, as if to think only that "we would learn!"

"None of "The Chosen", what a stupid name to call us," Burlga thought aloud, again, "really were very nice to him. That is, except Sheera. It would take someone like him, to defeat Kutulu Lucifer, in the end, though. His persistence and the way he always pushed himself to perfection, no matter how hard he had to work.

"Gods, and bloody Hell, I have to stop thinking about him!" Burlga yelled out.

Concentrating on an image. One she had not thought of in this past year, the image of her father's castle, her castle, came to her mind. Her father died shortly before she was taken by Merylon, and she was fighting to keep the lands.

Several of her cousins were attempting to lay claim, since she had the misfortune of being born a woman. If she had been married, it would have been a different matter, but who would marry a wizardress?

Pushing her mind to the basements under the Keep, she thought about the place, she wanted to arrive at. A medium sized room, square in shape and about fifteen yards to a side, deep underground, in the earth, the only way to enter or exit was from wizardry or sorcery.

She had dug it out, creating it through her use in the wizardry magiks, and chuckling, she thought of the treasures it now held. Secreting all the fortune of her dead father, as well as any of the art and memento's that she herself would not want to be without, she had made this room so easily, yet now, she was having a hard time bringing the exact picture to her mind.

"Even now, his thoughts invade my mind. He is so strong, yet pretends to be weak. His aura is easily that of Purana or mine. Why would he not believe he could do what we can? Gods and bloody Hells, I have to get my mind off him. I can't be in love with someone that does not love me back!"

Burlga thought, wondering at what the others would think. They were nobles, as well, with exception of the those two Terran's, of course, and she herself, was one of the more powerful of noble's daughters. If she had only seven years to unite this continent, she would need more money than the few hundred worth of gold and gems, Merylon had given her. She will need real money, and for that, she would take what was rightfully hers.

Finally clearing her thoughts, she managed at opening the gateway. Burlga stepped into the chamber. As the gateway closed, the darkness took her, and she tripped over something, falling to the pain in her shin after striking something hard, she hit her head on a metallic object and lost consciousness.

When Burlga first opened her eyes, she wondered if she did indeed open them. The blackness was complete and the panic in her began before she realized herself and created a ball of light a few yards out in front and above her. Momentarily blinded by the shock of the white light, cutting into the darkness, Burlga waited until her vision finally cleared.

Laying on her side, her head hurting and the scrape on her shin, she saw the dried blood and scab where a large piece of skin was removed by the table, gold and silver gilded, that she had tripped over, while stepping out of the gateway.

Wondering why her infra vision had not helped her, she soon realized, five centuries of just sitting here, the treasure would be no different in temperature then the rest of the room. Infra-vision of her elven heritage depended on heat to allow her to see in the darkness.

That and going from light to pure dark would have taken a couple moments for her eyes to adjust. Which she did not give herself, if there would have been anything to see, anyway.

Looking around, she saw the entire fortune of her father that she had secreted and stashed all those years ago. With her head still smarting, she realized when she touched the swelling egg-shaped lump, that the swelling was too large. She must have been laying there for a long time, if not hours. Her immortal regeneration was still not complete.

What was that word that JC and Sheera, would use in this type of situation? She thought, then smiled;

"Damn it!" Speaking aloud, she internally berated herself once again for turning her thoughts to that man!

"That wonderful beautiful man! I suppose I should not be surprised that he should have been more interested in her than me. She is from his own home world, after all!" And then Burlga frowned and added as an afterthought, "She wasn't really acting the flaming harlot. Sheera was a lot more subtle about her bloody intentions than I was, at times!"

"Do you always talk to the air?" A commanding feminine voice startled Burlga out of her reverie, as she whirled to see who had come up behind her.

The beautiful female stood some six feet two inches tall with sharp black eyes and sharply pointed elven-like ears. The slight overly long nose was almost pointed as well, and the long flowing black hair shined with an almost bluish tint under Burlga's white sorcery made lighting.

The devil's hair was worn over the shoulder, flowing down the female's front to cover her private areas emphasizing the too pale almost cloud white skin, nude without any clothing covering the rest of her. Holding a long-coiled rope in one hand and a jagged scythe like dagger in the other. If not for the almost transparent bat like wings sticking up from the woman's shoulders, Burlga would have thought the female quite striking.

"OK, demon, you have invaded my sanctuary, ignored my wards, and put me at a distinct disadvantage of not knowing who I address. Therefore, prepare to face the Creator!"

Forming the pictures in her mind of four different spells, Burlga released all at once, only Purana could do more at one time. But, before the first one connected with the demoness, the rope in its left hand uncoiled and covered the distance between the two women, wrapping Burlga from her waist up, pulling her arms to her sides.

It began to tighten, as the third and fourth spells flared and fizzled, the first two seemingly having no effect on the demoness.

"Now, elf, feel the power of Naamah, consort to the great and powerful Belial. Your insult at calling me a demon will not go unpunished. Know that your death will add much strength to my claim, and much power to my consort, as well!"

Forcing panic down, Burlga wrapped herself in flames as the rope quickly ignited and the deviltress was forced to drop the end she was holding, as the flames licked at her hands, she yelped with pain. Disappearing, she appeared behind Burlga and swung down with her dagger.

Burlga then, quickly sent out energy bolts from her newly freed hands and watched as all eight of the bolts shot out and turned to strike behind the half elf sorceress. All eight hit and staggered Naamah in the chest, forcing her back, Burlga spun as the dagger barely scraped across her shoulder and followed with a powerful gust of wind that sent all the treasure and furniture hurling upon the deviltress in its wake.

Continuing to push with her will, Burlga lifted more and more of the coins and jewelry from the room into the hurling whirlwind as well, burying the fear filled startled devil against the far wall.

Taking deep breaths, Burlga released the flaming shroud still surrounding her, and moved forward to the mound of treasure, piled atop the Hell's Greater Angel. Using her psychic will, she began moving the treasure away, pulling her short sword, which was ensorcelled by Merylon, himself, to kill the very type of Hell spawn, she was now facing.

If this creature really was whom she claimed to be, really was Naamah, then she was one of the twenty-seven Hell lords following Kutulu Lucifer. A true Fallen Greater Angel, sworn unto Hell! Her death is much needed and most welcomed. For Naamah was one of the more powerful females in all of Hell, according to the Ancient Ones' lessons.

As the pile shrank, Burlga readied herself, until the devil woman was freed of the sorcery made treasure prison. With an unholy shriek, and Hell spawned strength, Naamah launched herself at Burlga, attempting to hold the Immortal with a mind blast.

Already protecting herself from mental attacks, Burlga used a technique Sheera had taught her to use, when facing a much stronger foe. She rolled, backwards bringing her sword up in a short arc, driving it into her opponent's chest. At the same time, Burlga twisted to avoid the devil's dagger thrust and grabbed onto Naamah's wrist pulling in a downward motion. As the deviltress flipped over, landing hard on her back, Burlga rolled to her knees, twisting the blade of her short sword, and yanked it free.

With both hands on the hilt, the Chosen female quickly sliced down, removing the head cleanly from the shoulders as Naamah attempted a last effort at stabbing the half-elf. Instead, the twisted dagger fell to the floor, clanging on the hard tiles. Still on her knees, Burlga inhaled deeply, taking a breath as she surveyed the room ensuring no other hell spawn were present.

"Bloody Gods! That really did work!" She said with no small amount of excitement in her voice. "Thank you, Sheera, my very good friend!"

As she stood, wiping her blade on the devil woman's hair, the body began to smoke, disintegrating in an odor of brimstone. The head followed into an equal state, soon after, and from nowhere, a gust of wind came to displace the remaining dust piles into the air. No evidence of the battle, with the exception of course, of the broken furniture and other pieces of treasure in disarray, remained.

"So that is what happened to those Hell Spawn on the hill, before I was awakened!" She thought to herself, seeing the spot once occupied by the dissipating of the deviltress.

Burlga then found a couple of large sacks, just where she had put them, before being taken by Merylon, and began to load them with jewelry and other valuable lighter items of value. Tossing in about ten pounds of gold coins as well.

As she was collecting the part of the treasure that she would immediately take, she wondered if the others were having to face an attack so soon, as well. She would find out in a few months.

They had all agreed before leaving their most holy of training, to meet every quarter, every ninety days at the first spot on Zindar. Another of JC's ideas, but one that the others allowed themselves to be talked into. That way they could report on all their progress.

She had agreed too readily, she remembered. The others looking at her and Sheera, knowing that they agreed with everything he always suggested.

"Damn, him, and his hold on me, like this!" She once again yelled at herself.

What a lovely man, a strange one, to be sure, but such a beautiful man, never the less.

"If only..." She said aloud, before shaking her head in disgust.

Burlga tied the two sacks onto her backpack, and looking at the room and all the treasure remaining, she decided on a trap. Something she should have done in the first place. She pushed an invisible shield, a bubble of energy outward from herself, till it enveloped the entire room. Mentally thinking it as a rug of lightning, a tightly woven rug of threads pure electrical energy, able to cause pain, she marked it with her own identity, infusing into it with a small portion of her spirit.

"There!" She thought aloud. "That will certainly cause great harm to anyone else, with the exception of me passing through it, if not kill them."

"Now to see what kind of bloody condition and more importantly, what kind of flaming inhabitants now reside in my gods be damning castle." She thought to herself.

Forming a picture of the dungeons, her mind traced a specific cell. One her father had created. Hidden behind a wall of stone, several inches thick, it was created to imprison a very special prisoner. One that, she was not even supposed to know about.

The man that was to be placed in this cell to rot and die, was the man that was to be king. Burlga's father had planned to kidnap the heir in order to aid his own quest for the crown.

"Too bad he never made it", she thought.

The long war for the crown, between 18 nobles that claimed the power to take it was stupid, to say the least. The old king had spent his entire life pitting one noble against another, ensuring his position would go without contest, by keeping the nobles constantly against each other. And when he was dying, he had called for his son, the only heir, whom had been secreted away in another kingdom, hiding to avoid certain assassination by the other nobles.

When Burlga's older brother had died to assassination, her father went insane, claiming it was the king that had killed him, and vowed from that point on that no heir to the d'Noren line would live.

As the gateway closed behind her, Burlga put a spell of light on a large, half a fist sized piece of quartz, and held it out in front of her. The small chamber was empty except for the remains of what were bones of a man lying on a stone platform against the far wall.

Moving quickly to the stone door, easily visible on this side, she knew it would not be noticed on the other side. Made by dwarves, the secret door was solid and could not be opened from this side.

Her father had had all the dwarves that had constructed this cell slain, ensuring the secret would never be revealed. Of course, that also insured that no other non-human would ever build for her father again.

Pushing outward with the force of her mind, Burlga finally felt the stones begin to move. The door blasted outward, into another dungeon cell, as it finally gave way to Burlga's telekinetic push. Centuries of being unopened had seemingly welded some of the stones together, and it took considerably more effort than Burlga was expecting.

The dust from the blast caused her to cough and sneeze, as she stepped into the next cell, which appeared to have gone unused in over decades if not centuries, as well.

She knew that she had been gone for five centuries, but certainly, there should have been one cousin or another residing in the keep? This had been the jewel of the d'Venta clan, and was coveted by all the family line.

Coughing at the dust and with the dank unmoving stale air, each step she made seemed to make matters worse. The once iron bars of the prison were rusted and corroded away. Few were still in place and moving beyond a simple push sent the reddened iron to fall, most crumbling as it did. Surrounding herself in a bubble of fresh air, created by her sorcery, Burlga was finally able to catch her breath and avoid another bout of coughing.

As she made her way up from the dungeons, passing through wooden doors, rotting on unused hinges, if there were any doors at all, Burlga could not help, but wonder at the signs that pointed to none of these areas having been used, nor even visited in a very long time.

No signs of life, not even rats or other vermin associated with dungeons, nor were there any kinds of breaks in the dust that was thick enough for centuries of non-use. The air reeked of stuffiness, almost unbreathable, if not for her spell. How long, she wondered, had this part of the castle gone unused? She was not prepared for what came into her sight, as she reached the top of the basements!

The stone door leading into the first floor of the castle would not move. Pushing out with her mind, it took a considerable amount of psychic energy to finally push the jammed stone and iron door open. With a strong final thrust the stones gave way and she stepped out into a courtyard of heavy unattended growth of weeds and spring flowers. The sun was seen in its waning stages, broken walls showing the horizon easily. She stood shocked.

"This bloody hell should be the flaming assembly hall, not a bloody court yard!" She thought to herself in a stunned silence sure her memory was not that flawed.

Movement to her far right brought her back to her senses and Burlga reacted without hesitation. The fireball exploded on the three large ape like creatures. Standing ten feet tall, with greenish leathery skin, and tufts of lime green hair throughout their unclothed bodies, the trolls were toothless except for two tusks each, yellow sticking out of their mouths, wide and snarling.

Having been raised in the marsh lands of this kingdom, she was well aware of trolls and how to take care of them. Fire and acid came to her mind. Simple enough creatures to kill, but using swords or clubs on them would have virtually no affect.

And severing a limb was even worse, as the warrior would find himself facing two of the vile creatures, rather quickly. The more parts severed, the more trolls that would spring up from them. But fire decimated them and magical fire was overkill. The three monsters fell to a gelatinous pile of mush to her fire ball.

Several more began coming into view from all of the directions. It was hard to see in the dusk filled area, but with each flare of a fireball, Burlga had no problems eliminating the threat. After what seemed a very long time, but in truth, was little more than a few minutes, the keep was quiet and the only evidence of the troll infestation was the different sized mounds of greenish gelatin goo surrounding her.

At the least, now the overgrowth of vegetation, was burned away and she could see the floor of once smoothed slate stone, peeking through the debris.

"Its bloody hell has been flaming centuries since any flipping human inhabitants have lived here! I wonder what the flames hell happened to my family?" She spoke aloud. "Certainly, the entire d'Venta clan could not have moved on, or worse, been flaming eliminated?" Not expecting an answer, she was startled when one came.

"Actually, I am the last!" An aged half crippled filthy man, wearing a pair of ragged leather jerkins and a hard-boiled leather vest, equally spotted and weathered, spoke from behind up on a balcony.

His vest and pants were torn and in need of repair, showing signs of years of abuse. His hair was unkempt, hanging down beyond his shoulders, his beard equally dirty and in need of a good trimming. He was holding a long dagger, almost a short sword in a badly shaking hand, and leaning heavily with his other hand on a crumbled broken walkway some fifteen feet up the west wall.

"Who are you? And, I will forget that you are trespassing in my beautiful castle here, since you got rid of that nasty menace for me."

He laughed bitterly when he said that last part, but he never the less indicated clearly to her, that he considered this place his.

Creating better light, Burlga wanted to get a clearer look at the man up on the balcony. She was disgusted by the sight of such a slovenly man laying claim to being of the d'Venta line. His looks and the wary sense of insanity within his eyes, made her want to end his life right then and there.

"I am the Lady Burlga d'Venta, daughter of Lord Stellen d'Venta, high lord of the South Glenn Marshlands. This is my castle, my lands by right of lineage, and you unwashed one, are the trespasser."

Having spent a year around a man that abhorred her use of crude language, she had learned to hold her swearing down around others, not to mention the gods, themselves! With a deep breath at his heavy laugh, which ended in a cough, she continued.

"You will come down here, and give proper respect to your better, sir! Immediately! I have killed enough for the day and would not want to add your name to the list, whoever you are. But, I will, if you do not do as told, right this second!"

At the threat he regained himself, and a clarity came to his eyes. Even though facing a magi with obvious considerable power, the middle aged looking man, stood erect taking on the slight resemblance of a noble pride. He might have been able to pull it off, if not for the unsteady sway to his weakened form and the destitute way he looked.

"You, young lady is a liar!" He yelled out as he disappeared behind him, only to reappear a couple minutes later, entering into the destroyed assembly hall.

His talking never stopped and the echo came to the stunned sorceress' ears. She had been called many things in her life, but never before had Burlga been called a liar. If she did not want information, she was very nearly angry enough to disintegrate this man as soon as he entered the area.

It took considerable effort not to at least blow him apart with another fire ball. His limp from an unattended wound on his thigh that was festering, and she could see the gangrenous puss oozing down his pants as he limped closer to her.

"You... you little minx, are to bow to me. Magi or no, I am the noble here, and with what issues from your mouth, you certainly are not! I don't care who you claim to be, there is no such person as Stellen d'Venta, nor has there been for over 500 years, since that cursed name was stricken from the books. And his only son was killed and his daughter carried away by the invaders, my ancestors. And you, my pretty little girl, are obviously much too young and much too attractive to have been spawned from that demon's loins!"

The flipped compliment being interspersed in the insult caught Burlga off guard, and as she moved her hand to her mouth, she began tapping the index finger on her lips as she stood staring at the half falling keep.

"Hmm." She mumbled, "Obviously, things have not gone well for my family since I've been gone."

Looking at the man, standing only a couple yards from her, she resisted the urge to hold her mouth and nose at the smell. Instead, she asked after his name, since he still had not given it.

"I am Lord Quevit d'Venta, last of the cursed line that was once the proud holdings of the South Glenn Marshlands. Now, only a laughable destitute spot in the kingdom of Marintia!" He answered.

He did not bow to her, only standing on his one good leg, obviously in pain from the open wound on his other leg.

"That wound, Quevit," she purposely omitted the title, "is festering." Moving towards him, Burlga stopped as the man stumbled to back away, almost falling, as he brought his dagger up to an at ready position.

"Oh, bloody hell, man!" She cursed. "If I wanted to harm you, I would have just flamed well blown you off the wall." Burlga immediately formed a force field of energy around him, holding the man in a paralyzed state.

Then healing his leg, and while delving, noticed several other ailments and maladies within the man's body.

Not as elderly aged, as he appeared, maybe a little younger than herself, late thirties, she suddenly realized.

This man has had a rough life, indeed. She continued to talk trying to put him at ease as she healed what she could. She mumbled, something he could not understand, about healing, but as she worked Quevit did relax.

"There, that should at least get you moving easier. I wish I could do what my friend could, for you, but healing really isn't one of my strongest points." Burlga said stepping back and releasing the force field that was holding him.

Shaking from the shock of the healing, he did seem to be able to stand more erect and without the considerable pain that had gripped him. Lord Quevit could now walk without a limp at least.

"You need a bath, cousin, and a shave and haircut. Which of the brothers of Stellan do you claim? You probably are in need of a good meal as well! And we," she said waving a hand at the mostly destroyed keep, "have much to discuss." Burlga wrinkled her nose at the stench of the unclean man, and carefully kept her hands from touching her own clothes, having touched him.

Still not sure that this girl was who she claimed, Quevit was willing to listen. Spending a year on another plane of existence only to come back five hundred years into the future was a little more than he could believe. But, then again, she did know an awful lot about the prehistory of his family and the different family lines, including his own, before five centuries ago, at least.

She also had wiped out over fifty trolls in just a matter of minutes and had cleaned the great hall just as quickly.

And, her cooking, he had to admit, was actually rather good, he thought. He could listen, and maybe, this girl could lift the curse of the family name, as she claimed she was going to do, as well.

****

Purana was glad to be away from those others. Far inferior to her way of thinking, the thought of spending any longer grated her nerves. She was snapping at everyone, those last couple weeks, for reasons, she knew, were nothing more than minor annoyances.

She was a priestess and noble and should have had better self-control. To think that she allowed someone so insignificant to get to her, like that man did.

That middle-aged nobody, from a nothing world, where they did not even believe in magic, let alone have any practitioners. That she was beginning to have feelings for that short ugly old man.

"Well, maybe he was not so ugly, but, nothing like the other two men." she sighed before getting herself together as she looked around.

Now, Odyseus had been fun! He was a pretty boy, young, big, and, easily maneuverable She did enjoy the occasional bedding with him, when her urges came upon her. At least he did not pretend to know everything, like the others did.

"Blessed be to the gods, but this past year had been a nightmare. That insufferable old man we had forced upon us. Why would Selene have picked him, from all the worlds she could have chosen?" Purana thought to herself. "Certainly, she could have picked better. There is no way that she made him like that! Like Phaleg, Selene must have just found him, and thought he would work. Or else, she is really just trying to sabotage the others and is secretly, in league with Lucifer!"

Purana stood eyeing the surrounding, while she gathered her thoughts. She did continue to think on the man she hated to like, though!

"He had changed over the course of the year, but still!" She continued, within herself. "He was still, only average looking, no not ugly at all! But he was much too short." Almost a full hand shorter than she was, and her tastes in her toys had always been to the taller. "If you cannot bite down on the chest while copulating what good is the man?"

"And slow! Why JC couldn't even be a street sweeper back on my world, with his lack of intelligence. What those other two addle brained girls saw in him, I will never know!"

Why she had begun to feel anything for him, other than distaste, she could not understand either.

"It is good to be away!"

And with the time before having to put up with those other five, again, she could make use at getting her wits back in order.

Pulling out her sleeping blanket from the backpack, it would have to do, she thought. Purana spread it on the ground and began waving her hands, encanting a spell. She knew she really did not need to do this form of magic anymore, but she did want to find out if it still worked, and on this world.

Using the elements from nature instead of her own psychic will, was natural to her, and she could see the lines of power in this world as easily as she had back on *Haven*, her home world. She had memorized a few of her favorite spells, from before, this morning, and now was in the process of casting a simple *"flying carpet"* spell.

Of course, using a blanket would probably be a little like sitting on a feather bed that had too many years of not being refilled.

The blanket lurched on the ground, and then stiffened, moving to hover a few centimeters above the grassy green ground. The meadow extended in all directions for kilometers that of easy rolling hills. The mountains, jagged peaks sticking up were at the end of her considerable sight, off to the west.

Purana, sat down on the blanket, sinking only a little, and began to carefully spread out her dress, ensuring her legs, as she was sitting with them crossed, were properly covered, as befitting a lady of her stature.

She sat her pack and short sword on the blanket in front of her. Pointing north, she issued the command and the blanket lifted smoothly and evenly, moving forward gaining speed until she was flying about ten meters off the ground and gliding half again as fast as a horse.

Always head north, she was taught in her youth. When in doubt, north will be the guide to prosperity! And, here on this backwards world, in this small island called the continent of Atlantia, she would prosper. She was sure of it. Isis had promised her, after all!

After a few hours, the grassy hills gave way opening to fertile land of worked farms and the fenced areas of ranches. Men and women of all ages working the labors they were born to, plowed and hoed the crops. Irrigation lines feeding water to already growing produce and some cold weather crops were in the processes of being harvested.

As she sailed above, quietly on the stiff blanket, magically turned into a flying carpet, Purana smiled and waved at the startled peasants, like that of a parading queen. The laborers would point and wave back and some would even properly bow at her, as they should. She noted those that did bow, promising to remember those that were the first to acknowledge them soon to be, new queen. They would be properly rewarded, even if they did not know it, yet!

Of course, Isis had told her that here in Atlantia, all nobles were mages and sorcerers. And Purana knew that out of the six, only Burlga came close to her own power, and even that tart could not match the number of spells she herself could throw at once. What possible chance did any of these mere mortals have of matching her skills?

Purana was a great wizardress back on Haven, and now, she could do things with just a thought using her psychically endowed sorcery.

She knew what had to be done, and she knew she would need to subjugate the whole continent to gain that goal. Isis had picked her because she was the only natural choice for this destiny. Purana knew that of all the six, she was the only one that could become "The One Chosen Champion" mentioned in the prophesies.

After all, physical combat may be needed against the lesser denizens of Hell, but that would not work against Hell's leader. What good would combat do against a being that was a demi-god, and so powerful that the entire other six Ancient Ones were afraid to face him.

Even if that is not what they taught, Purana was sure she was in the right on that point. No, it would have to be her and her ability with the mind. But she needed to find another type of magic. Something that had never before been seen, something that Kutulu Lucifer had no defense for. Something so new, that it would make her even more superior than even Isis or Merylon.

But that would have to wait, for now! Purana continued gliding past the farms and ranches as another couple hours brought into her view, a sprawling city, at least twice the size of any on her home world.

With a command word, the blanket mount she sat on, stopped and hovered in place, allowing her to take in, at half wonder, the city glistening with buildings of white and gray, and many towers reaching great heights, with polished domes of gold and silver that sent reflected sunlight in all directions.

She was amazed at the wealth in the buildings of this city, and the artistic architecture had her excited at the thought of ruling here. She once again sent the blanket moving and soon arrived at the beginnings of the roads into Barach, the City of Sapphire!

Slowing her ride to little more than a quick walk, and lowering herself to only a couple meters above the ground, she realized she would stand tall in this land. The men were only about an average of 160 centimeters tall, even the old man was taller than these people. The women here were even shorter! At 176 cm, Purana would seem a near giantess here, let alone the power she would command with her sorcery.

"You there, peasant..." She yelled down at a man walking, a large cart following him unaided by any animal pulling. She could see the emanations of power on the cart causing it to move on its own, following its master as it would.

"Where is the Temple of Isis?" She finished.

The man, having been insulted by the title she had called him, was about to cast a spell of pain on her. But, seeing the power in the woman flying, as she readied a counter spell having noticed his building of psychic waves, he quickly released his own spell letting it fizzle out, and simply pointed in a direction and quietly moved off in another direction. She sniffed and headed on in the direction indicated. She would remember that fool, she told herself.

After gaining a couple more points or nods given in similar fashion, she was ready to raise the whole city in a purifying cleansing for the treatment she was being given. How dare they treat her with so little disrespect. These peasants would certainly pay dearly when she was their queen!

She finally found the building she was looking for, the Temple rising to something over seven stories high, made of white marble and topped by a bell tower that was gilded in lapis and gold. She dismounted, releasing the spell holding the blanket, and quickly rolled it up, stuffing it into her pack she slung the straps over her shoulder, grabbing the sword's sheath half way, she made her way up the stairs to the doors.

Anger boiling to a point of release, she willed the doors open, a little too forcefully, and they slammed echoing loudly deep into the church, as all heads within turned and saw the giantess standing, legs shoulder width apart, one arm down beside her leg, holding onto what looked to be a sword, and the other bent, holding onto the strap of her backpack. She looked ready to strike at anyone that moved.

"Who's the head here?" She voiced loudly, "I am Purana Bin Gage, Chosen One by the Holy Isis, and the new High Priestess to this land!" The temple went utterly silent!

The movement was slight and almost undetectable, off to her left. The lightning bolt suddenly sprang from an out stretched hand flying towards her. With but a thought she shielded herself against the bolt and at the same time tied the caster in a force field of unimaginable strength, the likes he had never faced before.

As he was lifted casually off the floor of the sanctuary, he watched as his own spell hit dead center on his target and instead of shaking or killing the sorceress, fizzled out on her body. She was far quicker than any he had seen, and she did not even seem to move as she stared at him, her head tilted to the side.

"Is that the best you have, sorcerer?" Purana asked. "Is this all the Holy Isis has given me to work with?" Turning to her right the nine acolytes standing together reading a spell suddenly found themselves flying backwards through the air, to stop hard against the back walls.

Purana moved into the Temple, calmly walking towards the alter, willing the bound priest to move in that direction as well. Any that moved after were just as steadfastly bound in a similar field of force, and when she reached her destination, she settled the flabbergasted man to the floor, but never released him.

"Now, again, I ask, who is in charge here?" Her icy calm voice cut through the movement as those that could, quickly exited the building. The remaining 13 bound in cocoons of air, the only ones still standing. The ancient priest, gathered his courage and answered that he was.

"Good, finally a show of wisdom. As I said before, I am Purana, and it is my pleasure to announce that Isis has finally sent your deliverance unto you." When he did not answer, she added, "You do know the prophesies, don't you?" At his nod, she continued.

"Good, then I don't have to bother with any of the drivel about you misunderstanding me. I'm here to whip this nation into shape, get all of you ready to face the hordes of Hell, and prepare myself to face off against Ancient Lucifer's champion. Maybe, even the god himself!

"Now, since I only have seven years to do that, I expect a little cooperation from you all.

"If I am going to have to destroy all the good wizards and strong sorcerers making my point, then I will be defeating my purpose at being here. Wouldn't you agree?" Her tone was so demeaning, her attitude too haughty, and the venerable High Priest was slowly losing his fear of this young woman that dared to defile his temple.

"Isis would not send such a person. This is not the promised one!" He thought. Mustering his courage, once again, he let out an equally scathing speech as the one she had just given.

"You, young woman, may be a very powerful magi, maybe even the most powerful I have seen! But, if you expect me to believe that the Queen of Love and Beauty would send an uncouth, loud mouthed little girl to us, regardless how pretty you may be, then you have another thing coming. And, if you do not release me, immediately, you will face the full wrath of the entire Temple. Strong as you may be, you will become eventually swarmed under. DO I MAKE MYSELF CLEAR TO YOU?" He finished with hard emphasis on each individual word.

Her laugh was soft, not even noticed at first. As the unconscious men and women began to awaken, she tied them up with hardly a thought. Finally, she regained control of herself, and eyed the priest.

"You do have courage, old man. Almost as much as the ones I've spent the last year with. But they have a whole lot more power than you possess. I will release you, but only because I do not want to damage any of the pretties here in Holy Isis' house."

All nineteen people remaining in the sanctuary found they could once again move. Purana was really quite pleased with herself. She did not think that she could hold so many people and yet she felt that while only binding no more than six at a time, she could have held onto many many more, if necessary.

As she was looking around at the others, all staring at her with uncertain fear, waiting for a signal from their High Priest, they simply watched the young woman.

When the priest was about to say something, nine dimensional doors opened in the sanctuary, pouring forth different types of Hell Spawn, and Purana did not waste time patting herself on the back, any longer.

Sending forth spell after spell, four and five at a time, even six on a couple of occasions, she quickly found herself in the midst of a life-or-death struggle.

The other priests and priestesses only hesitated long enough to see three of their fellows fall to the claws and talons of the creatures, before they reacted with their own sorcery and wizardry.

After less than five minutes, the gateways snapped shut, slicing four demons in half when Purana was finally able to close the doorways to Hell.

Fifty devils and demons lay on the floor and eight of the temple's clergy as well. As Purana turned to take in the carnage, the smell of brimstone hit her nose, and she could see the bodies of the spawn begin to smoke and disintegrate. A wind came from nowhere and blew the remaining dust into the air, dissipating the evidence causing the sanctuary to be clean of the sacrilege.

"Well, young lady!" The High Priest said, walking towards Purana, "Maybe you are who you claim. But you need to realize, that your attitude will need to change, if you think that brow beating the emperor is going to work!"

Purana stood eyeing the priest, in total disbelief that this world could be that much different than her own. If she would have possessed this much power back on Haven, she would have been crowned queen without a question. Could things really be so backwards?

"Perhaps, venerable one, you had better start telling me what kind of opposition I am going to face from the populace, then. I am accustomed to my word being law, and have little patience for politics. I have Hell Spawn to prepare for, not mortals!"

Purana's calm matter of fact statement only garnered looks of amazement, as the younger priests and priestesses began cleaning up the mess, and gathering their fallen brethren. Their head shakes and snickers did not go unnoticed by the Immortal, as she watched the elder priest before her.

The Immortal Chosen was perplexed to find that power, almost always ruled, but there were those that possessed the sufficient strength, yet not the skills, and the people could always rise up to over throw such a person.

"If you thought that might makes right, then you should just move south a few hundred kilometers into the continent of the makatiels and giants. Chaos reigns there, and you should make do, really well." The elder priest advised her.

Purana chuckled at the statement, but she heard, and began to rearrange her thoughts about how she could bring these people under her thumb.

CHAPTER 6
The flip of a coin?

From the east, should he come, he of the six, chosen of the
Holy Ancient Ones! By fire and lightning, he brings liberation.
And with it, the evil ones shall flee.

From the prophesies of the Order of the Sword

As he stepped through his gateway, Quen Dem Lurin rested his hand on the long sword at his hip. Imbued with sorcery, by Phaleg, himself, to kill any Hell spawn it was used on, he knew it would have to become his preferred weapon. But, instinct and long years of use, still pushed him to pull the one-and-a-half-meter bladed Bastard sword, sheathed on his back.

"I'll bet some blacksmith will be able to figure out how and what is needed to make me a proper bastard sword. Seems I remember JC saying he was a smith in his former days!" he wondered silently surveying the landscape.

The gateway closed and Quen's hand went for the hilt, reaching up along his right shoulder at the sight some twenty-five meters away to his front. He instead lowered his arm and began a slow walk towards the mark, some minor disdain showing on his otherwise smooth face.

Waving short swords and buckler shields, dressed in boiled leather armor or simple hides with chain links sewn down the chests and backs, Quen witnessed the ten brigands harassing the wagon and its owners.

None had seen him yet, as he continued to walk towards them. He watched the one-sided duel taking place, and wondered how he could handle this without the peasants being hurt. The middle-aged woman, one of two women, in the wagon, looked up in his direction, as though she saw him moving in.

The brigands were surrounding the man on the ground, while the two women were still sitting in the wagon. A few meters away, another of the farmers, male by the looks lay face down on the ground, either dead or nearly so.

The women were screaming to be left alone, one a middle-aged woman, with dark hair, streaks of gray running through it. The hair was tied up in a bun on the top of her head, coming apart in disarray at the activity taking place on the ground to the side of the wagon.

Her leathered wrinkly face, her dress a plain woolen kind, dark colored, with embroidery along the hems and seams, she might have been pretty in younger days.

The younger woman behind, kneeling in the bed of the wagon had her hands covering her lower face and mouth. Her hair a darker brown than the older woman's, was in a braid, hanging down her back to below her shoulder blades. Her dress, although a lighter color was of the same utilitarian design. Well to do farmers, to Quen's eyes.

The duel was taking place between a brigand and what looked to be the husband and father of the two women. The brigand larger of the two men, almost as tall as Quen's 192 cm, was lean and wiry. He held his short sword loosely with confidence, as his companions urged the skirmish on with obscenities and jeers.

The farmer, middle aged or older, had gray hair with a few streaks of black running through it. The hair was long, tied back in a short pony like tail. He was holding his staff out in front, at the ready, but showing an uncertainty at the situation. His eyes gave a perseverance, though that Quen recognized in those that had served in the military. The farmer kept to a circle ensuring the opponent could not get behind him. He was wary of those around him, but concentrated on the one in front.

When less than three meters away from the closest of the bandits, Quen pulled his bastard sword, quickly and loudly. The soft sound of metal scraping against hardened leather, got the reaction he was hoping for, as half the heads turned his way.

"Why don't you try your luck with someone a bit younger?" He growled just loud enough to be heard.

"Of course," he started, swinging his sword to gut the first one to step within reach of his sword, as his cross swing took the head of a second man, he finished.

"You will need more than just the ten of your filth!"

Forgetting the farmer, the remaining eight brigands attempted to form a circle around Quen, but never had the chance. Untrained bandits against a well-trained duelist, they fell quickly. As the ninth man fell to the ground, Quen turned to face the last, the one that had been toying with the farmer.

The thief had forgotten all about the staff. With a quick stab to the abdomen, the farmer followed through with a swinging club to the head on the bent over brigand.

Quen calmly wiped his blade on the shirt of one of the fallen bandits, sheathing the sword, he nodded his head to the farmer, who was standing warily watching, leaning lightly on his staff.

"My thanks, M'lord. The lives of my wife and daughter are in your hands. Who be thee that has come to this simple family's rescue?" The man legging a bow, but never lowering his head far enough to take his eyes off the warrior before him.

Quen nodded to the bow, noticing the bow of a soldier, not so simple a farmer, after all, he thought.

"I am Lord Quen Dem Lurin, most faithful to Holy Phaleg, High Priest of the Blade. And, I am sorry I was not soon enough to save your man, laying over there!" Quen returned the bow and then bowed to the wagon as well, "M'ladies! I trust you all are uninjured?"

"It is good that you came along, holy priest." The older woman exclaimed. "How is it that a warrior can walk out of the sky, like a god, as you did?" Quen could only smile, one that never quite touched his eyes. Not so simple farmers at all!

He quoted from the *"Law's of the Blade"*, only adding that he was sent by Holy Phaleg to insure their survival. Quen watched the reaction and could see the familiar hero worship from the daughter, he had seen the like back home, and the relaxing in the mother and father. Of the three, the daughter showed signs of psychic abilities to her aura. Quen was not sure how strong, not having a comparison, other than those he had just spent the last year with, but she could be taught.

After helping to bury the servant, and saying a quick prayer, the group left the area. The farmer had collected all the brigands' weapons, and left the stripped men to feed the carrion birds and hyenas. The mother had insisted that Father Quen, come with them and at the least accept a good meal, for his timely rescue. Hungry, Quen could not refuse.

That night, as he was about to bed down in a guest room, he heard a crash in the kitchen below. Grabbing his long sword, reacting to the screams that followed the crash, he took the stairs two at a time, where at the base of the steps, he was met by three large demons.

Standing over two meters tall, looking like oversized toads, with sickly green skin, and human arms in the place of where forearms would be, they emitted a force of fear around them. Resisting the urge to flee, Quen beheaded one, before any could react, and gutted a second one as the third attempted to claw at him with talon fingers. Quen's third swing missed as the creature leaped up and over him, landing four steps up, from where the Immortal was. With a wide arcing swing, Quen managed to sever a leg, and his fifth swing took out its heart. Without waiting, Quen ran into the kitchen where he could still hear screams emitting from.

Sir Mandoran Lem, lay face down on the floor, and the man's wife, Florentine, was beheaded near the door. Nileena, the young sixteen-year-old daughter, was backed against the wall, when Quen entered. Two more of the toad demons were moving in on the girl, one had her hair in its hand.

Quen yelled out and swung to eliminate the monster's arm, and as the arm fell away, to the floor, it pulled Nileena down with it. The two leaped over and around as Quen's blade flashed in and out, but within seconds, the demons lay dead on the floor, and Quen was standing, allowing the girl to embrace him, head against his chest, as she cried for her dead parents.

The search of the farmstead, found seventeen more demons, and six dead servants. After an hour of searching, with Nileena close on his heels the whole way, Quen was satisfied no other Hell Spawn were present.

"We shall get some sleep and leave at first light." he told the girl, emphasizing the "we".

****

"I sure be gonna miss those others!" Odyseus thought to himself as he quickly stepped through the gateway. As it closed behind him, he wiped the tear from his eye, staring at the space that once held a rift to another part of this world. The brown eyed, red haired, pale skinned man of nineteen summers, looked around.

Standing seven feet two inches tall and weighing over three hundred pounds, having grown some in the year he was with the others, in training, he was the tallest, largest, and by far the strongest of the Immortals, but that old man was sure of deceptive strength as well! Odyseus was especially going to miss JC.

No matter that none of the others seemed to like him, excepting for Burlga and Sheera, of course, JC was the one solid feature that he could depend on to lend a helping hand when none of the others would.

Never having known his father, Odyseus had adopted the older man as one, and JC never failed Odyseus in the year they had been together. Though, he had never openly admitted it when around the others. He was sure that JC would not even know how much the others really loved the man, after the past year.

The youngest of the six, Odyseus sometimes lacked the self confidence that the others all showed, but his wisdom was that of a man much older. Although, nineteen summers, his emotional development was that of a thirteen- or fourteen-year-old, boy.

Not a very good sorcerer, not agile with the blade, he could not understand why Minerva had chosen him, but it sure got him out of the trouble he was facing back home, so he was not going to complain.

His thoughts slid back to the day his life had been changed. His mother, sister to the queen of Athensoria, largest and most powerful kingdom on all of Muridian, was high priestess to Nike, Goddess of Victory.

He had been noted for his ability at battle strategies. All the instructors at the university lauded him with acclaims and citations every time he would present a new tactic that when tried in the war would work. Still shy of the age to command a legion, he kept to the university and eagerly awaited the twenty third cycle, his day of adulthood.

He remembered the seven men laying on the ground, and only five of his family members moving. Odyseus had broken the neck of the eldest son of the Queen, punishable by beheading, no matter the circumstances. He ran for the Temple of Athena, Goddess of Wisdom, in hopes to gain some answers from the priestesses there. He remembered praying to Athena for salvation, only eighteen summers old, he was too young to die such a dishonorable death, he begged the Goddess to have mercy on him and to give him guidance.

That is when she came to him, Minerva, not Athena, as she was known on Muridian. It didn't matter, to Odyseus, what she preferred to be called, he would listen to this woman. She was the most beautiful thing he had ever seen up to that point. Calming, wise and a Goddess. And, when she spoke to him, Odyseus readily agreed to her proposition.

And now, here he was, standing in Lemuria, smallest of the continents in this tiny world known as Zindar. It was fitting that he was given the smallest of the continents, he thought. He was too emotional to lead, and not old enough or confident enough to pull together a larger land. But, he thought, he would not fail his patron goddess.

"This do I swear, Holy Mother Minerva! I not be failing you!" He said aloud, half yelling to the forest he had stepped out into. His voice echoed through the trees, tall, thin, white barked, with many small leaves, coin shaped, the lowest of the branches still a few feet up, above Odyseus' own considerable height.

Unable to see the sun through the foliage above, he looked around trying to gauge a direction to travel. He was startled by the voice that spoke, and immediately brought his club up to the ready position as the aging woman, dressed only in skins, laced together loosely, stepped into view.

"You don't have to yell, young one. I was coming as fast as I could!" Her gray stringy hair was unkempt, and the walking stick appeared to be heavily used.

Worn twisted fingers spoke of hands often used for heavy work in this venerable woman's life. Her weathered face, like that of wrinkled leather was smudged with dirt, spoke of a woman that slept away from the cities. Her aura was only showing two spectrums, and he couldn't remember what that meant.

The inner one was gold and solid, he thought that meant she was good in sorcery, and the outer was a deep dark blue, solid looking as well. That meant she was sad, he thought. Odyseus never spent much time studying the auras, he thought they were too easily manipulated, but he was sure there was supposed to be three spectrums, and rain-bowed. He studied the old woman, and finally gave up.

"I knew you would come; the Goddess spoke to me in a dream!" She continued, moving slowly up to Odyseus, who was standing in stunned silence.

As the small disheveled woman moved up to him, stopping less than a yard away, she poked a gnarled index finger into his stomach and exclaimed.

"You are a big one, aren't you, boy? Couldn't tell in my dreams that you'd be so young, either!" Her voice was strong belying the rest of her bent form.

Standing only five feet tall, she barely stood to Odyseus' chest. But the sharp poke, hinted at a strength in her that this aged woman impossibly possessed. Odyseus was sure, as well, that she could use her cane as a weapon, if need be, regardless of age or her stature.

"Oh, close your mouth, boy. It's bad enough I have to get a crick in my neck looking up at you, I don't want to be slobbered on, as well. And, besides it is bad manners staring a woman, like that! One would think you were trying to undress me." She said with a wink that made the big man blush.

"Thy words do say thee, expecting me?" Odyseus stammered, asking with incredulous aplomb.

Stepping back from him, the woman looked up to catch his eyes, hands now resting on her hips in the way women do when they want to make a point. She sniffed before answering.

"You a little deaf as well as dumb? Didn't you hear me, boy? I said the Goddess told me you were coming!"

Anger forming, Odyseus calmed himself and answered the woman.

"I'm sorry, grandmother. Who be thee? And, do not ever call me dumb!" Standing erect, he puffed up a little more, towering over the diminutive woman, he was not trying to scare her, but he did not appreciate her attitude nor her lack of respect.

"That's a little better, boy!" She stated. Tilting her head to one side, still holding hands to her hips, she studied him, slowly walking around to get an entire look, Odyseus felt he was being measured for the slaughter.

"Well." She began, "you are a little on the young side, but your size will certainly do. You're even bigger than those on Brautania, the South West Continent, and they grow them the biggest in this world. I suppose, I can make a king out of you. You are a pretty one, too. Have to watch for the young ladies, I will!" Turning, she began to walk away, slowly, using her cane as she moved.

Dumb founded, watching the old lady, Odyseus was startled out of his contemplation when the woman turned, and spoke out, rather testily.

"You coming, boy or am I just out walking for my health?" She continued on.

Odyseus made eight quick steps coming along side of the woman, and slowed his pace to hers, asking again for her name.

"Oh that!" Was the only answer she gave, continuing to walk as if to ignore.

Eventually, she continued.

"You know, it has been so long since I've had to give my name, I had to think on it to remember. You can call me Hecate. But that will have to do. I don't remember the rest of my name, and it don't matter any, my Lord Brell. I remember everything else. Just not my name!" Her soft laughter was mischievous, sounding a little like a hyena after its dinner.

After a couple hours of walking, cramps forming in Odyseus from the slow short stepped march, the venerable woman stopped, claiming the need to rest. When Odyseus asked how much farther they had to go, he offered to carry her. The thought of walking for four more hours at this slow pace had him thinking the stiffness in his calves would be permanent.

"Hmm, that might be fun!" She answered with a wickedly immodest grin on her wrinkled face. "It has been a long time since a handsome man has handled this old body!"

Lifting her arms to him, Odyseus kept his blush in check and leaning down, Hecate wrapped her arms around his neck, as he moved his left arm to lift her. Sitting in his bent arm as if side saddle, she squirmed moving her legs so that her left thigh rested on his hand, she was sitting on his forearm.

133

Standing up, Odyseus could tell she sat comfortably, only weighing about eighty-five pounds, he thought he could carry her easily, for however long he needed to manage. Her smile never left her and when she kissed his cheek, he did blush, as he began moving through the forest holding his spiked club down in his other hand.

"You are a handsome, lad, aren't you? I'll bet you've had many a young maiden in your arms before. But, none with my experience, though!" She laughed, as he walked on, stumbling on something, the heat of his blush traveling down his neck.

The more she talked, the more he blushed, and when her hand followed the blush down his chest, he nearly dropped her, barely holding on, she only wickedly cackled more. His breath became labored, the heat rising as her lewd comments made him more and more embarrassed.

"This is going to be a very long trip, for you, young man. If, you don't learn to be more disciplined on your thoughts! Perhaps, I should cast an illusion and really test you by becoming your most desirable female. Hmm?" She finally announced breaking her incestuous banter.

Odyseus could only laugh! The nervous laugh, one gets when suddenly his arms were holding a woman, as desirable to him as even Purana had been. When she began to fondle his chest beneath his shirt, the big man had to sit her down.

"Hecate, if you please, thou do be taking thy proper form? I think thee a minx under that wrinkled skin, venerable one!"

She laughed, finally transforming into the woman she appeared to him in, and they resumed their trek until they finally came to a large oak tree, in the middle of the strange forest of aspens. The tree was out of place, for the type it was, but, more importantly, for its size. Over a hundred seventy feet tall, with a base of the trunk over sixty feet across. The small hole seemed natural, and when he squeezed inside, following the woman through, a natural made home existed.

Hecate explained, she had convinced the tree to grow this way, when he commented on not being able to see any cutting or workmanship in the walls.

****

As JC looked around, his gateway snapped shut behind him. Taking in the sights and smells of the open plain, a meadow in reality, small some two hundred meters between a forest on both the east and west, to the north the two forests joined about three hundred meters away. And to the south, about fifty meters, what looked to be a well-maintained road, and a farm extending beyond sight.

The road as he walked towards it, was seen to be heading east and west into the forests. Shrugging, he pulled out a coin, gold, from his pouch and looked at it. On one side was stamped with angel's wings, the other side, a stately woman.

"Must be the queen of these lands!" He said aloud.

Throwing the coin in the air, he caught it wings side up. Putting the coin back into his belt pouch, he shouldered his pack, and headed west. Smiling at the outcome, his only thoughts took him back to when he had studied seven of nine of the known prophesies.

He had asked for the other two, but they were not present in Launam, and the Ancient Ones didn't seem interested in making them available. Of course, Kutulu Lucifer's "Victory of The Light" and the Creator's "Histories of Past and Future" were not well accepted by the Ancient Ones. They considered it worthless reading the Creator's book, since it was a made-up church, with no real god, and Kutulu Lucifer was the enemy, so why need to read his story. Still, Jeasuas had taught some of it, to them.

"Should have known the coin would come up west, no matter which side I picked. From the east he will come! Depending on which one of the prophesies is read. But the east is the starting point." Still smiling he walked into the forest and continued to follow the road.

Keeping a strong pace, after several hours, he began to realize that it would behoove him to get a horse, or even a wagon.

"First town I come to; I will have to buy some transportation." He said aloud to himself. "I could really use a bath, as well!"

Whistling and humming songs from his past, he walked on, until the forest thinned and found himself staring from a hill overlooking a large valley. As the sun was ebbing, he looked below and saw about a half mile down, a large village. Almost a small town, he realized.

He had been walking for what he estimated to have been six or seven hours, when he left the forest and began the walk down into the valley.

A large square on the far side of the village was seen clearly, surrounded by three large buildings and about two dozen or so smaller ones. A river flowed past the northern end of town and a large building and another dozen smaller ones were at the river. A large lake was off to the west about another half mile beyond the town, and a good-sized castle could be seen in the distance close to the lake. Many small and large houses lined the road leading up to the castle.

JC noticed, coming from the square, in the direction of a part of town, thick black smoke was rising. The explosion of a fire ball, sorcery made was heard from that area, as well. He thought to himself the need for hurry, and he quickened his pace to a jog moving his scabbard from his shoulder to his hand.

He soon realized there were a lot more buildings, small houses and businesses that were scattered among many trees as he entered into the town. From the top of the hill, it looked more like a small village but as he ran past the few farms, he saw movement of a populace that was more like a medium sized town.

When he entered the eastern end, he immediately shrugged and stopped at the sight of devils and demons walking about, wreaking havoc on buildings and people. There were no warriors, he noticed, just farmers, and a few craftsmen valiantly, attempting to fight with the tools of their trades.

But he did notice that there were a few women and a couple men here and there that were casting spells via sorcery, and he assumed the Temple priestesses must be aiding in the town's protection. He also saw a very few men, using swords and even a couple casting spells via wizardry.

He noticed something else, as he eliminated a demon with a single strike of his katana, made by Selene, empowered to destroy any Hell spawn. He noticed that other kinds of magic were being used besides sorcery.

Making his way slowly through the village, JC's blade moved as if alive. Demon, devil, and other Hell Spawn fell, he continued to move in the direction of where he knew the smoke to be coming from. He only stopped along the way to reach down and heal those that were injured. Or, he said a quick prayer over the dead he came upon.

He hardly noticed the grateful smiles of the citizenry, as he helped a lady to her feet, while swinging out to behead a charging demon. With apparent ease, the spawn fell, and the people began to think they were seeing a god or maybe one of the Goddess' Angels, making his way through town, cleansing the Hell away. Shocked and surprised faces, as he leaned down to heal by placing a single hand to the injured's heart.

There was no shock nor was there the usual spasm or pain of the heal that most would feel when the Temple would perform theirs. The frown at times that JC would make would quickly turn to a smile as he moved on.

Any that were not conscious were given a small piece of himself, as he empathically took their pain into himself. Then he shifted the spell into healing the injury without any shock that they were used to seeing the priestesses do.

Always the touch was at the heart, those that watched noticed. The crowd that was following behind, at a safe distance, watched and some were shocked by the familiarity of his touch on total strangers. It was as if an angel was in their presence. Especially the women, noticed when he healed another woman, his manner in which he would inquire to their health.

Yet, none were ungrateful, and no one said anything, but simply continued to follow. After all, he was saving their village, easily, which was something all the Temple priestesses combined were having a hard time doing.

One young girl, about twelve, by her size, was hit by a blast of air as she surprisingly began to form a spell. JC noticed her aura and saw great strength in such a small person. She was already as strong as Quen, maybe even Odyseus.

"She must be an assimar!" he told himself, as he saw into her aura. "One that is first generation!"

The Chosen were told that they would not find this kind of strength amongst the mortals, yet here this little tiny girl who possessed it. He looked harder and noticed the angelic spirit in her, and realized he was correct. The one had angel's ancestry recently in her blood lines.
There was strength in the blast of air, and the girl flew back, rolling onto the ground to stop finally, at JC's feet. He sent out a flame strike to explode down on the minor demon lord, and knelt to the girl.

Still breathing, he saw her inner aura was silver and gold, and she seemed to be something more. Something familiar.

Barely conscious, the battered girl saw the fire erupt from this stranger's out stretched fingers, of his free hand, and the beast incinerated on the spot.

JC, seeing life in the tiny form at his feet, knelt down and laid on his hand. Her eyes jerked alert, with a start, from the normal shock of healing. Her own regenerative powers taking hold from there.

"Your safe, now, child. Help your friends, I'll take care of the Hell Spawn." JC said, noticing the crowd following him for the first time.

He continued on, more and more spawn died in his wake. He continued towards the square, where he was now feeling the use of powerful sorcery in great quantities.

"Strange this should not be happening!" he said allowed. "Too much power, Mother Goddess."

Stopping to render aid, JC saw the girl kneel down beside him, watching as he healed. She seemed, to him, to be seeing his use, and the way of doing it. Shaking his head as he smiled, he moved on.

"Who are you? How do you do that? No one can transfer psychic energy like that! Except for the Gods!" She asked in almost a command, as she walked beside him.

When they came to another injured, he saw her try and succeed with his form of healing. She staggered to the pain, as she tried to stand.

"Don't try and heal that way, child. You may be strong, but you will use all your energy, if not careful. You are not quite old enough to have the reserves. Not to mention the pain, you are taking in!" He frowned, knowing that no one else, including the other Chosen, could heal his way, yet this tiny little preteen girl had just done it.

"Who are you?" She insolently demanded.

"Who are you?" He sarcastically asked back with a smile. "I am vengeance!"

138

JC continued on as he approached the west side of the square. Entering to see twelve nine-foot-tall skeletal boned devils each with hooked boned arms, standing on overly long legs, with tails that looked like a scorpion's stinger. They were a bone white in color, and were fighting among nearly three dozen women all wielding sorcery.

A single large devil stood in the middle of the square sending fire and lightning into the largest building, where a tall female stood on the steps leading to the Temple of Selene.

JC recognized the larger devil as the devil lord, Abigor, a Greater Angel that was the Archangel Baalzebub's chief lieutenant.

Pulling the girl behind him, he only stated,

"Wait here, child. Don't let anyone else enter the square." Then he dropped his backpack and moved into battle.

The statue at the tiled court yard's center was a fountain with a large female holding out stretched hands from which the water was pouring forth. Except now, it seemed to be diluted blood that issued forth, as the red liquid was polluting the fountain.

The three large buildings, one little more than a ruin, now, still smoking from flames magically heated to burn even the stones. The other two, one at the north end of the square, a three-story stone, obviously an Inn of some sort, and on the south end of the square, where the dark-haired female was casting, was the five-story light colored stone building of the Temple of Selene.

The woman, seemed to be tiring, as her spells were not near what they had been, and the spells cast by Abigor were staggering her, beginning to penetrate her protective shields. She stood at the top of the stairs, and JC could see that she was linked to others inside the open doors of the Temple, in an attempt to boost the priestess' power.

JC could see by her aura that she too was a very powerful sorceress, even more so than the girl behind him. And, she too had angelic heritage. She was an assimar, as well. Although, her lineage was not as new!

He wondered how much of the power was hers, and how much was from the linking of several others?

Casting a lightning spell that split into three arcs, at the bone devils, he attempted to call out over the din, to use fire, on the larger one.

"Abigor is immune to lightning, use fire!" He yelled, but was unheard.

His next spell cast was a flaming tower of pure magical fire that started at the fifteen-foot-tall devil's feet and moved quickly up its brown body, until Hell's Greater Angel was fully engulfed. He then began to move quickly toward the now screaming dark angel, yelling to get its attention his way.

The girl, wisely stayed at the alley, they had entered from, but began casting lightning bolts at the nine bone devils, still standing.

The lone female at the top of the burned scorched steps leading to the Temple, hesitated only a few seconds as she saw a man, short, but powerful looking, holding a strange long thin curved sword, move towards the large devil she had been fighting.

The devil had turned towards the man, and now, the priestess could take a much-needed breather. Grateful for whoever managed to wrap the devil in flames, she wondered about the power of that spell, knowing she could not have done it like that, and yet she was the most powerful of the priestesses.

The High Priestess only took a moment to wonder, though, as she recognized Essmelda standing in the mouth of the alley that the man had walked from. Worry for the girl overtook her need for rest and the priestess began duplicating the girl, with lightning spells at the smaller bone devils.

Sending one last lightning bolt at the bone devils, as it arced, once again into three separate points, JC closed in with Abigor, who had finally dispelled the Immortal's sorcery caused flames.

Abigor's great sword wavered as he faced his new foe. A smile touched the too wide mouth, the large bug like eyes changing colors as he moved. The fire, extinguished, as the devil seemingly ignored the energy blasts coming from its left, cast by some priestess that had been relieved of battling a now dead bone devil.

"Abigor, in the name of all that's holy, I condemn you on this day!" JC yelled, as he pictured a flaming shroud around himself, and was suddenly engulfed in a blue fire shield that emulated the colors of the robes that the priestesses were wearing.

JC's own blade, his katana, became enshrouded in yellow and red as it seemingly turned to flames, as well. Tossing his scabbard aside as he moved into battle, The Chosen Immortal slowly methodically closed on the devil, as the angel Abigor began attempting to use psychic mind blasts against JC's mental shields.

The sparks flew when the two blades first met, the Hell spawned steel meeting the sorcery made steel of Selene. The duel was deadly, and quick, as both combatants appeared to gain and loose advantage. It became loud and bloody, spark filled war each time the blades would meet, and the cuts and injuries oozed blood from both devil and human, alike.

As the red blood from JC mixed with the flowing black blood of the devil, the tiled square was becoming slick with the crimson ichor and both duelists seemed to be slipping having a hard time with their own purchase.

All the bone devils finally eliminated, the priestesses and populace held back from the two duelists, one a four-meter-tall monstrosity, responsible for leading the days destruction onto their town, and the other, a short, but large shouldered man, enshrouded in a blue aura of flames, appearing very much, like some sort of Heavenly Angel of Selene, coming to their rescue.

To their horror, they watched as the human seemed to be gaining a winning edge in the battle, eight more smaller versions of the larger devil, suddenly appeared around the man, teleporting in to aid their master. JC appeared to ignore the smaller devils, as he pressed harder the larger one with swings, that appeared too quick to be natural.

Concentrating on the devil lord, JC began to move faster and harder with each series of his movements. He began to feel the drain of his *haste spell*, but still he pushed, knowing that Abigor was also, beginning to find a way through the mental shield JC was holding. When Abigor's stomach was suddenly opened and as the devil bent reacting to the evisceration, JC quickly removed its head with a back swing.

As the appendage suddenly rolled down the devil's arm onto the blood covered slick tiled square, JC turned to quickly eliminated the smaller devils, with a flurry even the crowd watching, could barely follow. His last spell that the cast was a

141

sheet of flame that erupted on the remaining fleeing spawn, as his own flaming shield dissipated.

When the fire would touch a building or a person it would leave them unharmed, yet when the eerie sheet of flame touched a demon or devil it would explode as the fire melted their bones from the inside out.

On unsteady legs, most of his strength gone, JC looked every direction and felt the nausea come upon him, seeing the carnage, human, and devil alike, littering the square. The smell of brimstone as the Hell Spawn began to smoke became over whelming, causing all to feel the nausea.

The sorceress, he saw, was now sitting on the top step, as more women had exited out of the building, beginning to stand or sit around her.

She looked as though she was as drained as he felt, but she watched the man warily. JC noticed, the awe-struck villagers moving into the square, as they realized the horror of the day was now over.

"Is everyone all right?" JC yelled out, but the voice coming through exhausted lungs was barely heard.

Before any answer came, JC dropped to his knees, his katana falling to the ground, as blackness threatened to overtake him. The last thing he saw before succumbing to unconsciousness, was the young girl, running towards him carrying his backpack.

The High Priestess on the steps yelled out as the girl was just arriving to JC's side.

"Essie, no, it is not known if he is friend or foe!"

The young apprentice checked and saw that the warrior was breathing as she turned back towards the Temple.
"Reverend Mother, he still breaths. I believe he is friend. Says his name is Vengeance!"

The orders to bring all the wounded inside the Temple were given as the town folks started to fill the courtyard. JC was lifted and carried inside along with several others that, if but barely, were still showing signs of life.

When all were stripped of their blood-stained outer garments as the lower-level priests and priestesses begin to clean the wounds and apply bandages. Essie, began to dab at the wounds on the self-healing warrior and noticed that his wounds were closing on their own.

"His cuts are closing, Reverend Mother." she told the older priestess noticing that the woman was holding away with a somewhat shocked expression on her face.

"What is it, Reverend Mother? Do you know this man?" one of the other novice priestesses inquired.

"It's nothing." Deanery quickly answered, as she turned to walk away. The Temple High Mother had called for a meeting, and all the seat heads were heeding the call. The council went behind closed doors.

As the Reverend Mother was leaving, she ordered that a shield be placed on the man, and that Essie would need to hold it, while they decided his fate.

CHAPTER 7
Claiming the Crown!

As the sun was falling the next evening, Sheera found a nice spot under a tree next to a small brook. Taking out her bedroll, she made a petite sized camp and settled down to watch the water. As a small brook trout was idly swimming by, she reached out with her mind and lifted it from the water.

The fish was cooking over the flames when she heard movement off to her left. Reacting with a mental shield, she readied herself, as a short being, only 102 cm tall entered into her camp. He was leaf covered, short, and wide, with deep forest green skin, dark reddish hair and beard, and striking violet eyes that seemed to be dancing in the fire light. His nose was wide and long, with an over-sized mouth full of yellowish teeth when he smiled.

He was wearing nothing on top, with pants that didn't quite make his ankles. They were a brown with many multicolored patches sewn all about, and appeared in need of more to be added. The rope belt was snug, and a small pouch and dagger's sheath hung from it. His hat was small and narrow, barely able to stay atop his round large head, slightly pointed ears sticking out of the long unkempt hair.

Demonic looking, except for the smile and the color of his inner aura, Sheera relaxed upon finally concentrating on the whole of the aura. He had good strong psychic abilities, more than she had seen around all the humans earlier today or at the Temple, yesterday. And, his outer spectrum was filled with compassion and joviality. She returned his smile and pointed across the fire, where the diminutive man finally, sat.

"Can you catch another of those, for me, little lady?" He asked pointing at the fish roasting on a stick. "I haven't eaten in several days." He finished.

"Here, then, take this." Sheera offered the stick over to him, which he hurriedly took, thinking she would change her mind.

"I am Sheera, and you?" She asked.

"Mm-mm, this is good. Leaf Loren at your service! Chomp, smack, Mm-mm, "he answered around his bites. The gnome ate the entire fish, bones, head and all, and sat the stick down, wiping his thin short beard and licking his fat stubby fingers.

"Most humans would have killed me on the spot, Sheera. You are from somewhere not around here, though, aren't you. The language you speak is not one I have ever heard spoken here, before." His eyes twinkled with glee and he smiled at her reaction to his last statement. He laughed and finished between the giggles,

"Yes, I know, you are en-spelled with a tongues spell. By the gods if I don't miss my mark by how strong it is. But that can't fool little old Leaf, it can't. I see through all that illusion stuff."

Sheera went the five meters to the brook and quickly returned with two more fish. Handing one over to the gnome, she started cleaning hers, noticing that he was not cooking his before devouring it, scales and all.

"If I may ask, good sir, what are you?" She inquired while working on her fish. She poked the unused stick through and set it over the fire.

"Why, I be a Gnome, little lady. Where are you from that you need ask such a question that any two-year-old could answer?"

Their conversation lasted into the night. Sheera was enjoying the teasing nature of the gnome, and the gnome seemed to enjoy the company. Sheera learned that the path she was traveling was filled with many Hells Spawn and that it would be awfully dangerous, even for her.

He decided that it was time for sleep and without asking if he could, he pushed some leaves into a pile and curled up about a meter from the fire. Sheera, just chuckled and leaned back against the tree, wrapping herself in her bedroll and drifted off to sleep.

The next morning, the gnome was gone, and Sheera was surprised at the four fish cooking over the fire, obviously stoked back up to a nice small cooking level. She noticed the leaf bed that was there the night before, gone and some lettering was scratched into the dirt. She read the message written in the Gnomish symbology.

Little Lady, you were kind to an old man. I was
glad for your company and will see you again soon.
Remember that the non-humans believe in you and
there is no need to have to convince us you are who
you are. Your own people will not be so forthcoming.
Fondly, Leaf Loren

Smiling at the note, she rubbed it away and sat down to eating the fish, saving two for the road ahead.

Sheera arrived at the next village, a tiny town-let of only four small huts and one larger building. The huts were burning, the two-story stone building was being bombarded with tree limbs and stones, and looked as though it was about to fall in, as well. The culprits were large three-meter-tall skeletal looking devils with a great bone hooked tail.

The creatures were bipedal, with two arms, which were being used to rip small trees from the ground and throw at the building. Their skeletal heads had glowing red eyes peering in the sockets. There were twelve at work, and screams could be heard inside the stone building.

Sending a lightning bolt at the Bone devils, it struck one moving onto the next and then the next, until all twelve were hit. The magically made lightning then dissipated into the ground.

Screaming at the attack, they turned from their former target and began moving towards the woman standing just twenty-five meters away. Only ten were still standing, and Sheera quickly pictured two more bolts and sent them out. By the time the Bone devils had closed the gap between them and her, there were only four left, and Sheera formed a wall of air, forcing them back.

One disappeared and suddenly was behind her, she only just managed to knock the strike of its tail away with her wakisashi. Her counter swing, cleaved the devil in half, and taking no momentary rest, she moved on to the other three. When it was done, the odor of Brimstone was permeating the air and a gust of wind blew the disintegrated devil dust away.

As she alerted the Inn, she found that only three young children, two boys and a girl, ages 8, 9, and 11, the girl being 9, were all that was left alive and that the rest of the village was dead or had disappeared. Taking the children, she made up a pack for each, and they left for the next village about six hours away.

****

Burlga spent the next several days cleaning out the castle and eliminating the debris. Her cousin had spent the time talking about the politics and changes during the past few hundred years. Using sorcery to make temporary fixes on the

146

walls and roofs, were all well and good, but she knew that she wanted to gain the use of contractors for more permanent fixes. Dwarves would be nice, if they had forgotten the curse against her father's actions.

"There are no more dwarves, cousin!" Quevit explained. "Most people believe they never really even existed; they have been gone for so long. Besides, we owe the kingdom so much back taxes and loan moneys, that we are lucky if they don't even confiscate what lands we have left."

Pulling out one of her large sacks, she opened and poured out the jewels and gems. Quevit only stared in disbelief.

"Will this take care of paying off the crown and gaining the proper castle repairs and servants, dear cousin?" The hundreds of thousands gold weights worth of jewelry and gems made him gape in disbelief.

"Where, what, ... how..." He stammered. Her laugh was light, childlike, as she shook her head.

"I told you; I am d'Venta, and the rightful heir at that. I have the fortune of my father. This will get us going, yes?"

****

The High Priest Anu, introduced Purana to Elder Priest Torel. Torel was easily the strongest in the Temple, and even though Anu was the highest ranking, she could see that the middle-aged priest before her was coveting the chance at following the Chosen One. Torel was ambitious, covetous, lustful, and more than a little useful for her purposes. Purana knew that she would have to keep an eye on the man, but he would be handy to have around.

Besides, Torel was the only man in the entire Temple that was above 168 centimeters in height. Giving the man her dagger, she instructed him on the use of certain destructive magiks, and ordered him to follow her whenever she would leave the city.

Purana had no choice, but to accept the small retinue that went with her, even though only four of the sorcerers were of any strength, and none of the sorceresses. There were a little over a dozen wizards of decent studies, and the muscle that came with the few soldiers was enough to keep the Hell Spawn cleared in what few villages she managed to visit.

Making her way from Barach to Atlantis, the capital, Purana cleared each village of the demon kind, and made more enemies along the way than she did friends. Those that thought her a goddess, found out quickly that she would be a goddess of unfriendly motives, and not the usual that their patron, Isis, would send.

Although, everyone admitted, the Chosen might be the most beautiful creature they had ever seen, she was not the Prophetess of Love and Beauty that they were promised.

"The Goddess must be sending us two prophets! The one of beauty has arrived, now we only need wait for the Prophet of Love to come!" She was constantly hearing the same comments everywhere she went, and soon, Purana began to ignore the peasants.

"They are only the uneducated cast offs of genetic impurities." She would say. "Not worth the effort of breathing, they should just find comfort elsewhere! I don't have time for them!"

****

Voices entered to his awareness as consciousness finally came. JC did not move, keeping his eyes closed, he instead listened. The force field holding him, kept his limbs from twitching, and he chose to find out more of what kind of hold he was under before reacting.

He was fully restored psychically and could feel healed of his wounds, as well. The shield while strong would not hold him if he were to exert himself. He felt all of his psychic ability available to him, meaning he was not shielded from its use. He was only being held, something not very smart if they knew he was as powerful as any of whoever it was holding him.

JC knew, though, they had tried to keep him asleep while under the hold and could feel it was three feminine beings he was being held. He could feel the warmth of the day, and the hard bench he was laying on.

He realized that it was probably early morning, and from the light seeping through his closed lids, he must be inside a building somewhere, most likely the Inn or the Temple.

He lightly probed the force field holding him, not wanting to alert the sorceresses holding it, and realized that it was the girl that had followed him through the town and two others. One an angel pretending to be mortal. This alerted the angel he was awake and he immediately struck out to all three and dispelling the field around him he placed a hold right back on them.

The angel pretended to be held, and when he sat up, he was unsure who it was that was secreting their identity.

The girl that was standing right next to him was very strong, and now that he had touched her mind with a tickle, could see that she was somewhat older than he first thought. Not a preteen, but maybe fifteen or sixteen, he would surmise.

He still wondered at her ability to learn his style of healing, that Burlga had told him would be unique to only him, according to her patron, Merylon. Although, since he knew Sheera to be his twin, she could probably do it, as well.

He would also have to think about the power he had seen used, by at least two others of these priestesses. Way too much compared to the warnings they had received by the Ancient Ones.

His immortal regeneration nearly complete in healing his physical wounds, he stood and stared around the room, noticing it to be the main sanctuary of the temple. There were several novices and other young priests and priestesses all tending the many wounded.

Through closed doors just off to the north near the statue could be heard a heated argument.

"He must be held, no matter the cost!" A female's voice was heard. There was urgency in her tone, though there was no sound of fear. Anger was propelling the loud conversation taking place behind the closed door.

"Don't be ridicules, Morella! You didn't see the power in his spells. Not all of us combined could hold him, if he chooses to leave!" Another female countered. Calm, no fear.
"We don't know if he was a part of the demon's attack." The one called Morella, stated.

149

"He is the reason we still live. Morella, you sound like a fool!" A different voice, musical and light sounding.

"Thirty-two of us are dead, Dyanea. Fifteen of them males. We don't have so many males in our order that we can afford to lose any."

"And he just miraculously appears and eliminated what all of us together could not? Don't you think that strange?" another woman interrupted.

"I think it miraculous, yes! I think it the Holy Goddess' blessing upon us!" The one called Dyanea stated.

A fifth voice entered,

"The convenience, that we with all our power were failing, and he just appears and succeeds is most disturbing. C'renan and Dyanea you two are too filled with stories in your heads."

"Not stories, Zaina, prophesies. You now, doubt the word of our Goddess?" The musical voiced one answered.

"Where are the others, then, C'renan? Where are the other five, if he is one of the promised ones?" The first woman asked, a touch of sarcasm entering into her tone.

"Yes, C'renan, where are the others?" Another woman asked.

JC continued to listen, and realized there were at least nine women in that conversation. And judging by the tones and content of what he could hear, only two seemed to be anywhere near, in support of him. The one called Morella appeared to be the one in charge of the group, and it was clear she wanted to control and hold him, if not outright eliminate him!

Thinking it time to get moving, he suddenly noticed he was nearly naked, only standing in his loin cloth, he studied the three he was holding and could not be sure which of them was the angel he had felt. The girl, next to him was surely an assimar, but he was sure he had felt a pure angel among those three. His eyes scanned the entire room, now under a silence spell, ensuring no call for help would be heard outside of the immediate room.

"Sorry for causing you any pain, child, but I have too much to do than to just lay here." JC said calmly as he moved away from the bench he had been laid on.

Stretching his muscles, he realized that his undressed state was causing the young ladies to close their eyes embarrassed by what they were seeing. All still held, they were unable to look away.

The girl's eyes had snapped shut, a blush filling her face, and he turned to movement from behind, to see six more priestesses and priests, all in their twenties or older, linking to cast a spell. Quicker than they were, he dispelled their link, and began to wrap all six in energy fields as well, duplicating the hold he had already done to the three others.

Thinking he would be able to hold all seven for as long as he needed, he looked at the auras of the six older women and found that none came even close to matching the power of the one girl. He also noticed that a half elf young female was showing moderate strength but had a strange inner aura of silver, normal for a human and gray, which would be normal for an elf, but he was sure that the half elf should only show one type not a blending.

Still standing in only his under garment, he began to move away from the girl, as seven shocked faces stared at him in amazement. Releasing the hold on the girl's gag, JC asked where his clothes were.

The girl instead asked,

"How did you do that? One person cannot hold so many!" She said as though fact.

"Maybe I would have a little difficulty if all were as strong as you, child. Now, where are my clothes, and what is your name?" JC asked, adding before she could answer, "And, child, how is it that you can do what not even the other Chosen can? You are a very unique individual, for a mortal! But then you are no pure mortal, are you? Assimar should not exist, I was told."

JC looked around at the sanctuary to find it filled with make shift cots and beds. More than forty individuals were laying in various extremes of injury.

As he began to move about, looking at each of the injured, the girl finally answered, with a little haughtiness and a touch of scorn coming across her tone.

"I am Essmelda, apprentice to the Reverend Mother Dyanea, Council of Nine, of the Brigitte Order to the Holy Goddess Selene. I ask you, sir... No, I DEMAND that you release us, now! Even the queens and kings do not treat Priestesses of Holy Selene, thus!"

"Probably because they can't." JC answered absentmindedly, as he continued to take care of the most critically injured amongst the villagers.

Not wanting to use his own strength, he began to draw energy away from the seven priestesses and four priests being held, and the looks on their faces, as their moans emitted around the gags, told him that they were feeling this happen for the first time. Before Essmelda could say anything, though, he asked,

"Now are you going to tell me where my clothes are, or am I going to continue to parade around like a dancer in heat?"

Her blush forestalled any further inquiry, and she once again closed her eyes. Sighing, JC moved to stand in between the clergy and looking at them one at a time, shook his head.

Seeing the awe struck looks in the older women, the near admiration in the men, JC realized that he had probably just sent them into a shock. They knew how to link, but to draw psychic energy from another to cast a spell with, like he had just done was something none would have ever seen nor heard about being performed.

And doing the type of healing, that only JC could, and now, Essmelda, had the six adult women staring in disbelief. They had known that a lot of the injured would have died to the shock of healing, yet using the strength of the priestesses, JC had managed to eliminate the shock to the injured's body.

And to still be able to hold against so many attempting to dispel his psychic binding on them, they all truly did think they were in the presence of some sort of deity.

JC could feel all but one attempting to eliminate his spell and he moved over to stand in front of the half-elf, nodding to eliminate the gag.
"You accept your fate without a struggle and do not even seem surprised what was happening. What is your name, young lady?"

"I am Pynora, sir. You are her we have been awaiting, are you not?"

152

"I am, JC d'Badger, High Priest to Holy Selene, Sword of Vengeance as promised in the tomes, one of six come to fight for Mother Gia in the War of the Gods. Yes, I am her you have been awaiting."

Her attempted nod as he released her hold became a bow. He pulled her up by the shoulders, shaking his head in the negative.

JC realized the villagers should all now, be strong enough to survive complete healing, and, the drain on the priestesses, while being enough to keep them from being able to attack him with any sufficient strength, they should still have enough to heal with.

"If I release all of you,"he asked, looking into the awe filled, paled faces of each of them. "Will you swear not to attack me, and instead continue with Selene's commands to take care of these people?"

He waved his arms as if to take the whole sanctuary in. He removed the gags on all the other six, as he continued to stand, half naked, arms crossed. Not getting an immediate answer, he softly exclaimed.

"I swear, under Heaven and the Holy Selene, as a High Priest to the Ancient One herself, and child under Mother Gia, the Creator, I mean none of you any harm." He added afterward, "Now, do you swear the same? I want you to help the people, they are suffering needlessly while you gape at me like I was some sort of monster! And, where are my clothes, please?" He finished, slightly elevating his voice on the last question.

All of the priestesses, including the girl, Essmelda, swore. As he released all their holds, three of the adult women and the three male novice priests, to include the half-elf, dropped to a knee and swore fealty to JC himself, thinking he must truly be a son of the Goddess Gia. As they rose on his command, he asked once again,

"Where are my pants, at least?" All seven women pointed to a corner of the room, and JC could now see his cloak covering a pile, that would have been large enough to be all his things.

"Thank you, M'ladies!" He stated as he walked to the pile, noticing his Katana sticking out from underneath the clothes, as well.

"I am the Priestess Mythalla, my Lord JC. We did not take anything of yours, so you needn't be concerned to be missing anything." He turned as he was pulling his soft dough skinned leather breeches up.

Tying the laces, he stared into the young woman's face.Pretty, dark complected, with large light brown eyes, and light brown hair. She stood the average height of five feet three inches. She appeared to be either late teen to early twenties, and JC could see by the nearly transparent middle spectrum of her aura, that she was only of slightly above average psychic strength, but still young enough that she would gain further.

She watched him, through awe filled eyes, and as he pushed his arms through his light blue blouse, and leather vest without lacing either of them, she knelt down to pick up the katana holding it in both her hands.

"The Council is a little put off by your use of such a weapon, that seems to possess a great power within it, and of such an unusual design, Lord JC. Can I ask where you got such a weapon? It is very heavily magicked!"

"Please, young lady, do not call me Lord JC. Father or simply JC will do! And to answer your question, the katana, as it is called, is a gift from Holy Selene. It is imbued with the ability to slay Hell Spawn!"

Her face paled as she dropped to a knee before him, and JC noticed that the other priestesses and priests in the room and a few of the injured that could, all had knelt to him as well. Shaking his head, as he took the weapon from Mythalla's out stretched hands, while he ordered the entire sanctuary,

"Kneel only to the gods, my children. Rise and never grovel to someone that walks the earth of Zindar!" As they all rose, Mythalla taking an offered hand by the High Priest Immortal, she mumbled, just loud enough for those closest to hear,

"So commands the long-awaited prophet, finally cometh to the Brigitte Order of Holy Selene, in Selene's name!"

Thus, was it written into the Holy Book of Selene, the first commandment ever spoken by the prophet, JC d'Badger, High Father of the Temple of the Goddess Holy Selene.

****

154

As Quen laid the girl down, after several attempts to get her to sleep alone, he agreed to stay with her, sitting in a chair beside her bed. When morning came, Quen was still sitting, sword across his lap, his eyes burning at the lack of sleep.

Convincing the girl to come with him, was easy after loading the wagon with food and clothing, as well as several valuables, and all the considerable money in the house. Nileena then set the house on fire, and the two rode out, wagon pulled by four horses, Quen riding another, as well as two more horses and four cows tied to the wagon behind. Quen grabbed a basket full of eggs and let the chickens go free, as well as undoing the gates penning the sheep.

Nileena stated that she would follow him to join the Temple, as she had nothing left to remain for. The house became a fitting grave for her parents, and Quen said a prayer as the structure burned.

They arrived at Vellium, the capital of the Grazia Empire, after seventeen days of travel. Having sold off four of the horses in one village, where Quen had to take care of twenty-seven minor Hell Spawn, and been asked to say burial rites over six graves, they sold the cows as well. In another village, where twenty more spawn were eliminated, he traded his horse for a war horse, and sold the swords taken from the brigands.

Eight villages total were liberated from more than three hundred Hell Spawn, and by the time they made Vellium, Nileena could even swing a short sword without hurting herself. When they arrived at the Temple to the Blade, Quen entered to announce himself.

Nileena was welcomed into the Temple, and placed in an apprenticeship program, and Quen spent the next month accepting challenges, until it was accepted that he was who he claimed. High Priest Meritt, the senior war priest and most powerful sorcerer among the Knights of the Blade, crowned him High Priest, and sent out word of the arrival, to the emperor.

Within three weeks after being named High Priest, Quen was crowned the new Emperor, the former man, High Priest Sveron Hurnd, surviving the challenged duel, was named and accepted the post of Regent. Quen would have too much to do, after all, rather than run an empire. The Temple of the Blade, had its promised savior, and the regent maintained his running of the nation. All seemed happy with the events.

Purana spent the next several weeks eliminating demons and minor Hell Spawn from the surrounding villages. She worked at maintaining her composure when someone would not give her the respect that she felt was owed, her. Being noble born and raised, she was accustomed to total acquiescence by the commoners. Here, even though being of the magi class guaranteed her noble status, she found that anyone could become a noble and those that were not were simply, not as impressed by it as they were on her birth world.

Purana still managed a calm, that had High Priest Torel very unsure of her, and he wondered that Isis would send someone so absolutely devoid of love. She was a very cold fish, and he could not believe that any man could have made her so lifeless. This person she would mumble about, Torel would very much like to meet.

"But that will come in time." He thought to himself.

Having just arrived in Atlantis, she found many of the demons and minor Hell Spawn in the guise of the common populace. When they were slain, her name was often mentioned in the same sentence with words such as brutality, hatred, and ugliness. Purana was becoming more and more frustrated by the lack of respect; she had arrived believing due her.

Purana finally cleaned the city and the surrounding farmsteads of Hell Spawn, and with only a week to go before the first meeting, of The Chosen, she sent out a challenge to the emperor.

She was not really expecting him to agree, since Torel advised her that usually, the most powerful person was given the crown, in order to avoid any bloodshed. When the acceptance to her challenge arrived, the High Priest was the most surprised.

Entering into the palace, the surprise was quickly altered to disgust, as the Temple of Isis found that there was no longer an Emperor to receive them. The High Priestess was advised by the head chamberlain, that he had accepted the challenge, as the demon that killed the monarch was still in the fallen one's rooms. That part of the palace had been sealed with magical wards, and they would welcome its elimination.

Purana dispelled the wards and entered into the room to find a succubus lounging on one of the divans, laughing at the sorceress' dumbfounded expression.

"I will enjoy so much taking your soul, my pretty little human."

Before it could react, Purana wrapped it in an air tight force field, and using old fashioned wizardry, cast a disintegrate spell on it. The whole situation was taken care of in a matter of seconds, and the next day, Purana was crowned Queen. The nobles would have to be sent for, but,

"You should be named empress by the end of the month, two at most," the Chamberlain, Doreen Faulin, told her.

Doreen Faulin, the head chamberlain was the typical sycophant. He showed a possible ability for sorcery, but insisted that he was just as happy with wizardry. Although, he advised the Queen, he was only of a limited order of studies, he had good strength in the spells he did know.

Purana, not being very good at reading auras, she had always thought that the study was a waste of time, did not pick up on the high strength of his psychic ability. Doreen Faulin was easily twice the strength of any other priest or priestess in the entire Temple, and was only a little less than half the strength of Purana, herself.

He was, though, an excellent chamberlain, and as head of the palace's staff, he was a very good administrator. His only reason for not killing the succubus himself, was the dream he had telling him that Purana would soon be arriving.

He was told in his dreams that the One of Prophesies would be her that could defeat the succubus. He also knew, that no other in the Temple would be able to. Excepting of course, for Apshai, who for some reason was also hiding most of his abilities.

The big secret that Doreen did not want Purana to know, was that he was the son of Nephthys, one of Isis' Archangels. Being an assimar It would be very important not to allow his full powers be known, as even Isis did not know what her favorite angel had done. Having a child with a mortal was certainly not forbidden, but Isis could be viewed by Mother Gia, as having cheated in the game.

It was bad enough that no angels were allowed, but for some reason, one of Gia's own Archangels was currently involved, and Doreen did not want that one to suspect his own heritage. Gia could only be spying, and Doreen wondered about the other Chosen as well.

"What angels would they have watching them? And, why was Apshai pretending to be a low-level wizard?" These questions haunted Doreen as he watched the Temple closely.

In the end, Doreen swore to Purana, and he also swore to himself that Torel would be watched. No one ever questioned, when he hired soldiers to look after the man.

****

Traveling via gateways, Hecate would teleport away only to return with their destinations. Odyseus, would then follow through her gateways into a village or farm and liberate the area of demons, minor devils, and miscellaneous Hell Spawn.

He never really questioned how she knew how to create something they had been told no one should know, and just enjoyed the company as they were clearing the country of spawn.

The battles were always short, and he would usually just walk away, with food or other gifts of minor needs, the two had. His reputation began to grow, as the hero god that would show just when needed, to defeat the monsters suddenly invading the land.

Hecate was always explaining the importance of reputation, in the elections.

"Get the people to remember your name, boy!" She was always saying. "It matters not, how they remember it, just that they know it, well."

Odyseus didn't argue, she was motherly, wise, and knew
the lands, and several times, when they would enter into a village or small town, his strength and club were really needed. The demons were many, here in Lemuria, and the more he defeated, the more he wondered where they were coming from.

"This no be how it should be, grandmother! So many spawns, dost remind of the first day. If no for JC, none of thy world's Chosen woust be here!"

"JC this, JC that! I'm going to have to meet this man, you seem to think so grandly of. You would think him a god or something."

"Just an angel, grandmother. No god, but more than the rest of us, I whilst think!"

"So, you say! Holy Selene's charge might very well be an Archangel, at that!" She slipped on that occasion. Odyseus saw her aura's change, but not knowing the meaning, he let it fade from his thoughts.

During one jump, Odyseus and Hecate landed in the middle of a battle between farmers and a few miners Hell Spawn. After the quick dispatching, they could hear screams coming from the village just fifty or so yards through the woods.

The men were falling back, the women and children running. They were all running into the forest, the two were walking out of. Odyseus was carrying Hecate, it being easier than walking beside her, with her too short legs that made him cut his stride in half of the normal. When a young elf maiden that was following the crowd, turned to cast a spell of fire into the three demons chasing after, Odyseus lowered Hecate to the ground.

Racing ahead, making his way through the crowd, he finally stepped in front of the young lass, her bow at the ready.

"Thy arrows no be harming those, lassie. Step back and let me handle this!"

Throwing himself into the fray, the seven feet tall, squat and broad looking demons, with small wings, large frog like head with mouths like a giant bull dog. The jaws are riddled with teeth, and the spike like nails on four fingered hands, were deadly weapons. The loose skin on the humanoid looking bodies appeared draped in shaggy folds. The three Shator demons rushed towards the yelling barbarian, as Odyseus felt the attack on his mind. His shields held, and his club went to work.

The battle was short lived, and when he saw the men of the village being slaughtered, trying to hold back against creatures their weapons were useless on, he began to run towards them. Hecate yelled out to wait, but he was heedless of her advice.

"Idiot man is going to get himself killed, one of these days." She mumbled standing beside the elf maiden. When the girl asked his name, from the elderly woman, Hecate looked into her eyes, with a down turn of her lips, and answered only before teleporting,

"He is none of your affair, girl!"

Odyseus seeing many fallen men, there are four more of the Shator demons, and they seem to be leading twelve tall nine-foot slender humanoid looking three fingered monsters of slime covered skin, with large fish like looking heads with jaws like barracudas. The Farastu demons, are quick, strong, and immune to most types of magic. But their slim frames are easily destroyed if a weapon that can hit them fall upon the monsters. Odyseus' could, fortunately for the village's sake. The battle is quick, Hecate's shields around the young man held, against the demons' mental attacks, and the protective shields that Odyseus raised against poison, helped him to fight off the stinging attacks from the clawed fingers. After a quick workout, all eighteen demons were dead, the smoldering odor of brimstone was permeating the air.

When the villagers that were still alive, finally moved forward to see their benefactor, Hecate was already fusing with his shirt, closing the tears with her magic, healing the wounds on him, as well.

"Village of Saturn's Run, it is my pleasure to introduce you to Odyseus d'Brell, Chosen of Holy Minerva, the promised one, has finally arrived." She yelled out.

The few men that could, began to move forward, and Odyseus spent the rest of the day helping to right the town. Hecate healed those she could, and when she noticed a Temple of Minerva, in this town, she whispered to the young man, his need to visit there.

"I am Bel ip Phon, Odyseus. I thank you for your timely aid, my large friend!" The elven maiden he first ran past, came to greet him.

Hecate attempted to move him away, but the boy, seeing the beautiful woman, with golden hair and amber eyes, could not be moved. She stood only five feet two, tall for an elf maiden, and was slender, but her large round eyes spoke of long-lasting beauty that seemed to melt the big man's heart. And when she spoke, the melodious song of her voice captivated him, till he almost forgot the venerable aged woman still standing by his side.

160

"I was the protector of this village before your arrival, but now, I see that Minerva has sent another even better equipped."

"The boy will not be staying, girl. Now run along!" Hecate almost sneered.

"Oh, do be quiet grandmother, please! We can stay for a few days. The village do be in needs after this little problem of Hell's creatures." He looked around the town, then back to the girl in front, noticing her eyes, belied an age of that many more years than he first thought.

"I be Odyseus, Bel ip Phon. It is an honor to meet thee. Willest thee honor me with a walk to thy yon Temple? I have needs of respect to my Holy Patron!" Smiling at the man, the elf looked at Hecate and even widened her mouth more, before accepting.

"It would be my most glorious pleasure to walk with thee, young man." Odyseus offered her his arm, and the two walked the street towards the far side of Saturn's Run.

Hecate, glowering, following slowly, using her cane for support. Seemingly forgotten by the man, she had spent every waking hour with over the past two months.

That night, during a celebration, the village had given in Odyseus' honor, Hecate had a chance at the elf maiden alone. Moving away from prying eyes and ears, she laid the law down.

"He is mine, elf, and you would do well to stay away." She seethed.

"Hecate, that you take care of him, I have no doubt. He is too well fed for a man to have done that on his own. But, in my more than four hundred years, I have never known a young man of, what is he, seventeen, eighteen, maybe? To want an old woman for a mate."
"He's almost twenty-one, a man, not some boy to be fondled over."

"He certainly is the size of a man, yes. But his emotions speak more of a teenage boy. I suggest you allow him to grow up, old woman. Look upon me, with that face, and you will be eating your words. I don't jump and run like some young farm girl, I imagine you chasing off, his whole life."

Hecate began to move to strike out at the elf, when she suddenly felt herself being held and unable to even cast a spell. The voice from behind, immediately sent fear through the elderly woman. Bel ip Phon dropped to her knee, bowing in respect.

"Hecartae Dryad, thy interference with my child, has gone on long enough." Minerva's tone was hard, but quiet.

When she released the hold on the elderly woman, Hecate turned to face the Ancient One. She did not bow, but she was not insolent, either.

"Minerva, please, I have to stay with him, he needs me."

"Yes, more so, than he would have, had thee not interfered in the beginning. Rise, Bel ip Phon, and face me as the warrior thou are!" The Ancient One looked from one woman to the next. Finally breaking the silence.

"Hecartae, thou will go with him, to the appointed upcoming meeting." Her smile, widened. "There, no amount of hiding will keep thine secret. The twins will all but notice you right away!

"Bel ip Phon, Odyseus is the one promised to Lemuria. Of that thee already suspects, now confirmed! That mine child is but a boy, matters not, in his battle prowess. This gift is thine, my faithful daughter. As protector to this village and this entire province, thy needs be even greater. Go now, and prosper in thy life! Know, that you can truly protect against the creatures that should not be in this war!" Minerva handed over three items.

A long sword, a short golden bow, and a quiver empty except of one arrow. When the elf maiden pulled the arrow out, a new one magically appeared in the quiver. Looking at the point of the one she held, she saw the magical steel of something that she knew would be able to hit the creatures of Hell. Bowing, when she stood, the Goddess was gone!

"So, you are an angel, as I suspected, Hecate." Bel ip Phon smiled. "I really have no need to fear you then. You would never harm one of nature's own!" Turning, the elf left Hecate to stew over the words ordered by Minerva.

"What are you up to, Minerva?" She mumbled.

Rejoining the celebration, Hecate watched the night, as Odyseus was kept busy dancing with every able-bodied woman in the village, young and old alike.

****

JC eyed Mythalla, as he helped her off the floor, his sigh at the bending of a knee that always would seem to bother him.

"Tell your council, "Standing with his vest untied, holding the priestess' hands, he looked at the others, slowly rising from their kneels, as ordered. Releasing his hands, Mythalla began to tie the laces on his vest, and the others moved closer to him.

"We shall have to get you some new clothes, Father JC. These are torn and unclean-able, it would seem." she mumbled to him as she held up the shredded shirt and noticed the many slashes in his vest.

"Tell your council that I will talk with them when I am ready and not before." JC took the shirt and using his sorcery, he began to mend the tears. They all watched in amazement as the shirt began to repair as if some invisible source was sewing it shut. "Tell them I'm a little put off with them at the moment, and," he added wrinkling his nose in disgust, "I can smell the battle on myself, so I know I am in need of a bath. It's a wonder any of you can stand to be near me." his chuckle was met with many smiles from the priests and priestesses around him.

Taking the back pack up and slinging it across his shoulder, he draped his cloak and shirt across his arm and picked up his boots. He noticed his stockings tucked down in the boots and left them there.

Reaching in his belt pouch, JC pulled out one of the medium sized diamonds and handed it to Mythalla. She looked at the stone that was easily worth several thousand gold credits and shook her head to the negative.

"My young Priestess, we will talk more later after I have addressed the council tonight. All those that swore to me, knowing that I am her whom is the coming prophet will each be addressed, after your council. Now, please take this and help those that have need. I noticed several buildings destroyed while walking through town. Tell the people to spread the word that I have come.

"I am sorry that I was late in coming, and that the Holy Selene will see the damages repaired. We teach charity as well as compassion, and the populace should know the ones who follow Holy Selene will not go without. Will you, please take care of it? And, is this enough to make the repairs?" He finished as Mythalla held out the

163

hand holding the diamond, and shook her head that she thought it was most generous and certainly would take care of getting the repairs started.

"If there is anything left, divide it up between those families that lost a father. As a matter of fact," he started to say as he dug for another of the diamonds, "use this for those families. It is time that the Temple was more than just a spiritual guide to the people. The war with evil is upon us," his voice rose, as he looked around the whole of those injured. "And Selene's Temple serves the people, not the people serving the Temple." Shifting his sheath across his shoulder as well, he placed his freed hand on the young woman's cheek.

Smiling, he looked over all the clergy pausing on Pynora before looking at the injured, as well. He noticed that those that could, were sitting up in order to see their savior. Walking to Essmelda, he looked into her eyes.

"You, child, and I will have a talk, soon. You are much too rare, and according to what I was told, do not exist. I will be most interested to hear your heritage and the explanation of its existence when next I speak with Mother Selene." Winking at the girl with a smile, JC then glided to the door of the Temple leading out to the square, and wills the doors to open before he reached them.

Turning to once again look into the sanctuary, the early morning sun, shining into the building, surrounding him in the soft blue of the sun, JC appeared as though haloed in the aura of a god, as he looked up at the statue of Selene at the far end. Mythalla only a couple meters away, having been following him.

"Whoever made that statue, obviously has never seen the Holy Selene! That is more closely resembling Brigitte than our Mother Selene. The Goddess' hair is shorter, just below the shoulder blades and has more curls, her eyes are rounder, her nose longer and pointed slightly upward, her lips are fuller, her bosom is smaller, waist is narrower, hips are fuller, motherlier, and her legs are longer with comparison to her torso! And," he took a breath before continuing. "She would never be exposing her cleavage like some dancer in a tavern. She is my mother, after all. Why you are using a statue of the Archangel Brigitte, well, one can only guess."

Taking a backward step, he turned and lightly walked down the steps, his bare feet feeling the coolness of the marble and sandstone he was walking on. Gliding across the town square, it occurred to him that he forgot to ask the name of this town. He stopped at the fountain, the statue of the goddess having been broken, and the fountain polluted with blood and bile.

JC concentrated and cleaned the water with a wave of his hand, burning away the liquid in the fountain and purifying the fountain. He then created water over it and performed a blessing.

"I will have to commission someone to make a new statue to replace the broken one." he said to no one in particular, but was overheard by those few that had stopped to watch the display.

He shrugged and headed over to the Inn, looking around before climbing up the five steps leading into the "Golden Hand Inn", across from the Temple at the far end of the square.

After securing a room, he found himself finally sliding into one of the seven tubs in the communal bathing room in the lower level of the inn, the water having been heated to a temperature that is nearly too hot.

His things were neatly stacked on a stool against the wall just a few yards away, and he closed his eyes, whispering a prayer to Selene that he had not made things worse by walking out on the priestesses like he did. He knew that the three that swore fealty to him would be a welcome for tutoring when he needed to know something, but he was not so sure about the young girl part angel.

Her aura was mostly that of a young woman, but there was something else in the mix. Something very angelic. Being an assimar that teenager could be trouble, and he needed some guidance or wisdom on how to handle that. He was shown how to detect demonic auras, but not really ever told what to do if he found a person with half a one, and besides, angels had nearly the same auras as the greater Hell spawn, since they were essentially the same.

Not to mention the six Chosen all had similar auras to the Greater and Archangels. The twenty-seven devil lords, made up of nine Archangels and eighteen Greater Angels. All the Ancient Ones, as well as Gia, have Archangels and Greater angels. Detecting the subtle differences was the hard part. He hoped it would be simple enough just to see the evil within. At least the young teen was not that!

There was something else very strange about her. His dream that he had during his coma all those years ago, came to his mind. This girl closely resembled the woman he had spent dream time with. But, much younger, of course!

Dipping his head below the water, JC scrubbed at his hair. The dried blood and sweat finally being washed away, seemed to relax him. As he moved to raise his head back above the waterline, he saw a tall woman, very tall for this continent, wearing the light blue robe of the Temple, step into the room. The darker blue around the collar, cuffs, and hem, indicating a priestess, very high in standing. She motioned towards the door, to forestall whoever was following her in, and shut it behind her.

Moving to within two yards of the tub that JC was in, submersed all the way to his neck, the priestess stopped to stand with her legs shoulder length apart, resting her hands on her hips. JC immediately flashed to his coma dream. This was that woman!

Standing some five feet eight inches, the tall woman, with long dark brown almost black hair, worn loose down her back, reaching to her buttocks, her too pale skin was smooth, that of a woman in her early to mid-twenties, but the dark violet oval eyes, had the look of experience in them, giving an impression of a woman that was much older. Her slight pointed ears of elven heritage and the aura of an assimar, he knew now, this was the girl's mother.

Her full lips turned a slight smile and JC knew he was facing the woman that had been fighting Abigor the day before, from the steps of the Temple.

He also could see the assimar bloodline in her, as well as, a slight touch of elven blood. JC knew he had met this woman before, however impossible that may be. The feeling of familiarity holding him deep in thought.

"You have quite shaken my apprentice, something awful, Lord," she stopped and took a breath, "no, I believe you said Father JC! As well as most of those others!" She almost turned the statement into a question.

Her voice was melodious and the power JC saw in her, belied what he thought possible in the mortals. Her aura was almost identical to the young girls to include the outer worlder part, the inner not wholly silver, either.

She appeared tired, almost exhausted, but the priestess still commanded a presence, as she watched the man.

"Did I, now? She should not have been treating me so, if she did not want to feel the same on her!" He calmly exclaimed. "You must be the Reverend Mother

166

Dyanea?" He added, while looking at the robe, flowing to her sandaled feet. JC eyed the woman up and down as she did the same at him lying in the tub. After a few moments, he blushed and sat up.

The woman's soft laugh was light, when JC covered his privates with his hands. Dyanea crossed her arms under her breasts and tilted her head slightly, her nearly black dark violet eyes narrowing to an intent stare.

"I'm not talking about your use of sorcery on her." She calmly continued, "Your description of Holy Selene has unsettled all of those priests and priestesses, as well as quite a few others that have heard it. Not to mention the villagers that were conscious enough to hear!" Still standing the two yards away, the Selenian Priestess remained calm, seeming quite at ease. But he could see in her aura a controlled nervousness.

"How could you accuse us of making a statue of Brigitte instead of the Holy Goddess?"

"Because you did. That statue is the image of the Archangel you all call yourselves. The Order of Brigitte! It makes sense, since it was the Archangel that gave unto the order the prophesies." JC matter of fact answered.

"You speak as though you have actually been with the Holy Goddess and her angels."

"I was trained by all seven of Mother Selene's Archangels and several of her greater angels, as well."

JC could see the disbelief in her expression, and noticed the dark circles under her eyes, and the exhaustion in her face, and realized that she probably had not slept all night, while he had lain unconscious. He could also see smudges of dirt on her hands and face, and the slicked down of once sweat filled hair.

Without really thinking about what he was offering, he created water in the tub next to him, and using more sorcery, lit a fire underneath, as well as heating the water immediately with a small controlled fire ball at the bottom of the tub's interior.

"You look like you haven't had time to clean up, nor sleep. You could use a little relaxation, as well, Reverend Mother. Will you join me?" After realizing what he had just said, he shook his head looking down into the tub he was in, and coughed.

"That was inappropriate, forgive me. Sometimes, my mouth moves without the thoughts forming first."

Her face visibly tightened and just as quickly relaxed. Taking on a slightly mischievous grin, the priestess walked around his tub, untying her robe, allowing it to fall from her shoulders. Facing JC, who had looked away she noticed, she slowly folded the robe, setting it on a stool next to his things, the woman finished getting undressed and walked to the tub, JC had filled for her, and slowly almost seductively stepped over the edge, one long leg at a time, until she could sink into the water. JC had been looking away, only catching glances from the side in his peripheral vision, not turning to look until she commented.

"I thank you, M'lord. I did have need of a bath, after yesterday!" Her laugh at the uncomfortable, embarrassed man sitting just one yard away, was wonderful in JC's ears.

When he looked up, JC was facing the woman, who was sitting with full breasts above the water line, calmly smoothing water up and down her chest. Quickly looking away, he licked his drying tongue across his lips, staring at the door since it was the first thing he could think of to study.

"I trust..." He started, then clearing his throat, finished, "you are Dyanea?"

"That would be me, yes. And, yours would be an interesting name for the one given unto us per our prophesies. If you are indeed him?" She added as if she was not already sure. "There are those on the Council that still doubt if it is true, or not." Her tone was serious, no longer joking, and she flicked water at him to get his attention. When he turned, she smiled, nodding to him,
"I expect to be looked in the eyes, if we are going to talk. You chose this arena for discussion, I will not be ignored, nor will I be treated so rudely!"

"I chose it?" JC quickly answered a small tone coming to his voice. "You were the one that came barging in on my bath. I told those girls to tell their Council that I would return. How dare you accuse me of being rude, when I am only trying to give you a little modesty, so as not to have an old man leering at such a beautiful young lady sitting so close to me, as the day she was born!" The words tumbled out of his mouth in a rush before he could stop, and this time it was her turn to blush.

She looked JC in the eyes, and he held hers, not daring to look down at her breasts or any other part of her, clearly visible in the still clear water.

Her blush only made her pale skin that much more radiant, and he could not understand what was happening to him. He had spent the last year with several of the most beautiful women in his entire life, three of them demi-goddesses, and did not feel once, the urges going through him at just a few minutes with this woman. All of Selene's angels did not stir him the way this woman was.

For over sixteen years he had sworn against feeling anything for a woman, and yet, he was feeling as though a teenager with his first crush, after only a few moments with Dyanea. And the feeling of familiarity would not go away, only getting stronger as each moment passed.

"Forgive me, Reverend Mother. I have had a recurring dream, a vision really of which you are the prime memory. I have not met you before, yet I know you, it would seem. I am most pleased to meet you, and wish I would not be so nervous as to have a moving conversation with you." he stated his eyes never leaving hers.

Dyanea dared not move. His eyes were like magnets, holding hers, she could feel the power of his charisma. He had to be the one promised by the Holy Selene. She could not understand the pull she was feeling. He was correct, she thought, she too had the feeling she knew this man. She had not gotten a good look at him, yesterday afternoon, as he battled the devil. She was too exhausted, then anyway, and he obviously was as well, the way he fell after it was over.

The worst part of it was how much he resembled the only man; she had ever lain with all those years ago. He was the right age, except for the lack of aging in his body, certainly, yet, even the eyes radiated the same power that man had, then all those years ago.

And, with all the gashes, cuts, and scrapes he had received, yesterday, where were the scars and how had he healed so fast. Essie had sworn that she did not heal him. She could only conclude; he really must be one of the Immortals promised in the prophesies.

But that certainly did not explain the feelings she was having being this near him. Why was she having so much trouble controlling her breathing. She could not let him see the discomfort she was having, nor could she let him know the womanly urges she was feeling, at that moment, so near him. She had to end this as soon as possible.

169

"Father JC, if I may ask, where are the others?" She managed to get out without any stuttering or breathlessness.

JC, jumped as her question broke the silence. He still did not move his eyes from hers, though. Instead, he answered.

"Each one of us was placed on a different continent. You, my lady, have the pleasure of this one belonging to me. Or the displeasure, if that is how you wish to look at it!"

"Now, if I may ask a personal question? Are you spoken for?" She asked, and then squeezed her eyes shut, as that was not what she had intended to ask. Blast her mind not staying to the course, she thought.

"It is my turn to ask forgiveness. I didn't mean to ask that."

Blushing, JC was still looking at the woman's face. She was blushing even deeper than he was and with her eyes closed, he reached across and placed his hand on hers that was tightly holding the edge of the tub she was in.

When her eyes opened, she looked at his hand, resting lightly on hers and sighed, mumbling under her breath that she should not be here and that she needed to leave. But she did not move.

"No, M'lady, I am not with anyone, nor does anyone have a claim to my heart. And, no forgiveness is necessary, as I was in truth, wondering the exact same thing. If I didn't know better, I would say that we both seem to be floundering under some sort of spell, or is it that fate is simply pushing us in a certain direction, neither of us wish to go, at the moment? In truth, if I wouldn't know it impossible, I would say I have known you at another time." He chuckled in that way he always did when he got nervous. "I have not been with another in over sixteen years, except in my dreams. You are my dreams, m'lady!"

He continued to stare at their hands, his on hers, which had noticeably relaxed its death grip on the tub.

"Perhaps, it is a spell. One woven by the Goddess herself? And, you, are also as familiar to me, if for the same impossibilities." She answered.

170

"Ahem," JC started clearing his throat, "yes, well, be that as it may, somehow, I have to convince you I am who I claim, and convince the rest of the Council, as well! I want the Temple's backing, and obviously, you will have need of mine in the next seven years. The war has begun, Reverend Mother Dyanea, make no doubt about that."

The talk was made easier as they discussed the prophesies. She never moved her hand, and JC never lifted his from hers. Finally, after about an hour, they decided it was time to get out. Turning his head, he allowed the priestess to rise out of the tub, then rose himself, keeping his back to her. After, she had quickly dressed, she left the room, only pausing at the door for one last look at the man, still toweling himself. Shuddering, she closed it behind her as she was leaving.

The next week was spent mostly in argument with the Council of Nine. JC would spend the evenings with Mythalla, Pynora, Galia, as well as, Dornar, Brell, and Thorm, the six that had sworn fealty to him.

Pynora, a thirty-six-year-old half-elf, making her roughly equivalent to a human of eighteen, was five feet two inches tall, with dark golden colored hair, worn short, cut just above her shoulders, and gray eyes, with the pointed ears high on the sides of the head as most elves have.

She was slight of build, weighing only one hundred pounds, and her aura indicating an only slightly above moderate strength in sorcery, but it seemed to vary depending on what she was talking about at the time. She did have a rainbow of colors in her outer that seemed to change from day to day.

JC could also see something else within her aura, but it never faltered so he chose to ignore it, for now! He was sure she was the one of the three he had detected as being angelic.

She was an accomplished magus, though, allowing her a certain ability to mix her spells. She was bubbly, pleasant and very inquisitive. Even if she did try to stay away from him as much as possible.

Galia, a twenty-year-old dark skinned, dark eyed and haired, woman of above average psychic strength, was quiet and reserved. The five feet four-inch-tall plump woman, was of minor noble birth, would only be inclined to answer questions presented to her, and then would only give the shortest answer necessary to complete the question put to her.

She was the hardest to get to know, and Mythalla was constantly at odds with the young woman, for one reason or another. Mythalla was an apprentice to Dyanea, as well, and Galia, of Berga, another of the Council members. Pynora was a newly named priestess, formally an apprentice to C'renan of the Council.

The three men were not apprenticed to anyone as of yet, since they were all newly sworn to the church.

Thorm, a tall, six feet in height, was slight of build and a former thief. He was light skinned and light brown hair, with an average psychic strength. He was caught trying to steal from the Temple and in the process of earning his freedom by converting to the faith.

His outer aura indicated some evil, but it was mostly gray and showed an indifference. He was sternly warned by JC that his chosen profession could be useful in the right direction, but would only lead to death if not monitored. He did not understand and JC would explain no further.

Brell was about JC's height of five feet seven inches and of medium build with a below average strength in sorcery. He was inquisitive and showed an eagerness to learn asking all the right questions.

Dornar was medium height, about five feet eight and slightly overweight. A former merchant apprentice, he was removed from the guild when he accidentally set the warehouse on fire losing control when he attempted to light a lantern using sorcery. His average strength would go far in the healing arts but not much else would be managed.

The moments that JC would spend with the Council, usually were cut short, by him leaving during the interview, when Reverend Mother Morella, the Leader of the Selenian Temple, would say something insulting, or would openly state that it would be better that a man that could not prove he was one of the prophesied ones, should just be chained or imprisoned all together, for heresy.

JC was on the verge, several times, of telling the other Council members what he had seen in the Reverend Mother's aura, but decided it better to keep it to himself. He did tell Morella in secret what he knew, and promised that when he could, he would expose her evil to the rest of the Temple.

They obviously could not read auras and he was not inclined to teach any of them how. Not, at least, until he had proof of the treachery that Morella had fallen into. He was not really sure what she had done, except that her outer spectrum was so dark, he could tell the woman was as evil as most of the demons, he had fought, and that her inner spectrum was black as well, indicated that she had sold her soul to some devil or demon. At least, he could see that the Council was made up of mostly genuinely good people and only a couple of the women, being somewhat less.

The Council of Nine, was entirely made up of women, and the order of their ranking was based on age, not strength in sorcery. Morella, was allegedly the oldest, claiming that she was over four centuries old, yet only looked to be in her late thirties to early forties. She was five feet four inches tall, with light colored skin, and brown hair and eyes. Her claim that she used sorcery so much as the reason for her near immortality, didn't hold wash, but JC kept that to himself, as well.

C'renan, an elven matron, was second, five feet two inches tall, slight of build, with long silver hair, worn in a braid and amber eyes, was nearly three centuries old as well. She was possibly the second strongest in psychic strength among the Nine.

Dyanea, was the most powerful in sorcery and JC was surprised to find out she was in her eighties, instead of the mid to late thirties that he had guessed. Her aura was the most pure, evil free of any mortal he had seen, since learning to read auras, and he often was caught staring at her.

Being told that she was one fourth elven, explained the violet eyes and the slightly pointed ears that were hidden most of the time by her full wavy nearly black hair. As well as the paleness of her skin. She was the tallest of the nine, and the one that JC seemed the most drawn to, easy enough for everyone to see.

JC did have it confirmed that Dyanea was one fourth angel, making her assimar bloodline known to him. All knew of the story of how her elven grandfather had mated with an angel that gave the immediate birth of a female child to him to raise. No one knew, however, what was the name of the angelic visitor.

Only C'renan knew of the circumstances of the first meeting between the two, and could understand the attraction forming between them. JC was surprised to find out that C'renan had been told so much of that meeting in the baths and actually had blushed when cornered by the elf, warning him to be careful of Dyanea's heart.

Zaina, a mid-sixties year old, gray haired, brown eyed priestess was the fourth of the nine. She was of above average psychic power, and very calm when questioning the Immortal. She seemed to be very interested in his description of the Goddess and of everything he knew about the other Ancient Ones. Although, she often acted like his answers were less than forthright.

Berga, a woman in her late fifties to early sixties, was also, gray haired with dark blue eyes, standing about five foot three inches tall. She was the third most powerful of the Nine, almost having as much strength as C'renan. Easily made to laugh, she was the most jovial of the Council.

Coigsta, a tall five-foot six-inch, plump bordering on obese, woman in her late forties, with brown hair and brown eyes, reminded JC of his grandmother, when he was growing up. Very serious, but, full of compassion and the ability to listen to all sides of a story before rendering judgment. She was almost as reserved as Galia, and took in everything with a wary eye.

Joreen, another in her late forties, was a very pretty five-foot four-inch tall, curvy woman, with seductive dark gray eyes and dark blond hair. Probably the fourth or fifth strongest in psychic ability, she was graceful in her movements and seemed not to notice that she was flirting whenever she spoke to the man.

Kyana, another tall five-foot eight-inch woman, with large breasts and hips, but a very narrow waist that made her figure look like that of an hour glass. She had a long torso with short legs that made her appear somewhat out of proportion.

An even personality, the light brown haired, mid-thirties woman was only average in psychic strength, but her melodious voice was deep and even that could melt the most hardened man's heart. Her big round brown eyes gave her a startled look most of the time, but that only seemed to add to her charms.

Mya, a tiny four feet eleven-inch tall, plump woman in her early to mid-thirties, was above average in sorcery strength, with training in fighting with a staff. She had spent one of the mornings sparring with JC, and surprised him with her agileness that belied her size. She also, seemed never to become winded, and when she managed a hit, it was with a strength the Immortal would not have thought she possessed, as well.

Dark blond hair and dark blue eyes, hinted at a non-Selenian heritage, possibly Brautanian, but the woman was otherwise quiet and reserved when not sparring with the man. She seemed to like him on the practice field, but then would be the first to side with Morella behind the closed doors. JC saw in her aura, a possibility to be turned evil and decided that she would need to be pushed to stay good, as much as possible.

JC had noticed that Essmelda was avoiding him the whole week and when he inquired with Dyanea, if he had offended the child, she only answered that Essmelda needed time to get to know him.

"Besides, telling her that only she could do something that no other mortal could do, has really upset her. It is hard enough on her, not having parents, let alone to be told something else about her is unusual."

JC told the Reverend Mother to apologize to the girl, for him, and that he would do so, if given the chance.

He did advise the Reverend Mother that he was going to teach his six apprentices how to read auras, so that it would be better if Dyanea spoke with the teenager about her heritage.

"If Essmelda hears from someone else that she is your daughter, that will make it that much harder on you. Please, for your sake, let her know. I know if she were mine, I would certainly be proud of the fact, not try to hide it." after sighing, JC continued.

"It was meant to be a compliment. When she reaches adult strength, I would guess that she could surpass all but, maybe three or four of my fellow Immortals, even. I really was told that no mortal would be as strong as us. To find you, C'renan, Berga, and Essmelda, is really quiet the pleasant surprise, Reverend Mother. You four are as strong as one maybe two of us." JC finished.

When the week was up, he decided he had answered enough questions and announced he would be leaving out, the following morning.

"I have a continent to clean of Hell Spawn, and only seven years to gather the armies for a war I have to prepare for. You either will be supportive of the Mother Goddess, or you won't. The choice is really up to you, and nothing more I can say, will convince you."

JC turned and left the Temple once again, leaving the Council speechless. They had become accustomed to his leaving unexpectedly. He sometimes would apologize for it, but most times, would just mumble as he left. This time he did neither. Simply walked out of the room, stopping at the statue in the sanctuary for a brief prayer, and exited.

Dyanea watched from the door to the office they had been in, and as JC reached the door exiting the Temple, he turned and bowed to the High Priestess, smiling at her startled look.

****

Three weeks of travel, Sheera had managed to rescue, eight villages, save over three hundred people, heal about half of that, kill or run off over two thousand Hell Spawn, and delivered nine children to orphanages. She had gained much support by the common people, but met with distrust by every priest or minor noble she had spoken with. She had also, spent many nights in conversation with Leaf Loren, who always seemed to show up, shortly after she was done with a battle. Or, right before dinner! When asked if he was following her, he only shrugged and stated,

"Only the gods know our destinations, Sheera!"

The Sho Gun's estates were about one hundred meters ahead and she could clearly see the two guards at the gate were Hell Spawn.

"Why would you want to serve a man that would hire you, demon?" She asked as her blade left the sheath cutting the head cleanly of one guard. The back swing caught the rising blade of the Katana the other demon was already swinging at her.

"Fast, aren't you? But quick enough is the real question." She was wiping the blood from her blade when she completed the sentence. She really didn't know why she felt the need to talk right then, maybe it was to keep her from using sorcery which would invariably alert the spawn with in the keep. More than likely, she spoke to calm nerves that were still unused to the casual taking of life, she was forced into, now.

Pushing the gate open as the armor of the two vanquished fell to the ground, no longer filled with bodies. The brimstone was on the air and the wind gust was attempting to dissipate the after effect.

Entering cautiously, Sheera quickly made her way along the wall heading for what would be the stables. Inside she found one more Hell Spawn and tied up in one

176

of the horse stalls, seven of the keep's residents. The devil was quickly dispatched, and she freed the women. Ordering them to keep still, she freed six more women and four children in another stall.

Checking each stall, Sheera found a total of fourteen women, twelve children, and six men, which were all moved into one stall. After getting a brief idea of how many she was facing and where the Sho Gun was, she left the stables behind. The newly freed prisoners waited near the stable's doors, until the noises started in the house. They then fled out the estate's gates, as ordered.

Sheera entered the house, quickly eliminating those Hell Spawn she could, with her wakisashi, but would turn to sorcery when necessary. She found herself standing in a large room, with many tapestries, and paintings lining the wall. She had found no other survivors in the four-story building, and was about to think the servants had missed the truth of their imprisonment, when seemingly out of the statues flowed six devils, standing nearly three meters tall, with a light reddish almost pink scaly leather for skin.

The devils' faces were large eared, hairless, as well as the rest of their bodies, they had tusks in place of teeth raising from the lower jaw, as well as fangs hanging down from the upper. The two large horns rising up from the top of their foreheads were curved inward towards each other, and looked as though they could be used as weapons, as well.

The large leathery pink colored wings rose above their heads and the long-pointed tails were weaving like whips that were alive. Each held onto a trident, large and deadly looking.

Sheera could feel the aura of fear coming from them, and quickly swallowed as she resisted and shook off the spell, before throwing herself into the battle. Using spells that were bolts of acid and lightning, she spun with her wakisashi, casting two spells at a time, all the while performing a blade dance. In a few minutes, a booming voice spoke out, and the only remaining Malebranche devil still standing, backed away.

"You woman, have dared to invade my sanctuary?" The voice spoke and a wave of fear gripped into Sheera's very soul. She knew it was a spell, but still, had a hard time raising even a simple protection shield on her mind. She knew that this was not the ordinary devil, nor was it even one of the lesser lords. She had never felt this kind of power emanating from anyone else, except the Ancient Ones.

Finally, able to slam her shield in place, she gathered herself and turned to look at the speaker.

Standing four meters tall, with blackened skin, he appeared to have a human body, but with the size. His robes were cut short just above his knees, purple and black, he had a large heavy sword through the belt. His hands were large, and callused, the fingers blackened even more. In his right hand, being held outstretched, was the limp body of the Sho Gun.

The Devil was holding the war leader as if a feather. The head of the monstrosity was fly like. Large eyes on each side of the insectoid face were half the size of the head, and multifaceted giving off a gaze that would stun most that looked. He had two large curved horns starting where it's ears should be, rising upwards as a set of bull's horns. The mouth covered the entire lower part of its face, and teeth, small and jagged were shown as it appeared to be grimacing. The room was filled with flies, gnats, and other kinds of flying insects, too many for any one place, and far too many for this time of year. With a casual toss, the body of the Sho Gun was thrown aside and it flew to the wall before falling to the ground.

"Baalzebub, you have tortured these people enough. You have killed too many, and in the name of the Holy Jeasuas, and the power that he has given me, I condemn you to an eternity of Hell." With a wave, she sent three bolts of acid into the remaining Malebranche, and turning the spell in the other direction, she sent eight tiny energy bolts into the devil lord.

He disappeared to reappear behind the woman, and Sheera felt its hands gripping her shoulders, as she was lifted off the ground. The devil was laughing at her struggles to free herself, fear and panic rising inside her head.

Sheera kicked out blindly behind her and felt her feet strike skin hard. The grip loosened slightly and with a sudden burst of adrenaline pumped strength, she rolled forward, while kicking hard at the devil's chest.

Her fall to the ground, she rolled coming up with a swing of her wakisashi, and turned to face empty space where the devil had been standing. She felt once again Baalzebub appear behind her, and sent an electrical charge of energy up his arms when he grabbed hold of her. The spell worked to make him let her go, and she turned, swinging her blade, and that time hitting the devil's leg. Baalzebub teleported after each attack and Sheera knew he was weakening, but too, she was tiring, as well.

Each mental attack the devil made struck hard against her mental shields and she was not sure how much longer she would stand against this devil lord. She wondered about the Hell Spawn's strength remembering she was taught that Baalzebub might be the third or fourth strongest of all of Kutulu's Archangels.

Her spell casting all but forgotten except whenever he managed a grab, she faced the devil lord standing some five meters away, watching the young woman before him with some uncertainty that he was not accustomed to.

Sheera holding an at ready pose with her blade pointed towards the beast, and her hilt being held in both hands. She was about to cast another series of energy bolts when Baalzebub disappeared. This time, without thinking, Sheera closed her eyes extending out her aura to feel all around her and kicked her superior quickness into full motion by jumping and spinning with a wide arc to her swing, her blade met with flesh, easily slicing into the devil's neck.

Sheera dropped to the ground, the blade lodging halfway through the devil's neck, she was jolted with a pain inside her head, even passing through her mind shield. She rolled at the ground coming up to see the devil staggering as it feebly attempted to pull the blade free of its flesh.

Sheera concentrated and sent out a tiny wall of air, she pushed at the blade as it began to finish its path through the lower part of the devil's head. With another push spell and a few bolts of energy to keep the devil's mind occupied, Baalzebub's head finally fell to the side, the clanging of Sheera's wakisashi as hit as it hit the ground was followed by a thud as the devil's head suddenly struck the floor, as well.

Still on her knees, Sheera began to vomit at the odor of brimstone and the smell of refuse and other debris in the house. Her protective shields having fallen away, she remained crouched over on hands and knees for a while.

When a moan and slight movement was heard where, Sheera remembered the Sho Gun having been thrown, she stood and moved towards the sound, stopping briefly to pick up her weapon and wiping the blood from it.

She staggered to the man and found him just barely able to hold his eyes open through the bruises and battering he had been taking.

Sheera delved for injuries and found that most of his wounds were surprisingly superficial and that his only real injury was of the mind. She healed,

179

eliminating the pain and bruising to the man, resetting his shoulder dislocation, and laid him back down, covering him with her cloak. She sat next to the man, and waited, making use of much needed rest from the fierce battle she had just been through.

"An Archangel, one of Hell's senior Lords?" She thought to herself.

"Could this have really been Baalzebub? He was certainly a very strong opponent." she finished her thought voicing it out loud.

She is not sure she could manage with any tougher. And he is supposed to be only the fourth strongest of Kutulu Lucifer's dreaded nine? She drifts off into meditation, one hand on the Sho Gun, the other holding her blade in her lap.

When finally, after a few hours the doors slid slowly open, the servants found the woman sitting cross legged in a corner with their master lying next to her. The room was empty now, with the exception of the bothersome bugs and the odor of offal throughout the keep.

Proserpine smiled watching Jeasuas' child tear Baalzebub apart. She had been sent to aid the devil, but had no intentions of committing suicide. That she could summon James Carl, was already causing an uproar in Hell.

"That idiot Martinith seems to think that it is no consequence that the two are linked in some way. He does not see the problems involved in this."
She watched until the battle was finally over, and moved out of the room.

CHAPTER 8
Cleansing the night!

The Sho Gun, Hachiman, finally came to his senses, after four days, the servants having all returned, and the Chosen One was called to the Master's presence.

"That I may owe you my life, I may have to accept. But you are not the Golden Dragon mentioned in the prophesies. You are too pretty, and too feminine, to be the one mentioned."

"I have read the "Golden Dragon of Peace" several times, Sho Gun, and don't remember ever reading that I would have to be an ugly man! Perhaps, your copy must have been written by a different person? Mine was given me by Holy Jeasuas, but perhaps it is an accidental misprint?"

"Don't get smart with me, young lady! Do you know how quickly I could have you placed under arrest?" The aging Sho Gun got upset.

"Oh, and how would you propose to do that? All your supposed soldiers are either dead, or running for the mountains, like little cowards.No, like little girls!" Sheera answered back.

"I am Hachiman, one of the most powerful men in the empire! I will not be treated like this!" He yelled out.

"You are a fool, Sho Gun, if you don't see what is right before your face. I will leave you, now. I see that you have much to learn in the way of what is to come. Next time, Sho Gun Hachiman, I may just have to pass by your little home, and allow the demons to remain!"

Feeling frustrated, not wanting to lose her composure, but at the same time, this man was probably going to be what she faced for the next seven years. Sheera shook her head as she left.

While walking towards the next province, after several hours, Sheera met up with a strange being, of very pale skin, almost cloud white with a bluish tint, long pointed ears, the golden hair and light blue eyes, big and round, are striking in the long narrow face, with a pointed almost sharp short nose.

The man, or she thought he must be by the melodious voice that reminded her of Jeasuas, when he first spoke with her. The man was 165 cm, and was seemingly in a very good mood. His auras spoke of power, according to the middle spectrum, but he claimed to be no sorcerer, just a simple wizard, on the down side of his life.

"You are the most beautiful human I have ever seen. You must be the prophet sent by Holy Jeasuas, the "Golden Dragon"?" He sang out.

The Elf, had been walking in her direction and Sheera's long stride caught up with the man before noon.

"I don't know about most beautiful, nor do I know about being much of a dragon, but, yes, I am Sheera, the prophet of Holy Jeasuas. What are you called, my fellow elven traveler?"

Smiling, the venerable elf, stood more erect, and turned to look into the woman's eyes.

"Before I go giving you my name, tell me about that pendant you wear. No mere jeweler could have made that. Not the way that the gold goes through the stone? I would say, its sorcery made, and someone very very powerful, to alter the elements."

She eyed the elven man, and met his stare, as the two, stood eye to eye, in the middle of the road, between the provinces, in central, Katiketa. Her suspicions alerted; she studied the man's aura.

The inner spectrum was a solid gray, almost white at the edge, indicating a long-lived elf, the middle spectrum was an azure blue, not as transparent as stained glass. This man's strength could be very high, if he chose to use psychic abilities, and the outer spectrum showed the six colors of the rainbow, in clear vivid brightness. As the two stared Sheera saw a wavering in the inner spectrum, and then it hit her.

"What are you? You are no elf, good sir?" She watched the outer, counting the colors, again. Red, yellow, blue, green, orange, and purple. Six, where was the seventh?
"You are very good, Sheera Lu Che! I would have thought that I could last a little longer, considering how trustful you have been, up to this point." The inner spectrum faded, and when it came back, it was a vibrant solid gold, indicating this was

an immortal, and one of at least Greater Angel, as well. But it was clear of any black that would have indicated devil.

"You have a need of me, Angel? Why have the gods seen fit to send one to me?" She spoke watching for an indication of a lie, knowing that the aura could be altered by this thing, if it was an Archangel.

"I was just wondering, have you thought about an easier way, as well as nicer way, to eliminate those bothersome demons? Not to mention, the fact that sorcery won't work on the Chosen of Kutulu Lucifer. Certainly, you have figured out the secret of this continent!"

"If you are talking about what I think you are, you are mistaken. I cannot do such a thing. It would most surely be forbidden by the gods. Technology like that cannot be brought to this world. Holy Gia, would never allow it!"

"Ahh, so you have thought about it, when you found the sulfur? That is good. Think on it, child. Why would it be forbidden, and then all the ingredients be staring you plain? It is just not known, yet. It isn't forbidden, Mother Gia, forbids nothing, to the mortals and their game. She just doesn't want us to interfere. But, you are not under such restrictions, you are a part of the mortal world. Why not make it better?"

"Who are you, and why have you come to me? Why don't you go to the man that can probably actually make the stuff? I can't!" She eyed the angel suspiciously.

"Ahh, you know the answer to that already, dear one. And as far as my name? I have been called many things, but, Gabriel, is my favorite. That you can call me, for I was the Angel of war, among the ancients, when I fought in the wars, those years ago."

"Who do you serve, that you would come to me, to try talking me into tricking my friend to making such a foul creation, as gunpowder?"

"I serve all the gods, child. But I belong to Jeasuas, I am of his spirit. But you are wrong, I don't come to coerce you into tricking your friend. I come to advise you of the missing element. The nitrate you need is found in saltpeter. You can find that in abundance, east of here.

183

Good hunting, child, and good luck, should you actually choose to ignore what's right in front of you!"

Gabriel disappeared, and Sheera found herself alone and deep in thought. She could not believe that Jeasuas would send such a creature, with such a vile suggestion. But, the more she thought, the longer she walked, it did sound like a plausible idea. She would have to at least see if JC could make it.

She moved on down the road, and Gabriel shimmered back into view. Watching the woman disappear over the horizon, he chuckled. Changing into a three-meter-tall handsome man, with diabolic features of blue-black skin, two large horns sticking from his temples curling upward like a bull, his red glowing eyes, are deep set and round.

The deep blue wings sticking up from his shoulder blades, and the large muscles of his arms and chest befit a being of great strength. The scaly skin has a sooty black color, and his too white teeth are pointed and jagged his laugh is like the whispering wind.

Belial, thinks to himself that was too easy!

"The girl is too trusting, and only she will be able to convince Selene's man into creating the stuff. Then the world will become mine. Even Holy Kutulu Lucifer will be able to be defeated, and I will become the new god of Hell!" His chuckle continued, as he disappeared through a dimensional doorway.

When Leaf stepped out of the trees, Sheera did not even see him, at first. Deep in thought, she continued to walk, until he moved up beside her.

"Good afternoon, Leaf. I was wondering when I would see you." She calmly exclaimed.

"You were being followed for more than an hour, and you just notice. Someday, you will get yourself killed, being so out of touch, little lady!" He spoke.

"That is what you are for, to watch my back. Is not that what you told me?"

The two continued on, Sheera slowing her pace to that of the gnome. She was fond of his company. He always had an opinion on everything, even if it differed with hers. She liked his joking banter, and the practical pranks he was always playing, never seemed to get anyone hurt. She most of all, simply enjoyed him being around!

"Gun powder, huh? You say that it can do what magic can, without the use of magic?"

"If something like that is available, do you think it would be forbidden by the gods?"

"It seems that if something was created that could make the non-gods, us, as powerful as the gods, them, then most likely they would not like it. Yes, it might be forbidden! But, not by Gia. By the Ancient Ones themselves, if it made you their equal.

"What I don't understand is, why would Gabriel, an Archangel of Jeasuas, the god of peace, come to you, if it was forbidden? That is what makes little sense, to me, Sheera!"

She eyed the short man, to her side, with something of a suspicious thought. She had mentioned the angel's name, but not anything about who he served. This little gnome seemed to know an awful lot more about too many subjects. He was always dropping bits of information, that Sheera thought too obscure to be simple knowledge.

"Leaf, how do you know who Gabriel serves? I had never seen him, and I spent a year with Holy Jeasuas! I only met with four of Holy Jeasuas' Archangels."

"I am knowing a lot more than you think, little lady. I'm well over four hundred years old, after all! You don't think I can't pick up bits and pieces of learning along the way?"

"Not stuff like that, I don't."

"Well, I did!" Sheera stuck her tongue out at the man, a habit she developed in childhood that never left her. Leaf only chuckled, as their subject changed to the prophesies. Another subject, that Leaf seemed to know a lot about.

****

185

The following morning, JC was stepping out of the Inn, packed and ready to leave, he had purchased a horse the night before, and was a little surprised when it was Mythalla that was leading his new horse around from the stables, holding the reins of a second horse, saddled for her as well. He smiled and thanked her, taking the reins she held out to him.

"I am surprised after all the yelling that went on yesterday, you are allowed to go with me. In truth, I am surprised you would even want to!" JC stated as he moved around to help the young lady up on her horse.

Lifting her all the way up to sitting side saddle, she smoothed her skirts, and looked down at him.

"Reverend Mother Morella may command the Council of Nine, Father JC, but she does not command me. And besides, Reverend Mother Dyanea said that all six of us should go with you, since we are sworn, but the council wanted to keep us all here to deprogram us.

"I decided that Reverend Mother Dyanea was correct and therefore will be going with you. Thorm and Brell should be here soon, as well." Mythalla smiled down at the man, a slight blush showing on her cheeks.

"Oh, and all your requests have been taken care of. The mayor was overjoyed by your charity and the hard work you put in this week, as you know, and even Reverend Mother Berga agreed to exchange your second donation to give to the families. She was very impressed by your show of charity, as well. I hope you will be pleased!"

Smiling, up at the twenty-one-year-old woman, JC patted her hand, and simply stated that he supposed it was time to get ready to head out then.

"I've not ridden a horse in over ten years, I hope I remember how. Now, where are those two others?" He said as he moved around to the left side, patting the horse's neck.

As he lifted his leg to the stirrup, he felt a hand touch his shoulder. Turning he lowered his leg as his eyes met Dyanea's.

"You didn't think I would allow you to leave without saying good bye, did you?"

"I was hoping, to see you again, M'lady!" He softly answered legging a bow to the priestess as he took one hand in his. "I am always hoping to see you, truth be told."

Taking her hand he brought it to his lips, lightly kissing the back of it. When he looked back up, she took his face in both of her hands, and stared into his eyes.

"Do not stay away too long, you have a lot of work to do, and by the time you return, I should have Morella and the other two convinced enough to support you.

"If I can find them, that is! They seemed to have disappeared late last night. We can take up our previous private conversation and explore where the truth of it lies. OK?" She winked at him as she let go of his face. Dyanea then turned to the young woman sitting the horse a few yards away.

"You take care of him, Mythalla. Don't let him make too much a fool! You know how men can be!" Her giggle was short as she turned a worried look towards JC.

Grabbing the saddle horn, he lifted himself up into his saddle, and winked at the lady standing to his side on the ground. He could see two men riding on horses of their own, coming into sight from the Temple stables.

When they came up along the father and Mythalla, Dyanea moved away. Then the four were off, at a slow pace through the square leading out into the village of Bornesta.

Mythalla was chuckling at the struggling rider for most of the way through town, when they exited out onto the main road into the forest, JC finally got back into the motion of what he was doing wrong with his horse.

"You will find yourself very uncomfortable after a day of riding like that, M'lord!" She explained.

"Mythalla, I am not as practiced as I should be. Where I am from, we don't ride horses except as pleasure. Perhaps I should have gotten a wagon, instead?" he calmly stated. "Young lady, there are a lot of things that I will need help with. Riding being the least of them.

"And, young lady! I am not to be called M'Lord, do you understand?" he added looking over to the young woman.

"Yes, Father JC, I understand. I see you as a warrior, is all. The Sword of Vengeance is the arm of the church against the evil, is it not? M'lord is just a seemingly proper title to be given the Paladin of Selene!"

"Where did you come up with that reference, Mythalla?" JC asked.

Thorm and Brell were both shaking their heads, never before hearing the word Paladin, before.

"I was reading a copy of The Chronicles of Marduk, last night. There is a whole chapter on the Chosen One of prophesy. He refers to you as a Paladin and explains that it is a Holy Knight."

"I'm a priest, not a knight. At least I don't think I'm a knight. I'll have to think on that one. It is a very honorable title to be given the name Paladin, in the world of my birth. I have not earned that here, yet."

He looked over to the three young people and smiled turning his head to the road ahead. Then he added several minutes later.

"Maybe, if we can stop this idol worshiping, we can, instead teach each other the things we all need, as well as learn from each other. It's going to be a six-week ride to where we are going, and I think that I will feel less than comfortable if you keep treating me like some sort of demigod! Do you not agree?" He looked at the others.

"If you say so, M'lord. Umm, High Priest JC." She quickly added.

"Yes, sir, Father JC." the two men added.

"Uh, children, can you just call me JC, please?"

"I will try, M'lord!" She blushed. It was going to be a very long ride ahead, indeed.

JC recited the prophesies as he understood them during the days ahead. Mythalla was very good at the Order of Brigitte Prophesies, but had never read any of the others. She constantly asked questions about the Ancient Ones, accepting his answers as gospel.

The men were even more curious, as neither of them had really read any of the prophesies. Eventually they had finally given up the term "M'lord" or other titles, but Mythalla did insist on calling him "Father" a term he could handle. Since many of his students during his long career as a teacher had called him that, it was not quite so much the shock. But, the implied "M'lord" every time she spoke, still touched a nerve every now and then.

"The capital, Father, of the Dragoran kingdom, is the largest city in all of the North West Continent, called Selenia, as you know, by most of us." Mythalla was commenting, with some noted pride on mentioning her home town, explaining on the eighth day of their uneventful travels.

They had gone from village to village along the way, managing to find an Inn to stay at each night, so far. The minor demons faced, in the villages were easily dispatched, without any fan fair.

Thorm was proving to be an excellent soldier, and could hold his own with a cudgel. Mythalla and Brell would attempt at sorcery, and even managed to assist with any healing that might be needed, but for the most part it would be JC's job to take on the monsters and let the three apprentice's aide with the people.

So far, they had found inside to spend the nights, but JC knew a time would come when they would have to sleep outside, but he hoped the weather warmed before that time would come.

The days were typical spring days, icy cold in the morning, they had started out heavily bundled up in their cloaks, riding out into the pre-dawn, and by the time noon came, with the sun high overhead, it had warmed enough to shed the coat and untie the top laces on their shirts, as well. Mythalla was finishing up her recitation at the question he had asked.

"It is called Alyndra, although it has had many names." She explained that with each new queen or king, the name of the capital takes on a new one. It is usually the new monarch that gives it its name. The current, of course, being Queen Alyndria d'Dragoran.

"She was once a very great lady, but some say that in the last year or so, she has fallen from grace. No one knows what happened, she just can't seem to hold her kingdom together any more. And what is worse, she doesn't seem to care, of late either!"

"Then why did the Council send me here, first?" JC asked. "Am I to try and put a new monarch on the throne? I assure you, the last thing I want is to be seen as a queen killer!"

"I think that is the Reverend Mother Morella's intentions, yes, but some of the Council, Reverend Mother Dyanea, being one, believes that she is under some sort of spell from an evil source." Her mention of Dyanea, emphasized when she said it, was a hot spot between them the past week. She had continually tried to talk the Reverend Mother up, like some little sister trying to attract a suitor for the elder.

"Do you not think she is most beautiful, Father?" Mythalla had said, more than once.

"Well, Mythalla," JC commented, "if Dyanea thinks that the queen is enspelled, then it must be!" He added with just a touch too much sarcasm tossed about. Mythalla went quiet for the next few hours, sniffing at any comment he would make afterward.

The other two men would only smile at the priestess' attitude change. They remained quiet, for the most part, allowing Mythalla and JC to determine the direction of the conversation.

As evening approached, the coolness in the air settled in, and they found a nice spot to settle for the night. JC set up camp, using sorcery, he created a large tent of twigs and leaves, and started the fire, boiling water that Brell had fetched from the nearby stream. They ate a warm dinner of vegetables and meat. Mythalla had purchased proper food at the previous village, and JC sat back, lighting his pipe, looking up at the stars. The charging demon almost caught him unawares.

Brell was caught off guard and thrown back, as the monster tossed the man into a tree, hard, breaking his back.

Mythalla, quickly regained her senses, and dove out of sight in a fearful half panic as Thorm jumped back pulling his cudgel from beside his bedroll. JC simply exploded the monster with a lightning bolt that took it squarely on the chest. Rolling to the right, he came up with his Katana in hand, pulled cleanly from the sheath and sliced a second demon in half, still in a charge. Standing to face the next, JC quickly eliminated the remaining three, and began searching the night for any others. When he returned to their camp, the familiar eke of brimstone was on the air, and the gusts of air were dissipating the fallen demon dust into the atmosphere. Mythalla came running up to him, dropping a knee, she buried her face into his left leg.

"Forgive me, High Priest JC. Forgive me for running like a little girl!" The tears were wetting his pant leg, and he could feel the shaking of a truly scared young woman. The death like grip she held to him with, was almost numbing, as he tried to lift her to her feet.

"Where is Thorm?" he looked around as he lifted Mythalla into his arms and moving over to where Brell lay unmoving at the stump of a large tree.

Finally, lowering to the ground instead, he allowed Mythalla to hug onto him tight, as he checked to see that Brell was no longer among the living. JC held her in a hug, allowing Mythalla to cry on his shoulders, before lifting her again in his arms. She continued to hold on tight, sobbing, her head tight against him, but her shakes eventually subsided.

After JC managed to console the woman, speaking softly almost a whisper that everything would be all right, he laid her down on her bedroll and began digging a grave for Brell.

"I'm sorry, child." He said as he was scooping the dirt on top of the body and a prayer was being recited to allow Brell's spirit to find its way to Heaven.

JC then searched the area for Thorm noticing that one of the horses was missing.

Mythalla's sobs were quiet now, and she almost seemed asleep, except for the occasional hiccup.

The next morning, JC still awake when Mythalla came out of the make shift tent. She noticed the mound where Brell was buried and the brewing of chicory. The absence of Thorm was obvious, as well.

"Sorry about last night, Father. I will try not to panic the next time."

"I never thought of the danger, you being with me. Tomorrow, I will send you back to the Temple."

"No, M'lord, not that!" Her head jerked upright, staring into his eyes, Mythalla forgot all about the nightmare she had earlier witnessed. "I will be disgraced, if you send me back. Please, Father, please?" She begged. "Oh, blessed Goddess, don't send me away. I will be better, you can teach me to fight the Hell Spawn.

"You can protect me! Please, I was given to be your apprentice, by Reverend Mother Dyanea, because I am her most trusted and I had sworn to you. She won't have me back, if you send me home in such disgrace. She cares for you, Father; that is obvious.

"That is why I was given to follow you!" JC watched the woman struggle to come up with reasons to stay, until she took a knee.

Then he pulled her up.

"Don't kneel, child, remember my command." She held herself straight, taking on what dignity she could manage, and looked up into his eyes.

At only five feet one inch, Mythalla was quite a bit shorter than him, something JC was not use to from a grown woman. But her eyes met his, and she looked, tears streaking on her cheeks, the swollen eyes, red from her tears, as he wiped her cheeks with his hands, leaving smudges of dirt along the way.

"OK, let us talk. If you are to stay with me, I am going to show you something that you are to give to no one, no matter what. Do you promise? Not even your precious Dyanea is to learn this!" Her head shake, eyes glistening with new excitement, she aptly watched and learned how to draw energy off of another sorcerer.

"Never take more than you need, child. As a matter of fact, never draw from anyone other than me. OK?" He explained. "I won't let you have more than I can afford to give, and I won't harm you when I sever the link. You take from someone that is stronger than you, against their will, and they can take it back and more, draining your very life! Do you understand?" Again, she shook her head, this time, horror filling her face.

"Then I should not do it to you, Father. I would not want to hurt you!"

"My child, you cannot harm me. You will not be able to take enough to more than inconvenience me. Just don't do it except when you face Hell Spawn. This way you will have enough strength to fight them."

"This is what you did to us, when you healed those people at the Temple?" His head shake, confirmed it, and she was amazed how easy it was and that no others had learned it before.

As they talked about the uses and laws of sorcery, her yawns became more and more frequent.

"You should go back to sleep. You have not had enough."

"I'm fine, Father. Lets ride a little. What happened to Thorm? Did you send him away?"

"No, I did not. I think he decided that traveling with me was more than he bargained for. If we run into him, don't think unkind of him. This is not going to be an easy journey. Are you sure you are up to it?"

He tried once again to send her off to bed, but she refused, asking more questions as they started to tear down camp.

In his element, JC was enjoying teaching, again, and would relent with more answers and more guidance. After she finally fell asleep, during the first couple hours of their ride, he pulled her from her horse, to hold her safely snug to allow her to sleep.

That night as they made camp, Mythalla began again asking questions about auras and the more subtle parts of sorcery. It was several hours later that she drifted off to sleep in front of the fire, once again.

JC lifted and carried her to her bedroll, covering her up against the cold, he stood outside the nature made tent, maintaining a watch until long after the sun had come up. He was still standing stoking the fire when she exited the tent and joined him at the fire.

"So Dyanea is a quarter elf. That explains the young appearance to her eighty some years. I have to admit, I find that hard to believe she is as old as that. But, what about Essmelda? Why does she look so young? I still can't believe she is 15, she doesn't look a day past 10." JC didn't look at the young woman, as she cleaned her face and using salt and a brush, scraped her teeth.

He already knew the answers to the questions, but wanted to see what Mythalla knew.

He continued to stare at the fire, watching the flames jump about, as if deep in his thoughts. She kept silent until she had brushed out her dark hair, tying it up into a braid to let it hang halfway down her back.

When she rejoined him at the fire, he was kneeling, filling a bowl with some oatmeal like mush sparsely spread throughout with nuts that he had made, he handed the dish to her.

"Some say she is Reverend Mother Dyanea's, but, that has never been said to her face, more than once, anyway." Mythalla quietly spoke. "some say that she is Hell Spawn. But that is met with the wrath of the Reverend Mother, as well! So, none, say it aloud in her ear shot, now!" Her tight smile said that she had faced that wrath and JC could quite imagine the outcome if Dyanea had lost her temper.

"The only Hell Spawn I saw in that Temple was Morella." JC quietly calmly stated.

Mythalla dropped the bowl she was holding, and quickly turned to face him. The anger touching her eyes, the hold of her mouth said he had committed a sacrilege.

"You can't say that!" She hissed. "Even in jest, never say such a thing! I don't care who you are, they will destroy you!"

"Oh, she is marked, child." He calmly answered. "She bares the mark of Kutulu on her. If you all knew what to look for you all would see it. Now, I just need to figure out what to do about it. She has sold her soul to the devil, and that is why she appears so young compared to her age. Not sorcery, it doesn't slow the aging down like she claims. And if she is the oldest on the Council, even more so than C'renan, who is a full elf, then she has gained immortality from the Ancient One, himself. Believe me, Mythalla, I am not jesting now!"

Looking over at the horses, Mythalla only noticed hers. JC's and Brell's were missing.

"Where are the other horses, Father?" She announced trying to change the subject.

"They are out eating. I told them not to wander too far. Hopefully, tonight we will find an Inn." His matter-of-fact answer, he still was appearing deep in thought.

"Yes, how am I to handle Morella?"

Cleaning up the camp, JC did it without the use of sorcery. Carrying water up from the creek, nearby, he doused the fire, last, and spread dirt on top to ensure no heat would escape to fire up again. When he was done, he considered the tent that he had created with the magic and decided to leave it like the one from the previous night. The forest would reclaim it eventually, and if some other traveler could make use of it until then, so much the better.

Retrieving the horses, he checked them out thoroughly, and found them all in good shape. He decided that walking would be good for him, anyway,

"Besides," he told Mythalla, "I'm not the best rider in the world, and the walk will help get the feeling back into my backside." Her laugh at his joke broke the tension, and they tied their supplies on her horse and both took out up the road, their horses following behind. No other mention of Morella was made, nor did they talk about the Temple, at all, for the rest of the day.

Late that evening, they finally arrived at a small township. The next day, after trading in the horses, and buying a small wagon and two draft horses, they took off, both riding in the seat, where JC could continue his lessons of the politics of Dragoran Kingdom, and Mythalla hers on sorcery.

****

Burlga and Quevit spent the next several weeks fighting with the magistrates and finally managed the back taxes and paid off all the debts. With the legal problems cleared, she was able to set Quevit up as the token Lord of the lands, and she would handle the finances. She did not like that arrangement, but it quickly became clear that some things hadn't changed, and it would be difficult for a woman to hold onto the lands.

She hired servants and a few soldiers from the local mercenary guild. The thirty soldiers would help in clearing the lands of the Troll infestation, and she would need protectors for the contractors she had to hire. Seeing that things were finally moving forward, Burlga was a little put off, by how empty her first bag of treasures was, and by how much everything had cost to fix.

Stocking the pantries, purchasing the needed furnishings, weapons, and armor for the keep's armory, as well as, a few dresses for Burlga, and some finer clothes for her cousin, the second bag of gems and coin was half gone as well.

"This is becoming quite a bit more expensive than I thought. Just what the bloody hell, have you all been doing to my lands, cousin? You only had five hundred years to flaming ruin it so?"

He could only shrug. Quevit had not really taken over yet, when his uncle had died heir-less only a few months prior to Burlga's arrival.

Moving around the villages that were promised allegiance to her holds, she managed to clear out several hundred minor demons, and a few devils. The people were glad to see the sorceress come, but seemed gladder when she would leave, after introducing herself. The d'Venta name was infamous, and the use of claiming to be the daughter of Stellen, was causing her much too many problems. She would have to accept the fact that he was thought of as an insane criminal, and she would need to stop claiming any heritage to that. Quevit had suggested a more obscure line within the family that had died off a couple centuries ago, without an heir.

"That way your fortune would be accepted without question, and little was known of Remus d'Venta, other than he was quite eccentric in giving away most of his money to charities and inventor's."

She finally agreed, philanthropy would help build her name in the people's eyes, and make her claims as a priestess much easier.

She also, decided to approach her mother's side of the family, but Quevit had advised no humans were allowed into the groves. It would be questionable if Burlga would even be allowed.

"Only one way to find out, and besides, they don't really have the power to take me down if I don't want them to." she said with a wink.

****

Quen walked the city of Vellium. His escort was two women and one man. The Knight of the Blade, Brother Darin, was made to be Quen's royal body guard, even though the emperor thought that a little wasteful. The best sword dancer in the world, if not the entire universe, the thought at having a body guard was a needless expense.

"Appearances, M'lord, are often times the most important. The people will expect it, and you must remember, they are the tax payers in the kingdom. You must give them what they expect!" High Priest Meritt had instructed.

The High Priestess Lalia, was very strong in sorcery, maybe even as strong as Meritt, but the middle-aged woman never carried a sword, and Quen wondered how she had managed to become a Blade.

"I am a good administrator, Emperor Quen. I have never needed to master the sword." Lalia stated.

"Then it is time to learn. Even an administrator needs to protect themselves."

"Yes, your majesty. I will begin attempting it, again." She reluctantly answered.

The other person walking with him, was the almost seventeen-year-old young woman that openly idolized the man. Near to worship, Nileena, was rarely far away from the emperor, when she could get away with it.

After just eleven weeks she was actually becoming practiced with the sword, and she could cast spells as well as any of the apprentices. She only knew a few, but she was easily one of the strongest young people, and Meritt commented on her becoming almost as good as Lalia or maybe even himself, when she obtained adulthood.

"A rare find, you have made, M'lord. How did you know?" Meritt had asked.

"I can see it in her aura, Father." Quen had attempted to teach the use of auras, but was unable to, and quickly lost the patience to try.

As the four were coming down one of the side streets, about to enter on the Empire's Road, the main street leading to the palace, a group of fifty dwarves were marching, in a loose squadron march, led by a large man, standing almost 130 cm, tall. He was wearing a small gold band around his head, a broad sword across his back, and a hammer tucked in his belt.

When the dwarves did not stop for the emperor to walk by, Duarin yelled out.

"The non-humans have forgotten their manners, not to step aside for the emperor?"

All fifty came to an immediate halt, and the one wearing the coronet, moved to the priest.

"He must be invisible, priest. I only see a couple little girls and their play toys." The chuckles are quiet moving through the ranks.

"You will regret that insult of the emperor and his clergy, dwarf. Before I got you in a fair duel, I would have your name. You are about to face Brother Duarin, Blade of the Holy Phaleg."

The large dwarf looked over at Quen, standing calmly with an emotionless expression. The women had both moved to either side of the man, who was only two meters behind and to the left of Duarin.

"If you are the prophet, human, then it is you that I have come to see. Call your boy down, and trade swings with Moradin, King of the Durin Clans."

Quen nodded and as he stepped forward, the visible paleness that suddenly moved into Duarin's face, was replaced by relief.

"It is said that you have never been beaten in a duel, your highness. I, myself, have only one loss, that being too Holy Phaleg, himself. I accept the challenge, but it will not be to the death. I have no wish to eliminate one that I hope to make an ally."

The dwarves all laughed at the comment, and the grin on Moradin's face, showed teeth through his beard.

"Quen Dem Lurin, your confidence is most wholesome. If you truly are the Prophet that our prophesies speak of, then I think that we will be getting very drunk tonight, after, we see which of us the better." He stepped back and pulled his sword from over his large broad shoulders.

The dwarves moved to block the street, as all traffic came to a stop. The two royal leaders, circled each other and the first couple passes were tests, of which both combatants already had decided their opponent was one of skill. Quen broke a smile, knowing he had finely gotten a worthy opponent.

After three more passes, the dwarf found his own sword in Quen's off hand, and when the Emperor Chosen, turned it hilt first to hand back to the King, he stated, simply.

"Your Highness, I thank you for finally giving me someone with which I can respect. I am only wishing my own Temple had someone of your caliber with which to practice."

The dwarf not knowing if he joked or not, the duel being over so quick, having never lost a battle or duel, Moradin looked at the man, with a new respect.

"You say that Holy Phaleg is your only defeat, I can easily understand, Your Majesty. That you ended this so effortlessly, I hope your words are not a joke at my expense."

"I don't joke, when it comes to blade dancing, Your Highness. You are very good. I am, though, simply the best!"

The two walked up the road, towards the palace, the group of dwarves silently following behind. Nileena, smiling in awe of the demigod, she shared a bed with!

CHAPTER 9
The heroes have arrived!

Thirty-six days of travel, they finally had arrived at their destination. Nineteen villages, six hundred Hell Spawn, one major demon, all removed, along the way, and Father JC and the beautiful Sister Mythalla had healed over three hundred people. Finally, on the forty sixth day total since leaving Bornesta, Alyndra, was within sight.

It was early afternoon, the morning rains had dissipated, and the sun was shining weakly through thin clouds. A musk hung in the air, as they passed a farm that had not yet been plowed. There were no signs that any labor had taken place, nor were there any of the usual noises one would expect to hear from a working farm in the morning. The place looked deserted.

On a hunch, JC turned the wagon up the dirt path leading to the farm house, and when he entered the yard, he told Mythalla to stay put.

Slinging his Katana over his shoulder, he cautiously walked up to the door, hanging open, off all but one hinge.

"Yo to the farm!" He called out, not hearing an answer. "Is anyone home?" He tried again.

As he came to the door, he probed out ahead using his sorcery, until he finally found the occupants. He also found something else, in his probing. The pure evil of what could only be Hell spawn. Pulling his weapon, he looked back at Mythalla, holding her arms crossed her face showing a little fear, JC put on a tight smile and stepped in through the door.

Finding the imp, a small mischievous devil banging against a door that led to the cellar, he tapped his blade on the ground to get its attention. When it turned, JC removed its head with a quick sweep.

"You can come up now, it is dead and gone!" He called down the stairs after he unsealed the locked door.

"Nothing is going to hurt you, now!"

After several tries at coaxing, the father of the family finally came up, looking disheveled, unwashed, and half insane. He also showed signs of cuts and other injuries that had not been taken care of.

Calling out to Mythalla, JC wrapped the man in air, and laid him on the couch. When Mythalla came into the house, she got a large pot of water that JC asked for, and immediately began to tend the farmer's wounds, using some sorcery to heal the infection that had begun to set in. JC went to the stairs and climbed down into the cellar.

The smell was bad, and he had to cover his nose to keep from gagging. What he found was a woman, in just as bad a shape as her husband and two small children, both boys, looking like they were about to fall over. He wrapped them in air, as well, and floated them all up to the living room, laying them on the floor rugs. Where, he and Mythalla could help them.

After the family was cleaned and healed as best as they thought they should, JC finally was able to get some answers out of the mother. The father was still too far upset to be any real use, and probably would be that way for a very long time.

The imp had shown up about two months earlier, and after simple harassment, things began to get worse. It would not let them get the fields ready, only allowed them to play with it. Finally, when they decided they had had enough, about a week ago, the imp attacked. The family was able to escape to the cellar and bar the door. They had been down there since, with very little water, and only the jarred foods that were canned the previous year, left to eat.

JC gave them a few gold pieces saying only that the Temple of Selene was their benefactor. He and Mythalla left, the priestess as tear filled as the farm wife was. He wished them luck, and turned the wagon back towards the city.

"Can Hell Spawn really be walking the streets of Alyndra?" Mythalla asked once, aloud as she sat next to the High Priest. "I cannot believe even Queen Alyndria would allow that!"

"We shall see, as there it is!" JC commented as he saw the sprawling city ahead. The farm lands had given way to homes and warehouses.

On top of the hill, a tower could be seen, spiraling up several stories attached to a sprawling palace. Just below the palace grounds were businesses and large houses, almost small castles as the king's road circled up the mountain.

****

When she entered a small sixteen building village, named Inan, Burlga saw the usual count. There were many dead or injured people, and something amazing, two men, bravely facing down eighteen minor demons. Their swords were mostly bouncing off the hides of the spawn, but occasionally, one would actually break the skin causing some minor damage to it.

Sending two lightning bolts out from an outstretched hand, she caused both to branch out in four directions each, she managed to kill eight of the demons on her first volley. When most of the remaining spawn turned to see the sorceress sitting a horse, they began lumbering quickly in her direction.

The remaining ten demons were slain before any more villagers were harmed, nor were any able to even react.

Burlga rode her horse forward, to the two warriors that had been gallantly facing the demons, and when she approached, they both immediately dropped to their knees, bowing.

"My Lady has arrived at a most fortuitous moment. I am known as Persides the Wise, and bless the arrival of she who can only be the Prophet of Holy Merylon!" One of the bowing men looked up stating.

"Rise, wise Persides, you do indeed face the High Priestess Burlga d'Venta. And, who is your equally brave companion, good sir?" Burlga motioned them to rise.

"I am Sorlons the Strong, Holy Priestess. We had heard of your coming, and were hoping to find you."

Both men dropped to one knee, again, looking up at the sorceress, still sitting her horse, and swore their blades to the Prophet, finally come!

Spreading gold coins to the masses, like she had been doing in each village she had been in, while the two warriors followed, Burlga walked her horse throughout the large village.

202

She arrived, finally to the largest building in Inan, a three-story stone keep, with the words "The Sorcerer's Guild" inscribed over the main doors. When she began to climb the stairs, the two soldiers stopped refusing to enter.

"It is forbidden for non-guild members to enter, My Lady. Certainly, you know, that!"

"Flaming Hell, if Holy Merylon's Temple is forbidden the general masses! What has happened to my country; that this would come to pass?" She seethed, as she slammed the doors open, walking through, hearing the echo throughout the hall. She loudly announced,

"I am The Lady Burlga d'Venta, Chosen One of Holy Merylon! Where is the guild leader that dares blasphemy in My God's name, by keeping the Holy Word from the people?"

When eight people, four men and four women, rush in, beginning to cast the slower wizard spells, Burlga easily wraps the first four in holds of air and turns to do the other four, when she was hit with a reasonably strong psychic crush. It would have seriously hurt her had she not already had a mental shield in place.

Smiling at the thought of a sorcery using guild member, she wrapped three in hold spells and crushed the mental shield of the sorceress that had attacked her. The pain from the backlash of having her mental shield dispelled, caused the woman to fall to the ground holding her head.

"Good, a real sorceress, among you! Too bad, you're going to be in too much pain to cast for a couple days!" Burlga almost laughs.

Eyeing the woman that had so easily incapacitated eight of the guilds' best, a wizard named Palomides began.

"Who are you, woman? That you have so much power in you?" Elderly, with white hair and beard, the man was short, only about five feet six, thin and frail looking.

Turning to the entrance door, where she saw her two followers standing just outside, she waved them in.

"Persides and Sorlons, do come in, please! These idiots seem to be deaf as well as dumb!" Turning back to the wizard, after ensuring her men were coming in, even if hesitantly, she once again spoke.

"Are you indeed, deaf, venerable one? Or, is it that you have not read "The Prophesies of Kraylon", sir?" Her sarcasm was heated, and the man showed open fear in his eyes. But, his comments back to her, are haughty and full of disdain.

When Burlga and her two men-at-arms, finally left, she was disgusted with the guild, and forgot her language. The two soldiers were blushing red when the three eventually left the village.

"Mistress Burlga?" Persides quietly asked, after a few minutes on the road. "Should you not have released your spell on the magicians?"

"It will wear off, eventually!" She calmly answered. "Those flaming bloody fools, follow themselves, not our Holy Merylon! They deserve to bloody rot, for all I care! And, a little flaming humility will do them some good!"

Sorlons just nodded agreement as Persides advised Burlga about the guild throughout all of Marintia was pretty much just like that smaller guildhall, in attitude!

"Not for bloody flaming long, will it be!" was all she said, as they took on a silence until, that night, they arrived at her and Quevit's keep.

****

Sheera wandered down the road heading towards another village, her mind thinking about Leaf.

Something was off about him, even if it was for the good! Sheera was determined to figure it out and was readying herself when he next would appear. She was about to stop for the evening near a large river when she noticed a suitable tree not too far away.

As she approached, the Gnome in her thoughts was there making a nice camp, even arranging some leaves across the fire from the tree as if a bed for himself. Sheera returned his smile, as he grinned to her approach.

"Leaf, I was just thinking about you. You must have mind reading among your other talents."

"I am never too far away, little lady. You just seem to be always going my way, of late. I may just have to be around more often, since you cook better than I can." his wink made her laugh.

"Lephorisal Prignome" she suddenly said.

He did not seem startled as he pulled a couple fish from the brook, but Sheera thought she saw a little flicker in the inner spectrum of his aura.

"Did you say something, young lady?" Leaf commented a couple minutes later as he approached the fire having cleaned off one of the fish for Sheera.

Per his usual, he was only going to cook the fish for himself a few seconds to slightly burn the scales off. He never cleaned the fish much more than that.

Sheera watched him studiously before answering and his eyes never wavered from hers as he sat down to eat.

"Thank you, sir. I only said a name I remember reading in Gia's prophesies. One of her nine Archangel's is called Lephorisal Prignome. Humans mispronounce it all the time, The Ancient Ones all admitted. It means."

"First Gnome, yes, I know the story you are referring to." Leaf finished for her. "I've read the scrolls several times in my centuries of life, young one."

"Of course, you know the story. I'm just commenting on how very close to the name of your creating Archangel, your name is."

"Who knows, maybe my mother just liked the name and thought I reminded her of an Oak Leaf when I was born." he chuckled.

"How come there are no shrines or temples to Lephorisal? There are a few to his first creation, Garl Glittergold. But, none to Lephorisal."

"Maybe he didn't like being bothered with stupid questions from youngsters that had better things to think about." Leaf answered a little too abruptly.

Sheera shrugged with a slight frown and leaned back against the tree. There was no more conversation that night, and after watching the gnome for a few hours she finally fell asleep.

The next morning, she was awakened by singing birds and an empty camp, the fire having long burned down, even the coals were cool to the touch.

She smiled as she noticed that Leaf's makeshift bed had not been slept in.

The small hovels and large single storied buildings were interred mixed with some small businesses here and there. The city had been built below a large hill, and now could be seen to surround the hill. At the top of the tallest of the hills was the palace. Walled all the way around, the sides of the hill having been dug out to create short cliffs below the walls. Rising above the dark stone that was the walls, a lighter colored tower rose to easily a height of over fifty meters. It was huge compared to the rest of the city, as no other building could be seen to come close. The streets were dirty and unkempt, and for a city this large there was very little traffic moving about. The sun was still up, not quite evening yet, this place should be awash in people. He pulled the wagon to a stop and watched ahead, in amazement. Mythalla, who had been raised here, could only sit dumbfounded by the sight she beheld.

"My home." She half choked out. "What is going on here?"

JC looked around carefully, and then drove them to what looked to be an Inn.

The next day after listening to the rumors spread by men too far into their drinks, the only ones that JC and Mythalla could find willing to talk at all, they decided to tempt the streets and make their way to the Temple of Selene.

Not as large as the Temple in Bornesta, which was considered to be the first and main Temple, it was the next largest in all the kingdom and was supposed to house over sixty of the Order of Brigitte Priestesses. As well as the only four High Priests to serve the Goddess. They had been told that no one had seen any of the "witches" in over three months, and that to travel to that part of town was certain death.

"It would seem, my dear child, "JC turned to Mythalla, "that what those farmers we rescued, might have been telling the truth. Even if our information is slurred through the wine, it could not be all false."

206

They left their belongings in their rooms and left the Inn late in the morning just before noon. Walking through the too quiet town, JC felt Mythalla's hand grab his arm, occasionally squeezing as she eyed the city.

When they came to what appeared a quickly made wall that possessed the emanations of sorcery, where one should not be, blocking a street, they stopped to view the soldiers guarding a stout solid wood and iron bound gate, barred on this side.

"You do not want to go in there, sir!" The guard told JC as the two clerics approached.

"I am High Priest JC d'Badger, and this is my apprentice, Priestess Mythalla d'Blaze. Stand aside that we may visit our Holy Temple." The comment was not a request, the commanding tone, he used, spoke volumes to the wary guard. But the soldier still would not move from in front of the thick iron bound wooden door. It was barred on this side, and strange noises could be heard on the other side, as well as the occasional scream from somewhere far off.

"I am sorry, good priest, but this section of the city now belongs to Lord Graz'zt, and his... Ahem, kin! If your Temple still stands, it is beyond being defiled. Please, I cannot truly stop you, I know. But I beg of you don't go in there!" His adamant plea was only half ignored by JC, who looked at Mythalla and pulled her hand free of his arm.

"How many demons are running free under the demon lord's protection, sergeant?"

"Corporal, sir, and at last count was somewhere over a hundred. Most of our weapons just bounce off their skins, so the walls were erected with the help of a few of the surviving witches. You can find those that are left, over at the Inn of the Green Brook."

"Your weapons may not be able to harm them, but mine can. I will enter, sir, and by night fall you will have your city back." Turning to Mythalla, he said, "Go and find our brothers and sisters. Tell them that there will be need of much healing when I come back out.

"Also, advise them that The Sword of Vengeance is upon them and demands their presence." hmm, he looked at the wall. "And, I think that we have

207

found out who is troubling our queen, Mythalla! Now hurry, child. Bring them all. Tell them I am not requesting this. And, find out if any of them know what happened to Morella!"

As she took a step to comply, she turned back to see JC still watching her.

"You will be careful, Father? Remember what happened after you faced Abigor, in Bornesta."

"I'll be fine, child. This one is not nearly as powerful as Abigor was. This one only has numbers to send against me."

The guards listened to the two clerics as though they were insane. Certainly, this man was. He had never even heard of any priest that could fight before. And the calmness with which the spoke of facing that many demons had the guard wary.

As JC turned to the gate, he looked up the wall, standing over twenty feet tall, he made a leap, using sorcery, and landed atop. Looking down at the destruction ridden streets, on the east side, seeing minor demons and major ones as well, moving from building to building, he felt as though he had just stepped through a gateway into Hell. Shaking his head, he pictured arrows, acid dipped in his mind and began sending them forth from his out stretched hands, two at a time.

As she took a step to comply, she turned back to see JC still watching her.

"You will be careful, Father? Remember what happened after you faced Abigor, in Bornesta."

"I'll be fine, child. This one is not nearly as powerful as Abigor was. This one only has numbers to send against me."

The guards listened to the two clerics as though they were insane. Certainly, this man was. Who ever heard of a man claiming to be a High Priest of Selene. He had never even heard of any man that could heal before. And the calmness with which the spoke of facing that many demons.

As JC turned to the gate, he looked up the wall, standing over six meters tall, he made a leap, using sorcery, and landed atop. Looking down in the destruction ridden streets, on the other side, seeing minor demons and major ones as well, moving from building to building, he felt as though he had just stepped through a gateway into Hell. Shaking his head, he pictured arrows, acid dipped in his mind and began sending them forth from his out stretched hands, two at a time.

After several demons had screamed out in agony at the magical arrows embedded in their rough hides, the hoard began to form a mob of Hell Spawn directly in front, down on the street. Seeing some thirty plus demons in so close a proximity to each other, he sent the wrath of his power into their mist.

Ice, followed by fire, followed by gases, followed by more fire. Spell after spell he sent into the mob, and after less than half a minute, he had washed the area with nineteen spells of destruction, killing or disintegrating over forty demons. Pulling his Katana, he stepped off the wall disappearing from the onlookers that had gathered to watch the fireworks and the noise the human was causing.

Some even said a prayer for a speedy painless death for the man, when he jumped down. They knew the reputation that Lord Graz'zt had earned for torturing any who trespassed into his domain.

As JC moved down the street, eliminating all the demons that attacked him, they continued to pour out of the houses on either side of him. JC knew where he had to go, and following the directions that Mythalla had given him, he made his way to the street of the Temples.

There would be three, when he got to the Street of the Gods. The largest would be that of the Creator, and then Holy Selene's would be the Temple on the left. The one to the right of the "Church of God", would be that belonging to Gia.

It was an amphitheater, she had told him, but would have a large oak growing from its center. He could see the Oak tree from the wall when he was standing on it. The tree stood over a hundred feet high and was filled with leaves even this early in the year. He moved in that direction, and any that tried to stop him, he eliminated.

Catching one that somehow avoided his blade, by the neck, he looked into its eyes and inquired to Graz'zt's hiding place. The demon slashed at him, saying only that the great lord would find him. Willing his hand to be aflame, the demon burned to dust crumbling as JC squeezed. The slashing wounds on his arm quickly closing as he healed himself.

209

Supposedly, no one could heal themselves due to the pain and shock to the system. But JC had tried, and since he was able to empathically handle the pain while healing another, he had figured that he would be able to heal himself, as well. He did not do it often, but little wounds that could fester, he would not hesitate in doing.

Wrapping himself into a protective force of air, JC continued his process until finally he made the street he was aiming for. On one side of the long straight brick road, was a park. The grass burnt away, crucifixes were erected, each of the twenty-six crosses holding a person; some were still alive, though barely so. The Hell spawn that was torturing those people, he eliminated with a blade dance, as Quen would have called it.

Not all the crucified people were human, and the first one he came to, was a Dwarven female. Her beard having been pulled out or burned off, and her nude body was covered with welts and lacerations and cuts that would surely have killed a human or more fragile elf. She painfully looked down at JC, and whispered,

"Please, good sir, finish me off. I cannot withstand this pain much longer!"

Instead, using sorcery to release her, JC lowered the dwarf to the ground, using his cloak to cover her, he delved and then using conventional healing, allowed the dwarf's own superior constitution to withstand the shock of the body regenerating. With a deep breath her eyes fixed on JC, and she mouthed a thank you.

"Thank you, m'lord. I wondered when you would come." she exclaimed.

"You were expecting me, then?" he responded.

"I was, and I am yours, M'lord. The Chosen Badger comes!" was her only answer.

"You are a free creature of the world, M'lady. you belong to no one, least of all a humble priest of Selene." Standing, JC turned to the temples across the road.

"Now, if you can begin to let those down that are still alive," he said as he pulled a sorcery enspelled dagger from his boot. Handing the female, the dagger, he finished;

"I have a demon to kill. Are you able to heal, priestess?"

210

"I could if I had my hammer or a holy symbol."

"Here, then. I am a holy symbol and don't need a trinket. Use mine!" he stated handing her his necklace, the symbol of two serpents wrapped around a staff, facing each other as if kissing.

The dwarven female took the symbol and felt the magic flowing from it. She nodded to the man and smiled.

"You are the Chosen Badger that Gia promised. Finally, you have come." she pulled JC by the collar down to her height and kissed him.

"You wouldn't know which one he is in, would you?"

Grunting she pointed the blade at the middle building.

"You'll find the big one in the Church of God. Too bad I don't have any more clothes on than this oversized cloak. I'd help you with that one. You are going to need it."

Smiling down at the four-foot-tall woman, he winked.

"I'll be fine, M'lady. Help those that you can and then wait for me here. I think most of the Hell Spawn are dead, but we can't be too careful. That little stickler your holding will hurt any of them it touches. It was a gift from Selene, so I would kind of like it if you would keep an eye on it, while I go and take out the garbage." JC marched off towards the Temple.

The dwarf nodded and watched as JC gracefully walked across to the Temple. She took on a wry smile and only commented in a tone just above a whisper;

"Mother Gia, this the one of prophesy you told me was coming? Then I am his, whether he wants it or not!"

Entering into the Temple, JC was immediately assaulted by several minor mental spells that his shields easily warded off. The demon lord attacked from behind, but as his sword bounced off the magical air surrounding the Immortal, JC eliminated the left leg of Graz'zt and cut deeply into the inner right, with the same swing. Avoiding a jab by the demon's sword, and feeling the mental shield being attacked as well, when Graz'zt attempted to teleport, he suddenly found JC's sword in his chest, where the heart should have been beating, but now, was simply sliced in two.

Graz'zt's own sword did manage to slice across the Chosen's arm and JC only barely managed to keep a hold on his katana as he twisted the blade while pulling it free.

When JC walked out the door about half an hour later, he was wiping his blade off with a piece of cloth. The glow of his sorcery made protective shield still surrounding him, and it appeared to the former crucified few that could see, that The Creator himself stood at the top of the stairs, in the door of his very own Temple.

Sheathing his Katana, JC allowed the protective shield he had formed to wink out.

Skipping steps, he walked back to the park, where the dwarf was now standing over sixteen others all laying or sitting on the dirt under cover of a tree. The dwarf had taken off the cloak he had given her and used it to help the others.

"M'lady, it is done. I trust you met with no resistance?" JC legged a bow to the small gathering, immediately bending down to look into their needs. Some minor healing on one man, resettling a broken leg on another. The worse of the wounds were on the women, that JC could see, and he found it hard to keep back tears that settled on his cheeks as he healed a child that was not yet thirteen years of age. He knew she would need a whole lot longer to heal the mental injury she had obtained.

No one said a word while the priest worked, and finally as he stood, he heard a voice ask his name. Turning to face the middle-aged female dwarf he had first freed, she was proudly standing, her nude body no longer showing the bruising or cuts she had before been healed, holding out his dagger for him to take it back.

"Killed no demons with it, but it sure cuts rope easily enough." She had no smile, but her eyes carried a hint that might have been an attempt at a joke.

Reaching to the empty sheath in his boot, JC pulled it free and handed it over to the dwarf.

"Well, perhaps you can keep it until you get a chance to see how well it works? Unfortunately, M'lady, I left very little alive coming here." JC's smile was met with one from the woman, and he thought he was beginning to understand the offer that she had made earlier.

"My name, forgive me for having no manners," he bowed to the seventeen people, five men and twelve women, "is The Father JC d'Badger, High Priest to the Holy Selene, called The Sword of Vengeance by her angels. To those of you that can walk, let us make way now to the Temple. Those that can't walk we will carry. I'm sure we can find something to cover you all up in my Goddess' Temple. The Mother's Temple needs to be cleansed anyway, and I really think we should find something to clean all of you up, as well."

"The Holy Selene only has four male high priests and you are not one of them! Especially carrying a Katiketain sword!" One of the women on the ground shakily spoke out. She was middle aged, obviously pretty when not in such disarray, and JC assumed by the look to her that she was at least part elven. Pointed ears, sharp nose, and overly large eyes. And she had the aura of a sorceress, but one that would be even weaker than Galia.

"Priestess?" JC asked.

At the incline of her head, JC continued.

"I was first called High Priest by Holy Selene, herself. The Archangel Brigitte taught me healing and the Archangel Inanna taught me the sword." he smiled as he took a breath before finishing.

"I am the Sword of Vengeance! Mother Selene has given me unto Gia to work for the world, to help rid the infestation and prepare you all for the war of the gods that is already upon us. Do you not know our own holy book's words?" JC finished with some small amount of sarcasm in his tone.

Taken aback, the priestess could only look on the man as he leaned down and picked the young girl off the ground, gently cradling her in his arms.

As he turned to hand the girl to the outstretched arms of the dwarven female, he stopped suddenly aware he did not know her name.

"Forgive me, M'lady, but I have failed to ask your name. I really am being rude, this day!" With a short chuckle, he nodded his head in apology.

213

"I, my good sir," as she accepted the child, "am Massy Thistle, of the Thorn clans. Once wife of Limb Thistle, lord of the Thistle clans. Now, just plain servant to those that once taught at the Temple of Holy Mother Gia." Shifting the girl's weight to handle her more gently and comfortably, she followed as JC picked up a human man, still unconscious but breathing easier after the healing he had received.

"As I said earlier, I am now your servant, Father JC." She continued after they had walked some ten yards.

The others were following, holding on to each other for moral support as well as needed physical support. He looked over his shoulder at the fourteen others to make sure they were coming, and stopped to look at the dwarf.

"I told you before, no other person is my servant. I would welcome another hand in our war against the Ancient One Kutulu, or even a friend will do, but I will not have you bowing down to me every day. No one should bow to another except to the gods themselves. "

"M'lord is most wise. I shall help you as I can, then, if you will have me?"

"And please, M'lady, just call me JC, or at the least, simply Father, will do."

Her nod was sufficient as they entered the Temple, to find the sanctuary in chaos, and the stink of offal on the air.

There were no signs of demons anywhere, and the ten humans, four elves, two half-elves and one lone dwarf, all visibly relaxed as they found robes to put on, and a fountain, in which JC had created water in, to wash with. JC wrapped the man he had been carrying in a robe and laid him on a bench to rest, whispering as he did,

"I will take care of you better in a while, after I have rested. At least, I can insure you will see another day." JC felt a hand on his shoulder and looking up at the owner, a somber Massy stood looking down on the sitting priest.

"You are more tired than you pretend, Father?" It was not intended to be a question, but that is how it sounded. "Fighting demons can be exhaustive work, and I saw the healing you did. It was not like that of the other clergy of Selene. There was no shock in some of those others, like that I felt when you healed me. It's like you gave a part of yourself to those that really were near death." Massy finished.

"You are a most observant woman, Sister Massy." her eyes opened a little wider as he gave the guessed title.

"As are you father." she chuckled.

"Yes, it was different. The normal kind of healing would have killed the ones that needed the type I sometimes use. They are not as strong as you. But it does tire me out more to do it this way."

Standing, JC now looked down at the woman, her hand never leaving his shoulder. He smiled and leaned down to whisper in her ear.

"Thank you, my lady. I will have need for much more of your wisdom. I will need more than just friendship, before this is all over." She only squeezed where her hand still held onto the Immortal's shoulder.

After a few minutes rest as they all cleaned themselves and dressed in the borrowed robes, JC had been leaning back as he watched the others.

Massy watched him, closely, but allowed him his privacy as he maintained his watch. After they had moved away from the fountain, he moved to it and dipped his head into it submersing all the way to his shoulders.

When he rose wiping his long hair back over his ears, he smiled and announced that they should get moving.

When they walked by the Amphitheater of Gia, JC laid a hand to the great oak and said a prayer. The leaves began to change colors and no longer appeared yellow and dried. The green suddenly was changing, as he smiled.

Without another word, he turned to join the others and they made their way out of the Street of the Gods.

"Now, my friend, we can leave." The father commented.

"May she continue to bless you, JC d'Badger."

Most of the others were not overjoyed by the Father's insistence at searching every building in this walled off section of Hell on Zindar. It was only a couple blocks around the Street of the Gods, but it took a few hours to complete, and they met with many minor demons along the way.

However, they may not have been happy with it, but they did not want to leave the warrior priest, either.

Massy got her chance at using the dagger, as three spawns exited a door to a small dwelling, JC swinging to kill two but, failed to hit the third. Massy caught it in the chest with a jab, and actually smiled as she pulled the blade easily from the creature's chest.

"Your Mother Selene makes a fine blade, JC! A fine blade indeed." The emphasis on the word "mother" brought him up a little short, but he only nodded smiling at the Dwarven warrior-priest's matter of fact statement.

A few hours later, sure the section was cleansed as he had promised the corporal, they arrived at the gate.

The gate opened on its own, JC, using sorcery to remove the barricades on it, and pushing it with a blast of air, only six hours after he had first jumped down off the wall.

Walking through the now open hole in the wall, JC carried a human male, and was followed by thirty-nine humans, elves, and dwarves, some being carried, most walking or limping on their own.

Mythalla gave a happy jump, clapping her hands as he came through the gate first, and quickly ran to meet him.

"I knew you would be all right, Father." Her excitement barely contained. "I just knew you would do what you promised."

Looking around at the crowd that welcomed the others to freedom, he noticed that there were no other light blue colored robes in the crowd. The half elven female on his right, wearing a robe found in the Selene Temple, sniffed at the actions of the young woman showing her excitement over seeing the warrior.

"Show some dignity, child," the elder priestess exclaimed, bringing Mythalla to a startling halt immediately. "You are a priestess of the Most Holy of Goddesses and you act the child on dance night."

"Mother Tetheran, I will act happy at seeing my mentor safe, if I want." Mythalla almost pouted. "And, don't give me that look, I am his apprentice, given freely by the Reverend Mother Dyanea, herself."

"Yes, well that remains to be seen after Reverend Mother Morella finds out."

"She knows! She was there!"

Watching the banter JC finally tired of it, and asked where the others were. There was much healing to be done and it would be good for the Temple to be seen as the benefactor here.

Looking down, Mythalla's face took on a saddened look.

"You were right, Father! A note arrived before us, and they are not going to help you. They nearly threw me out, for just being with you!"

JC's laugh, cut through the throng of well-wishers and wary soldiers crowding around. The small crowded square became quiet, as he held out the man he was still holding to a couple of the soldiers.

"Take him to an Inn. He needs rest most of all, but will need to be given a lot of fluids and watched for the next few days."

Turning back to the two priestesses' side by side looking at him as if insane with his laugh, he announced.

"So, the Temple here in the capital chooses to follow the commands of a woman that is..." He stopped what he was about to say at the tightening look that showed in Mythalla's eyes, suddenly and corrected himself,

"Unaware of the prophesies. Our most high Reverend Mother has a whole lot to learn before this next seven years is over, and I mean to teach her. Even if I have to force feed it down her throat.

"Come, let us go and talk to these misguided sisters!" He started off in the direction of the Inn of the Green Brook, followed by Massy, still holding the girl, who was now holding the woman around the neck tightly, not about to let go. Massy showing no signs of the burden, followed without a word, only a slight determination on her face.

"Is this going to get nasty, Father JC?" She asked after a couple minutes when they were away from the majority of the crowd.

Turning to look behind, he noticed the two priestesses were following but, farther behind than he thought necessary, as well as a good throng of people, that was strolling behind them as well.

"It could be, but I won't let it go too far. They will not openly attack, no matter what the letter they received said. Their leader is a little misguided right now, and I need to correct that. But that will have to wait.

"Is the girl heavy, Massy? You need me to take over carrying her?" He calmly changed the subject.

Her head shake, Massy just tilted her head to that of the child, in a loving gesture.

"I am fine, Father. She is but a feather in my arms. But, thank you for asking." She added after a moment.

Walking into the inn, the five new comers were met with open stares by the thirty or so women sitting at the tables in the common room. All were dressed in the light blue robes of the Temple and all turned towards the man, standing with legs shoulder length apart, hands crossed across his chest, and a finger lightly tapping the hilt of his Katana as it stuck forward from his side.

"So, Morella has told you not to help the people?" He calmly said, purposely omitting the honored title he should have given the High Priestess.

"Has she forgotten what our Most Holy Selene's commandments have been? Have you all forgotten, as well? Do the people no longer matter, to the Holy Mother's alleged followers?" He watched, before he took a deep breath and calmly stated, "I am The Sword of Vengeance, Father JC d'Badger, High Priest Chosen of the Holy Mother Selene.

"I do not care if you follow me or not, but the people will not be ignored. Mother Selene will be most displeased, as I am, when she finds out that the people were neglected, because of a minor temple being scared of a few demons! Not to

218

mention the misguided commands of a woman that seems more evil than good, in her letter to you."

Embarrassed looks flowed through the women, most now standing at his use of their leader's name with such disdain. Gaining the reaction he wanted, he turned his back on them.

"Mythalla, you can stay here if you like, I will go to an inn that is not tainted with so much of the evil, as those that turn their back on Holy Selene's commands and the people. I will not dine with those that commit sacrilege in our Goddess' name." Saying it loud enough to be heard by the entire room, he then walked out the door to the street easily dispelling any attempts at sorcery to stop him.

Stopping a few yards away, he turned to wait. Massy had followed him out and stood there, head shaking, she gave him a concerned look.

"My Lord JC is most abrasive when trying to gather priestesses to his cause."

He started at the comment, and instead smiled wryly.

"I have a queen to heal, Massy, and have need of rest before then. Let us be away. There are those in the Selenian Council that already follow my cause, and I will leave it up to them to bring the others around.

"I do not have time to debate with those that refuse to look at the portents. As soon as Morella and her demonic taint is removed, they all will see the light. Come let us get you some proper clothes. Temple garb does not suit you; I think!"

They walked down the street and stopped briefly at a trading post so that Massy could order some clothes made for her. Instead of the dresses that JC only half expected, she ordered made, a boiled leather vest and stout pantaloins. She asked that thigh pads and knee pads be added, and then purchased good walking boots and under clothing. JC added a few extra golds to have the vest and pants made and delivered to the Boar's Inn, in less than two days.

Massy actually smiled when JC granted her a new war hammer and a small buckler shield, the hammer was tucked into the belt of the robe she was wearing next to his dagger also belted there.

She also purchased some clothes for the girl, and then offering to retake the girl from JC, which he refused, they made their way to the inn, where he secured another room, across from his. Mythalla was waiting in the lobby, when they arrived.

"Not a very good way to start things, Father. They all admitted that you might be the prophesied one, but with an attitude like you showed, they wonder why Reverend Mother Morella would have let you go. I was unable to convince any of them, to include Tetheran..." Mythalla said joining them, as they walked up the stairs to their rooms.

Taking the girl into Massy's room, JC told the women that he was going to get some rest.

"I expect a rather eventful day at the palace tomorrow. I would think that you both should not stay up too late, but do get something to eat." Turning to Mythalla, he simply put a hand on her cheek.

"Do not fret over the priestesses, child. Selene will open their eyes as soon as Morella is exposed. You, Pynora, Galia, C'renan, and Dyanea know the truth, no one else matters at the moment." He said the Reverend Mother's name with a little too much smile to his face. Adding a frown at the casualness of his comment.

"Go and get to know each other. I suspect we will be spending a lot of time together over the next few years. Priestess Massy of Holy Gia, again, I thank you for coming with me. I will have need of those I can trust, and I know the reputation of your people. Your word alone, is enough for me to welcome you, as a friend at the least, if not so much more." He tucked the girl in bed giving her a kiss on the forehead,

"We will talk in the morning, child." he whispered before turning to the door. As he reached the door of the room, he turned and legged a bow.

"Now, if my ladies would excuse me, I am more tired than I let on." He smiled as he tossed his money pouch to Mythalla and walked directly across the hall entering into his room.

The next morning, JC found himself joined in the common room, by the three women. He had been there a while when they finally came down the stairs, Mythalla expecting him too already be there.

The young girl sat where Massy pointed and immediately began to down the fruit that JC had a large plate of, on the table. As all four ate, he noticed that Mythalla and Massy were chatting like they were long time friends, and he smiled at the intervention of fate once again.

His thoughts drifted to the long black-haired woman back in Bornesta. The one that had been haunting his dreams ever since his coma after the accident. His face took on a dreamy look, when he was interrupted from his reverie.

"Father, are you all, right?" Mythalla asked.

"Huh, wha.., oh, yes, I'm fine. Just thinking of someone, I mean something."

JC smiled and immediately brought his cup of tea to his mouth.

Massy, started, unknowingly easing his embarrassment,

"JC, this is Natylia. She is a ten-year-old orphan of the Temple of Selene. Natylia, this is Father JC, High Priest to Selene and it would seem, your new benefactor."

The girl looked at the priest across the table from her, and nodded.

"Never saw a man priest with a weapon like that one at the Temple before." She mumbled.

Before Massy could chastise her for the disrespectful attitude, JC shook his head looking at the dwarf.

"That's because I'm the first, so it seems. Things have changed in these new times, child. Has anyone ever told you that you have the spark in you to be a sorceress?" When she did not answer, he continued. "Well, you do! You will be really good at it someday, I would imagine. Maybe even as strong as Priestess Mythalla, here."

Mythalla looked at the girl, trying to see how he could tell, and remembered what he had taught her along the way. Concentrating on Natylia's auras, she viewed the middle spectrum and saw the soft blue, transparent, indicating someone that was average. Knowing her own strength was about average in the Temple, she wondered if that was how hers looked.

Turning to JC, she saw his aura, and noticed the bright solid golden inner spectrum, indicating he was an immortal of angelic beginnings, his middle spectrum a deep blue, solid, not able to see through it at all, and his outer spectrum a light rainbow of colors showing his compassion and easy loving mood at the moment.

Proud of herself for seeing it all, she exclaimed,

"I can see it, now!" A smile almost childlike on her face, JC forced back a chuckle and patted her hand.

"Good for you, I told you it just takes practice."

Massy watched the exchange with bewilderment and Natylia began to say something, but closed her mouth in a hurry. Then after a few moments, she finally began to open up.

"They said at the Temple that I would become a priestess one day if I wanted, but..."

As JC softly guided the conversation, the girl opened up more and more, until the flood of information was finally released, along with her tears at the horrifying experiences she had just gone through. Massy put an arm around the girl's shoulders and smiled at JC, seeing in him the real priest and loving counselor, he claimed to be.

After a couple hours, JC told the others that perhaps, Massy and Natylia should stay here, while he goes to the palace. The dwarf agreed and taking some coins from the man, agreed to have some more clothes purchased for the girl, and for herself as well.

"You might go and see if you can get some sort of armor made, whatever you might prefer. At the least something with more protection than the boiled leather you ordered. Assure them that whatever else you come up short will be taken care of."

"It looks like you have two apprentices, now, and a woman at arms, M'lord!" The dwarf said a little to wryly for comfort. Her chuckle was dry, and she went back to her stoic face almost immediately.

"I will make you happy one of these days, Massy. Mark my words, you will feel joy before I'm finished with you!" His sarcasm was not lost on Massy, whom grinned.

"But, my High Lord Father JC." She said a little too drawn out, "I am oh so happy just being near you! See my smile?" Her grin was almost evil and the spark in her eyes told him the joke.

Laughing while he got up to leave, JC held out his arm for Mythalla to take.

"I may not make you laugh, my dear lady at arms. But you will surely bring joy to this old man's days ahead."

Mythalla took the arm offered and the two left the Inn. Leaving the wagon and horses, they chose to walk, taking up to the palace, the long winding Queen's Promenade Road. It was still quieter than a city should be, but the two could already see noticeably more traffic out on this day compared to the previous.

The word had already begun to spread through the city about the man claiming to be The High Priest of Selene, and the way he cleaned the whole part of town called Hell's Prize, in just half a day.

The two, also could hear, the wall being torn down near the section that was until recently closed to the road.

Mythalla did not comment the whole way, and JC was equally quiet, only waving at the few people that recognized him, or thought he might be, the rumored priest.

Arriving at the palace just before noon, the guards at the gate let JC and Mythalla in only to ask them to wait nearby inside. A runner was sent off at the expected arrivals, and a few minutes later, a middle-aged man, with salt and pepper gray brown hair, standing the same height as JC, about five feet seven inches tall and wearing the braids of a high-ranking officer on his lapels, a shined bronze breastplate that was repaired in spots and a long sword at his hip. He came walking up with the runner.

Stopping a little more than two yards away from the clerics, the man eyed JC and nodded.

"I thought you would be some sort of giant, the way they have been talking about you! You are the one that liberated the Temple area of town?" The question was more of a statement, this man already knew the answer. "I would have words with you before you see our Queen."

JC gave him a nod and followed him away from other ears. Mythalla heeling behind. The Officer looked grimly at the priestess before finally deciding to speak his mind.

"I am General Hanlon d'Boar. I am the Knight Protectorate of the Queen and leader of all the Dragoran armies. What I am about to tell you could be considered treason, and get me my head served; you understand that I only do this because I love my country and my queen?"

JC nodded and swore confidentiality.

"We are clergy, M'lord. Anything told to us in confidence must remain so! And, if it is the Temple you are concerned with, fear not, for I have issues with some of the priestesses myself. My apprentice, Mother Mythalla, here is not one you need worry about. She loves our Queen as much as she does me, I suspect."

Mythalla smiled nodding at the high respect he just afforded her.

After a deep breath, the General continued,

"Lord JC, or Father JC if you will." Another deep breath before finishing in a whisper that Mythalla only barely heard. "My queen is possessed. And I think that your Temple is responsible. More precisely, three of your witches. I'm no expert, mind you, but I know; or rather knew my queen!"

The gasp and quickly stifled "NO!" By Mythalla, as JC signaled a hold to her, by raising his hand. He quickly looked around to insure they were still out of ear shot of the guards, his eyes falling onto the generals hard. A practiced look he acquired when a teacher, JC glared at the General, who did not flinch at the stare.

"Those are hard words to throw my way, General d'Boar. I am not going to dispute them, but I hope you have some sort of proof that I can devour. The accusation at my priestesses is most troublesome!"

"Your Reverend Mother Morella, and two others, Mother Nevah and Mother Lenara have been coming in the past three months, almost every day, for nearly a month before Graz'zt arrived.

"That in itself is only alarming in that we use to not have more than one visits a month from the Temple, and until this all started happening, Morella had only made one visit, sixteen years ago, when the queen was crowned." His sigh at knowing that was not enough, he continued never taking his eyes from the priest.

"The Queen started becoming moody, and making unreasonable demands of the people almost immediately. Taxes where there should not be any, confiscation of lands from the Lords, and false accusations of treason to the crown, against others. Then the day before Graz'zt arrived, she ordered no more patrolling of the guards in the Temple areas, and ordered the wall built, which your Rev. Mother agreed to. Then it was like Hell opened up in our streets."

General Hanlon, took hold of JC's arm and began leading him towards the palace. He continued to speak softly as he led the clerics, looking around at all times.

"What I ask is a lot. I want my queen back, and unharmed!"

The emphasis on that last part was more of a warning.

"She has become even worse since yesterday, and has ordered you beheaded. I have been able to put a stop to that so far, but I don't think you are going to be in for a good time. I am sorry to tell you this, Father, but I have to send you in, otherwise, I have to arrest you. You understand that my hands are tied on this, don't you?"

With a slight chuckle, JC nodded. As they made their way to the Throne room, JC noticed by the auras that the guards at the doors were in reality Hell Spawn. Getting to within hearing range of them, he smiled and said aloud.

"General, did you know that demons guard your Queen here at the doors?"

They attacked immediately and were quickly removed with a bolt of energy, two each from JC's outstretched hand. As they disintegrated, JC winked at the General smiling.

"Mythalla, wait out here. I have never performed an exorcism before and this could get messy, and if I am to keep the queen alive, I will have to get creative."

"We can link, Father, if you like. But she is my queen as well, and I will not run for hiding, anymore." Mythalla responded, some fear peeking through the brave

225

statement. He nodded and immediately took her into his mind, as he felt some of his energy being drawn into her. At the point he felt comfortable, he put a shield up to stop her, and only said,

"That is enough!"

The two-clergy entered through the doors, the General following behind, his sword in hand. Almost immediately they were assaulted with the stench in the air. The over powering reek of a room that had not been cleaned in years.

"This has only been a couple months?" he received only a nod from the General.

The woman sitting on a throne, at the far end from the entry door on a dais raised about two yards up some steps, looked in disarray. From the door, JC thought the queen was far older than he had been told.

Debris was thrown on the floor all around the dais and there were a few of what he assumed might have been servants lying face down on the floor, some very badly twisted. Gen. Hanlon did not follow the two in beyond the door.

Through the link, JC could feel the fear in Mythalla rise, and when he turned to once again tell her to wait, she only shook her head and regained control of herself.

They walked down the twenty steps into the grand hall. There were fourteen demons walking about, and another dozen humans wearing the livery of the keep, indicating they were servants to the crown. They were jumpy, obviously scared, and all looked about ready to run.

JC thought that it would be better if they did, as he and Mythalla walked across the hall towards throne on the dais.

He marched, head held straight, only the balls of his feet hitting the ground, hands at his sides, eyes watching in all directions ahead. He almost appeared an animal at the ready.

The young woman walking warily behind him, attempted an airiness of uncaring, but her head jerked too much, looking every which way and behind as she never let the priest get more than a couple yards ahead.

JC could feel in the link that she had about half a dozen spells ready and probably would use all of them as fast as she could, if startled.

"Calm yourself, child." He whispered. "Remember, we are not here to harm, hold spells are what you want. Let me do the destroying, you just hold."

Her mental images changed, and JC could feel the priestess relax a little.

"So, this is the Pet of Selene?" The dry scratchy voice issuing from Queen Alyndria, was not what JC expected.

She had obviously been yelling all morning and was going horse from the efforts. The debris on the ground created a hazard as the clerics approached the dais, and JC stopped at the foot of the steps, legging a bow to the woman.

"Your Majesty, is well informed. But I am only her priest. Her pets all live in heaven, a place you will never see, so it would seem."

His eyes never left the woman, with dark brown hair, uncombed standing out in all directions as if she had just risen out of bed, and light brown eyes that were blood shot and swollen, her skin was a deeper color than he had seen on this continent, almost a true brown color.

She was a handsome woman of middle age, or at least would be if she was in better straights. Wearing a red silk dress, with many beads and embroidery sewn at the hems. The top was unbuttoned causing the gown's neckline to plunge way too low for appropriate modesty, and the rips and tears in the sleeves and the collar indicated that it had been through much abuse the past few hours.

In her hand, she held a scepter of gold and platinum, with a large ball on the end that was damaged from obvious use as a weapon. Her eyes never strayed from JC as they moved up and down his frame.

"You have slain my man, killed many of my children, and now dared to destroy my guards. You will die this day, pet, and I will do so most unmercifully."

"Ahh, so I have the pleasure of audience with the master of the demon lord Graz'zt? Then I can only be addressing Cerodagon. You are truly a scourge that will be driven out of this city."

"Kill them, she screamed." And the fourteen demons moved in from the circle they had been forming around the couple.

JC immediately felt the force of power being used behind him, and waved his hand as a wall of forced air seemed to leap out at the six moving from his right. The demons flew backwards hitting the pillars and the far wall, hard enough that three did not move nor attempt to rise from the floor. Another wave, this time by his left arm and the same happened to the four moving in there. Mythalla wrapped the remaining four in air hardened force fields quickly thrown around them one at a time. She began to squeeze mentally, as if trying to pop the demons.

"This is ridicules, Hell Spawn. I command you to leave! You are defeated here, and all will know your failure." The Queen's scream was one of pain, as JC's first attempt at the exorcism failed.

As he began to climb the stairs of the dais, he waved his arms once again, to send the lesser demons flying as they renewed their charge. This time he added fire to the spell and all ten he was facing burned in screaming agony.

"What in the name of The Creator"General Hanlon yelled out entering deeper into the room, at the screams.

"General, please help me, kill your queen's attacker!" The woman's voice yelled across the hall. The General did not move more than ten yards from the doorway. Holding his sword hilt hard, his hand turning white with the death grip he had on it.

The Queen waved her own hands and a wall of force slammed into JC, which he barely was able to withstand, as he slid back a few meters before stopping the slide. He sent a force of air, his own spell, back onto the queen. She jerked in the throne chair, as she felt the force field shield being slowly wrapped around her.

The demon in control of her was strong, JC realized. The power of the demon lord equaling many of the fallen angels in Hell. His shield was having a hard time to be laid in on the Queen, but finally it snapped into place and JC took the moment to look around the room.

Noticing the four demons that were being held by Mythalla, one seemingly about to suffocate, he sent out bolts of energy into them, pelting each one with two

228

or three until they all died in her hold. He turned to the servants cowering along the walls, and yelled out for them to run.

Those that could move, did, and JC finished climbing the dais, until he was face to face with the Queen.

"Now, snake of Hell, Cerodagon, I am commanding you to leave this woman. In the name of all that is heavenly, the name of the Mother Gia and Holy Selene, I command you to leave this woman, now." Her jerk and stiffness as she tilted her head upward her mouth attempting to scream but for the force covering her from talking.

"I will, if I have to, take this place apart, and destroy you all. Run back to your master, Cerodagon, and tell Forcas, that the next time he sends anyone, I will destroy him as well." The statement was a low whispered growl, and the eyes of the queen turned from blood shot to pure red.

The demon within was struggling with its anger, as JC continued to whisper insult after insult, until finally the queen spasmed and only his shield was holding her in the chair.

JC stepped back, slowly down the dais steps, until he was a few yards away. Still watching the spasms, he yelled out one more time.

"Cerodagon, with the power given me by the Holy Selene, and favored by Mother Gia, I command you to flee this woman's body. I command you to crawl back to the pits of Hell where you belong."

With a scream of agony, that pierced through JC's gag, the Queen finally succumbed to unconsciousness, appearing dead on the throne. A black smoke poured from her mouth as suddenly standing before the throne, was a sixteen-foot-tall creature, with bluish snake like scales a long tail, ending in a fork, and two baboon like heads. In the place of arms were tentacles long and whip like. The two heads both turned towards JC and the red glowing eyes imparted a force on his mind that he was only barely able to stop.

As the stun of the mind whip hit deep within him, JC's arms lowered as he was beginning to sway from the pain. Both arms whipped down on the man as he was lashing out with his own mind blast. JC barely noticed the psychic hit from behind that was only just shielded.

Probing quickly, he found the source, as he was thrown back from the whip like arms and as he rose from the floor, JC sent a sharp bolt of pain disrupting the spell that held him, just long enough for JC to break free and roll out of the way from the oncoming second attack by Cerodagon's tail.

The fork like tail scraped across the immortal's back and JC could feel the poison begin to take effect on contact. First the numbness then the paralysis began to take place.

He noticed across the room, Morella and three other priestesses all holding their heads as if just struck with headaches. The room was suddenly cast in darkness, from Mythalla's own spell, backfiring on the shields the other priestesses quickly erected, and she began to move in that direction, the soft yellow glow of her strength boosted aura visible to JC.

His back becoming paralyzed, JC began to attempt to roll to a kneeling position. The poison was acting quickly and he saw the tail once again striking down on him. He pushed out with a wall of force sending the demon flying backwards away until it landed some twenty yards away.

As he stood up, he concentrated on neutralizing the poison, and just cleared the sluggishness as the demon lord was charging back towards him.

Pulling his power infused Katana, given him by the Holy Selene, he turned to the strongest aura of evil in the room, and found the demon, moving towards him. Another mind blast bombarded JC, and he deflected it with some difficulty, but he managed to slice through the tentacled arm that flew towards him.

His sword cut through causing the demon to scream a cry of pain, as JC danced around the wildly swinging tail to cut through a leg. Not as strong as devils, this demon still required all of JC's considerable strength to cut a clean wound, as Cerodagon began to fall, missing the lower part of his left leg.

Cerodagon's tail and right tentacled arm came flying into JC, at the same time, and the priest found himself in a mental battle with both of the demon's heads. Concentrating on the auras in the room, JC did not even notice when the darkness was lifted, but his quick movements and shining blade of his favored Katana met the demon lord in a quick battle that was over in less than a few minutes.

The wounds on JC's back, legs and arms already seemingly beginning to fester in infection. The poison even affecting his great constitution, even with the paralysis gone. The body of the demon, began disintegrating to the now familiar odor of brimstone.

As JC turned towards the battle at the far end, he saw Mythalla holding off two of the sorceresses and attacking the other two with air and water spells.

She may only be able to cast one at a time, but with JC's spirit boosting her own power, her spells were effective against the weaker women. Morella was the only one in the group that could still come close to matching Mythalla, now, and even she was not nearly as quick.

JC wrapped the four in a force field and gagged them with air to stop them from being able to cast. He then moved across the room, as General Hanlon raced in the other direction to run to his Queen, still sitting in a force field of air on the throne. Still unconscious!

"That is enough, Mythalla. They are incapacitated." JC calmly stated.

When she turned, she noticed the puss filled wounds on him, and immediately made to heal. His head shake stopped her, as he told her it could wait.

"Morella, I charge thee, marked by Kutulu Lucifer, you have sold your soul to the devil. I will not allow you lead My mother's Temple, anymore. You are removed from the Council of Nine, effective immediately, and are charged with treason towards our queen, treason towards our country, and charged with atrocities against humanity.

"The only thing left for you, is to face judgment by the laws you have sworn to protect. The Queen will decide your fate!" He turned away from the fear filled eyes of the woman, as she seemed to age around those eyes slightly. Tears falling onto paralyzed cheeks.

He turned to the other three women, and closely examined them finding only black marks in their auras, but only one with any in the inner spectrum. The other two only had the knowledge that they knew they were committing evil.

"I have need of all the clergy of the order, but if you three do not forsake this devil's ways and swear fealty to me and Mother Selene, right now, I will send you to

Kutulu wrapped up as you are a present. What say you?" Their looks of horror as the words sank in, and the realization that what their leader had ordered them to do, and they had been following willingly, came to them. With a nod, JC adjusted the hold on them allowing them to speak, and they all agreed.

Releasing their holds, he told them to swear and they fell to their knees, before him, vowing before Selene and the Creator that they would follow JC's ways and forsake all other commands that have caused them to become the evil infected priestesses they have been. Accepting the oath, JC left them on the floor as he marched back to the throne dais.

"Let me see how she is, General. The ripping of a soul out of an others body cannot be good."

Examining the woman, JC found her physically unharmed, but her mind was comatose, he lowered the energy field holding the queen, and took her up in his arms.

Handing her over to Hanlon's outstretched arms, JC told the man to take her to her rooms,

"Cover her to keep her warm and place something under her feet to lift them slightly higher than her head. Have her watched and I will check on her in a little bit. I can do nothing now, until I see what else is in this place." He then turned and allowed Mythalla to heal him.

The wounds did not close, but the infection was gone, and he insured her that by morning the cuts would be gone, as well.

"Right now, we need to ensure the castle has no more demons in it. And with me being weakened by the healing, you will be doing most of the cleaning." His wink told her he was only half joking.

The three priestesses, still on their knees, Morella still standing in the holding spell, JC sighed and asked Mythalla to tell them about bowing like that. She shook her head in amazement at him, and moved quickly towards the women, as more guards followed into the hall.

"The former High Priestess Morella is to be incarcerated in a cell. She is charged with treason and awaits the Queen's judgment." The startled guards eyed the man, and then the woman being held, and after being told to do it one more time, two of them lifted the paralyzed woman and carried her from the room.

The other two guards, standing and listening to the instructions being given to three priestesses by a younger one, watched the affair, as JC moved towards them.

JC walked to the stairs leaving the hall. As he watched the women, a palace liveried man entered and announced that General Hanlon had requested Lord JC to come to the Queen's rooms. Nodding to Mythalla, to continue with what she was doing, he followed.

"Father d'Badger, I am afraid that I cannot allow you to leave until the Queen is better. Please, I know I cannot truly stop you, not after what I saw today, but I do ask you to honor my wishes. I am sure things will be taken care of once she awakens."

"Understandable, General. If you can, though, please have some guards go to the Boar's Inn and escort my other followers here. I would not want them to wonder why I have not returned. A dwarf named Massy is in charge. She is with a child, named Natylia!"

"Consider it done, Father. Princess Massy Thistle-thorn is well known to all of us here in the castle. I have also had a suite prepared for you and your people. Also, it would seem, that it will not be too long, as the Queen was sleeping even easier, last I checked, than when I first brought her here. You did what you said you would, I just hope that her mind is able to recover as you said. She is unharmed, physically and for that, I thank you!"

JC gave the General a soldier's shake, hands to the forearms, and then went inside to check on the Queen. She was being treated for shock, legs elevated by several pillows, with her head on one.

JC removed that one, and lowered the legs by two layers of pillows, and readjusted the blankets. He advised that he would check on her one more time before going to sleep and then first thing in the morning.

"Please have the servants and guards said that I will be coming in and out. I will also, have Mythalla, the young priestess I came with, stay with her for the night, in case there are any changes."

233

General Hanlon only nodded his head, and had a palace maid show JC to his rooms. Before heading into the suite, JC asked the maid to send for a palace guard. He then thanked her and turned to enter. Mythalla and the other three were there, in the sitting room.

"Are we free to go, Father?" Mythalla asked as he entered. "They brought us here saying we had to remain."

"I told Hanlon that I would stay until her majesty is up and around. I also told him that you'd stay with the Queen tonight. I hope you don't mind?" JC added.

She curtsied, and left for the Queen's rooms. JC, sat down with the three priestesses, Marina, Gulnara, and Evellina. He studied them all, each returning his look.

Marina was a tall woman, about his height, at five feet six and a half inches, early thirties in age, with dark blond hair, light brown eyes, and a light brown complexion. Her eyes were rounder than the average local, and she looked as though she may have a little of the Lemurian Continent blood in her.

Her aura showed only a passing strength in psychic abilities. She was plump in the hips and had very little curve to her waste. She was average looking at best, and the outer spectrum of her aura showed her to be the most filled with evil. But her inner spectrum was still untainted, so JC was sure she could be saved.

Gulnara was of average height and size, as well as being the oldest, nearly in her 40s. Only about five feet two inches tall, with light brown skin, dark brown hair and gray eyes. Her psychic spectrum showed above average strength, with a clean inner spectrum as well. Her outer spectrum was hardly tainted with evil, and she carried the most fear on her face, and indicated the most regret by her actions when JC laid his eyes on her.

Evellina, a striking woman of about early to mid-twenties, with dark blond hair and even darker blue eyes, a light walnut toned complexion. Her eyes were held tight at the edges, and she frowned when JC brought his eyes to her.

Her inner spectrum was slightly tainted, and the outer spectrum told him she had performed many atrocities in her young life. Her psychic ability was about average, the light blue almost transparent to look at. Mythalla, was easily stronger

234

than two of these women, and she was one of the weaker ones at the Temple in Bornesta that he had met.

But Gulnara was a strong woman. At least she was the least evil of the group.

Looking the longest at Evellina, JC finally sighed and spoke aloud,

"Tell me young lady, Two others were mentioned. Where is Nevah and Lenara? And, tell me why I should believe you will honor the oath you gave? You were Morella's apprentice, am I correct?" She started at the accusation and just as quickly regained her composer.

Her first reaction was enough for JC, though, to tell him he had guessed correct.

"You should believe because I am a High Priestess of Selene!" She answered. "And, because I am not Morella's apprentice, just one of her followers." She did not answer his first question.

"The Holy Selene, don't you mean, sister?" JC purposely called her by an apprentice title of sister instead of the title Mother, as any High Priestess would be given.

"Broth… Father, I assure you I will not go against my oath. You said that all we had to do was promise to follow you." The strain in her voice as she ended, was showing the fear that was quickly filling her. JC still had not taken his eyes off her, when the door knocked.

"Come!" He spoke aloud, still staring at the priestess.

"M'lord, you asked for a guard?"

"Yes, I did. Thank you for coming, sir. I would like you to form up in groups of three, and search every inch of this palace for anymore of the demons that might still be about. Check with General Hanlon, if you doubt my request. If one is spotted, then send one of the groups back here to me. Two can probably handle the monster, unless it is one of the kinds that cannot be hit by your weapons. Let's get this place back to order before the Queen wakes up. OK?"

"Yes, M'lord. Good suggestion. I will take your request to Gen. Hanlon, immediately, but I think he will order it done. You sure you want to be bothered with it, M'lord?"

"Sir, I assure you that you should all be quite done before I go to bed. Now get to it." JC's request came like more of an order, but he had gotten used to that this past year. And, as a teacher for most of his adult life, he was usually the one giving orders in the classrooms. Some thing's just never die out, he thought to himself, as he still stared through the woman in front of him. Finally, she broke the silence.

"Father JC, if you do not trust me, then send me away. I won't be mistrusted at every turn, even if you are who you claim to be."

"And, child, who have I am claimed to be?" He asked with his tone filled with malice.

"The Chosen One that will face Kutulu Lucifer in the final battle, of course."

"I never claimed to be that Chosen One, child. I am the prophet of Holy Selene that was promised to come. I am the Sword of Vengeance, and I am a Chosen. The Chosen one to face Kutulu is still to be named. Big difference! I am only one that might be the final savior!

"And, child, as far as trust goes, it is earned. You have lost trust, when you followed the path of Hell. Trust is hard to come by after it is lost. Especially in the way you lost it. I would say that you need to find a corner and meditate.

"Meditate hard and long. And, ask Holy Selene for forgiveness and to clean your aura. You are touched by Evil, and it is something I am almost willing to bet need's burned out of you."After a few seconds and the young woman had not moved, JC added more forcefully, "I said do it now, child. Get in there and pray, now!"

Evellina jumped to the command, but the glower never left her face, she did move to one of the rooms and did as he said, however. At least as far as he could tell. When he returned to the chair across from the remaining two, he turned to Marina.

She became increasingly uncomfortable, and shifted several times under his gaze, as well as continually looking down to avoid his eyes.

"Marina, you have not fully given yourself to the Lord of evil, yet!" He finished.

"Nor will I, my lord Father. I have no excuse, but I can give a cause if you will listen. Oh, and to answer your question, I am Lenara, Evellina is Nevah!" At his nod, she took a deep breath, tears flowing freely down her cheeks, she continued.

"I was seduced by power. I only have a moderate strength in sorcery, and Morella offered me the chance to rise in political power I would never have obtained. As I said, Father, I was weak in will, as well as in the sorcery, and I fell to follow the one that would gain me the most. I swear, Father, that I will work every day for the rest of my life, to earn my place in Holy Selene's heart again. Please, do not send me away. Please, Father, let me follow you.

"I do believe you are the one that was promised us. I do believe that through you I can gain forgiveness." She was on her knees, clutching JCs, as he sat watching her, a cold expression on his face.

Taking her hands and undoing them from his legs, he simply said.

"Did you not believe, Mother Mythalla, when she told you my first command. Do not grovel on a knee to me, ever! I am not a god. I am simply, what I am!" JC shifted his eyes to the last woman still sitting across from him, watching Marina, in her grovel.

"Well, Gulnara, what say you?"

Sighing, shaking her head, she simply spoke, as she slowly rose to her feet,

"Marina, pull yourself together. Haven't you realized Father JC is not impressed by weakness? Nor by those that enslave themselves?" Looking up to meet his eyes, she continued.

"High Father JC, I am sorry for what I did. I have no excuses, nor would I insult you by offering to give any. I knew what I did was wrong, but knew not how to stop. I was too far gone, before finally seeing wisdom, and I have continued to pray to the Goddess Holy Selene, every night for salvation.
"I believe, that today, it has finally come. Do with me as you will, Father. I gladly accept the penance as you see fit!" Her matter-of-fact statement was spoken with tear filled eyes, but she maintained her composure throughout the speech.

237

Watching her aura as she spoke, JC could detect no lie in it. Finally, he spoke after a long moment of watching the two women.

"OK, here is what we will do. I am thirsty, hungry, and I am tired. It would not be fair for me to issue any judgment with the state of mind that I am currently. You will join Evellina for a night of meditation and prayers. You will not come out of the room until morning, and by then I will have hopefully gained guidance by the Holy Mother.

"At the least, I will have a better frame of mind. I believe you are both to be saved, ladies. I want very much to be able to give you over to the Council of Nine as the High Priestesses that you are. But, hold no doubt in your hearts, right now! I am most displeased at the moment! Most displeased that any of the Selenian clergy could be turned to evil so easily."

The two women turned to leave, and as they got to the door, Gulnara turned back to look at the man taking a seat hard, still watching them.

"You are a very wise and charitable man, Father. I think that I will enjoy serving once again as an apprentice. As your apprentice!" She left for the room she was sharing with the other two.

JC finally rose to leave; he noticed two guards outside his suite's door. Smiling at them he began to move down the hall in the direction he had come from the Queen's quarters. One of the soldiers fell into step slightly behind.

When they reached the outer door to the royal sitting room, one of the guards on duty, opened the door with a single knock. JC walked through.

General Hanlon was sitting in a lounge and across from him was Mythalla, who stood on his entrance and gave a report as to the condition of Her Majesty. JC, ate some fruit while talking with her, and then spoke with the General.

"Any word on filth in the keep?"

"No, not as of yet. It shouldn't take long; I have everyone looking. I think that with the one you got rid of this morning, and the one yesterday afternoon, along with the hundreds more that you have taken care of, we are pretty well off. I will send guards out in the morning to scour the city.

Alyndra will be cleaned by night fall tomorrow. Thank you, Father for the good suggestion. I was too far in worry to think straight, it would seem."

JC bid them both a good night, and placing his hand on Mythalla's cheek, he winked at her, and asked that she come and get him if anything changes for the worse.

"Tomorrow, I will attempt to wake her from the coma. Try and get some sleep, child."

"Yes Father. Thank you for letting me stay here. I do not think I would wish to be near those other three, this evening." JC snickered as he left.

Massy and Natylia arrived to the suite, and JC advised the dwarf of what happened.

Massy was wearing her new outfit, a light brown hardened leather vest worn over a good pale colored cotton shirt. Her padded pantaloins were tucked into her boots, and she now appeared the warrioress as she led Natylia into the room, she would share with the girl.

JC, slept in the room between the fallen priestesses and his lady at arms, and raised a detection of evil shield around the whole suite, then he laid down to meditate.

CHAPTER 10
The arrival of the Chosen One!

When the forsaken Queen bows, he will return her
Nation to glory. Once again, they will stand proud.
Holy Selene's blessing will be Hell's release.

From the Order of Brigitte Prophesies

Purana walked the palace, looking for others. The cycle has fallen, and she needed to have a clear head before meeting with the other Chosen, tomorrow. Her blood was boiling, and she could not believe that it had been a month since last she was forced to endure bedding one of these lesser creatures. She had thought about searching for Odyseus, but Isis had come to her and forbidden it.

"My daughter, if you would only open your heart, you might see there are those near to quell your urges. My mistake was in forgetting the strange biological habits of those from Haven." Isis had commented. The Goddess smiled, and shaking her head, looked down on the young woman with an almost dissatisfaction to her expression. Of course, Purana mistook it for being upset with herself for not knowing Haven's biology. Purana would never have thought that the dissatisfaction could be directed towards her.

"Purana, you will stay away from the others, until you have need of them for use with the Hell Spawn. Only on the scheduled meetings will you visit your companions."

"They are hardly companions, Holy Goddess. They are, but fodder to be used as distractions while I take care of the master!" Purana confidently answered.

"We shall see, daughter. You have a lot to learn!" Isis said before disappearing.

Now, Purana was forced to use one of the priests. She had thought about copulating with Doreen, but he was just a commoner, and she could not bring herself to be that desperate. She did wonder why Torel had disappeared.

"You would have thought, after last month, the man would be overjoyed to be picked. He is less than adequate, but at least the urges were taken care of!" Purana told herself.

Torel woke that morning and quickly left the palace. Remembering what she had told him, he looked forward to this time of the month, until last month, that is. After the beating and injuries, she had given him, it took nearly three days to recover, he was not going to go through that again! Let one of the younger priests sate her urges. Not only was the woman without any love or other kind of decent emotion, she was an animal in bed.

Between her biting and her spells of longevity, his fifty-seven-year-old body could not handle another bout. Purana was not what he would have thought, Holy Isis would send to them.

"She is a woman of evil, and how can I use her, when she would just as soon kill us all, as look at us? Isis, what have you sent to me?" He mumbled. Disappearing to Silver dust Grove, the gnomes all laughed at him, when he explained his dilemma to Larg Silverdust, the Gnomish Chief.

****

Dreams are often times destructive at best. JCs are little more than a war zone. This time he watched as a beautiful woman was running from Lucifer, JC unable to catch up as he ran harder and harder. Just as he rounded a corner on some building, all current one hundred ninety-eight of the Order of Brigitte Priestesses were there standing linked and shielded against him.

Dyanea, the woman that had been running from Lucifer was now in the Ancient One's arms smiling as she pointed her finger at the Immortal. JC sat up in a sweat just as his dream body exploded, his waking head pounding with a sharp pain that had awakened him. He could see the shadow moving towards his bed, in the darkness, and knew that was what had set the alarm off, passing through his protection shield.

Too small to be Hell Spawn, he concentrated on a light directly in front of the creature still moving in the darkness. The brightness momentarily blinding him as well, the female was caught off guard with the light suddenly in her eyes as she dove for the corner.

241

With a roll, JC cleared the bed and moved towards Morella, she was holding a dagger. He reached out catching her dagger hand, while attempting to hold her in a new force field. She had a shield protecting her this time, and JC did not want to waste time with a psychic struggle.

Morella sent out a psychic blast that would have staggered him, had JC not been ready for it, instead it slid off his own protective shields and she screamed as she attempted to free her hand.

She clawed out with her free hand, and caught JC under his eye, barely missing the socket. Still struggling with the woman as she sent mental blasts at him, one after the other, sometimes two at a time, all the while kicking, hitting, and biting the man. All he could do was hold on to the wrist that was holding the knife while trying to grab the other.

She screamed as her wrist snapped; JC was squeezing so hard. Morella suddenly went limp, and JC still holding the wrist, saw Massy standing in just her shift holding her hammer at her side.

"You slay demons with but a thought, yet, you can't even handle one small woman?" Massy calmly stated, without any embarrassment for her state of undress, nor his.

"What can I say? I have a hard time hitting a woman. It's how I was raised." He shrugged, as he took the knife from the woman's right hand. The large knife, small dagger in reality, was probably one of the guards.

"I'll bet this little demon has left a trail of dead from the dungeons. I thought my hold on her would last at least until morning. Won't make that mistake again."

JC looked up, to see three of the four other women, in this suite, all standing just inside his room. They looked at Morella, as JC placed another energy field around the former High Priestess.

"Where is Evellina?" JC said as Natylia came to stand next to him, watching the energy used in forming the holding spell.

She wanted to ask a question, he could tell, but wisely held her tongue, at the moment. JC thought he saw something strange happen with the girl's aura, but it was so quick, and he had other things to worry about.

Gulnara shrugged her shoulders, answering uncertainly.

"I had drifted off to sleep, Father JC, I am sorry. When I awoke, she was gone!" Gulnara looked up over at Marina who also admitted to have fallen asleep. Both women sounded surprised that they were unable to meditate any longer than they had.

JC only nodded, and spoke in a whisper,

"I should learn that not every woman can be saved." Gulnara's firm head shake, mirrored by Massy, was all the answer he got.

"All right everyone, go back to sleep. My lady at arms managed to pull my fat out of the fire, this time." With a smile, he advised Massy that he would take care of the woman, after she offered to take the "garbage out," using his own phrase. Putting on a robe, then throwing Morella over his shoulder he moved to leave the suite.

Natylia caught up with him at the door touching his free arm on the hand.

"Father, may I ask what is used for that spell?" The girl spoke and when Massy called out to wait till morning, JC smiled and offered to show her.

Wrapping the girl in a light energy field, one that would be easy enough to break out of, he smiled and told the girl to study the hold, and learn how to shut it off. If she could figure how to do that, she would know everything about how to make one that could not be removed.

"I will be back in a little while to check on your progress." JC told her. The frustrated look, she gave him, changed to concentration and JC turned to Massy,

"Place Natylia in her bed while she is working on the lesson. I'll be back shortly. Thank you, M'lady! I guess it is I that should be serving you!" He added, as he left the room.

Most of the guards were not dead, he had pleasantly found, on his way to the dungeons. The two at his door were merely asleep, and easily awakened. JC ordered one to stand inside the sitting room, that another woman was loose somewhere, and had the other Guard follow him.

243

Still carrying Morella, he found six other palace personnel, four of them dead, and two easily awakened. Morella had used mind blasts, and the reaction to the pain can be anything from unconsciousness to death, depending on the mental strength of the victim.

The weaker the person's psychic strength, the less damage done to the brain. JC did not tell the people he was waking up, that last part. He finally arrived at the dungeons to find both guards there, quite dead. One with a dagger sticking out of his head, the other a victim of suffocation. Shaking his head, he turned to the guard, tailing him.

"Not only a traitor to the crown, but now a murderess, as well."

He roughly laid the women in the cell, and placed an anti-magic shell around the small cubicle. The iron bars glowed a deep red as if being heated, then took on a crystalline like appearance to them, as the spell took effect. JC closed the door and locked it with an equally crystalline looking lock.

"She won't be able to escape that, if or when she wakes up. I don't know what you do to murderers, and I don't want to know. If she does not make it to trial, I will only be mildly put off by it." He left the dungeons, walking purposefully back towards the apartments, heading to the Queen's quarters on the far side of the castle. He was relieved to find the guards alert, and General Hanlon asleep in the lounge he had been in earlier. Mythalla was reading a book she had found on the shelf, something called *Impossibilities of the Prophesies*. She was not at all happy by the words she had been looking at.

Advising her that Evellina d'Nevah had escaped, he checked on the Queen, and then advised the guards at the door. They both knew who Mother Nevah was, and would certainly alert the sorceress inside, if she was seen. JC returned to his rooms.

Natylia, appeared to be still working on the hold, and when she advised the father with a smile to not touch his spell, he grinned and went into the sitting room to lounge in one of the divans. This time, the protection shield he put around the whole suite would alert everyone of anything entering the suite. He was awakened by the sun, as it entered the room, early the next day.

Morning found JC outside in the court yard, exercising at some kind of a dance. At least, that is what the guards thought it was as they watched him perform. Sometimes with Katana sometimes with staff, most of the time without any weapons, the guards just thought it a peculiar dance to limber the priest's muscles.

"Pretty," Massy said as she came walking up. "Very nice for a ball room, but I don't see much use in a battle. Care to trade blades with me?" She said, tossing him a practice sword.

"You'd be surprised at the effectiveness using my dance in a duel." he shrugged at her smile.

The two traded blows slowly for a few minutes and began heating up. After about fifteen minutes of practice, Massy stepped back and spat.

"Never have liked the blade very much. Hammer is a real weapon, never have to worry about it breaking."

Taking up a staff, JC severed it in half, using sorcery, and, offered to allow Massy to use her hammer. The two went at it. With a clear advantage going to the staff, as Massy barely avoided being clobbered in the head, when she looked up after a few minutes with an angry scowl to her face.

"You holding back on me, Father?" She asked. "I know you are a whole lot faster than this. If you think just because I'm a woman I cannot handle you?"

Chuckling with a slight embarrassment, JC admitted holding in some, but not because she was a woman.

"Massy, I would be holding back on anyone that was not of immortal or demonic blood. I would feel a fool if I hurt someone unintentionally. And, besides, I would not want to harm such a beautiful lady!"

"You think a beautiful lady would not gut you? Thoughts like that are gonna get you killed, one of these days. Almost did just last night!" With a quick toss of her hammer, it struck JC fully in the chest, knocking him off balance. Followed by another quick motion, he found himself looking down at the dwarf, holding the dagger he had given her, at his groin.

"Gonna get you killed, for sure, my lord! Women are even more dangerous than men. We cheat!"

Picking up her hammer, JC handed it to the dwarf as she re-sheathed the dagger. They worked a little more, as Massy pushed him harder and harder. Working almost at his non-sorcery potential, Massy stepped back when his shortened staff snapped on her hand and the hammer flew to the ground.

"That, Father JC, is much better. You are showing a little more regard to proper training. We'll have to do this every day, till I can break you of your little bad habits."

JC chuckled, and put an arm around the short woman.

"Massy if I were a hundred years older, you would have to worry about me, making a pass at you. Hehe, it will be an honor to work with you whenever we can find the time."

"You think I'd want a shriveled up old man, do you?" She returned his joke.

One of the guards looking on, Sergeant of the Guards Marcus d'Wind, cleared his throat and stepped forward. Thumbing the hilt of his long sword, he eyed the priest and dwarf, before finally speaking his mind.

"Lord JC, if you would want to work with a real warrior, I am sure I can give you a better workout than the woman. Especially a Dwarven woman!" Standing a little over six feet, he was tall for an Selenian.

His frame, supported by hard muscles that were being flexed as he gripped his hilt. Massy, was eyeing the twentyish young man, not showing any emotion on her face. At two hundred thirty-four years of age, she had heard too many human insults in her life, to allow another one to really bother her.

JC, on the other hand, was not going to let it pass so lightly. He stepped towards the guard, stopping only a little more than a yard away and crossed his arms. Looking over at the two other men, each in their late teens or early twenties, they carried the same facial expressions as their leader, Marcus.

"What's your name, sergeant?" JC quietly asked.

"Marcus d'Wind, Sir. Me and my friends think your dancing was nice, but fighting against a dwarf with a hammer, is not going to win you any battles against real soldiers!" His tone took an arrogance, the self-doubt he had a moment before, gone.

"I'll tell you what, young man! I'll take an army of dwarves, any day, if they all fight like her." JC walked over to Massy, pulling his shirt off, he handed it to the female, and then turned. Pulling one of the last two diamonds from his pouch, he held it up.

"I will practice with all three of you at once. If just one of you can touch me, before I count you all out, I will let you have this gem. If you all are tapped out, or quit, before you can hit me, then you will apologize to the lady, knowing that she alone, has done today what I don't think the three of you together will manage." Raising his eye brows, he looked at the soldiers, and picked up the practice sword, from the rack, where a servant had put it away.

"JC, you are a fool." Massy started, "There is something called luck, and you can get hurt over a stupid insult that I was not worried about." Massy sternly told him. "It's not worth the trouble, Father!"

Smiling, he looked up and waved the wooden sword back and forth waiting for an answer from the soldiers. He whispered.

"Now, I will show you what my dancing was really all about, M'lady!"

"I think that we will accept, My Lord Priest." Marcus said after talking to his partners.

They began removing their steel chest plates, and under padding and chains. Selecting wooden practice swords for themselves, they moved to surround their opponent.

"Sergeant, I think you should just apologize now, and save yourself a lot of pain." A booming deep voice announced from behind. The soldiers immediately moved to attention as the General came walking up.

"I heard that bet you just made, and the father is playing you for a fool, boy. You don't stand a chance, unless you really do want to be humiliated."

247

"Three at once, General. We only have to touch him. He's not that good. We were watching him for the last hour practicing. He's a priest, we are trained soldiers in your guard. He's tired, we are fresh." The man was coming up with excuses and General Hanlon finally raised his hand.

"Marcus, you don't need to give me excuses. Boy, if you think you can take him, it's your funeral." Stepping over to Massy, the General legged a bow,

"M'lady! Hope you were not too offended, by the stupidity of youth."

"General, the kids will learn. I just hope the father does not slip on those tired legs of his." Her words were dry, and loud enough to be heard from all, and Hanlon was not sure she was joking or not.

Dwarven humor was like that sometimes, he had to tell himself.

Eyeing the soldiers, JC told himself the sergeant was the more superior of swordsmen. The others seemed to be the most eager, as well.

Marcus feigned a step forward and quickly stepped back. The other two charged in from the side. JC, ducked one overhead swing and side-stepped the jab from the other.

Bringing his sword down atop the two hard and fast, his own practice sword snapped about ten inches down the blade end. The guard's sword on the right was shattered.

Tripping the man with a leg sweep, JC lowered his jagged edged stick to the man's chest and tapped him out, with a small scratch of the wood's newly sharp edge.

The second guard used the momentary stop in the action to attack, as Marcus led in with a jab of his own. Ducking under the sweeping swing, JC grabbed the man's wrist taking the sword from his hand, and turning the man into the attack of Marcus' jab. As the man went down in pain to the jab in the groin, JC tapped him on the back of the head, indicating he was out, using the man's own lost sword. Spinning to an erect position, JC faced Marcus and smiled.

Marcus had backed off out of range, as soon as he had felled his own partner, and now looked uncertainly at the father a few yards away from him.

248

"How much longer, Father?" General Hanlon asked. "The Queen is requesting your presence."

"She's awake, then?" JC looked over asking in surprise. Marcus used the apparent lack of attention to choose the moment to attack.

His sword lowered; JC barely raised it in time to knock the attack away. Dropping into a leg sweep, JC connected behind Marcus' knee and the younger man went flying onto his back.

"Give me one minute, General, and then we can go. I have one more lesson for the day, to point out." JC said, as he moved back away from the sergeant, allowing Marcus to roll up off the ground and retrieve his thrown wooden sword.

JC buried the tip of his own sword into the ground beside him and indicated the sergeant should attack him unarmed as he was.

As Marcus moved in, JC feigned with his right leg another sweep, the sergeant snapped his blade down where he thought the leg would be, and found JC's left leg, just above the foot, connecting to the side of the sergeant's head.

The Sergeant dropped down dizzily, and quickly found his own sword being held point end to his throat. JC standing over him, smiling, the High Priest nodded and held out a hand to help the young man up. The whole battle taking less than 2 minutes.

While JC moved to the water basin and toweled himself off, Marcus moved to face Massy, and dropped to a knee, taking her left hand in his right, he placed it against his forehead.

"M'lady, I do apologize with all my heart and honor. I have wronged you, and wronged your Lord. Please accept my sorrow for any emotional pain I might have caused, and know that from this day forward, your honor is mine!" Marcus stood, looking her in the eye as he rose and then turned to face JC, who was pulling his shirt on. He looked at the General and then back to Massy.

"What he did to us, and that you at least could stand up to him, I wonder why your people aren't the ruling race of Zindar."

"Sergeant, I accept your apology, but I may someday hold you to your oath for my honor. Remember who you gave it to!" Massy said, looking up into Marcus' face. "And we do rule exactly what we wish to rule, son."

The other two guards, Guardsman Borre d'Boren, and Guardsman Lionel d'Wind, Marcus' younger brother, offer their apologies as well, though, with less sincerity than Marcus. Massy accepts and grabbing JC's belt and Katana, follows after the father and General Hanlon. Sergeant Marcus d'Wind falling into step with her as he watches the backs of the two men in front.

"He really is unorthodox, in his fighting, but I have never seen anyone do what he just did. Maybe his dancing does have a purpose?"

"Son," Massy starts. "I don't think the world has seen the likes of him, before. He is the man of prophesy, young man. Remember, that! He is to be our savior. If we can keep him alive long enough!" She added.

The Queen, was sitting up in her bed, blankets pulled up to just under her shoulders, but her hair noticeably combed and some bits of powder added to her face. She was fussing over Mythalla trying to force food down her, when the maid announced General Hanlon and The Father JC d'Badger.

"Gentleman, come on in, please! Save me from this retched child trying to fatten me up as if for feast day!" Alyndria d'Dragoran is a pretty woman, with striking brown eyes, now that the demon's presence was not within her. Her smile radiated her face, and the wariness of the past few months seemed gone over night. She showed a strength of will, and a small amount of humor in her face as the men entered. Bowing General d'Boar walked over to the bed and kissed his queen's ring on the middle finger of her right hand. JC moved to her left side and legged a bow, never fully lowering his head. He stood erect once again, placing a hand on Mythalla's shoulder.

"She is just following my orders for your care, your majesty!" JC calmly spoke, with a light squeeze on Mythalla's shoulder.

"Ah, so it is you I should blame for trying at making me fat?" She lightly laughed.

JC's smile and nod, only made her more gleeful, and she looked up at the General, still holding her hand.

"Hanlon, my dear, I think the good Father should be flogged for making your queen look so unsightly before the holidays." She said with a wink.

"Only if you hold the whip, my queen!"

JC intoned, with a little spark of joviality himself.

Mythalla, held out the bowl and spoon, filled with fruit and porridge, and insisted,

"Please, your majesty, just a few more bites. You will need your strength back." she smiled, "If you are going to whip the High Father, after all!" She added after a pause.

Laughing aloud, the Queen leaned down and took a bite, squinting her face as she finally swallowed the cereal.

"Not the usual stuffy crowd from the Temple, are they, General?" She announced as she watched JC intently. "You could have at the least added some honey to the globe."

JC watched her auras seeing the inner and outer spectrums clean of any residue of the demon, and now he could see the light blue, transparent middle spectrum, indicating the queen's potential for some slight sorcery.

"You are a sorceress, your majesty? Or at least you have the potential with training!" He asked.

"So, I have been told, good priest. Alas, I have a country to run, not a god or goddess to appease. But I can see in you something that does not belong.

"You, young man, are not as young as you would appear. You look in the face, at least to be about early to mid-thirties, the body of a mid-twenties man at his peak. Why do you have the aura of someone much older? Much much older indeed! Several centuries, at least!"

"So, your talent lays in reading behind the aura, your majesty? Just what exactly does mine say to you?"

"Oh, I would say your spirit is hundreds of years old, if not thousands. You are in your thirty first or second body or incarnation if you will, and that in this life, you have met with both great joy and great sorrow. I also, young man, see in you the ability to love, but you have forsaken the love of a woman for some sorrowful event! You want me to go on?" She said when she saw JC stiffen, as well as the looks that Mythalla turned on him.

JC forced himself to relax, and then sighed.

"You see much, my queen! You indeed see much. Perhaps we can be friends during this little seven-year problem we are about to pursue!" he smiled before sighing his next response. "My incarnations and age, well, I do know I am two thousand years old, and this is my thirty first life. But, alas, that is about all I do know. It is being hidden from me by my mother, for now! I am forty-nine years in this life and indeed have forsaken a woman's touch. For the reason you gave. If you wish to continue, I cannot stop you. Fear not for my apprentice, for I really do not fear my past. Some things just do not really matter anymore, for me nor that of my past."

The queen nodded and smiled.

"Yes, you do not fear much, do you, High Father? You fear most for those you consider to be your family.

They spoke on into the morning. The four people becoming increasingly comfortable with each other. When lunch was served, Queen Alyndria ate hers on her own and finished off every bite.

The others watched her, and after a delving, Mythalla announced that the Queen was physically perfect, and as far as her mental state, she seemed fine, there as well!

JC and Mythalla left the Queen and General alone, returning to their suite, after lunch was completed.

"Have you really, Father?" She asked as they moved down the hall.

JC looked down at her, and nodded.

"You mean what the Queen said about me, yes, child, she was correct in all she said!"

252

"But, then what about......" She stopped as she was about to say someone's name. Wisely, she caught herself.

"I love whom I love, child. What do I need with a woman's touch as long as I have a full heart?"

"Father, I would think that any man, or woman, for that matter. I mean," she stumbled over the unsaid sentence, and when she did not finish it, JC chuckled.

"Mythalla, I am about to enter into a war that a lot of the world may not survive. I may not survive! You all think I am the One to end this, but I still believe it to be one of the others. You will meet them when I go to see them in just a couple weeks. I'll let you figure out if I am still the one you think I am."

Spending the rest of the week at the palace of the Queen, JC and Alyndria quickly became friends. He had explained to her that he would not kneel to her, but easily could swear fealty.

"I only bow to the gods, my queen. But, as far as promising you my friendship and my loyalty, I can guarantee you that."

"You will do so in the public's eye?" she meant it as a question, but it came out as a command.

JC smiled and taking an at attention stance, crossed his arm across his chest.

"As a priest out of the Bornesta Temple, my taxes belong to the Queen. My sword, however, belongs to the world, and I will live or die at Gia's bidding." he advised.

They argued often, when they got into their philosophical discussions, and usually the room that they were in would clear of all the palace's people. Alyndria had a reputation for a temper, and the father usually goaded her every chance he could get.

They would end up laughing at each other, and in the end, neither really cared who won the arguments. The Queen was still the queen after all, and even the father, in public, would admit to the Queen's wisdom, and give in. But, in private, that was another matter. By the end of that week, it was obvious to anyone that the two were friends, and that the father was more relaxed when around her majesty. Even Hanlon was becoming fond of JC.

Not sure how to handle his humor, it seemed too sarcastic, but he never openly admitted to not understanding a joke.

The Queen was also, becoming very fond of the young priestess that showed no fear, when the father was around. She found it quite amusing to watch the young apprentice, and her devotion for the man. Alyndria wondered what kind of woman it would take to make the man give up his vow against women, though. She would have to work on that. She told herself!

"No man should be without love. Besides, Massy, how are we ever going to get him to survive until the end, if he doesn't have a lady to live for? Humans are like that, you know? Especially the men, such simple creatures!" The dwarf would smile at Alyndria, and shrug.

"He loves, Alyndria. He loves deeply, just not whom you think. I will be most interested to see these other Chosen, next weeks. Then I will have a better answer for you!"

"I will be most interested in meeting these other Chosen. Maybe I can get the meetings moved here. How can he go to Pan and still be back within a couple days? Ships can't even sail that close to Pan!"

"He is taking a few of us, he said. I will find that out for you, as well." Massy chuckled. "Be advised, though, before you go trying to play match maker. Your cousin, Alyndria, has a very strong hold on his thoughts, according to what I have heard and what Mythalla has said."

The Queen once again advised JC on the morning of the trial, that if he was to be a Paladin then he needed to be knighted. He countered with the fact that he was a war priest did not make him a Holy Knight.

"That is Mythalla's idea from some story she read. I am not a knight, my queen."

"You, my Lord are going to accept a knighthood if I have to force feed it to you. Much as you made your apprentice do to me, do you understand?" she sternly countered.

254

"My Queen, please. I do not need to be tied down to honor you. I do not need to be given some reward for something that I was placed on this world to do. I was given life for one purpose, and will die bringing it to fruition."

He did ask her to give her support for him, in the upcoming war, with the other monarchs, though.

Alyndria wondered what kind of woman it would take to make the man give up his vow against women, though. She would have to work on that. She told herself!

"Too bad that Massy is a dwarf. He seems very fond of the Princess and she of him. She is also, the only person not afraid of him." she counseled with Hanlon one morning.

"The soon to be queen of the dwarves is also very content being his sounding board, Alyndria. She gives him counsel often and is usually with him when he goes to your library."

On the third day of the second week after Alyndria's exorcism, the trial of Morella was held and she was sentenced to beheading. JC had tried to talk Alyndria out of it, but to no avail. Treason to her person was enough, and the death of the guards, that she had caused, put the decision over the edge.

"If she were a man, Father JC, would you be so adamant about her not being put to the head block?" The Queen asked. When he said no, he would not, Alyndria responded,

"If she would have been a man, I will bet you, she would not have even made it to a trial." Massy added.

By that evening, the entire Council of eight remaining had arrived as well as, over one hundred priests and priestesses of Selene. They all tried to speak with the Queen, but Alyndria would not speak without the father present and none were comfortable with him present. None that is, excepting for C'renan and Dyanea.

C'renan, a two hundred plus year old elf, was the new council head. And, she was one of only three that agreed with Father JC of the need to bring more men into the church. Of course, the fact that her human husband was a sorcerer as well as a minor priest of Selene, might have had something to do with that line of thinking.

Yet, even she could not like seeing one of the priestesses beheaded in public. And she tried to talk the Queen into making it more a private affair.

"Father JC, certainly you would not want this to be so public?" Dyanea added to C'renan's plea.

Shaking his head, JC was not given the chance to respond.

"Father JC has already begged for clemency, Reverend Mother C'renan. He seems quite put out that I want this woman removed from Zindar, at all. It was not his body, though, that was made available for becoming a vassal to the demon lord.

"It was my person that was violated, and it is my decision. Now, ladies, I am sure you want to talk to the father alone, so if you will excuse me, you are all dismissed." Alyndria wondered at the looks JC kept giving to the one priestess.

As well as, the looks she gave him when she thought no one was looking. Maybe, this could work. Mythalla had said something about Council member Dyanea. And, Massy thought her cousin was the one JC was interested in.

"The looks given by the priestess; she certainly had a school girl's crush on the man." Hehe, Alyndria silently laughed as they exited the room.

"I will get you a wife, yet, my soon to be Lord d'Badger. I will have you cemented to me, before you know it. I need you, and you will make the prophesies my own deliverance. And, Hanlon, if it is Dyanea that he cares for?" she left the question unfinished.

"Is she not your grandfather's illegitimate sister, Alyndria?" Hanlon asked, quietly when they were alone.

"She is the niece of my grandfather. Her mother was the illegitimate sister." Her smiling nod, told him the rumors of the palace were true. He understood, where his Queen was heading.

They all left, JC with the two most powerful priestesses walking beside him. One each side, they both took an arm.

"Father, you will need to come back with us to the Temple." C'renan said lowly enough that only the three of them could hear.

When his eye brows raised, she held up a hand to his lips, an effort at forestalling any comment, and they ducked into the first room that was unoccupied. Both women rounded on the priest.

"This is not to hold you to us, like you think." Dyanea quickly said.

The feelings in JC were there again, with her so close, and her eyes boring into him. And, he thought he could see in her eyes the same uncomfortable emotions rising.

"Well, maybe it is to tie you to us, but not the way you think we want."

"We want to get you nominated to the Council of Nine before anyone else thinks to stop us." C'renan announced. "You are the most important man in the world. At least you are to our Temple! Also, you are as powerful a sorcerer, as any to come along, you are easily the best among us, maybe even in the world. And, you are old enough for your words to carry a lot of authority." She added.

Stunned and a little dazed, JC eyed both females.

"If I come and allow myself to be tied to the Council, then you will support my bid to unite the kingdoms for the upcoming war?"

They both nodded without delay. C'renan adding,

"Father, that you are the Sword of Vengeance, we accept and those fools that have decided to ignore the minor things in the prophesies can be ignored." After a moment, she smiled, her head turning towards Dyanea, before looking JC back in the eye.

"I think that the words you used to your woman at arms, was..." C'renan lowered her voice in a poor imitation to JC, *"There are those in the clergy that already follow my cause, and I will leave it up to them to bring the others around. I do not have time to debate with those that refuse to look at the portents!* Those where your words were they not?"

JC looked at the two, before taking a hand from each, in his. He knew the prophesies of all the known religions, except one. He knew that he would be united with the Order of Brigitte council and uniting it with the other two factions of the Selenian religion. According to the "Nature's Blessing", Gia's prophesy, *"The Badger shall unite the church under one flag and bring the northern continent to its glory."* JC wondered how that would be accomplished, but now, he could see the way. Nodding, he took a hand from each of the two Reverend Mothers.

"This day," he started as he formed a blessing and a prayer spell around them, "is the day that I unite with the followers of Brigitte, with the entire church of Selene, as hinted at by the prophesies of Gia, and told to me, by my Mother Selene and Father Jeasuas.

"I call on her to witness, as I give my word to you both, as a High Priest of the Holy Mother Selene, and a Chosen of the Ancient Ones, a child under the heavens of Mother Gia, that I will support the Temple and lead into the battle that is to come.

"I also, swear this day, C'renan and Dyanea, that my love and support extend to those that follow my mother's word, especially, I give my support and backing to you two. May Holy Selene bless this union of three, and help guide us in her will." JC then kissed both their hands, resting his lips just a moment longer on Dyanea's, before looking back up.

C'renan was the first to respond, as she took Dyanea's free hand in hers, the three stood in a circle, and the high priestess added her own spells of prayer and blessing to the circle.

"This day, I give my word, JC d'Badger, to both of you, Dyanea, as High Priestess to the Holy Selene, and High Council member and leader of the Order of Brigitte, calling upon the witness of the Holy Goddess, herself, that I will accept your support and your guidance, and that I will do all in my power to ensure that you arrive at the appointed battle to gain us the victory over those that would destroy us.

"I also, swear, that my love and support extend to those that would lead in her word, I give to you JC d'Badger, and you Dyanea d'Lyon.

"May Holy Selene bless this union of three, and guide us to her will." C'renan followed the father's example kissing each of the other two's hands.

Dyanea was watching the other two, taken in by a ceremony never before performed, and cast forth her own spells of blessing and prayer. With a deep breath, she squeezed JC's hand and began, never loosening the grip as if he would pull away,

"This day, I give my word to you both, James Carl Tigara, now known as JC d'Badger and C'renan ip Breylan that I will give all my support to you and to you, and to the circle of three that we now form.

"May the Holy Selene witness, guide, and bless this union, to her will are we bound. I give freely my love to you both, and seek the day that we stand together against the forces of evil, as they will come."

She kissed C'renan's hand and then moved JC's hand to her lips, hesitating slightly as her eyes found his. When she kissed his hand, JC thought he felt a shiver on her lips, and knew for certain that something had passed between them.

As the spells began to fade from them, a sudden soft blue glow enveloped the entire room, and a loving calm came upon the group. The room was filled with peace and love, and standing behind JC, was a tall female, exactly matching the description that he had given to Essmelda and those others, that first time he was in the Temple. Without turning, JC knew who it was that stood behind him.

"Consider this union blessed, my children, and also think wisely on what you have just done. Whenever the three of you are together, no man nor woman will be able to deny your will, nor your suggestions. Never let this power go to evil, nor allow it to be abused."

She rested her hands on JC's shoulders, and the two high priestesses dropped to their knees in awe. JC, turned to face his patron, and nodding his head in a bow, he calmly took hold of Selene's hands and kissed them both.

"Thank you, mother. I had hoped you would hear us and come." His voice was steady, after having spent a year with all the Ancient Ones. He looked up at Selene deeply in her eyes, and she bent to kiss his forehead.

"You are doing fine, my son. I am always with you, should you need me. Remember this, child, you do not need to rush things. I have been watching you and your sister for two thousand years. Let things happen as they will. Just remember the teachings. Not everything is as it seems." After a moment's pause, she continued forcing her mind deep within his, as JC's dream came to the forefront of his thoughts. "My child, you do not need to fear falling in love again. Your past is your past, walk into the future, my son. Your choice is a good one, and it is not entirely of my doing, as you suspect!" she paused and with a smile, adds;

"And, James Carl? Just what do you mean my hips are more rounded like that of a mother?" Her tone on the last was somewhat sarcastic, and, JC only smiled. The snickers coming from the two priestesses only adding to his embarrassment.

"I love you too, Mother!" He answered.

When Selene had finished, she hugged the man, blessing her two highest priestesses, and disappeared. The two women were still on their knees, now, bowing to JC, they knew he must be a god to be so blessed by the Mother Goddess, Selene.

"Get up, ladies. Never bow to me. After today, you are my equals if not my better. Never bow to anyone that walks the earth of Zindar. And, besides, the Holy Selene would not like you to throw your worship my way instead of hers."

C'renan looked to Dyanea, as the two rose to their feet, each taking a hand offered by JC. She spoke wryly as they rose.

"Well, Reverend Mother, I would say that if there were any doubts, all have been dispelled. He is who we thought he was! He is the Sword of Vengeance!" Then she looked at the way that Dyanea was looking at JC, and added.

"Perhaps you two wishes to be alone? JC, the voting for the new council member will be in four weeks, you are so ordered to be there with all priestesses, priests, and apprentices in your gathering. I will issue the summons to all the Selenian Temples, immediately." She left the room, once again kissing JC's hand before giving him a hug. Turning, she left stopping at the door to see the other two standing alone, still holding hands only staring into each other's eyes.

"Well," JC started before clearing his throat, "I guess you have a lot to do and we can talk at another time. If you like?" He added a little too hastily.

"Now, is as good a time as any, if you have something you wanted to say?" Dyanea responded a little too curtly.

Taking a deep breath, JC fell into a chair motioning the priestess towards another. When she moved to take it, he stood up hastily, then only sitting after she had sat.

"Forgive my manners, it would seem they leave me whenever you are near me."

260

JC accepted her nod, and noticed that her troubled face eased some, but not entirely.

"I told you once, that it had been too long since I had been able to speak of private matters with a woman that I had an interest in." He started.

"When we were bathing together, yes, I remember!" She interrupted him; then added, "Are you saying that you have an interest in me, my Lord?"

Holding his eyes with hers, he noticed for the first time the true violet in them, had an almost blue tint, and the beautiful way they were slightly tilted like that of an elf. He also noted the slight way her ears were almost pointed at the top, instead of the more rounded human. JC began anew, after once again clearing his throat.

"You are a very beautiful woman, Dyanea, and I had thought that Holy Selene had placed some sort of spell on me to attract you, I was wrong, according to my mother's last comment. It would seem that the feelings I am having after only a brief time of talking with you, are of my own making!"

"So, you think that it would have had to be a spell cast on you to be liked by a woman that is not entirely human?" She stated a little anger hinting at her tone, "Or perhaps you thought that I had cast a spell on you to make me act like a teenage girl with her first crush?"

Leaning forward on the edge of the chair he was sitting in, JC reached across with his hand that Dyanea only hesitated a moment before taking.

"Dyanea, I do not know the customs of this world on these matters. I do not know if it is proper or not, we never were taught about relationships, so do not take this next thing I say as anything more than how it is intended. Perhaps you can teach me the customs, properly.

"But I wish to know you. I wish to learn everything there is about you. I wish to find out if these feelings I have, that we have, I think, can grow to become something more. I wish to find out if you can be with me for the rest of my life.

"You are the woman of my dreams, and even though you and I both know the impossibilities of it, we have already spent time together, knowing each other. I want to court you, Dyanea. I want you to want me the way I want you!"

She smiled, watching his hand as she put her other, atop his, now grasping his hand in between both hers. She continued to watch the hands her smile never more than a tight glimmer in her beautiful eyes.

"Are you asking for my permission to marry, my Lord JC? I know about love, Father, and I know about feelings between a man and a woman. Your intentions are so noted, and now I wonder of mine own."

"I would never be so bold to ask to marry you without even us knowing each other. I have never had a wife before. I have, as you can tell, a hard time talking to women like this. And, tend to make a fool of myself. Most women do not enjoy long the company of a man that makes such a fool. Not where I come from, in any account."

"Most men are fools!" She answered, too quickly. "Most men make fools of themselves for women. I would say you are from a strange place if that is not true." Looking now into JC's eyes, Dyanea swallowed hard, and softly added,

"Most women are fools for love as well, my lord. And if you wish to express your desires to gain my attention, then I say, good for you! I will watch, and I will accept them. When, or if, love deepens from it, I will order you to marry me, as you say, when it is proper."

JC nodded, and took a deep cleansing breath. He had not realized he had been holding it, until he let the air out. Taking two gold coins out of his belt pouch, he began imagining a pendant in the shape of the symbol of their temple. Recreating the gold, he instilled a blessing into it, as well as a protection against psychic magic.

When he finished, he opened his hand and extended the newly formed Holy symbol to the priestess. Shaped into scales, with coiled snakes rising up to face each other as if in a kiss.

"I will more than make my intentions known, my lady. Know you this, I have not felt this way in many years, and even though the short time we have known each other, I do believe in destiny, and think you are mine!

My full name, as you know, is James Carl Tigara d'Badger. JC is how I go by, but with this name, you shall have power over my heart as it is freely given to you, my lady." He finished as Dyanea took the offered gift. She looked on in wonder at the man, as she held tightly to his first gift,

262

"Made from his own mind, so casually, so easily. Imagine the power in sorcery at his command!" she thought privately.

Before anything else could be said, the door knocked and Mythalla entered, only mildly embarrassed when she saw the two holding hands.

Her smile grew, before she quickly replaced it with a stern look of business.

"Father, Queen Alyndria has ordered an audience with you in the grand hall. Shall I tell her you will be awhile?" She added hopefully.

"No, Mythalla, tell the Queen that he will be along shortly." Dyanea said. JC's face was now, sober looking as he turned to the priestess still holding his hand.

"Our young apprentice was most forthcoming on her intentions for us getting together, my lady. I heard many things about you, in the past few weeks. Many good things, you can be sure of! And, none bad!" He looked to see the frown coming on Mythalla, and before she could say anything Dyanea interrupted.

"Then I guess she should be thanked for opening your mind to the suggestions that your eyes were making on that first day, and your male mind trying to ignore. Hmm, Father?" With a curtsy, from Mythalla, Dyanea sent the young lady out closing the door behind her.

JC rose as did Dyanea, and when the two turned towards each other, he lifted her hand to his lips. Then bowing to her he left the room. Dyanea fell back into the chair and was still sitting there, fumbling with his gift, when C'renan walked back into the room.

"Well, Reverend Mother, is he truly, firm in our camp?"

"Yes, Reverend Mother, I think he is at that. Or, at the least, I am in his!" She lowered her head to her hands to cry. After a few moments, she rose and followed with C'renan to the Grand Hall.

JC entered to see the Queen standing with many people, mostly scribes and clerics. He moved to the dais, until he was only a few yards from Her Majesty, where he legged a short bow.

"JC, you are going to be welcomed properly the day after tomorrow evening. You will be there, and you will be properly dressed. Please see my seamstress, when you leave here today! Mythalla, you will take him there promptly!" It was not a request and the young Priestess curtsied in response.

"What is this about, your majesty?" JC asked.

"You will know, then. I told you; you will be given to the people that should know you. The lords and ladies of the realm. I need make plans for it, so do be a good boy, and run along. No arguments, this time, please! Get something nice to wear, and I'll talk to you tomorrow. Most are already here and will be wanting to get into seeing you early. Do try and stay out of sight so as not to be bombarded by their intentions."

"As you say, my queen. Alyndria, please, I ask you, don't do anything foolish!" He lowered his voice, as he nodded a quick bow to her. Turning, he exited to his apartments.

"Yes, Mythalla, I did get something appropriate to wear. Is this not good enough? You were there when I picked them out." JC said, standing before the priestess, wearing his leather jerkins, now cleaned, with a brand new light blue linen shirt. He looked at the mantle laying on the bed, and the hose beside them, shaking his head. Mythalla gasped, rolling her eyes.

"Father, the Queen will not be happy with those clothes. She had all those others made up for you, why can't you just wear them for tonight? You will be meeting all the lords and ladies of the realm."

"Mythalla, why don't you leave us alone for the moment?" A familiar voice said at the door. When the two turned, the Reverend Mother Dyanea and Massy were standing in the entrance to JC's room.

"Father, you will listen to the woman, or I'll hold you down while she changes you, herself!" Massy calmly stated. No smile was on her face, but JC thought he could see it in her eyes, the joke.

"All right, if you all think this is really necessary, I'll change! Now, all of you get out of my room!" He finally gave in. When he turned to untie his shirt, he heard the door close.

264

"If you are going to be my future husband, you will learn the proper court etiquette." Dyanea said, startling him. He turned to see her standing near the door, hands on her hips. "You are aware, JC, that I am, or was a noble?" She finished.

"I guess I am now!" He removed the shirt, and turned back away from the woman, as he removed his jerkins.

"Good, now this is what you will do...." As the man was forced to dress with the High Priestess giving him directions on the evening, he was amazed at how easy it was for him.

Being around Dyanea, had become much easier, it seemed, since they had the talk the past couple days. JC, only wished, he knew more about the customs concerning, courting a woman. That she had been rather secretive about, and even Mythalla would not talk about it.

Massy had told him that if he was a dwarf, he would just take Dyanea and challenge her to a duel. If she won, she would leave never to agree to be with him, if he won, then she would be his for life. JC just laughed.

Entering into the Grand Hall, JC was announced and he noticed as he was walking down the steps that present were not only most of the High Lords and Ladies of the Realm, but many of the Selenian Clergy, as well. To include, all eight remaining Council Members of the Brigitte Order. Rising from her throne, Queen Alyndria, took two steps down from her dais.

"Ladies and Lords, it is my supreme honor to present to you the man that rescued your poor misbehaving Queen, and saved the Street of the Gods, as well. He not only drove all the demons away from our glorious city, but destroyed the lord of demons that had taken hold of my soul.

"I present The High Father JC d'Badger, High Priest of the Holy Selene. And as of this moment Lord of the Dragoran estates in Bornesta, from now on to be known as the Badger Forest. Bornesta from this day forward, is to be stewarded by Lord Father JC d'Badger. So, say I."

The claps of the crowd, only slammed the stunned feeling he was having as JC came to a stop in the mid room. Staring at the Queen, he had told her he wanted no gifts. He quickly quelled any anger, before it showed. Slowly, JC moved forward, once again, a calm look placed on his stilled face.

Reaching the dais, he legged a bow to the Queen, and stepped one foot on the first step, placing both his hands to the bent knee. Watching to see what Alyndria's reaction would be at him not giving a proper bow, she only looked on with a slightly amused look.

"As I have performed rather poorly over the past few months or so, under the control of the Demon Cerodagon, and his priestess, Morella, formerly known as a Selenian Witch. "She paused looking around for reactions from the priestesses present, as well as the nobles, she continued,

"I have ordered all lands confiscated to be returned, any charges of treason expelled from the books, and any nobles still in prisons to be released. This command was signed several days ago, and those of you that were affected by me during my possessed behavior should have already been notified.

"I ask for your forgiveness, and I trust that we can move forward, placing this all behind us, knowing that with Father, no, with High Lord Father JC d'Badger to watch over our kingdom, this will never happen again. Is that not true, Lord Father?"

"So, say you, my Queen. I do swear that the lands placed so into my hands, are forever yours, and that I am and forever will be the protectorate of the crown. I also, my Queen, swear that not only will you have my protection, but the entire Dragoran realm will have that of the Temple of the Holy Goddess Selene, from this day forward. For so long as she is held high over the realm."

The roar of the crowd started slowly at the words of the Father. They rose thinking that he had sworn fealty, but the brief frown on Queen Alyndria's face, quickly removed though it was, she knew full well how that speech was intended. She turned and whispered something to her scribe who with a scroll in his left hand, leaned it to the queen.

The crowd fell silent as she quickly scanned until she came to the passage she was looking for. Looking up, she smiled down on JC and began to read.

"*Selene's child will spread his wings, bringing all the nations to his call. The Hells will tremble with Heaven's smile. The Lord Marshal of the North will then lead the armies against the Ancient One's own.*" She paused rolling the scroll back up handing it over to the scribe.

266

"It would seem, my Lord JC. That, you can refuse me, goes without saying, but you cannot refuse destiny. And, from this day forward, I command that the Dragoran Kingdom is securely held under the angelic wings of the d'Badger banner, and that our glory will forever be in the chronicles when The Armies of Hell are sent back, under the smiles of Heaven." She looked hard at JC, knowing she had just trapped him where he did not want to be.

Their discussions had led her to place this burden on the man, but she was neither sorry for it, nor regretful. It had to be done, and she could think of no one better suited to unite the world, as she interpreted the prophesies. The crowd of nobles and clerics alike, stood in silence, until one short stocky Dwarven female stepped forward.

"Your Majesty? It is time I should speak." Massy announced.

"Of course, your highness, the hall is all yours!" Alyndria answered.

JC smiled at the title given as several of the nobles stood shocked. Massy smiled as JC turned to a slight bow towards her.

"I thank you, your Majesty for keeping my little identity secret, but as all that has come to pass, it is time for the prophesies to be heard. Listen to Mother Gia's words, and hear the prophesy according to my people.

"When the day that the solitary beast is named overlord, the lands that first names him thus, will be raised above all others. In the mother's gardens will his name be blessed. Hear me, now, High Lord Father JC d'Badger." Massy eyed the man, and then watched the whole audience before turning back to JC.

"The oath I gave you in the park still stands. I now add this. I, Massy Thistle Thorn, Princess and heir to the throne of the Thorncave Clans, and High Priestess to the Holy Mother Gia, do hereby swear to you this day. Just as I swore to you on the day you freed Mother Gia's Temple, all the peoples of the Thorncaves give support against the armies of Hell.

"We will stand by our human brothers in the great battle to come, and from this day forward, Queen Alyndria and all of Kingdom Dragoran will be granted treaty of trade, so say I." When she finished, the stunned nobles, thinking of the trade and money flowing into the country's coffers, immediately cheered.

Alyndria walked the rest of the way down the steps to stand by JC who only looked upon Massy with an amazed look to his face. Massy walked forward, grabbing his arms, hanging down at his sides, and reached up to kiss his cheeks. Her smile was not sarcastic, nor was it anything, but genuine.

He returned the kiss to her cheeks, and for the first time since arriving at Zindar, he dropped to his knees. Spreading his arms wide, he looked up to the ceiling, exclaiming through tear filled eyes,

"Holy Mother Goddess, your will be done! It has begun, may we forever be granted Thy wisdom and Thy blessings!" He then rose, and embraced the two monarchs.

The noise of the nobles and priestesses rose to a roar, and JC found himself repeating too often "rise, bow not to me," as each stepped forward to meet the new Lord Marshal of the Selenian Continent, Lord of Badger Forest, JC d'Badger.

****

Martinith sat his throne seething. He fingered the bone made arm, peeling the copper gilding away under his finger, using his god like strength, as a normal person would peel lacquer off a table.

The demon that Samael had sent to deliver the message was afraid, standing under the Chosen of Lucifer's gaze. Never having feared a person from Zindar, the incubus knew, now, why Lord Samael had sent it, rather than coming himself. Just looking into the death watch of this half human, had the demon shaking.

"You say that the three weakest of the Chosen of those weakling lessor gods, have already killed three Greater Angels and one Archangel?" Martinith started. "I suppose in their arrogance, no ground support was in accompanist, and they attempted to take on more than one at a time?"

"Not true, my Lord Martinith. Your Majesty, they had many of the lesser angels with them. The Selenian Chosen, by himself battled over two dozen Lesser Angels, while still fighting Lord Abigor! That does not even count all the angels that his Temple eliminated, as well. And, some say, my liege, that the Katiketain is as fast as, even you!" The demon continued.

268

Rising from the throne, made entirely of human bones, shaped with copper and gold gilding, Martinith stood to his full seven feet six inches of height. The shorter incubus flinched when the half-makatiel's large hand found its throat. So fast did the emperor move, the demon could not react.

"Please, M'lord, mercy! You would kill the messenger?" It pleaded.

"So, it would seem! I shall have to put an end to these nasty rumors. I'll go and kill the little girl myself. After, of course, I have a taste of her. Since all you pathetic little creatures are too incompetent to handle the simple tasks yourselves, I'll get to have some fun out of it!"

He squeezed until the head was ripped free of the body. The demon began to smolder, the aroma of brimstone began to permeate the air, and Martinith inhaled deeply, filling the nostrils in his pink pig like snout, with the sweet perfume of Hell.

His course laughter filled the room, as his eyes turned a crimson, seemingly glowing in his reverie.

The half-makatiel opened a gateway to the Gates of Hell, and summoned Lilith, the Greater Angel of the sixth level of Hell, and once, the consort of his father. When the most beautiful and possibly the most powerful of all the female angels of Hell, arrived, out of the dimensional fold, Martinith felt his lustful urges take hold.

"Ah, my pet, you really are as lovely as they say! I will enjoy making offspring with you!" He leered.

Lilith, standing seven feet five inches tall, slightly above the half-makatiel's, she shimmered as her nude muscular body, with large transparent dragon like wings, and black hair and eyes, suddenly took the form of a human queen wearing a very modest high collared gown that touches the ground at her feet, as well.

"You may be my former lover's son, makatiel, but being Lucifer's offspring, does not grant you any privileges. Your hands, nor any other part of you, will ever touch this body." She calmly stated. "What is it you want, Martinith? I have a real man to get back to, so let's make haste."

Feeling the slight, it took all his control not to reach out and snap this devil's neck like he did with the demon, earlier. Only the knowledge that she commanded so much of Hell's lesser angels, kept his hand.

"I need to know why the weakest of the Chosen are still alive. Has Samael forgotten my orders?"

"The weakest are still alive because you sent the devils after the strongest, Martinith. Your orders, fool, has the weakest easily skating through lesser scum. Even less than the lesser angels. You are an idiot, Martinith. You want the Selenian slain, then do it yourself. You have nine bodies to waste, after all."

His hand was like lightning, as he reached out taking her around the throat. She was barely able to concentrate as she teleported out of his grasp to appear behind him. Feeling the pain, suddenly, Martinith looked down to see the point of her twisted long dagger, sticking out from his chest.

"Don't move, makatiel! It rests next to your heart, and, it would be a shame if your first death was caused by one of your own!" He relaxed in her grip, knowing that of all the devil lords, this one Greater Angel could and would do it without a thought.

Lilith was the only one to stand up to Kutulu Lucifer, on several occasions even, and still is alive. Once Lucifer's Consort, her only punishment was being given to Molech, the Archangel, as a gift.

"Now, listen closely Champion! JC d'Badger is not the weakest, as you seem to think. And, going after his pets, only makes him that much stronger. You want him dead, do it quickly and silently. You are an assassin, aren't you? One thing else, Martinith. All the other Chosen are considered his, as well. Except for one!" She added, lying, a thought suddenly coming to her. "Remove the Lemurian and he won't be so inclined to seek vengeance. But, beware, he may not be as fast as you, but Odyseus is stronger!"

Lilith disappeared, leaving the long dagger sword still inside his chest. Martinith carefully pushed the tip, until he could safely remove it, out the back. The pain driving through him, as he labored in his breath.

"That witch will die, someday!" He mumbled throwing the useless pointer to the ground.

"I am an assassin. I'll take the man out myself." After he healed himself, he opened a dimensional door to the Astral plane and stepped through.

270

As the door closed, Lilith reached to the ground, and picked up her weapon. She smiled, becoming visible.

"Yes, little brother, go and get yourself killed. With the Selenian Chosen, I could finally rule Hell. With his aide, I might even be able to eliminate Kutulu Lucifer, himself!" She contemplated the victory, with her sitting queen over all the angels, as she stepped back through the door called the "Gateway to Hell."

"Now, to eliminate Samael, Belial, and Nebiros. Perhaps, I can even get James Carl Tigara to do that, for me, as well!" She laughed, a not nice sounding chuckle that emanated from her slightly parted lips.

****

Working in the yard, his morning kata were feeling exhilarating to him. Dyanea, he noticed was watching. Her knitting needles were moving without her watching the intricate weave, she was creating. Instead, she watched JC

When the dimensional door opened, right where the man would have been, had he not stumbled forward. JC was hit from behind by what felt to be a strong gust of sorcery made air, pushing him, just before the half-makatiel stepped out swinging his one and a half meter long bastard sword.

No time to wonder who shoved him, JC rolled under the quick swinging blade and came standing just next to the weapons rack, where his favored katana was resting. The cut across his back as he was moving, was not deep, but still he could feel the pain as it came precariously close to his vertebrae. He could also feel the poison coursing through his body as his own constitution began to combat the drug.

He rolled to the side, as he saw Marcus flying back into Dyanea, from an offhand punch by the large half-makatiel. JC concentrated on speed, when he saw Dyanea and Marcus hurt, and more importantly, in danger.

He concentrated on closing the dimensional door, and moved into Martinith, quickly and smoothly. Kutulu Lucifer's Chosen, felt several attacks on his mind shield, as the human before him, moved in.

Faster and stronger, Martinith was still no match for the controlled fury, nor the battle prowess of JC. The duel was ended quickly, when the half-makatiel was eviscerated by two quick slices across the mid-section.

Only his god like speed kept the cuts from being any deeper, but he knew he was in trouble. He barely blocked a third swing, and swinging out with his free hand, landed a punch to the man's shoulder, instead of the face, when JC managed to move his head away.

Knowing he was dying, having taken another slice across the midsection, Martinith cast a teleport to the Gates of Hell, and quickly entered his father's palace, as he died upon the tiled floor in the onyx palace on the planet Hades.

Lilith's lips turn upward into a diabolic smile, as she stood, invisibly, watching the duel. Knowing that Kutulu Lucifer's Chosen was out classed, she still seemed amazed by the abilities of JC under such duress. The wound he took should not have allowed him to still stand, let alone....

"Such a wound and it did not even slow him. Even now, he shows more concern for his pets, then his own injuries. Yes, James Carl Tigara, I will have you. You will make me Queen. Maybe even a goddess!"

Her smile widened as she teleported back to Haden where she could open a dimensional door back to Hell.

CHAPTER 11
Troubled thoughts, nervous solutions!

Quen was working out in the courtyard behind the Temple with six of the Temple priests. Some of them were not too bad. At least they were better than the other Chosen, the first time they all were together.

He remembered thinking back on the first time all six had come together in that dimensional planet that was Merylon's creation. Odyseus was the only other warrior, besides Sheera, of course, but even those two were not really that good with swords. Sheera's form of non-weapon fighting was interesting for exercise, but JC was the only one that seemed to understand it. Of course, they are both from the same world.

"I still don't understand the pull he has with any of us, nor do I understand why he never acted on the attention that all the girls gave him. Sheera and Burlga never really denied the feelings they had, not like Purana, but those last few months it was fairly obvious that even she was beginning to notice him more. There is something about the man. I can't really dislike him, even if he is only a commoner." Of course, Quen thought,

"We all are so much more than just commoners or nobility, now!"

He barely avoided the four blades coming at him, and decided it was time to stop thinking about the others. It had been eleven weeks, he had single handily taken out several hundred Hell Spawn, and he still hadn't figured out how to gain weapons that would allow his fellow priests to hit the scum of Hell.

"I'll have to try and be nice to the old man, I guess, not that it will be too hard. I really do miss those people. But I know the old man, among us, will have figured the secret to the swords!" Quen was thinking as he disarmed two of his sparing partners.

"If any of us have, it will be him!"

After less than three months, he had established himself as the leader of this part of the church. Looking around at the yard, he realized that during his brief reverie, he had managed to disarm all six opponents and one laid on the ground with a deep wound in his arm. The other priests that could, were healing him.

"Sorcery, what a waste! If it would have been so important, Phaleg would have made sure I was more endowed with it!" Quen took his thoughts into another direction as he watched the others perform their magiks.

"Will he be all right?" He finally asked. Thinking to himself the need for being nice, was starting to grate on his nerves.

"Make sure he rests up and gets enough fluids in him!"

The priests only gave him that look that indicated the frustration of being told the obvious. This world was a strange one, indeed. There were hardly any wars. Usually just skirmishes between minor kingdoms or lords, and here he was trying to figure how to prepare a people for a worldwide war against a foe most would not even be able to fight.

He thought of Sheera and her "martial arts" he was thinking she had called it.

"I wonder if I could get her to teach us that kind of skill. Maybe with even a little bit of sorcery, the people could succeed against the spawns of Hell." His thinking of Sheera brought another woman to his mind.

Nileena was becoming quite the little soldier. Her strength would still need improving, but she showed a good courage, and would make a good companion on the long road ahead. He thought of Burlga and how Nileena reminded him of the other Chosen. Of course, Nileena was not a non-human, and she had a cleaner mouth.

When Burlga was first being taught the sword, she nearly cut her own foot off. Now, she was at least comfortable with a blade in her hand. Nileena showed the same kind of intensity for learning it, and he thought she was doing so for the same reason Burlga did.

Burlga would try anything if it meant being near JC, and Quen was sure that Nileena was doing the same for him. He chuckled to himself, while outwardly, still showing the calm emotionless appearance.

Quen stood looking down at the priest on the ground, his arm healed, he was working his limb to test the mobility, and Quen would have to apologize for injuring the man, for the man's inadequacies. Sighing, he offered a hand up.

274

"My mind must have wandered, I am sorry for your injuries, Brother Duarin."

"Your mind has been wandering more and more of late, Brother. What is the problem?" Father Meritt asked from the side.

"Just been thinking about how all this practice really only serves me. What good if I am the only one that can hit the Hell Monsters?" Quen answered.

"Perhaps, as you say, one of the other Chosen, will be able to help. Maybe, when you go later this week to meet with them, you can take a few of us that are...."

"Better in the sorcery than me?" Quen finished the father's statement. "Yes, I had thought of that. I'm not too sure how the others will feel about you being taught, but I think I know one that will help. All I need to do is swallow my pride and ask him." Quen thought out loud.

"Ask? Could you not just command? Certainly, none are as great as you!"

"Command? No one of us commands the other. We are each talented in our own ways. And, JC d'Badger, is the least of us, yet the best." Looking at the questioning face on the middle-aged priest, Quen, thought he must be confused.

"Just accept it that JC will need to be asked. He does nothing without manners, first!"

"Ahh, an elder, then!" The high priest said, as if knowing.

"I leave it to you Father Meritt. Gather the best of you at sorcery. Those that can do more than minor healing, at least, and you will be coming with me, of course!"

The rest of the week went by and on that day of their scheduled meeting, Quen opened the gateway and four priestesses and three priests stepped through ahead of him.

****

It had been a long time since a woman had made him feel like a little boy. Yet, here he was following an ancient woman, she had to be at least eighty, he thought. Hecate was smoothing his shirt, insuring it was just right.

275

"Can't have you going looking like some sort of barbarian, can I? Even if you are one, you don't have to look the part!" If he was going to be king, then he needed to look like it, she was always saying.

Neat and tidy, even if he had just finished a battle with a few dozen Hell Spawn, she expected him to do it without mussing up.

Odyseus laughed, and allowed the woman to dote. In truth, he enjoyed it.

"Yes, grandmother, so thou hast said. But I will be king as soon as is needed. Are these quite through, yet?"

In the past three months, the big man had killed over eighteen hundred Hell Spawn, and liberated thirteen villages and sixteen farmsteads. Hecate was a strong wizardress, but her use in sorcery was even less than his, or so it seemed.

He often wondered about that. Some of her spells, were used with different incantations yet yielded the same results. He wondered what kind of magic she was using, but when asked, she would just shrug and say "my kind!"

But she was a wise woman, and managed to pull him out of some foolish situations he had found himself in, on a number of occasions. Of course, Hecate was usually the one that got him into those situations. Grandmotherly one minute, and the next?

Well, those times when her mouth would run, she could be downright nasty. Forget the Temple of Love, back home, those Holy whores had nothing on this woman, when her mouth would get going. Odyseus chuckled at the thought, until Hecate jabbed him in the ribs,

"What's so funny, boy? You laughing at me because I want you to look all pretty for your friends? You don't want them to think that I haven't been taking good care of you, or watching out for you? Don't smile at me like that, your precious Lord JC, if he's like you claim, will not like me much if he thinks you are not what you should be!"

"Oh grandmother, he be nothing like that. He's a good man. If I like thee, then he will. And most of the time, I do, anyway." He said earning him another jab in the ribs. Hecate was short for a Lemurian, Odyseus had found out. He was not the giant that he thought he would be. True, he still towered over most, by a few centimeters, but if not for his bulk, he would be just above average. This little woman, though, was more than a head shorter than most of the people. At only 150 cm, she was even shorter than most of the elves, they had met.

There were times, though, when she would show a physical strength that belied the little frame Hecate was in. And, then when she would put on an illusion of a young woman, in order to try and seduce him. "Testing" she had called it, but he wondered. Admiringly, he enjoyed it. She could appear the beautiful woman. And, there were times when he had to admit that if he didn't know what she was really like, he would have been persuaded. He shuddered at the thought of that, happening.

He did enjoy her company, though. More of a mother to him, than his own had been, yet, too, Hecate was a friend. She reminded him a lot of an older female version of JC. Odyseus was looking forward to the meeting.

Seeing JC, and those girls chasing after him. That was the most fun to watch. Burlga and Sheera, both stunning women, all but throwing themselves at his feet, and JC never seeming to notice.

"He couldn't be that blind, could he?" Odyseus thought to himself on more than one occasion. He never treated them like he was interested, only like they were just two more of the "kids".

"He used to call me or all of us, kids. That be bothering me at first!" He said aloud, Hecate fussing with his boots. "Then I figured it out, if he didn't say kid or child, when talking to us, that meanst he be mad at us, or at himself. It wast an affectionate way of talking to us, I think!"

"Like when I call you, boy!" She said, tying the laces on his shirt. "You know that I really do not use it to hurt you?"

"I know grandmother. It bothers me not. I do be liking it."

Yes, he did enjoy Hecate. He would be alone, if not for her. Even after he would free or rescue someone, they would look upon him mostly with fear. Lifting wagons off a person, or throwing a fallen horse at an oncoming demon, had earned him a lot of stares.

277

He had a great strength here, and he had to learn to tone it down a bit. The people were afraid he was some sort of God or demon himself, and it had caused trouble with making friends.

Not, understanding why he could not befriend anyone, Odyseus was glad to move on to the next stop that Hecate would take them. Her dreams were never wrong. She knew every time where they should go. Her visions were never wrong, but in reality, he would not have cared if they were. He was just having fun, on this little adventure of his.

Raised a pampered lord, he was enjoying the life of a not so common mercenary. And the life seemed to suit him. He was making a name for himself, and it was now preceding him into the villages.

Hecate would tell him, on more than one occasion, he needed to more generous with his help.

"Lift a boulder out of the way, for a farmer, rescue the occasional dorcal from a tree, free the horse, fallen into a marshy bog." She would tell him to do the things he wanted to avoid. The things that made the locals afraid of him. But she would claim,

"It's the little things, boy, which will make you a king. We do not have a lot of time, the elections are in less than two years, and it would not hurt if the people thought you a demigod, or something. Get their attentions now, and make friends later." She would say that same speech over and again whenever he would try to figure a non-heroic way out of things.

Whenever, he did try to do something as a normal person, trying to catch some young ladies' eye, Hecate would force him to do the quick and easy thing, saying only,

"You don't need to impress some young floozy. You have me, boy. What do you need with any of those creatures, for?" Hecate almost seemed jealous of those girls, but certainly she could not be that.

Finally, Hecate was finished fussing with him and he opened the gateway before them. Opening a gateway was near the very limits of his powers, and he was surprised when it would be big enough for him to go through. Just big enough for the two, as it turned out. Hecate walked through, quickly followed by the big young immortal.

****

As the date approached for the first meeting of the six, Burlga was becoming excited and a little fearful.

"So, what is this "JC", you are always going on about, really like?" Quevit asked. "Sometimes you make him out to be an old man, and sometimes a god of some sort." Quevit understood none of what she talked about, only just beginning to believe the things she said.

"He is just a man, Quevit, though, more of one than I have ever met. Not a great warrior, but he is better than good, and much better than he lets on. Not a great wizard, but he is a good sorcerer. He is a great priest and a very good teacher. And, yes, he is a little old. Almost 50, I think."

Burlga, had not realized she spoke about him so much, thinking that she was doing well to have him out of her mind. JC would have found a woman, by now. One that was more to his liking, whatever that could be. She needed to concentrate on the matters at hand.

"Any word from the Guild of Sorcerers, or a reply from the King.?" She asked him, changing the subject.

She had sent messengers to both the King asking for an audience, and to the guild, announcing her presence. Yet, neither Merylon's priests nor the King had responded. She would have to take care of Merylon's group when she got back.

They would feel the wrath of ignoring their new High Priestess' summons. And as far as the King went, well, he would learn, as well.

She pulled out her journal. She had been keeping it ever since she first went into town. It was her first purchase and she tried to write something in it every day. Especially when she faced with Hell Spawn or other creatures. She was keeping a tally off to the side.

Besides, the devil lord, Naamah, Burlga had killed three hundred thirty-eight demons, forty-seven devils, and at least six hundred other minor Hell Spawn. That

279

number was inaccurate as it was hard to keep up with true numbers when fighting a battle. She had disintegrated so many with one fireball during the one attack, last week. She had also, killed over 200 Trolls, and thought the marsh must be almost cleared out. Soon the laborers could begin mining the minerals from the swamps, again. That was how the d'Venta fortune was made, to begin with.

Her father's grandfather, had built the castle with the minerals and methanine from the swamps. And the way she was spending money, she would need those mines opened again. Besides, one of the mines was mythral and she was sure she could get a pretty penny for that stuff, if she could get it out.

Her cousin had been right, of course. There were no more dwarves. And the Gnomish miners still remembered the d'Venta curse and wanted three times the money to return to the mines. She was thinking how she did not want that, but had little choice. And the only other non-humans were the elves, and they were so full of themselves, that most thought that no sane person would ever deal with an elf. Of course, Burlga could claim her heritage with that, she was descended from the King of the elves, and being one of the princesses, should carry some weight. That would be another thing she would look into when she got back, she thought to herself.

Using sorcery to aid the contractors, the keep was almost half completed by the end of the three months. Burlga sent more runners out to the royal palace, and this time she had Quevit sign the permissive, since he was to be the figurehead.

When the day finally came for the appointed gathering of the Chosen, early that morning a reply from the King arrived.

Lord Quevit d'Venta.
It has been granted, one hour's audience with
The most exalted, to be attended two hours
Before noon, on the third day of the month.
Emperor Ulfa d'Sveta, most exalted, will then
Entertain your petition to claim your rightful
Position, as heir to the d'Venta holdings.
Missing said appointment will be cause for
Immediate dismissal to your claim, and seizure
Of all holdings by the crown.

The note was signed and sealed by the High King.

"Emperor?" She exclaimed, nearly fuming with the anger building over such a dismissive letter. "I'll be back by tomorrow, if not tonight, and, in two days, cousin, we will show Ulfa, believe me, we will show him what it flaming means to question the bloody d'Venta claim." Her anger barely held, Burlga stormed out to the stables.

After she had saddled her own horse, slapping the groomsman away, Quevit watched as the gateway was opened. Burlga rode her horse through it, followed by Persides, and as it shut down, Quevit could see others, already there. None looking old enough to be who she had called

"Her Lord JC"!

****

The gateway opened and four women, three wearing the light blue robes of Selene Priestesses, and one a dwarf, in full padded leather armor of a soldier, and two men, both wearing plate armor chest plates, painted crimson red and baring the black symbols of a dragon on their chests, step through. One of the soldiers was a human and one was a half elf, of rather large size for the race.

But Sheera was more interested in the man following after them, wearing a light tan leather vest over a blue linen shirt, and utilitarian heavy tan cotton pantaloins. His small silver holy symbol dangling from a leather thong around his neck, that of balancing scales with a rod and two intertwined snakes meeting at the top as if kissing.

The priestesses all had similar symbols around their necks as well. JC's Katana was worn loosely across his back hanging from a tightly braided cord over his shoulder. He had longer hair, than before, and a tanned face and neck showing above the V-neck cut of his shirt unlaced at the top two laces.

He smiled, with his clean-shaven face, at the young lady who looked up from the campfire she was sitting at, brewing tea over the small fire she had made. She looked to have been there for a while, waiting for the others to arrive. She was alone, and JC noticed some apprehension to her auras.

Sheera eyed the three human women, seeing one of an age, JC might not think too young. She wondered, he could not have found someone, already, could he? The other two were young, about her age, and the dwarf, looked to be in her early middle age, but was without a beard as if in mourning. The dwarf also had

281

several burn scars on her neck, forehead, as well as her head being nearly bald as if the hair having been burned off.

She appeared to be the leader, by the way she carried herself as well as the most relaxed showing in her own auras. All the women appeared to be sorcerers, although far below in strength of the Chosen.

The one woman, mid to early thirties had Sheera the most concerned. Being guarded by, or so it seemed, by the two soldier's demeanor as they flanked her on both sides. She had an aura showing much evil in it.

Not the possessed kind that she found in one of the Sho Guns, but the kind of someone that had committed some grievous act, willingly.

"Why would the man have someone like that?" She thought to herself as she stood.

A smile forming on her face from the frown. When JC's smile leveled upon her.

"I knew you'd be one of the first to arrive." Sheera exclaimed, a touch too excited, she thought, as JC stepped to the front of his retinue.

A slight touch of jealousy was felt by Sheera at the sight of the women, before she quickly smoothed it out mentally.

"Sheera," he said with the full tenor tone that she had come to love and missed hearing.

Even more relaxed than when last, she had heard it, she noticed the smile was genuine and the love in his eyes still there. JC came to her, meeting her halfway as they took each other's hands. He kissed her cheek before finishing his comment.

"I'm glad you are here. I take it we are the only ones, so far?" He said as he looked around.

"I've actually been here since yesterday. I wanted to be the first to see you, James."

Looking at the mortals with him, Sheera forced a smile before returning her own kiss to his cheek.

Introductions were made, and Sheera saw the one young girl, about twenty-one, as she watched them, with open scorn. She smiled at Mythalla, and tilted her head, seeing concerned envy in the young woman's aura.

"You collecting your new class, teacher? Let me guess which one is the teacher's pet?" She chuckled.

Tilting his head to the side, the smile a little too wry, he answered,

"So, it would seem. Old habits die hard and all that, don't you know? What is the matter, my dear? You appear somewhat distraught!"

Sheera sighed, and holding back tears, suddenly threw herself into him, embracing, no longer able to resist and they stood for a few moments before she wiped her tear streamed face on his shoulders.

"I've missed you, old man. I really needed to see you right this moment. Your presence is needed in my heart. I'm not doing really well with the Sho Guns, nor with my preaching." Her embrace tightened its grip once again, and JC just held on to her, knowing it to be what she needed most at that moment. Feeling the closeness of his sister Chosen, he returned the tight hold and hugged her back.

As they spoke, Massy was the only one of the "mortals" that seemed to interject into the conversations, Sheera stated that her only real success was with a gnome that knew who she was, but none of the other races would even spend time talking with her.

"Humans are not welcomed in many of the non-human towns until they prove to be less prejudice. Go to them with that gnome friend of yours and they will come around. But, be wary, young Chosen! Dwarves and gnomes have a rather interesting sense of humor, so don't take any insults too personal." Massy stated.

"How is your temple accepting you, Sheera?" JC added.

Her head shake was not a positive answer.

"To include my own Temple!" she gasped. "No one seems to believe that "The Golden Dragon" could be a male.

"Just as we wondered if "The Sword of Vengeance" could be a male, father JC!" Gulnara mumbled gathering head shakes from the other women.

"Seems Gia wondered why Jeasuas made you to be female. She knew you would be hard pressed." JC absentmindedly added.

"I actually have wondered why I was not made male and you female? Things could have been easier were it so." Sheera shrugged.

Massy advised that she knew the King of the mountain dwarves by reputation and he is a fair man if approached with respect.

"I have tried to gain an audience with him but to no avail, so far. I have been in and out of so many villages cleaning the Hell spawn out that I have not really had time to enter the mountains. A few traders her and there, I have met and told them I would like to talk to their king."

"That is your problem, m'lady! The merchants may take months before going back home. They will carry your message, but on their time line not yours." she chuckled.

The group grew larger with the morning. Odyseus arrived with Hecate, and gave both Sheera and JC big bear hugs, nearly forcing the air out of the small woman's lungs. She kissed him on the cheek, only mildly telling him to put her down.

Then Burlga, on horseback, followed by a late twenties soldier, arrived as a queen in an obvious huff over something.

She quickly melted her ire, though, when JC gave her a hug and kiss on the cheek. Her usual lewd comments left unsaid, as she only held onto him, longer than any of the others thought necessary. While holding the man, she eyed the three human women that had come with him.

Burlga turned to kiss the man, and surprisingly he did not push her away, until that is, she tried to make it more of one than was appropriate. His laugh, was calm and relaxed, no blushing, Burlga noticed.

284

"Some things, never change, do they, young lady? I did miss you, though!" He laughed when Burlga patted him on the buttocks. Sheera only gave Burlga a disgusted look and a light slap to the shoulder.

What was not missed by the two female Immortals, was the looks directed at them, by Mythalla, the young twenty-one-year-old priestess that watched everything, as though making notes at what was going on.

Seeing the young priestess so interested, only helped to make Burlga even more brazen with JC, and Sheera seeing Burlga's actions, did not want to be left out.

Long before noon, the two women had finally managed to make the older man blush with embarrassment, and the young priestess red with concern. The dwarf, Massy, seemed to find the whole thing amusing. As did Odyseus and Hecate.

Finally, as noon approached, Quen arrived with seven priests and priestesses, a part of his retinue.

All were surprised with Quen's arrival, as he seemed the most emotionally changed over the past few months. He walked directly to JC ignoring the others, and grabbed the man's arm in a soldier's shake, adding his left hand to JC's arm, as well.

The familiar form of shake was equally returned by the father, a smile on his face that he had given to all.

"My Lord, High Priest d'Badger, it would seem I have missed your sermons and speeches more than I thought I would." The warrior smiled a thin break from his usual tight stoic calm.

Quen's people went to where the other mortals were standing, just a few yards off to the left of the Chosen, while High Priest Meritt watched his lord, talking to the shorter man with an ease and familiarity, he had not seen in him, the past three months.

After being introduced, to the other Immortals, Quen's people stayed a bit apart from the other mortals, only nodding slight attention to the priestesses of Holy Selene, who returned similar slight nods to their brothers and sisters of Holy Phaleg.

Meritt watched, looking at the man that seemed to effortlessly control the young Chosen. Looking to be about his late twenties, except for his eyes, and the slight graying of the temples, the High Priest of Phaleg could not understand why Quen had said he was almost fifty.

Meritt was forty-six, and looked more the elder here. With the exception of the dwarf, of course. The two women Chosen, were absolutely beautiful, and based on the youth of the half-elf, he assumed her to be in her mid to early forties, where the Katiketain female would be in her early twenties.

The boy mountain, was a late teen, and, seemed to be just as emotional as most Lemurians that Meritt had met. That would mean, he probably had the mind of a young teenager.

"These are the saviors of the universe?"He thought to himself, in a mumbled comment.

"It is interesting, isn't it, High Priest?" Massy mumbled over hearing Merit's comment.

His head shake was all he returned.

"We have a lot to do in order to insure these people get to the designated end, I sure hope they grow up quickly." Massy added.

Meritt turned and smiled at the dwarven female.

"How long have you been in mourning, m'lady?" he whispered.

"I was just over a year, and my beard had started to grow back. My capture by demons is why I have no hair, now. Thank you for asking, High Priest. You know our ways?"

"I am a fan of the clans in battle, yes ma'am." he nodded. "Although, I would have thought that your Selene temple would have been able to heal you without the scars."

"JC tried, but I would not let him. I hold these like a badge, and will see how Mother Gia allows my own constitution to heal."

Meritt smiled and nodded again. He gave a small bow of his head in understanding before turning back to the Chosen and their conversations.

286

The group was sitting in the grass, green and lush early in the late spring, and the day was warm, with a nice cool breeze. The sun was high, and the normal paleness of it was brighter here, than it was when they left in their homelands that morning. The clouds seemed to not be moving, hanging in the sky as though it never changed.

No matter what time it was in their homelands, each Chosen arrived at a time when appropriate to the conversations. JC thought it the work of Gia, and knew that this meeting was being watched. He was not sure by who, or which if not all of the Ancient Ones, but the manipulation of time was not something any of the Chosen could have done.

Relaxing his thoughts, he allowed them to turn back to the younger Chosen and the discussion on how many and what types of demons and fallen angels, the devils, had been dispatched.

They were all surprised and made Sheera relive her battle with Baalzebub, as the smallest of the Chosen had faced and defeated an Archangel considered by many to be one of the most powerful.

Quen seemed to be the most impressed and showed the most pride for his fellow Chosen.

JC had brought a banquet of meats and cheeses, and when Burlga created wine out of the water, they all were enjoying the discussions.

Mythalla watched closely as the Immortals would argue, and talk mostly about something called gunpowder, whatever that was.

The one Katiketain female Immortal wanted JC to make it, and he was refusing, quite soundly. The other Immortals did not even seem to know what it was. What was not lost on Mythalla, was the way the two women seemed to never take their eyes, nor their hands, off of Her, Father JC!

"Haven't you noticed it, Massy?" She whispered.

"Girl, don't you worry none about that, look at all the ages of them. These are the saviors of the world, and yet not one except JC is more than a child." Massy answered in an equal whisper.

"But he is promised to Dyanea, well sort of, anyway. And they are so beautiful, so young, and... and, so immortal. Certainly, he will forget about our Dyanea, with them the way they are acting."

Her laugh, brought Mythalla up.

"Look at them, Mythalla! They are little more than school girls to him. The way you are! You are a very beautiful woman, yourself, and has he ever tried to take advantage of your obvious affections?"

Mythalla started and slowly shook her head side to side. She still worried over it, though.

Hecate moved to sit by Massy, and looking over at Mythalla, she said a little too loud, for their comfort.

"Mountain girl, they are all a little too young at that, aren't they? Let me ask you something about the JC. You all belong to him, don't you?" She finished as she plopped the rest of the way sitting.

Watching the woman suspiciously, Massy answered.

"We follow Father JC, venerable one. We do not, though, belong to any ground walker!" She finished, using the father's own term attempting to even sound like him.

Hecate's cackling laugh cut through even the Immortals' talk as all heads turned towards the venerable old lady.

"Good answer, dwarf. Good answer!" She stated loud enough for all to hear. Then just as quickly regained her serious look and lowered her own voice to a whisper, so that only the two females beside her could hear. Meritt edged a little closer attempting to hear the whisper.

"What's he like? My boy, over there, thinks awfully highly of him. Speaks sometimes like he could be The Creator himself!"

Mythalla shook her head slowly and breathed out barely an audible whisper,
"He would not like hearing that! He has even forbidden any to kneel to him, nor even allow us to call him more than lord. He's simply Father JC, to all he meets."

"I have heard him say that except for Lady Sheera and Lady Burlga, none of the others really cared for him. Your boy's affections would come as a welcome surprise to JC." Massy added.

Meritt had been listening, and was beginning to look at the man harder. Quen still would argue, but softer, and with less command, than he would use with the Temple or palace back home.

Meritt thought his Lord was putting on a very good show, acting less prideful with the man, in order to get what he wanted. He also, noticed the eyes. The man was indeed, older than he looked. The lines around the man's eyes, and the slight graying of hair around his temples, was missed upon first sight.

Their tone took on a more normal speech, as Massy and Hecate talked, both trying to feel each other out. It was obvious to the priestesses that the Dwarven princess had little trust for the old woman. Mythalla and Gulnara both listened, adding comments where appropriate, with Marina standing quietly behind, the two guardsmen flanking each side of her.

"What I really, need," Quen exclaimed, "is for you to tell us, or me, if I am the only one to not know, how to make more swords, like ours!" He said it to JC, but looked to Sheera and Burlga, as well.

"I haven't been able to make one last, Quen. The spells dissipate, eventually. But they are good enough for the short battle. You could probably even do it, at least all your people could if they are as strong as the ones you brought." Sheera answered, looking over to the sorcerers and sorceresses that came with him.

Burlga just shook her head, exclaiming she had not had the time to try and learn anything, yet.

JC looked at Quen and Odyseus and nodded.

"I've studied the blades, yes. And I think I know how. But, until very recently I have not had a smithy in which to attempt anything. That and the metal used is mythral. Not even sure what that is, in reality!"

"I knew you'd be the one, to have figured it out. You were always the best of us at that sort of thing." Quen announced, calmly, matter of fact. "Besides, you were a blacksmith, yes? I remember you mentioning it, once."

"I think, though, I am not sure that you nor Odyseus would be able to make them, Quen. I don't say that to be mean, unless you have eliminated that block of yours. Just as I am not sure, I am strong enough to do a couple of spells needed." Sheera eyed the man, and knew he was not being fully truthful about that! She had seen what he could do, as she played with the pendant hanging down her front. JC looked at her and smiled.

"Either way, the mixture of metals is why Sheera's spells didn't work. Common sword steel won't work, it is made of." He continued.

****

Purana had ordered her soldiers to ready themselves. She knew that nothing would happen, but in order to ensure her little muse would work, she needed her troops to be at the ready.

"Remember, do not attack, unless I give the word. A show of force, is what we want. We will march in, I'll get my answers, and then we will leave. No bloodshed!

These people are not normal, and although, I could survive, most of you, if not all would die, to go to war, against them. Pay attention, and look ready!" The captain only nodded. Purana had given these same orders six times in the last three days. He was sure that even these battle starved soldiers would not attack, unprovoked.

Captain Hebron was just not sure how long they would be held back, if those the Empress was going to face, did provoke them. He turned to his men, and simply nodded.

"You've heard her majesty. Any one of you goes against her orders, and she won't have anything to punish when I'm through with you!" The soldiers all saluted.

****

At the moment when JC was about to give the details of his research, a gateway opened up. The sun was a little lower than two hours beyond noon, and out marching in an almost perfect military unison, five abreast, were twenty priests and priestesses of Isis, forty fully armored soldiers, each holding a ten-foot-long spear high into the air, and a banner man, holding the flag of Isis' Ankh in a pool of pink water, surrounded by stars rising over a falcon. Floating behind on a stiffened carpet, about three yards above the ground, Purana sat, stately with the air of a Queen.

"OK, people, I have too much to do and haven't the time for this, so let's get it over with." Purana arrogantly called out as her gateway snapped shut.

"Glad you could make it, Purana." Burlga loudly stated, with a bit of sarcasm to her tone, "We were about to leave without you!" She finished.

"Good, how many, if any, of the lords of Hell are dead?" Purana ordered, but none of the other Immortals seemed to react fast enough. "I said how many? Are you all deaf? I will not be ignored!" She all but screamed. The frost to her tone, did not go unnoticed by the rest. Her soldiers standing twenty to a side of her, shifted as though to attack.

Calmly, JC stood from where the other four were still sitting. They seemed stunned in awe of the woman's attitude. The others looked up at JC, as he turned to face Purana still floating a couple yards above the ground. Sheera saw by the way the man's jaw was working, that JC was about to say something that would most likely upset Purana. She took on a calm, and watched, ready to react, as would be necessary.

"You are even more arrogant than you were, before, child. I see ruling suits you most fine?" He stated, the sarcasm evident by his tone. He broadened his smile as he looked up at her.

"Child?" She screeched, barely able to contain herself, "CHILD? You dare call me like I am one of your whores, old man?" She pointed over to the other two female Immortals.

Burlga, reacting to being insulted, caused the carpet to lurch. She was trying to dispel the magic, without actually alerting everyone around. But, with only half of the force of her mind, the spell on the carpet, resisted Burlga's simple attempt. The magic was obviously made by Purana, herself! The half-elf Chosen thought.

Still floating, the flying carpet did lurch before being brought under control, like it was a live horse under Purana, instead of a simple weaving of string and cloth. Purana's face twisted in anger; that ruined the porcelain beauty normally present. Thinking JC caused the carpet's momentary malfunction, she was about to lose her composure.

Her people formed a line quickly in front of her as a challenge. Quen's and JC's people, all moved to stand beside their leaders quickly and quietly, aware at how outnumbered they are by the sorceress' forces. JC only lowered his hand palm side down, as an attempt at calming those behind him.

Mythalla saw the others put up mental shields around themselves, the Immortals as well as the mortals. Massy watched JC; she had been holding his Katana. He had not reached for it, yet so she did not offer it up. Instead, she placed her free hand to the hammer, resting in her belt. No one seemed to notice how very calm JC had become.

JC took on an even more of a calm stance, arms resting in front of him, hands loosely crossed, he shifted his feet to shoulder length apart. The smile he assumed radiated outward. The other four Chosen moved to stand behind him, as he began once again, to speak.

"You come here, much too late, Purana, ordering us like we were a part of your little entourage. You treat us as if you are the mistress, acting like the child, you so evidently are. You dare to threaten us with your less than adequate untrained lackeys? Yes, My CHILD! That is exactly what I called you!" Placing an emphasis on the word child, JC did not move, only watched.

Quen watched the two. His hand tightened on his long sword's hilt, he could only think, how very calm JC appeared. Purana had all of them in a bunch, everyone had placed shields around themselves, and yet, JC just stood calmly. No shields, no anger, just his usual calm priestly appearance.

"What is going through the man's mind?" Quen thought.

Thinking hard, Purana, had not moved, either.

"He's baiting me wanting to see how far he can go." She thought.

Purana seemed to be struggling with herself, as she contemplated her next move. She could see that JC was the only one not ready for an attack. She struggled within herself.

The conflicting emotions raged through her. She wanted to eliminate this man. Yet, at the same time, she wanted to love and follow him. Even from so far away, she felt the tug on her inner senses, and wanted to scream. She refused to love him, yet felt more for this one single man than she ever did anyone, even her own mother.

Purana was visibly shaking with fury as she continued to stare down at the man. Never before had the conflicting emotions been so prevalent.

All the other Chosen would easily waste her people, before any could move. JC would fall, though, easily enough. But the power that was in his and Quen's people was very high, and Odyseus' lone crone with him was above all of them in strength.

Equal to that of some of the Chosen.

"Yes, he would die, maybe. But I would be severely harmed before I could finish the others." she thought.

Finally, after moments of silence, she took a deep breath and in a more normal tone, spoke out.

"That I could eliminate you, all, where you stand, is not in doubt. Your bravery was always that of a fool, old man! But, since it has been forbidden for us to fight each other, and in the end, I may, just may, mind you, have need of you to keep the spawn busy while I take on their master. So, you will live this day, and we will not see each other again, until that appointed time.

"Remember this charity, JC, that I have let you live another day. Know this, old man, the mortals are more powerful than we were led to believe. When I face off in the final battle, I can make do without you. You all may need me, but I am not hampered with such weaknesses!"

"It was only forbidden in Launam, Purana. Try, if you dare!" Burlga snarled, still feeling the sting of being called a whore. JC raised his hand to her. Shaking his head.

Purana's gateway opened behind her, and with a single word command, her army did an about face and walked through.

JC smiled even wider, and nodded to the group leaving. With an apparent over emphasized sigh, he answered.

"Purana, I thank you for your kind words, this day. Just remember, child, I still care about you, and wish you luck! We shall see you in a few months." JC calmly stated as Purana's people filed through the gate. The other Chosen turned an eye at the priest's comment.

Purana made her carpet back off, without taking her eyes off JC, until she flew through the rift and the gate closed.

When he turned, JC noticed that Quen's fingers were still white where he had been gripping his sword hilt, Odyseus still had a mental shield in place, and the women were just lowering theirs. JC seemingly the only one unaffected by the exchange, calmly stated.

"Well, that was interesting! Did you notice her aura?" He smiled. The looks from the other Immortals, caused him to briefly laugh.

"Ah, my wonderful children, you did not even take note of her aura, did you? No wonder you are so upset. I don't know for who, but that was just a show." They all brought their stare to JC, questioningly.

"What dost thou mean, Father?" Odyseus asked, concern in his tone.

"There were strong feelings in her aura, boy?" Hecate spoke up before JC could answer the big man. "And the feelings were good, kind of, not the evil of hate like her words!" She finished.

Having seen and heard enough, Mythalla no longer kept quiet,

"Who are you, Hecate? And, why don't you show your true form, Immortal one?" Mythalla spoke out. "Your inner spectrum is as gold if not more so than any of theirs!" She finished spreading her hand towards the Chosen.

JC smiled at his apprentice.

"I was wondering if you would notice, young lady." His pride at her showing brought a smile to Mythalla.

Mythalla may not be as strong as some of the others, but she learned well, and studied even harder than JC ever did. Gulnara studied the aura more intently,

294

wondering what she missed. The Chosen five moved to the venerable woman, JC stepped forward, stopping only a yard in front of Hecate.

Forcing his mind to dispel illusions, he slowly forced the old woman's form to change. She began to fight his spell, with a power that matched his own, and was almost able to slowly ebb the illusion back into place, until the others added their strength to JC's.

Hecate's shield dropped, the illusion was dispelled and suddenly sitting on the ground where the backlash of her spell, sent her painfully, was a beautiful young-looking lady, light green skin, immortal green eyes, like JC's, the only thing showing any age. For a brief moment, another form had been taking place, but so fast did it disappear into this one, no one seemed to have noticed it, except for Odyseus. The form was the woman, that Odyseus assumed was just Hecate's illusion, he now, suddenly realized was her true form.

Sitting on the ground where she had fallen, Hecate, the first dryad, shook her head.

Shaking her head, to dispel the pain from the backlash, of her spell being forcibly eliminated, the woman regained her feet, standing five feet nine inches tall, she reached out and accepted the hand of support, offered by JC.

"Blood and Ashes! I thought I had you beat, James Carl, though you are stronger than I even, would have thought. I just couldn't handle all of you, though!"

She radiated a charm that began to affect all those present until JC wrapped a dispel magic around her and smiled.

****

"May I ask what that was all about? Your Highness." The High Priest Anu asked, as Purana lowered herself to the ground.

"I don't have time to be fighting a spell that only one of The Ancient Ones could have created." She answered as she rolled the carpet into a tight roll. Turning to face the man, she dismissed the rest of the attendants and taking his sleeve, she guided him and High Priest Torel, to a more private area.

295

"Every time I get within a few yards of that man, I find myself doing what he wants. When I get away from him, I am back to normal. It is some kind of charm spell that even I cannot detect, nor can I seem to fight. I just wanted today to be done with, now, and then I don't have to deal with him anymore." Purana was talking, more than normal, and the High Priests were willing to let her talk. Torel had need of this girl, but she was too closed mouth, most times. Torel needed her, for him to ever gain the throne. They remained silent and let her talk on.

"My year spent with The Chosen and the Ancient Ones was good at first. But, sometime along the way it changed. And everyone saw it. It was just that only I seemed to notice that sorcery was involved.

"That man, has some type of spell on him, Selene is the only one to have placed it. Even I fall victim to it." Purana sat down hard into a large soft heavily padded chair. The fire place was built to good flames, she took a glass of spiced hot wine, and sent her maid off for food. Taking a long deep swallow of the drink, she continued.

"And the biggest problem, Holy Isis, finds it amusing, and refuses to remove the spell, or even admit there is one. Is everyone blind except for me?" She yelled out.

Taking another drink of the hot cider, she readjusted herself in the chair, pulling her legs under her, she finally was able to get comfortable. Taking deep breaths, staring at the flames, Purana calmed and continued.

"He is not even attractive. He's too old, too short, too dumb, and most of all, too stubborn! He even refused to bow and grant any of us our titles, like any other good commoner would. He is just a peasant and he won't treat me like the noble born lady, I am!" Purana turned away from the fire, looking at her priests.

"You saw him, Torel, Anu! The nerve to call the Queen of all of Atlantia, a child! Who does that low born old man, think he is?"

"He does have a sense of confidence to him!" Anu spoke quietly.

When silence went on for over an hour, the priests bowed and took their leave from the room. The maid found a corner after retrieving food for Purana, and sat, leaving the Empress alone in her thoughts.

For the remainder of the evening, she sat and stared at the flames. It was nearly morning when Purana finally moved off to bed.

"The Queen is losing her mind!" High Priest Torel, thought to himself as he walked away from her quarters. Anu nodded to the younger priest and left for the Temple. Torel continued to think.

"Holy Mother Isis, why did you send me an insane woman?" He continued, making his way towards his own rooms. The man was so deep in thought, that he did not notice the servants bowing and curtsying him as he walked by. Nor, did he notice the guards that take up behind him, as he moved swiftly through the halls.

"How am I to ever control the throne, if Purana continues to act the fool. She has barely risen from her studies, the last few times that we have been attacked by Hell Spawn.

"Then, the spells she casts half the time end up killing a few of our own in the back wash. I have had to tell everyone, to protect themselves against spells coming from their own Empress, as well as from the spawn." Thinking to himself as he continued to walk the halls.

The guards following him were ordered by the chamberlain. The man was sure, that Torel was up to something and meant to protect the Queen. He found it easy to convince her majesty of "protecting" the High Priest, and now Torel was shadowed everywhere, but his chambers by four guards, all were very strong in wizardry.

Torel continued to think, even after he reached his suites.

"Maybe, it is as she says. Maybe this man does have a spell on him that curses women." He continued to think to himself as he entered the suite and closed the door.

His own private maid came to him and placed her head in his outstretched hand. He comfortably massages her scalp as the thoughts continued to roll through his own mind. After some time, he abruptly stopped and lifted the maid, by her head to look him in the eye. He kissed her soundly and then spoke out loud.

"I will go and meet with this man, Lily. That is what I will do! We shall see what this really is about, from the other's point of view!"

Taking the girl by the hand, he led her to the bedroom, where she had already prepped the bed with warmers under the sheets. As he let his robe fall, the maid walked the room extinguishing the candles.

****

Hecate became agitated as the five Chosen interrogated her. Questions were being directed at her from all sides and she could feel the power of a couple of them attempting to bypass her mental shields and force their way into her mind.

"James, can you get into her mind?" Sheera telepathically sent to him.

She smiled when he seemed surprised that she could do such a thing.

"I tried reading the surface, but I cannot get past her shields. I know we are dealing with a dryad, but one of way too much power!" he thought back to her.

Odyseus seemed the most upset by her illusion and that bothered her, the most for some reason. She should not care about how the big child felt. Finally, falling into tears, at his feet, she yelled out,

"All right, enough! Enough already!" Sitting still on the ground, hugging Odyseus' left leg, she looked up into the big man's own face, tears holding at the edge of his eyes. She might have broken him, if she could not regain control. Her heart tugged, though, at the look in his eyes.

"Who would have thought, I'd be found out by a mortal? It would be one of yours, James Carl! Only you, would think to teach them some of our ways! And, why did you not say anything, if you noticed, earlier?"

Leaning down in front of the woman, JC felt the tug of a sorcery formed charm and managed somehow to snap a mental shield in place.

She was very beautiful, an appearance almost that of Gia, only with lighter brown hair, sparkling green eyes, with that same gleam of mischief in them, tanned brown greenish skin, the woman could make any woman jealous, and any man's heart pound, without the use of sorcery.

Her hair flowed down her back, with a slight wave, all the way past her knees if she were standing. JC looked into the woman's eyes and suddenly smiled.

298

He had seen a break in her thoughts when Hecate tried to charm him. He suddenly saw who and what she was.

"Why would Gia send a spy to watch us, Hecartae Fairydom? Are there one of you in each of our little followings?" He turned to look at his three priestesses and two soldiers. Before shaking his head.

"It is true, James Carl, that I am one of Mother's Archangels." Still holding on to Odyseus' leg, she reached a hand out to pat the older priest's face. "But the mother did not send me. No, I'm here on my own. And, even if you all did have one of us with you, you must know, boy, that I would not betray one of my own siblings. I may be a foolish woman, fallen to love, as is my nature to make others love me, but that does not mean that I am so far gone. But, you, boy, do not have one of my brethren watching you!" JC saw a slight lie in her last statement.

"Then why or what interest do you have in my young friend? Certainly, it isn't love that makes you stay an old woman, around him? Have you decided that the strongest of The Chosen has need of a mother?" JC could be most forceful, without the use of sorcery, and even the angel was feeling the strength in his demand.

The probing against her own mental shield was hard, and feminine, and she looked at Burlga and Sheera trying to decide which of the two was doing it.

"Well..." She started.

JC noticed a spark of light move across her eyes, the same mischievous twinkle of Hecate's mother creator. "Well, boy, if I have to answer that, I guess I should just say this!" Her face took on an embarrassed look briefly then with a quickly added smile, she stated,

"Purana's rage was for your benefit, JC, not the other boys! Hehe", she chuckled.

She felt the combined power of a spell hit her as Sheera joined with JC and the two immediately began to crush her shields. They were about to fold as she struggled to maintain herself.

"Answer my question, Hecate! If you are so, in love with Odyseus, why the guise of an old woman?" JC stayed calm, but his voice became cold, almost as emotionless as Quen's could be at times.

299

Realizing the woman was going to twist and stall, he added more forcefully,

"I do not like forcing anyone, but I will have my answers!"

Startled, her eyes grew big and dangerous. Hecate slowly stood up, using Odyseus as a ladder. As her hands grabbed onto his upper thighs, the discomfort could be clearly seen in his face.

When she grabbed his belt, Odyseus took her hands away and lifted her to an erect position, still holding her hands above her head, for a moment before letting them go.

JC had slowly stood with her, never taking his eyes off hers. He felt the press on his own shields, and forced out one on hers.

"How many do I have, then?" he interrupted.

"We feared you would not be so easily watched. We were obviously correct!" She knew immediately, that she had said too much!

Feeling the tug of compulsion on her, she could tell it was not a spell, but a natural part of his spirit.

"What is it about this man that makes people want to talk?" She thought!

Hecate could feel her shield weakening to a power that this man should not have, even linked with one of the others as he was.

"You dare threaten me, boy? With sorcery, even?" She hissed, lowering her hands to her hips, legs slightly apart, she continued.

"You may be able to dispel my illusion, youngster, with help, but do not pretend to think you can mentally force me to do anything you wish." She wondered, though, if he could.

"And you, boy," she added with a couple strong finger points to JC's chest, "Yes, I see, your weaknesses, I know all of your weaknesses. And, JC, yours is mine's advantage. You cannot hurt a woman. You would never ever physically force a woman!" JC held his ground with the finger thrusts, and only tilted his head slightly to the left, but his face remained blank and unreadable.

"The man may not, hag, but I would have no such flaming problems!" Burlga said, stepping up behind JC, slightly to his right. Her hand had taken hold of his right arm in a tight grip.

Staring at the Immortals, Hecate knew she was too outnumbered and besides, she had to regain control of Odyseus, somehow. Looking down, she took on a demure look.

"Listen, it is as you said, and more. Certainly, you can see that I really do love this big bear. I only am here because of him." Still seeing no emotion in JC, she continued.

"I had to meet all of you, which is the only reason I came, today." she took a breath letting the rest of what she was about to say fall away.

A calm had come to her and she continued.

"Besides, the way he talks about you all, you would think you were his family or something. Maybe, who really knows, you really are. I only am here because of love."

JC looked around at the mortals off to the side, and the Immortals around him, finally he looked up into Odyseus' face, to see the torn look almost begging him for an answer.

"We are on Pan, Hecartae First dryad, Queen of the Fairies. What would Holy Gia say if we were to call her forth? I would hate to gain her intervention in this, but will do it if I cannot trust you." Sheera stated.

"She at least, now is speaking the truth!" the voice was coming from all around them, before the one it belonged to appeared.

All those present bowed, as Minerva suddenly appeared off to the side. All bowed except for JC, as he lowered his head in a short sign of respect.

"I wonder if she really can be trusted, Holy Minerva." JC started seeing the fear in Hecate to Sheera's statement. "Holy Minerva, you have been with us all day, thank you for your visit. We have need of your wisdom, in this, I would think!"

301

"No wisdom is needed in anything more than you already have. I have seen that all of you have watchers, though my son's is more active. Odyseus, you have my heart in whatever way you choose. James Carl, you will continue to love all the Chosen, I know. Gia will not be happy in this, Hecartae!" The Ancient One disappeared and the feeling of being watched left with her.

"I still wonder what your true intentions are, angel? The trust or mistrust, on my part, is one thing. But it is not my place to say. Odyseus, my boy, she says she loves you, and of that, I do believe.

"Her other reasons for all of the subterfuge, well, who can say? I'm a poor match at trying to understand women, as you all know.

"Therefore, I leave it to you to make the decision. I trust you, Odyseus, and I trust your judgment. You are wiser than we give you credit for. You decide! It would seem that your own goddess is amused by this angel's interference." JC said, still watching the angel before him.

Hecate had moved to grab onto Odyseus, but when he stepped back, she was stunned and allowed more tears to form in her eyes.

"I would never hurt you, Odyseus. You have to at least know that!" Hecate choked out between sobs.

Odyseus' eyes moved between her and JC. He took a deep sigh, and finally stated.

"We do be at things that need discussed, woman, but not here and not now. Right now, my friends and I do need talk, so, go and sit over there until I'm ready to leave. Please!" He added when she made to protest.

Sullenly, she moved away, looking back at him, with tears holding at the corners of her eyes.

Meritt could not believe his eyes. An angel? And, one that claims to be an Archangel! And, the Goddess Minerva shows up. And, this father JC and Lady Burlga threatened her as if she was just another mortal follower.

"Not to mention that the one named Sheera so casually threatened to bring Gia present." suddenly he became aware what she had said.

They were all on Pan, the mythical island of Mother Gia that had been disappeared from Zindar for eons.

"Who are these people, that my Lord Quen calls companions?" He thought to himself.

Massy watched the movements of JC. She thought to herself, how very calm he can stay, when others might be threatened.

"He has absolutely no fear when those he cares for, might be in danger. This is quite the man; I have chosen to follow! You did well, Holy Selene!" She thought to herself.

"Well, where be we, now?" Odyseus stated, taking a deep breath. Sheera moved to him and gave him a hug, as Quen patted him on the back.

"Hey, instead of used up old woman, now, I be getting to eye a pretty girl, trying to teach me. This be wantin fun!" He laughed, but he never took his arms from around Sheera and she could tell by the quiver in his entire body, that he really was hurting. "Say something, JC." She thought, still holding the big young man.

"I think, Father, about thy discussion, thine lecture was telling us about our swords?" Odyseus finally, broke the silence. JC still looking at him, smiled.

"I think, child... young man, that I am very proud to be your friend right now! Prouder than ever before! If I ever have a son, someday, I hope he turns out, just like you!" JC finally said. Odyseus relaxed in Sheera's arms.

The smile that broke on the big man's face, was childlike, but everybody relaxed at that moment and they were able to move on. Turning to the mortals standing off to the side, watching with stunned disbelief, JC waved them closer,

"Come on everybody. You too Hecate, though I would imagine what I am about to show is not unknown to you. Let's get this over with, so we can all get back home. We have had a very trying day!"

Quen smiled, inwardly. "JC always knew how to relax the group. He really is the High Priest, of the Chosen. And, the leader of us, for all our arguments."

JC asked for the dagger, he had given Massy and she produced it, hilt first. She was smiling at him as well, and patted his arm, with her free hand, as a gesture that she thought all had gone well. JC nodded to her before continuing.

"The blade is made of mythral, silver, and cold iron." He started. "Ten parts iron, to four parts silver, to one-part mythral..."

The spells were simple but required a lot of strength, and as he showed them, discussing the differences that Sheera had used, he changed his mind on a couple spells as Burlga added her own ideas of alchemy.

Sheera's way would require less psychic strength, and Burlga added ideas on using alternate spells that would not weaken the blades. Although they would not gain as good a blade as the Immortals were given, at least the metal that would be made should be able to hit any of the Hell Spawn.

"And if, the magic is done while the metal is being smelted, then more weapons can be produced with fewer spells. "JC concluded. "A simple permanency spell on the finished product, and the blade would be completed. Bless and another permanency, after the blade is attached to the hilt, and you have a sword, or whatever other weapon, you are making, that no denizen of Hell could avoid."

As the others went to leave, JC took each one in his arms.

"Quen, I am so glad you came. I was fearful that you would have felt as Purana does, towards me."

"I admit, JC, that I use to think your overbearing priestly attitude a little hard on the nerves. But I came to realize over these past months, that I needed it, as well. I can be somewhat overbearing myself, at times." With a wink, he left with his sorcerers, sure that all would be better off, now.

JC made sure to shake all of Quen's people good bye and even held on to Meritt's arm a little longer adding.

"Look after him, please, High Priest. We all will need to be taken care of by our churches." Meritt smiled and gave an assurance he would.

"See you in a few months, Father JC d'Badger!" He yelled out as his gateway closed.

When Burlga left with Persides, she gave Sheera a hug and JC a passionate hug and kiss, while soundly patting the man's buttocks. Laughing at the startled look he gave, "as he always does" she thought, she winked at him with a comment on what he was missing, and hugged Odyseus hard before gaining her horse and riding through her own gateway.

As Odyseus was leaving with Hecate, JC took hold of the big man in a solid embrace and wished him luck.

"You can let me know how things go, in a few months. Remember, I'm proud of you, son. I always have been!" Turning to Hecate, he gave her a stern look.

"I think awfully highly of this young man, Angel. If you hurt him in any way, I will not think well of you. Don't misuse our trust! Become our friend, Hecartae, not our enemy!"

She only nodded, and grabbed Odyseus' arm, this time he did not pull away. They disappeared.

Sheera was putting out the fire and cleaning the area with Massy's help, when he came to stand with her. Taking her necklace in his hand, he set it back against her chest.

"You still have that, I see?" He smiled. "I figured you would have sold it for some palace or something." he chuckled.

"Yes, it was given to me by a very special friend. My brother, actually. I'll use it too, one of these days. But, of course, he probably will be in the arms of some beautiful woman, and won't come." She faked a sniff. Then winked.

"If you are in enough trouble, that would make you use that, I will come, no matter the circumstance. Remember, it was given out of love, Sheera. And I don't give my love, lightly! I will not lose you, to any curse!"

"I know, you don't. No such thing as a curse, James! I hope she is as good to you, whoever she is, as I know you are to her!" Sheera patted his cheek when he stared dumbfounded at her. "A woman always knows when the man she is connected to is in love with someone.

"You were raised with females, James, I would think you would not be so innocent, still." she laughed. "Now, by your reaction, I know that it is true!" She looked askance at the group of women following him, and shook her head.

"No, it would not be any of these. She would be someone you might think recognizable, but possibly unobtainable. And it would not be a woman of common means, either, would it? Someone you rescued? No, if you rescued her, you would want to protect her. One of your high priestesses, maybe?"

Massy started to laugh openly, and Mythalla chuckled. JC was glad for the setting sun, as his skin is burning with embarrassment. He quickly gained control, and took Sheera's hands.

"That is enough, my dear. You don't have to show everyone how well you know me, maybe even better than I do, myself."

JC gave the other women laughing, a stern pout, and then smiled himself, at the joke. The two embraced taking up where they had begun, that morning. Mythalla nodded, thinking to herself,

"This Chosen is very astute, and very much, loving towards our father. She would be someone that could help or hinder, Dyanea."

As they were saying their farewells, Massy came forward and took Sheera's arm.

"Are you going to ask him, young lady, or are you going to make the coward? He isn't that intimidating, you know."

"What are you talking about, Massy?" JC asked. But the dwarf only looked at Sheera, who was taking a deep breath, before she blurted out.

"I want to take Massy with me!" The startled looks everyone gave to the Immortal, was overlooked only by the shaking head of the Dwarven priestess.

"Children!" Was Massy's response. "What she means, Father, is that she and I were talking and maybe I can go and round up support for her with the dwarves and other non-humans on her continent. With that, then she can gather the human lords a little easier. Especially if she comes at them from a position of strength."

"It could work at that! That was a good idea!" He answered. "I'm going to miss you, your highness, even though we didn't have time to really get to know one another, better!" He added. "You've become my best friend, here."

"And I will miss you too, young man!" She answered. "Give me a year, and then I'll be back home. Besides, you will see me every few months anyway."

"You take good care of her, now. Sheera is a very special sister to me." Giving the dwarf a hug, the princess was a little taken back by the show of affection towards her.

She wiped at her eyes and turned to go, with the young female Chosen. As they approached Sheera's gateway, Massy stopped and took the dagger that JC had given her, off her belt.

"Keep it, your Highness. It may come in handy. Besides, it was a gift to my friend." JC stated, as he rubbed at an eye.

They disappeared through her gateway, and JC opened his own, back to their suite at the palace. The gateway closed, and he found his eyes tired and burning for some reason, as he excused himself to his room. The women were all, smiling as the father closed his door.

Mythalla, turned and quickly exited out the door for Reverend Mother Dyanea's suite. The only thing on her mind was the absolute beauty and power she saw in the group that was amassed today.

That, and the gorgeous men, named Quen and Meritt. Whew, if they only had noticed her once, all would have been a great day. She thought to herself.

When she arrived at the Rev. Mother's suite, she knocked on the door, and gathered in her blushing, before entering.

CHAPTER 12
The night's blessing!

After giving her report to Reverend Mother Dyanea, leaving nothing out, to include the actions of the female Chosen, Dyanea had her open a gateway to the Temple of Selene, in Bornesta.

"No need to mention the appearance of the Goddess Minerva, nor the angels. We don't need interfere in that." Mythalla agreed as she stepped through the gateway allowing it to close behind the Reverend Mother.

Later that evening, the council was brought together.

All eight members of the Council sat and listened as the young priestess relayed what had happened. Mythalla, now, apprentice to Father JC was also, the Reverend Mother Dyanea's former apprentice.

It was beginning to bother her that she was spying on the man for the council, but since she was under orders she would comply. So far none of what she had been asked to do hurt the father, and she was going to be away for stretches at a time, anyway.

She smoothly outlined the meeting of the Chosen to the council.

"So, there is a way then that weapons can be made, sisters!" Dyanea, already having been told everything, to include parts that Mythalla was omitting to the rest of them.

"Yes, Reverend Mother. Father JC was teaching the others, to include even all of us followers. The Holy Merylon Chosen, called Burlga, she seems the most powerful in sorcery among the group, a half-elf and the one called Sheera, Holy Jeasuas' human Chosen, seemed to think by altering two of the spells, it would not affect the effectiveness of the weapons, but would still allow us mortals, as they call us, to make them as well. Jay. Umm, the father, agreed!" Her near slip did not go unnoticed by Dyanea, who smiled.

Using Mythalla as a spy was a good idea, even if a less than desirable action. But it was obvious to anyone, that she was truly beginning to become enraptured with the man, and the Reverend Mother wondered how much longer, the young woman would be of any use.

"Mother Mythalla, did any seem to think gaining mythral would be too difficult?" The Reverend Mother C'renan asked. Thinking a moment before responding, Mythalla, only shook her head.

"Only Father JC hinted that he didn't know how to get any. And, Lady Sheera said only that she didn't even know any smiths, as of yet, to be trusted with the information. Nor does she have the support of her own church, yet. But she seems to be the closest to our own Father. Spiritual siblings were the term Father JC used." Mythalla stopped, not meaning to add the last sentence. She cleared her throat, looking at Dyanea, before continuing.

"The Holy Phaleg's Chosen, called Lord Quen," her voice almost sang, "acted as though he easily had access. He has already become the Emperor of Grazia. I spoke with his most trusted priest, High Priest Meritt. Also, it should be noted, Emperor Quen is the weakest in psychic strength, among the Chosen, although, it still out strips most of us priestesses."

"Who is the leader of the Chosen, Mythalla? Is it this Lady Burlga?" The Reverend Mother Mya, asked.

"Based on what I saw, it is probably Father JC. There is no real leader, they all agree and disagree, but there is one that is not a part of the six. Purana, I believe her name to be, is Queen of Atlantia, the Holy Isis' Chosen, and, it was our own Father JC that called her down. She was only at the meeting for a few minutes and actually threatened the others but Father JC advised that was just for show.

"No, if there is an unspoken leader within the group, it would be him. He's the elder of the Chosen, all the others being about my age, and the Father is the one, they seem to defer to!" Carefully choosing her words, Mythalla had told Dyanea about the girls' fawning on the man, as well as about the Angel. But, at Dyanea's command, was leaving this part out with the rest of the Council.

"So, if we can send someone to speak with this Odyseus of Lemuria. He's the boy, correct, Mythalla?" The Reverend Mother Kyana spoke out. "Certainly, one of us could manipulate a boy, and then we could use him to bring our father JC under control."

Mythalla looked at Dyanea, a frown on her face and turned to Kyana after choosing carefully structured words.

"The Chosen One Odyseus, has a very powerful adviser with him. One as strong as even, our own Dyanea. And, Father JC thinks, he might be "The One Chosen Champion", of the prophesies. I would not go after, nor interfere with the boy, if we hope to hold onto the father."

Facing the Reverend Mother Kyana, Mythalla spoke slowly and carefully. Hoping that she would not be noticed, leaving something out.

"Why do we need to control the man?" C'renan finally spoke up. "Why not bring him into our Council and hold him to our laws? He is our prophet, after all! We chase him away and one of the other orders may gain his counsel. He also, has been made our new Marshal. You want to control him? What is wrong with you women?"

The argument that ensued among the women, lasted for several minutes. Most of the eight still held to the old customs that men were too violent to be healers, and although, The Father had proved to be a good healer, he was also, very violent!

"He even carries that strange sword of his like it is a part of him!" Reverend Mother Joreen stated, disgustingly.

"It was given him by Holy Selene, herself!" Mythalla quickly answered. "And, if I may?" She looked to C'renan for a nod, before continuing. "I have been with him, twice when the Goddess has appeared. He is the Sword of Vengeance, from her own mouth."

"It is probably just an illusion for your benefit, young one!" Reverend Mother Coigsta, interrupted.

"Why would he need do that, Reverend Mother? I already know him to be the prophet I don't need any convincing!" Mythalla almost sounded angry before getting her composure under control. The amused looks she received from the Council brought her up short.

"It would seem our pretty young priestess, here, almost worships the man!" Reverend Mother Zaina calmly stated, with no hint of sarcasm to her.

"Perhaps, then we should not be discussing Father JC with her in this room?" Mya added.

"Enough!" Dyanea rose from her chair. "You talk of control? Do you control me, Mya? Do any of you control anyone else, or are any of you, controlled by anyone?" The Reverend Mother Dyanea's temper was well known.

The quarter elf was known for her fiery disposition and all the Council could see it coming to a boil at that moment.

"Dyanea is right!" C'renan said, attempting to calm her closest friend. "We hold him to us, by putting him on the Council. We do not need to control the prophet of Selene. And, I for one, do not want to see his power reigned in, if we even if there was a way we could!

"Mythalla, what has the Goddess said on those times you have seen her talk with Father JC?"

"Only that he needs to not rush things. Whatever that means. Oh, and, that the Chosen One Purana will need his help. She is quite adamant about Father JC's need to keep forgiveness in his heart at all times."

C'renan nodded her head, and then looked around the room. Dyanea still standing, her fingers turning white gripping the pleats of her robe. C'renan took a deep breath before resuming.

"Reverend Mothers, you talk of illusions. Dyanea and I have both seen the Goddess with the man. Are we too, so susceptible to illusions. I think not. Elves are immune to those types of magiks, as you well know! And, I tell you this, ladies. The Holy Selene's manners with this man, as Dyanea and Mythalla can both attest, is not one of Goddess to subject!"

"It is, mother to son! And, you all want to control, this man?" Dyanea added, quietly through gritted teeth.

The other six Council members sat, looking stunned or in disbelief. Rumors of Holy Selene's visit to the Palace had spread, but they were just rumors. Now, the two ladies were admitting to them.

"You manipulate us all very well, C'renan!" Reverend Mother Berga spoke up. "You are almost as good as Morella was at this!"

"Except, I do this for all of our good. I also do not have a demon controlling my every move. I'm not Hell Sworn, as she was!" C'renan smiled. "And, you, Berga, are already sure of the man, or at least you have said. Holy Selene, Goddess of Healing and Vengeance has, finally, sent to us her Sword. Should we not all, just embrace him?" C'renan looked at Dyanea and Mythalla, before eyeing each of the others.

The unanimous vote to put JC d'Badger on the council carried.

****

As he exited the chamber, Martinith stopped to look at the mirror he passed.

"Not too bad!" He thought.

He could feel the spirit of his brother, within, battling for control, but he simply willed it back to sleep.

He knew that eventually his brother's spirit would meld with his own and then a new personality would emerge. But for now, he must plan his revenge.

"The luck of that man, tripping forward, just as my door was about to open on him. It would have been so much easier, and he would be dead, right now. I was too over confident, and, that bitch, Lilith, had me in too much of a snarl. I won't make that mistake, again!" Martinith spoke to the other vats, still in the stasis chamber. One vat now empty, and the other seven containing his brothers. Not, really to be his brothers, he was looking at the other "shells", new bodies should his next attempt end like the first.

"How did that man take that kind of injury to the back, yet still, manage to fight like he did?" He mumbled.

"Because, brother, he has the constitution of a god. Like you do, now!" The voice behind was soft, lovely sounding. Martinith turned to see Proserpine, eyeing him.

312

"What do you want, Proserpine? Come to harass me and goad me into a battle like Lilith did?" He snarled.

"Did she tell you to go after the Archangel unaccompanied, Martinith?" Proserpine responded.

"Archangel? He is nothing but a man with power, Proserpine!"

"He is Selene's child, Martinith. Much as you are our lord's. Her seed, her control. You want revenge, take one of our Archangels with you. Match his power with our power. Take Nebiros, maybe. He's one of our father's most loyal, or even Molech would do. And, Martinith? Be sure to take a few of the lesser angels, as well! Pit Fiends would do nice!"

He looks at his sister angel and smiles. Not as pretty as Lilith, though, she is nearly so. Proserpine is easily as powerful, and very appealing.

"Come here, Proserpine. Mammon is a weak, in comparison to me. Let me show you what a real man can give you."

Martinith was not ready with his mental shields. Only awakening a few minutes ago, he forgot what the devils and demons in Lucifer's Palace were like. The mind crush hit him and he fell before he was even aware she had killed him.

When the second vat opened and Martinith stepped out, Proserpine was gone. He shook his head, remembering their conversation.

"She's even more touchy than Lilith. That's two bitches that will learn what it means to go against me. Yes, they will learn."

****

Sheera and Massy were walking and the dwarf asked about gun powder. Not being able to follow, the conversation that the Immortals were talking about, she had a curiosity about any type of weapon.

Sheera explained that it was something she had thought about, only as a last resort.

"Katiketa has all the elements for it, but it is a dangerous fool that tries making it, without knowing how. I thought James, uh JC, would be able to, since he was a scientist, back on our home world." Seeing the look on the dwarf's face, she added. "A scientist in our world is similar to alchemists, here. They experiment and make substances out of other things. JC use to teach that sort of thing, before coming here."

"Why was he so against it, then? Could it be, that he does not know how, and did not want to admit it?" Massy asked.

"No, not our JC! He would freely say if he couldn't do something. As a matter of fact, that he fought so hard against it, says exactly what I thought. He knows how, and maybe even has thought about it, as well. Somehow, someone must have convinced him that it is forbidden. He speaks with our mother's angels so much that who knows where he gets some of his ideas."

The voice that spoke behind them, had Massy turning, the hammer coming into her hand, with such quickness, it seemed almost alive.

"So, Chosen One, Selene's Chosen refused you, this time!" The angel said. He had the same face, as Gabriel had, but, now, the angel stood over two meters tall, and had a golden skin tone, with long high feathered wings. The long flowing hair of gold tresses, waved between the appendages. His bright blue eyes, seemed to pierce the dwarf's mind.

"He said it was forbidden. Who would forbid him, if Jeasuas says I should do this?" Sheera said.

"Perhaps, JC just didn't understand what he was told? If it was forbidden, would I have told you about it?" Massy did not have good feelings about this being, but not being able to read auras, she had to let Sheera handle it.

"I will ask him one more time, but he was getting into his stubborn mode, and when there, he cannot be moved. If it is so important, why don't you tell me how to make it?"

"My dear, we are not supposed to interfere, remember?" Gabriel told her. "Oh, and one other thing. Be wary of that gnome that occasionally follows you. He is not so very trustworthy."

314

"What do you mean by that? He has been a good friend, for almost three months."

"Just keep an eye on him. He is not what he seems! That is all I'll say! Good bye, young woman." And with that last, he disappeared.

Sheera only shrugged when Massy asked about the bad feelings, such a creature would make her feel. They continued on.

When Belial shimmered back into his true form, he turned to see Leaf standing on the road

"So, you are the one that is Gabriel, Belial. Perhaps, I should just tell the girl, to disregard your advice."

"And give yourself away, Lephorisal? You have more to lose, than I do!"

"Stay away from her, devil. She is under my protection. We have been forbidden to fight, but I will certainly disregard that, to keep her safe from you!"

"Ahh, you have a little pet, cousin How cute! Don't threaten me, you have no more power than I do, and I would imagine, even less." Belial disappeared through a dimensional door this time.

"How to tell her, without admitting what I'd seen?" Leaf thought, aloud.

****

The gateway closed, and Quen felt a little nostalgic, for some reason. The usual stoic matter of facts attitude, that had become his life, was suddenly rocked by the strength of character, of a not so common man.

"It would seem that JC has become even more dominating a personality since being around the mortals than he was around us! It only seems to add to the mystique of the man."

"An impressive man, indeed, my lord!" High Priest Meritt exclaimed as the rest of the group left after the gateway closed.

"I see your hesitation at crossing him. Very well played, if I may say so, Lord Quen."

315

"That was no game I played, Meritt! I really did find myself failing beside him. I could not have remained so non plussed with Purana, as he did. No fear, that is easy enough, but to not even have anger.

"His was no show, my lord priest. All he was feeling was sorrow for the woman. I am the one, that will face the last battle, of that I have no doubts, but I know now, that it is most imperative, that Father JC d'Badger, is there with me. I will need him! I had forgotten about the confidence that he instills to others around him."

The priest looked at the young man and only nodded.

"Perhaps, then, we should pick our best blades, and send them to the father for his protection? Perhaps, as a good will gesture, with some mythral. He did not say it, but I don't think he has the resources, himself. He freely gave you the way to make swords without any demand for recompense."

"Yes, I told you he would. All I needed was to ask, and he gave. That is his way, with those he cares for. And, he really does care for us all. He has always seemed to care!" After a moment, Quen stopped and turned to the older man.

"But it would be only proper manners, as you say, if we were to gift him for the gift, he gave us."

"As you say, Brother Quen. It shall be done! Would maybe say, 100 kilograms be enough?"

"Make it 150, and send along four of the first blades, after they are made. That way, he can tell if they are done correctly."

"Very good, my lord! A little smoothing is always needed the first time we try new spells. Very good, indeed! And, I will be the one to make these gifts, of course."

"Of course, who else?"

"What about the protection, M'lord?" Meritt added, thinking his emperor never even commented on it.

"That would be taken as an insult, Meritt. I know that I would. Mention something about creating the Blades Elite, and see where he goes with that."

The priests walked into the Temple's smithy, and immediately began the directions to the armorers. The first of eight long swords were completed by the next evening.

Quen, looking at the swords, not yet mounted to hilts, wondered at the last of the spells. Eyeing the blades with that of a warrior use to holding only the best, he found very little flaws to the balance.

Almost perfect, and the edges sharp and true. Yet, when he pulled his own sorcery made long sword, given to him by Lord Phaleg, Holy Ancient One, and his benefactor and mentor, Quen saw a difference almost immediately.

The mixture on his peoples' blades was evident. He could clearly see three different metals making up the finely tuned blades. On his own god given sword, there was no mixture of metal evident. Only a bluish tint to the honed steel that never needed sharpening, and never break.

He recalled having swung completely through a demon, only to strike against the stone wall, behind, and ended up having to pull the blade from the stone. A not too easy task, that one time. Even the stone did nothing to tarnish or damage his blade. This first batch of blades will certainly not handle that kind of punishment. He could feel the sorcery in it, though, and it felt similar to his, as far as the probing went. Alas, the differences, still troubled him.

Handing the steel shank back to Meritt, he looked again to his sword, and re-sheathed it.

"They are similar, yet different. Damn, I was hoping for a bastard sword. Not yet! The sorcery is the same, but the blades look different, and the fact that stone can still damage the tips, make me believe we missed something."

"I did what Lord JC had said. The only thing missing is the blessing and final permanency on the finished product. Of course, these are not the exact same spells that Lord JC had first mentioned. Maybe the lesser type casting spells that the Ladies came up with are the differences. I am sorry that we failed you, my lord, Quen!" High Priest Meritt finally said.

"You did not fail, my friend. If you did, then I did as well. I watched and I know you did exactly what the old man told us. Maybe, the slight altered spells that

Burlga and Sheera came up with, were the differences, as you said? Maybe we do need to make them, the original way that JC first said?"

"If that is so, he did not think, even he could cast a couple of them. What chance would any of us?"

"Good point, Meritt. That is why you are the High Priest!"

The slight smile that was quickly replaced by the emotionless face almost went unnoticed by the older man. He sometimes had a hard time knowing when his Lord was joking, and on a number of occasions that had gotten him into some trouble. Meritt, now, smiled, and calmly retorted.

"Perhaps I should gather the gifts, and go and see our Lord JC. It might be that we just didn't hear something the way we thought we did."

"How much does it cost us for the mythral, Meritt?"

"I pay the miners, a little over two hundred gold weights per kg. We can gather about one thousand kilograms per week, if we have to. Each blade costs four kg and another two kg of silver, M'lord. That will be the real problem. I think we will run out of silver long before we do mythral"

"Hmm, OK, gift the first hundred fifty, as I said. Then when he asks, and he will, barter him to two hundred fifty per kg, providing he pays in silver, and no more than two hundred kg of mythral per week. And also, ask him how much mythral would it cost for him to cast the original spells on a thousand kilograms of mixture. I know him, and he can cast the spells, you can be assured of that!

"And, if he wants to give something more, ask him if he could make me a bastard sword. I'd love to see what he can really do if it was a gift. I'd bet it would be a real piece of art!"

Smiling, Meritt looked at his emperor,

"You are most wise, my Lord. I shall go and rest, and leave tonight. Until later, Lord Quen, good morning!"

Meritt walked away, only bowing with his head. Quen, did not allow the High Priests to give him a groveling bow, as he thinks it demeans the church. The Immortal smiled as he finally had broken most of the priests from that practice. Realizing he himself had been up all night, he took off for his own rooms. Nileena walked by, dropping a quick curtsy, and with a winning smile, nodded to take up beside her lord. The two arrived at the emperor's suites and Quen ordered a wakeup call in six hours.

****

Walking the halls of the castle, Quevit watched as the laborers continued their work on the keep. It was only an hour before sun set and he wondered that his cousin was not yet back. He had been wondering all day, about her and this JC, of hers. Is he really so much better than Quevit?

"He is not even a noble, how could she prefer that man to me?"He said aloud. "She admitted that he is too short, and shows no notice in her like she would like, but yet, still she pines for him like some young girl and her first crush! I'm not so old, younger than he is if she is telling the truth. I may be almost thirty-five, but I'm still healthy! I will have to tell her how I feel, when she gets back. If, that is, it is not too late."

"She is a fool, not to want you, my lord!" The sultry even pitched voice, seemed to settle in his mind, as he felt the pull of it.

Quevit turned to find himself face to face with one of the most beautiful of women, he had ever laid his eyes to. His eyes could not pull away from hers, as she held him entranced.

The black eyes, perfect circles within the perfect face, too pale, but that just added to the exotic appearance of the rest of her features, he thought! At least the features he could see.

Quevit was unable to take his eyes anywhere, but where they continued to stare. The light yellow almost white hair, flowed in waves, as though it had a life of its own. Something was behind her, but he could not focus on the two moving arches beyond her eyes. Nor could he focus on the pale exposed shoulders, below her head. He was sure he had seen them bare before he locked onto the eyes.

The woman, smiled and began rubbing against him, pushing him backwards until he stopped at the wall behind him. He felt himself becoming aroused, wanting to feel this magnificent creature, take all of her in with his eyes, as well as his mouth, but Quevit never took his eyes from hers. He was sure he would not be able, even if he wanted to.

She wanted him, he could tell, and his hands finally were able to move, touching bare skin at her hips. As he moved his hands slowly, exploring, to find that more than her shoulders were bare. No clothing was on this woman, the only thing he felt other than cold skin was her hair hanging down below her shoulders to just the top of her round strong muscled buttocks. Quevit tried to look down, wanting to see the perfect body that his hands were caressing, but the woman took a grip on both sides of his head and her mouth parted slightly as she moved closer for a kiss.

Her body was too cold, but her lips were warm, and moist. And they tasted as though she had spread honey on them, as her tongue forced its way into his mouth. He closed his eyes as he began to feel weak.

His eyes opened after a few seconds, they were still kissing, but now he was able to focus on the arches rising behind her. Shocked out of the charm, he saw finally, that this goddess of a woman had nearly transparent, leathery bat like wings growing out of the top of her shoulder blades. Somehow, he had missed them when his hands were devouring her body.

His hands caressing her breasts, suddenly squeezed tightly, the trance he had been in, now broken. He tried to push while he squeezed, but she was too strong. He twisted his body trying to move, as she continued the hold on to his head, tightening more with each moment, and her kisses becoming a vice on his lips. Yanking, scratching, and punching her chest and stomach only succeeded in gathering a moan, as though she was aroused by it.

The longer her kiss held him, the weaker he was becoming. His teeth began trying to bite down on her tongue, but it was like biting into hardened leather, and she just giggled. She continues to moan with pleasure as he was weakly battling her.

He is steadily weakening, as it became increasingly more difficult to fight. He could feel himself wanting to give in to her. She was draining his soul from his body, and his will was going with it. Worse was that he no longer seemed to care.

Burlga had finished with her horse, letting the stable boy take him away. She dismissed Persides, telling him to go and get some sleep, they would be getting up early on the marrow. Turning to the castle she entered and made towards the sleeping quarters. Quevit would be glad to know, he would soon have a sword, a real sword to aid her in the battles.

"Leave it to that wonderful old man, to have figured it out! Not a bad kisser, I'll bet, either. His lips are still soft, and pliable. Just the right kind for a woman to bite down on. And he almost responded, this time. I bloody will win this game yet, old man." She smiled as she thought about the man. Burlga was just turning the corner in the hall, when she saw Quevit and a devil struggling. Or were they?

Quevit was about to pass out in an ecstatic death, when the devil was suddenly ripped away from him with an agonizing scream. He had something moving in his mouth, something like leather, yet still moving, as he slumped to the floor. He could see his cousin, throwing the female devil hard against the opposite wall, swinging Baalzephon by one of her willies succumbed to unconsciousness, as the building seemed to shake at the devil's impact.

Burlga realized the seductress was eking Quevit's spirit out of him, a piece at a time with that kiss. She could tell, he was almost dead, before she entered the battle. The devil was never aware of the sorceress' presence until too late, and now Burlga drew her sword as she placed a force field around the momentarily stunned devil.

The energy field held, while Burlga stabbed with her sword. With the devil battling the field of energy holding her, Burlga continued to stab and cut at its neck. The garbled scream came through flowing blood, where Baalzephon's tongue had been half bitten off. Burlga chopped once again, at the neck, and the head rolled off onto the floor. Watching it roll over to her cousin, she kicked the head aside and leaned down to Quevit. His smile as she lifted his head, told her he would survive.

****

"So, grandmother, what we to do now? Thy dost look no so old, anymore!" Odyseus asked as his gateway closed behind him. The young-looking angel hanging on his arm still disturbed him, especially since he did not know how to handle this. JC had told him that he trusted his judgment, but Odyseus really was out of his element here.

Give him a war, and he could devise a plan.With love, well, he still remembered how Purana had just used him once a month and then ignore him the rest; and then on this day, well that said, exactly how did she feel towards the love they had shared. Or rather, the love he had given, he was sure now, that it was never returned.

He was deep in his thoughts that he did not hear the woman's answer beside him. The jab to his ribs brought him out of his reverie.

"Pay attention, boy, if you want me to stay."

"Well, that do be the question, is it not, Hecate?" He stopped turning to look down at her, as she had taken on her form as the old hag.

"You really are not going to just toss me away, are you? After all I've done for you?" She sniffed.

"What hast thou done? Let's see. Gotten me almost killed, lots at times. Gotten me into kinds of problems be with nobles. Gotten me nearly cut to half by a lightning bolt, cast by thy hand, claiming thee only trying to save me. Be I missing anything else, woman? Oh, yes, and chasing all possible female friends away." His tone was that of anger, but Odyseus never really showed it in his face. He managed an outer calm, only the tightness of his eyes, the tears being held back, and the tone of his voice told her his true emotions.

"You do not want to do this. Have you never heard the phrase that Hell is cooler than the heat of a woman that has been cast aside? Well, boy, I am a heavenly lover or a very vindictive angel. You make the choice!"

Odyseus looked at her, and started to shake. The inner chuckle rumbled his insides at first until he was laughing aloud. Tears were rolling down his face when he realized that he was the only one laughing.

"Thine anger be misplaced, Hecate!" He said between sobs. "Thine own mother, not to mention all the Ancient Ones woust never allow thee to bring harm unto me. I think Mother Minerva be watching right now, wondering this be turning out. And, as far as heavenly lover?"

"The Ancient Ones are not so omnipresent, boy. Only The Mother Creator can so easily know an other's thoughts. Gia, even only when she concentrates on

322

someone. I could make your life very miserable if I wanted and it would be months before any of them would notice.

"Do not be so sure of yourself. I will have you! And, I will have what I need from you. You know nothing of what my purpose is, and only when I tell you, will you know!" Realizing that she had said more than she wanted, the impetuous angel stepped back snapping her hands to her hips.

"What be thy purpose, Hecate? Tell me now, there be no more secrets betwixt us."

"Or what, you big bear? What will you do, put me over your knee?"

"I can, but the way thine talk leads, I thinks that thee woust actually enjoy it overly much!" The sarcastic answer came between clinched teeth. No joke to the tone.

The slap delivered rattled his jaw. Out of nowhere, Hecate swung with a strength that she had only hinted at having. Odyseus was staggered backwards a couple steps before stopping only the stare, with his hand involuntarily rubbing at his cheek. Tears were falling on Hecate, and she stood there watching him, arms crossed across her chest, as she herself was involuntarily shaking.

She had resumed her real form, that of a light green tinted dryad standing over one hundred eighty cm tall, her mystically beautiful face streaked with tears and the long yellow green hair flowing down the front of her covering her breasts and midsection. She was otherwise, nude and Odyseus felt the charms of her kind beginning to work on him.

"Why, my love, why did you have to say that?" She sobbed. "Can't you see that I have fallen so hopelessly in love with you?"

"Then tell me!" He screamed.

No longer holding his frustration in, the echo of his voice through the forest, his own face nearly in tears. Dropping to his knees, Odyseus still came to just below the angel's chest, as he pleaded with her.

"Just be telling me of what thou intend with me, please!"

"I am making you a king, my bear!" she grabbed his head and pulled him into her, feeling the moisture on her stomach as he was crying. "I am making you a king."

With her arms around his neck, she held onto him, allowing her dryad beginnings to take hold. Odyseus let his arms remain dangling at his side, as he allowed her to take his head into her. He could feel that if it were not for his immortal spirit, he would be making love to this creature right now, but his will allowed for him to fight off the urge.

"I have need to know, that thine plans be not interfering with Holy Minerva's." Odyseus exclaimed. "I need thee tell me the rest, Hecate. If thou love me, if thine heart wants mine, love thee back, then no secrets. No secrets betwixt us. I be not used by any woman, ever again! PLEASE!"

They stayed as they were for several minutes, before she finally started talking. The more she said, the easier it was. After a while, Odyseus was even returning her embrace, his big arms wrapped around her tiny waste. When she was finished, he looked up into her tear-filled eyes, and they kissed. Not the kiss of grandmother to child, but that of lovers, as they laid down onto the forest floor.

CHAPTER 13
The War begins!

Persides and Sorlons, were loading Quevit onto the wagon, when he arrived. Burlga had placed a holding spell on her cousin, he was awake, but a thirty-five-year-old man with the mind of a one-year-old, was not someone that any would want roaming free. Belusa, the newest maid at the keep, a thirty-four-year-old woman, that had lost her husband and only son in one of the demonic attacks at one of the villages that Burlga had liberated, was named the nanny, to watch after, Quevit. The short five-foot six-inch, green-eyed blond-haired woman climbed into the wagon bed after the Lord of the keep was gently laid down.

The new arriving man, as Burlga was just sitting her horse, was a tall six-foot four-inch, hazel eyed man, with light brown hair. He was wearing the robes of someone from the Merylon Guild, and introduced himself as Marut. His auras were a perfect mix, in all three spectrums, and Burlga thought to herself, too perfect.

They spoke, he was not from the main Guild Hall in the capital, nor was he from any in all of Marintia Kingdom. He claimed to be out of Uleran Kingdom, the far western part of the continent, and the smallest of the four Kingdoms. The man appeared to be in his late thirties to early forties, and was a minor sorcerer at best. He would be even weaker than Quen, pretended.

"I'll have to help awaken Quen's true potential, one of these days!" She thought.

Looking back to Marut, she pointedly asked, receiving a startled expression, but no changes in the aura, that would have indicated lying.

"So, tell me, Marut, are you a bloody angel?" She said it with a smile, but her tone was hedging on anger. The stunned look upon the man, he only shook his head, before finally answering.

"My Lady, although some women may have told me so, I do not feel as though, I am all that angelic!" His look attempted to take on a seductive one, with the answered joke. Burlga continued to study his aura, and finally shrugged.

Too perfect, but then again, he was handsome, in a rugged sort of way. His answer certainly indicated that he thought highly of himself, either that, or he had heard of the reputation for the Lady sorceress to carouse the Inns of the villages she was saving, these past couple months. But, if he was from Uleran Kingdom, he would not have heard anything, yet!

"OK, Marut, that you have come all this way, you can ride with us, to the capital. We go to see the guild, and find out what can be done for my cousin, here, and what kind of Hell, I can raise with those idiots that think they can keep my Holy Patron from the people. Hurry up and go get a fresh horse. We shall give you the count of one hundred before leaving you behind." Burlga was smiling, and the priest/sorcerer moved his horse, tired from the long journey into the stables.

"This is not going to be so easy. She is already suspicious, for some odd reason." He thought to himself. "It has to be Hecate or Lalia's doing. Neither of them would have concealed their power. It is too hard to control an aura, if one tries to appear psychically powerful. "They had been warned of that, but he knew his sisters."

As he quickly moved his saddle from his horse to another, the groomsman taking his horse to feed and brush it down, as Marut was leaving the stables, Burlga was already leading her party out the gate onto the road. Marut, jumped up into the saddle and booted his horse to a gallop, as he thought.

"This woman, is one of the, if not most powerful, of all the Chosen. She even rivals Selene's child, in pure raw strength, although he does not know it, yet! Too bad, she is so impatient, she would make great and strong babies, with that man, if they could get together. Good thing, no one knows, that JC has had two sent to him. He will be the hardest to hide from, but the two are smart enough to not go in with blazing power."

He caught up with the group, looking into the wagon, as he passed forward, Marut saw the man, laying in back, and immediately saw the loss of soul. Thinking carefully how to answer this, he went with a question, instead.

"Mistress Burlga, what has happened to your man, here? I see a loss of some spirit, yet, no injuries."

"You can heal, Marut?" She answered with a question. "Few of the Holy Merylon's Temple would know that talent."

"That is about the only talent I possess, I'm afraid to say, Mistress!" Marut decided along the way, it would be the most important around one of the Chosen, that way no mistakes in battle would be made, and it was a talent that required the least amount of Psychic strength, since most of the power would come from the victim. Her head shake told him that she accepted it.

"My cousin was in the embrace of Baalzephon, last night. We go to the Guild Hall in Ussfan, now. I need to find out how long it will be before he recovers. I also, have to meet with the King on the marrow."

"We will not make it by tomorrow, M'lady! It is three days travel from here, just to get to the outskirts of the city." Sorlons calmly exclaimed.

"We travel by that door in space, I tried to explain to you, brother!" Persides stated.

"It's called a gateway, a minor spell that even Marut there can do, if he pays attention when I cast it. All one needs know, is a vague idea what the other end looks like, to open it. I spent many years growing up in the capital, and should be able to do it. Of course, if things have changed too much, we may have to go via a dimensional doorway, which does not require you to know so much of the destination. It is just a little more dangerous!" She seemed to be talking to herself, but the others thought only that she was trying to make the newest arrival understand, teach him something. Marut pretended to listen.

When Burlga's gateway spell failed, she appeared surprised that things would have changed so much. Opening a dimensional door, she concentrated on the Temple of Merylon where she had grown up, and saw the building materialize. They rode through the rift in the fabric of space, to find themselves in the court yard, and a man screaming having lost a good part of his foot, when the door suddenly appeared in front of him.

Burlga jumped down, hurrying to him, and immediately healed the man, to include regenerating his foot. When, the shock of healing hit him, however, he succumbed to the pain, and Burlga ordered Sorlons to carry him to the wagon.

"That gentleman, is why I did not want to use a dimensional door. It will not care who is in front of it, and can quite kill, if the person was to be sliced through their vitals. At least a gateway just opens to the side of someone, if they happen to be in the area." She turned to Marut, and ordered him to go in and announce the arrival of the Holiest Merylon's prophet, promised of the prophesies, Chosen of the Ancient Ones.

Marut, smiled at the title she ordered him to use, and thought only, as he walked away, how she may be a forty-two-year-old woman, but she certainly acted like a child, having slept for twenty years of her life. He walked inside the building, while the rest of them waited, at the wagon.

"That is a most infamous name, you have chosen, young lady!" An elderly man stated, as he led over four dozen from the guild out of the court yard. Marut was walking besides the man, and Burlga thought she saw an imperfection in his inner spectrum, but she decided she could be wrong based on the many imperfect auras coming towards her.

"My name was given me by my father, Stellen d'Venta. My name should be in your records as the fastest ever to obtain master status. I was but sixteen years old, when I left this Temple, over 500 years ago!" She matters of fact answered.

"I am Karomal, what is your real name, young lady?" Burlga recognized the name from that given her at the guildhall in Inan. He was the head of all the Guilds, the one that would be called High Priest of Merylon, if the church had not been so perverted over the past century. It really had just become a magic user's guild, now. What Burlga found suspicious was the man was supposed to be well over one hundred years old, and yet, the one before her, could not be more than sixty.

She smiled at his question, when she felt the psychic probing come from him. She easily blocked it, and forced the man's spell back upon himself. The elderly man winced at the pain, his knees began to shake before Burlga released the spell, all the time, continuing to smile.

"You will ask before probing, old man. I am she, who you call infamous, and much much more! According to the prophesies, if you would bother to read them, I am the new head of the church.

"And, that you have so obviously failed the people, this last century or so, it is a good thing, Holy Merylon, has finally brought me upon you! There will be changes, and you will start them, immediately!" As all the wizards and sorcerers began to shift, Burlga raised a dome of air around Karomal and herself.

The protective shields would stop most spells and she did not see many that would be able to break through. She reached a hand to help the elderly man off the ground and as he stood, she was still smiling, he noticed.

328

"So much strength, this one has", he thought to himself while he rose. "May I, Chosen One, verify the truth of your words, please?" He stammered out the words, as though they were being pulled from him. Karomal was not use to having to ask, anything. When Burlga nodded with a simple warning against doing more that truth seeking, Karomal hesitantly reached out with his mind.

Burlga watched the others, the wizards with material items for spell casting, or pointing rods or wands at her protection to dispel it. She could feel the many minor spells being cast at the shield she had erected and after a few seconds of probing, Karomal raised his hand, for them to stop.

"You idiots, could have hurt me if she would not have been so strong to stop your castings. That she did manage, with the ease of which she performed, should prove she is what she claims!"

"Good, now that we have verified, let us get to talking!" Burlga dropped the dome shield, but never dropped her mental protections.

When they all left the Guildhall that night, to take an Inn close to the royal palace, she was in an uproar and decided what was needed was getting thoroughly drunk.

"Those flaming idiots know who I am and still refuse me? Useless, bloody trash, all of them! Maybe I should just take my cousin to JC. Not only could he probably heal him, but that would get me the chance to finally get the man into bed! Get my bloody frustrations out with the old man!"

Persides and Sorlons were use to their mistress by now, yet, still managed to blush at the forwardness of her suggestion.

As they were leaving, Karomal talked with Tristoly.

"When in her mind, I saw a man from Selenia. He must be the Chosen of Holy Selene. The girl is in love with that man. Go to Selenia and find out as much as you can. I would start with the main Temple in Bornesta of Dragoran Kingdom." She nodded and went to her room to pack for the voyage."

The next morning when Burlga woke to find Marut in her bed, she could only groan. Not for the pounding of her head from the drink, but for the realization she really had done what she feared would happen. Her lustful nature had taken hold while drunk.

"This is why I don't drink, Marut!"

"Better me, than with one of the young men that would have fallen in love with you. And, my lady, truth be told, I didn't mind!"

"You flaming idiot man, of course you didn't bloody hell mind! Damns and bloody hell, but I'll never win JC's heart, if he thinks me the whore!" Burlga turned over to cry, as Marut slipped out of bed, and quietly left the room.

****

The rumors spread of the prophet having come. With the tiny beautiful young priestess at his side, all of the spawn from Hell was on the run. Odyseus d'Brell was finally coming, and whenever he entered a village, or drove out some demon from a farmstead, he would be cheered and idol worshiped.

Hecate improved on her speeches, ensuring his name would carry on. After each rescue, or each slaying of evil, Odyseus was given the full credit. Most did not even know the tiny woman's name, but all knew her power equaled his own.

When rumors of invasion fleets landing on the beaches, Odyseus sent messages to the senate at Jupiter, the capital, that it was time to begin for war. None came back, nor did any men come forth. Odyseus began to send them directly to the king, only garnering equal responses.

****

JC was performing his routine of morning rituals, when he noticed that besides the audience of his protective guards, Dyanea was sitting watching his "kata", as he called them. She had knitting needles in hand, and was working with yarn, as she would look up to watch the man, seemingly perform like a dancer at the king's table.

Except, she could see more to this dance, than the jovial kind. The guards had mentioned that JC had called it martial art, and she could certainly see the battle in the movements. It was certainly an art form, but definitely was it a martial skill. She

330

thought to herself, the beauty of turning war into artistic actions was almost disgusting.

Looking over to Essmelda, off to the side, she could see the girl attempting to mimic the man, and shook her head. JC noticed it and waved the girl over and began to show her some rudimentary moves, ones that the girl would easily perform. She smiled and began attempting the arm movements he was showing her.

"There is a total of twenty-four moves in this form of Tai Chi. We call this moving meditation because it stimulates the mind, spirit, and body. Learn this and it makes everything else come easier." he began and Dyanea watched as he worked patiently with the girl. She continued to work her knitting while watching the two.

"She is his daughter, I wonder if he has figured that out, yet?" she thought to herself. "How much does he understand of what happened all those years ago? He thinks it a dream, it was so far from such a thing. C'renan agrees with him, I should let her know she is mine, and him know that she is his." Her thoughts dominated as for the next hour or so, the girl worked with him, never getting frustrated as he never got impatient with her.

"I will join you every day, Father JC. I want to learn this Tai Chi." she said as she concentrated on her slow movements.

After his "kata" was done, he took up the practice sword and with the newly promoted, Lt. Marcus d'Wind and Sgt. Brenan, both dueling at the same time. Dyanea sighed, as she thought, this is a man, Berga and Zaina thinks can be tamed? Essie continued to do her slow dance.

"Maybe as tame as a badger!" she thought, smiling. "Do I really want him tamed? Do any of us really want him tamed?" She continued to think amusingly.

After an hour more of working, the three men washed off and put their shirts back on. JC, then, put his arm around Essmelda.

"That is enough for now, child. Don't overdo it."

They walked over to Dyanea, and bowed.

"My lady is enjoying the morning air?" He asked.

Dyanea sat her needles to her lap, and looked at him, as she allowed him to take her hand to his lips. She only stirred a brief moment, when she smiled.

"Your lady, is more than happy to feel the cool breeze in her face, while you seem to enjoy making yourself stink of sweat!" Her mouth wrinkled her nose as she gave him a look of disgust, but then smiled. "As well as, now you make Essie equally sweaty."

"Ah, well in that case, you would not wish to join me for a leisurely walk through the forest?"

She rose, and took his other hand in hers.

"I would like that very much. I shall go and prepare a repast for us and meet you at the gates, in say one hour? That should give you time to clean up, properly!"

Chuckling, he answered.

"Even now, I find that my, true queen, can command me to her biding! One hour, then. I shall eagerly await, Reverend Mother." He kissed her hand once again bowing, and turned to leave. Dyanea shivered, again, as she walked to the keep.

"What am I doing?" She thought. "He could not be the same man, could he?"

"Yes, he could be, my daughter." The voice entered her head, and she was sure it was the same one that had spoken to them the other day.

Only this time, when she looked around there was no one present. Dyanea, sat at the first chair available, until a palace servant stopped to inquire of her.

Startled, she looked up.

"Huh, oh, yes, I'm fine." The Reverend Mother rose and headed to the Queen's quarters.

Walking through the woods outside the palace's northern gate, where the forest turned into mountain range, JC looked at the woman, beside him and smiled. She was watching the trees, seemingly deep in thought.

Her left arm wrapped through his right, she held her hand on his muscular forearm, bared with his sleeves rolled up. Her index finger idly tracing the veins coursing through the Immortal's lower arm. Her right arm hung at her side, the basket dangling in her fingers, looking as though it was ready to fall.

Dyanea appeared in good spirits.

Following discretely some forty yards behind, was Lt. Marcus d'Wind, sworn man at arms, two other soldiers, ordered by the queen and with him two young priestesses, Mythalla, apprentice to JC, and Essmelda, apprentice to Dyanea, and two priests.

JC tried to ignore them, following, not use to the noble title, forced upon him, he was not use to the shadowing.

"What is wrong, my lord?" Dyanea asked, revealing to JC that she was not so lost in thought as he was thinking. Before he could answer, a crash was heard behind, between the two High Priests and their followers.

Turning to see a dimensional door pouring forth Hell spawn into the dried leaves of the once quiet forest.

Feeling the use of sorcery coming the forty meters back, Essmelda and Mythalla were already reacting. Dyanea was casting as well, her strength in sorcery far and above what the Immortals were taught mortals capable of. JC concentrated and a fireball exploded into the dimensional door, stopping the flow of spawn.

The doorway disappeared, with his second spell dispelling it, and the minor demons were quickly dispatched.

As the six people came together towards the elder couple, JC cast a protective shield and placed it down over all the mortals. Being able to hold off most psychic attacks, his shield might keep them alive if they were attacked again. He then readjusted the shield so that it was like that of a wall of force as well, only domed around all of them. They would be able to cast out, but it should keep anything from coming in.

When the new dimensional door opened, eighteen devils, all seven feet tall, with skin like scales, horned and barbed throughout, and long tails with ends like that of a morning star.

The talons for fingers on their two arms, fangs hanging down from too wide mouths, and tusks extending from their foreheads just above the large round eyes.

Using a wall of force, JC attempted to push them back through the door when his wall was dispelled. The back lash sent the man staggering.

When JC regained himself, he saw the being that dispelled his spell walk through, with eighteen more of the barbed devils.

Standing over fourteen feet tall, the devil had a humanoid body with golden skin, covered in chain and bronze plate armor. Holding a large morning star in its right hand, in the left a large square shield. Its head was elongated and looked to be a bull's head with golden hair covering all but the eyes, large and oval shaped, and the long broad nose.

With protruding pointed ears and two small curling bull's horns pointing forward from above its eyes. The door closed behind it and the thirty-six devils and devil lord faced the nine people, only one with a weapon of any use.

"Stay in the dome!" JC yelled, as he could feel Mythalla reaching out to draw strength and courage from him.

He let her, only stopping when she doubled her own strength. Stepping forward, he released lightning bolts into the devils and continued to move away from the mortals. Unable to go beyond the dome, they were in, they stood watching the Immortal cast spell after spell as lightning seemed to jump from his hands.

JC was even greater than when he fought Abigor, and she wondered at where this was coming from.

Never before in her eighty years had Dyanea seen the kind of power being wielded by a single man. Casting more spells than he claimed he could, JC seemed very much the angel they all believed him to be.

Devils began to fall, and even the Greater Hell's Angel could not stop the sorcery from hitting into the group.

Essmelda added lightning of her own watching the father and using the same spells he was using. Then the other two priestesses cast bolts of energy. When

JC had finally reached the hoard of devils, he already had sustained minor injuries from the larger one's spells, but only seven of the smaller remained still in the battle.

They broke off letting their leader deal with JC, and flew to the protective dome, in an attempt to get at the mortals. The priestesses were still casting damaging energy into the devils and although it was weakening, the protective force of air was holding back the spawn long enough for the three to eliminate six of the seven.

JC and Bael, were in a deadly duel, as both were delivering and taking terrific injuries. When the devil began, after a few moments to doubt the battle's outcome, he tried to open a rift, but found that JC managed to dispel the doorway.

Bael was weakening as the battle continued, yet the High Priest seemed to still possess the same surprising strength.

Bael teleported behind the Immortal, and JC dropped to the ground kicking back catching the devil just below its knee. As Bael's great morning star descended down to the unprotected chest of JC, a blast of energy hit it directly in the back forcing the morning star's aim to just miss above JC's moving head.

Essmelda nodding at her well-aimed spell, sent another into the turning devil lord's chest knocking him back a step. JC, instead of rolling away from the staggered devil, swung his leg in a sweep, upending Bael.

The last of the barbed devils managed to break through the dome shield and grabbed Marcus by the neck, when the man stepped in front of Essmelda, the devil's original target. As the soldier's sword bounced off the thick skin of the devil, unable to even cause pain to it, Marcus slowly succumbed to the squeeze of the Hell Spawn. All three priestesses reached out with energy blasts watching the creature explode in the sorcery made destruction.

JC rolled to his feet just as Bael was beginning to stand. The two rushed in to battle, once again, as the priest turned his sorcery in on himself, boosting the speed of his katana. After a few seconds of quick short slices, the devil's arms feel free of its body, and with a final spinning sweep, the katana sliced through the mid-section, cleanly cutting Bael in half.

Staggering after the release of the energy draining spell, JC turned to see Essmelda leaning to heal Marcus. Her hand was about to touch his heart, when JC yelled,

"Essie, stop!"

The young teen flinched and looked up at the bleeding and bruised priest running towards them. JC added in a softer tone,

"His neck is broke, are you prepared for that kind of pain, child? It could kill you to heal him that way."

"But, Father, he saved my life. I can't let him die." Her tears started to form at her eyes, as JC fell to his knees next to the guardsman.

Essmelda had a sense of honor for the man she believed to have just saved her. JC knew, she certainly would not allow him to die. Delving to find what injuries there were and how well off the man was, JC realized that the only way to heal was with empathy, the way that Essmelda was about to try. He took her hand and forced a smile to his face.

"Then you will do it, but I will take most of the pain. Let me take some of your energy like I did that day at the Temple. OK?" Her nod, he took a little as he felt the energy flow into him. JC then placed his hand on Marcus' heart and almost screamed as the pain of the broken neck was added to the cuts and broken bones, he already had taken from Bael's battle.

His muffled groan caused all the soldiers to wince as they saw the neck on their lieutenant straighten and the bones grind back into place. They could see on JC the twist of his own neck as he took the majority of any pain away from the fallen soldier to absorb it into his own superior constitution.

As Marcus began to breathe easier, the priest was barely able to stand, and Dyanea wrapped her arms around him in a worried loving embrace.

"I think we need to figure out how to get some mythral, my love. You cannot continue to fight alone, like this." she whispered in his ear as they held each other, she supporting most of his weight.

****

"Eat up, Quevit. You need to keep your strength up." Burlga was a little worried, even those idiot Merylon wizards didn't know if he would ever heal. No one had ever survived an attack from a succubus before. They would not even believe her

336

when she tried to explain that it was not a demon succubus, but a real live devil lord. Those idiots barely admitted that Burlga was the one promised to them by Kraylon, all those centuries ago.

"What a bloody waste of human flesh that is going to be, cousin!" She blurted aloud. "They are less in strength than the girl that JC had, and he claimed she was only moderate. Well, at least they will be sending a large contingency of representatives here to live at the keep. We will have to build a tower, but they can finance it.

"I'm not going too, they can just live in the Marsh, for all I care. Merylon, where are you, my patron? Why did you not warn me of the problems within your own fold? Bloody Hell, man, I get more help from JC than from you, my God!"

Burlga continued to feed her cousin, talking about the meeting with the King. Another worthless piece of humanity, as far as she was concerned. It would be years before he could muster an army, and that is just not possible.

"I thought he was going to fall over with apoplexy when I told him he would either conform, or I would just burn his entire kingdom to make room for the army. Hehe, you'd have bloody loved it, cousin."

Burlga was interrupted by the chamberlain as she was finishing the feeding of her cousin, announcing that the first two thousand kilograms of mythral had arrived from the mines. She ordered it taken to the smithy and tell them to begin heating it in the cauldrons. She would be there soon.

After leaving Quevit in the capable hands of Belusa, his personal maid, she made a gateway to her treasure room and collected the 800 kilograms of silver she would need. 25000 silver coins would have been impossible for her to carry a year ago, but now it seemed only heavy, as she cast a floating disk of air and moved the silver onto it. Working with the Ancient Ones had greatly increased both her physical as well as her psychic strength. Also, as well as, a lot of other aspects to her body. She was always a pretty woman, but now she felt beautiful.

Even JC, gods but she wanted that man, had told her a few months ago, that he thought she had gotten prettier since her attitude had matured. She thought that the greatest compliment he had ever given her. Although, she still wrinkled her nose that he would have thought her immature, before. Oh well, she didn't exactly think him all that great when he had first arrived, either.

"That's not true! I did think him, with pretty eyes when I first saw him. I just wish I was a little older, or maybe he a little younger. I know that is the problem between us, in his mind. Perhaps traveling with all those young women, will ease his feelings on age difference. Then I will move in for the hunt!" She smiled, that half tilted smile she had every time she thought of a way to get what she wanted. So sure, in the end, she would not fail!

At the smithy the armorers were readied and the mythral was barely warm. She broke the mythral into sixteen equal sections with sorcery, and then she mixed, in the steel cauldrons that she had made with sorcery to handle extra heat that would be needed, the proper balance of silver and raw iron.

Forcing her spells of lightning, fire, spirit, and bless into the mixture of metals she melted the blend until all sixteen cauldrons contained a liquid mixture of one single pinkish glow. Into that she cast enchantment, and cutting her hand at the palm, allowed the blood to mix into the goo of each.

After allowing it to cool slightly, thickening the mix, she finished with a permanency spell on the mix, and thinking why not, added her own psychic energy into the mix until it boiled, anew. Changing the use of spirit to that of JC's original plans, she could see why he thought the men would have trouble. It was exhausting even for her. Only one cauldron did she use the original spells with, the other fifteen were done with hers and Sheera's modified spells.

"We shall see the differences in those his way, and those of mine and Sheera's!"

The weapon smiths went to work immediately, telling her that there was enough of the mix to make at least twenty blades from each cauldron.

"Three hundred twenty new weapons that can kill Hell Spawn will help our cause very well. Good, and the first ones you do will be given to you twenty. I want them all done as soon as you can, and remember, as long as the mines hold out, we will be making more. I need hammers, flails, and daggers, as well. This time make five of the mix's swords. Forty short swords, and sixty long swords. With the others, make one mix all hammers, five into flails, three into daggers, and the other into arrow heads and spear tips. This one, into long swords, as well." She pointed to the one she had used all of JC's original spells on. "I will finish the last two spells when you are ready to mount them to hilts, so I shall see you in a couple days."

Burlga walked back to the castle, skipping at the exhaustion she was feeling. Those spells were simple, but they do make one tired. It would take her at least an hour to regain most of the drain she felt. But she was happy and thinking of the man she wanted.

"I will make him some as a gift. He is going to need to build an army as well, and he acted as though he didn't have access to mythral when he was teaching us. Hmm, it would be just like him to not want to ask us for help. Perfectly willing to endure all kinds of pain and whatever else we need, anything for us, but ask for a simple loan, he never would." She frowned at the thought,

"What an idiot! No, just a typical man. But, a good man, none the less!" She smiled. Dreams of him holding her, she went into her rooms.

****

When Kuan Yen approached Sheera and Massy, on the morning she was leaving the Sho Gun's Palace, Sheera eyed the smaller priestess with suspicion.

Vastri, Sho Gun for the eastern Nim Lang Province, had been a waste of time, the Immortal thought to herself. She had dispatched several hundred Hell Spawn that he himself could have handled, in several of the villages under his control, and even drove the minor demon lord out of the man's wife. The second time she had done this, in only three Sho Guns. This time it was no different, than the first two.

Vastri's gratitude was a few small pouches of gems and an amused smile, when she asked for soldiers to help in the cause. He of course refused.

"The prophesies speak of six champions, young lady. If you claim to be one, then find the others to help you!" He had said.

"We, venerable one, are spread out on each of the six continents. Read the "Golden Dragon of Peace", again, if you do not properly, remember it! It says one will come here. I am that one, yet, you allow logic to leave your mind, because you think I am not fit?"

"As you say, Sheera Lu Che, the Holy One, Jeasuas would not have sent a woman. You are unfit to lead an army. I have paid you for your efforts, very well, I might add. Now, be happy with that, and leave. Now!"

Sheera was not happy, even her Temple only half accepted her claims, but being a church dedicated to Peace, they would not help in a war, anyway.

Now, here was the only person of real psychic power, that Sheera had seen, standing before her, and the tiny 152 cm tall priestess was dressed for travel.

"Kuan Yen, you want something to be spoken, then speak up! I'm in no mood, today for the game of guess." Sheera cupped her right hand inside her left, bringing both to the level of her chin, before giving a short bow. The greeting was returned by the High Priestess, although, Kuan Yen lowered her eyes as well, something Sheera never did!"

"Holy Sheera, I wish to join you in your Quest!"

Towering more than sixteen centimeters taller than the priestess before her, Sheera could see in her aura, a strength that exceeded even Quen's and Odyseus'. Even the three that were with JC. Yet, she knew the woman would never use her power for anything destructive, even in the face of Hell Spawn!

"All are welcome to Holy Jeasuas' cause, sister, but what has changed your mind, since last we spoke?"

"The Golden Dragon of Peace! You commanded our brethren to read, once again!"

"So, you accept me to be the Golden Dragon, finally?"

"Sheera Lu Che, it is as you say. Holy Jeasuas would need send us a warrior to battle against Hell. That he sent a woman, only shows his thoughts for compassion and charity, as no man who follows war, would have such."

"You have not met the man, I call my brother, then. The Chosen of Selene is a man you say cannot exist!" Sheera smiled as she fumbled with the sorcery made pendant hanging down her chest.

"In any case, I would be honored to have another travel companion. Especially one that can aide in healing the people. Come, we can talk while we walk."

The next few days of travel was spent in training the priestess in protective shields. Kuan Yen, although far beneath Sheera in psychic strength, was very strong, and learned quickly and with ease. Being able to place a shield over Massy to protect the dwarf against psychic attacks, would leave the Dwarven princess to do what she did best. Swing that hammers she carried.

"Too bad, Burlga isn't here. I can show you how to read the auras, but she's the best at interpreting them. Just remember, the seven colors on the outer spectrum, will be lighter for positive and darker for negative. I don't really remember more than that. Sorry! Leaf, you can read auras, can't you?" She turned to the gnome, startling him, briefly. His eyes narrowed, before he answered.

"Some. The outer spectrum as you call it, I can. I look mainly to health and attitude." He nonchalantly answered.

"High Priestess Sheera Lu Che, what need do I to see auras?"

"Kuan Yen, health is the reason. If the yellow, blue, and purple are dark with it. Green and bright orange then the person is very sick or injured. Injuries are obvious and easily healed, but even some illnesses can go undetected with simple delving. The aura can help in that instant."

"And the white?"

"If missing, or black is prevalent among all the spectrums, then that person is evil. If black is in all the spectrums, especially the inner, then they have either made deals with Hell, or they are dedicated to doing evil!"

As the four approached the mountains, Sheera felt a tightness. Her nerves were wound and even Massy nor Leaf, could calm her. Kuan Yen watched in wonder.

Six battles over the past few days, with minor demons, and each time, the easy eliminations would cause Sheera to fall down and get sick, or at the least nauseated. At least she did not always vomit, anymore, but it still caused her to feel as though she would.

"You really, are not a warrior, Sheera Lu Che! For all of your battle prowess, you still have the heart of a lamb!" Kuan Yen exclaimed, after the fifth battle.

"She is as much a one as she needs be, Kuan Yen!" Massy answered, with a small bit of concern to her voice.

Massy knew, now, what JC was going through, when he feigned being tired.

"Being a man, he just hides it better!" She thought to herself.

Coming down the path towards them, were twenty Dwarven soldiers. Dressed in chain mailed armor, each with a hammer and short sword, tucked in their belts, holding small shields in their left hands. When they come up to the four, two human females, a gnome male, and a Dwarven female in hardened boiled leather armor of obvious Selenian design, the middle-aged female only having a beard of a few weeks' growth, they stopped.

"We have watched you, Sheera Lu Che." The obvious leader, stated. He was middle aged, about three hundred plus years, broad and only a couple centimeters taller than Massy, standing about 122 cm. The younger soldiers were all armored the same, but most of their shields did not have nearly as many dents as the elder.

"Then you know I come in Peace, bringing with me, the one of prophesy!" Massy spoke stepping in front of Sheera.

"You claim so, but the only man with you is a gnome. A rather puny one at that!"

Massy crossed her arms across her chest and eyeing the man, gave a single shake of her head.

"Is it so hard to believe that Holy Jeasuas would send a woman to Katiketa?"

"Perhaps, she certainly is a big enough human, even if a woman. A bit too pretty for a warrior, though, and she has no beard!

"And, then there is her little problem, after battles. Would the one of prophesy retch like a child after so great a battle?" The dwarf grinned, his joke lost on the two humans. Leaf, grinning back, as well as Massy, the chuckles moved through the other nineteen dwarves.

"She would, if she was a child sick from eating your obvious mush you call food on this continent! I am Massy Thistle Thorn, High Priestess to Mother Gia, Princess Queen of the Thorncave Clans of Selenia. Are we to stand here all day, making jokes at the girl's expense, or do you escort us to the Shang Dragon? I wish to formally meet my cousin!"

342

"I am General Horotu Wing, commander of the Shang Dragon armies, and Prince, brother to the King of all the Shang Dragon Clans. Undefeated champion in over one hundred campaigns. I welcome the Golden Dragon and her escort. And, Your Highness, my cousin's unexpected presence will please King Dormathin Wing, even more. Come!" Horotu bowed first to Massy, then to Sheera, who gave her half bow, right hand cupped in left.

Dormathin eyed the women before him. He smiled at the Dwarven princess, before returning his scour onto Sheera.

"How long were you in mourning, Princess?" The king asked, still not taking his eyes off of the Immortal.

"I have been widowed for over ten years, Dormathin. My beard had long grown back, but for recently. This time, it was burned off and yanked out by demons." She matters of fact stated.

"Yet, you still live? I would think you'd be wearing the teeth of those for a necklace, then!"

"Didn't have my hammer to knock any out, at that moment. Now, they run from me for fear of it!" The laughs moved through the cavern, as Massy continued to stand easily in front of the largest dwarf she had ever met.

Easily almost 150 cm tall, he was larger across the shoulders than most, and she could imagine, in his younger days, he would have been quite the man. Now, at more than six hundred years, his beard was gray and the dark hair long down his back, was white streaked, as well. His arms still showed signs, though, of good use in swinging his hammer.

"So, our alleged human savior!" The King started on Sheera. "What is it that I owe this visit for? You thinking that Dwarven blood can be added to the fodder, where even humans dare not go?" Sheera had been listening to Massy on the way into the mountains.

Come with a show of strength, and do not be afraid of giving insulting humor. And, take no offense to that given. She smiled at the king, before responding. The chuckles continued from some of the warriors.

343

"Your Majesty is wise!" Sheera began. Bringing one hand up so she could look at her finger nails, she continued.

"Why should I risk breaking a nail, or denting this pretty face, when there are so many strong arms willing to destroy the makatiels and goblins, in my stead?" The smile on the King widened as he nodded. The laughter in the cavern seemed somewhat constrained. Sheera continued to smile, thinking not insulting enough.

"You may be cute, girl, but no beard on your face makes you still a little girl. Why should I follow a little girl into battle?"

"Because, King Dormathin, this little girl could throw your overly large soft lazy butt, across this large cavern!" Sheera eyed the dwarf, bringing her smile tight into an evil grin.

She leaned forward, placing her right hand to lean on her knee, as if to insinuate her intentions. She hoped she did not issue the challenge too soon. Massy had warned her, she would have to at the least fight one of the dwarves, just needed to do it correctly.

Dormathin laughed, a booming sound that echoed throughout the cavern, joined by all several hundred presents. Massy even was laughing, and Leaf grinned. Kuan Yen saw no humor in the threat, issued by the High Priestess of Holy Jeasuas.

"Well, King Dormathin? The little girl has challenged you, what say you, now?" Massy spoke.

"Why or even how did a human of non Katiketain blood come to be traveling with a Selenian warrior queen, cousin?" Dormathin almost ignored the challenge thrown his way.

"I am the sworn body guard to her brother Chosen. He wished to ensure The Golden Dragon protected until she gains a suitable escort here in Jeasuas' lands. I came to meet my distance cousins from a side of the world I had never been on." Massy matter of fact answered.

"Sheera Lu Che, you do not insult enough. But you will learn, if you choose to hang around with us. But you should know, if you are going to challenge me, that we don't practice with wooden weapons, like your soft kin, girl. You really want to face my champion with real weapons?"

344

"Better still, King." Sheera stood tall and faked a yawn. "Your champion, Horotu, I believe, can use anything he wishes, and I will still beat him without a weapon, using only my hands!" Massy shook her head, seeing the same foolhardy boast she saw in JC. She only, mumbled.

"Fools and children!" While the laughter and bets began to flow amongst the cavern, Sheera even saw Leaf placing a bet, dropping silver coins all being placed on her winning.

"Sheera Lu Che," Dormathin began, seemingly the only one not laughing among his clan. "That you are the Golden Dragon given unto Katiketa, by Holy Jeasuas, I already have believed for weeks. Do not be foolish just to impress us with your bravery! I have seen you against the demons. I know you are brave."

"I am only as brave, as I need be, Your Majesty! If I am to lead, then I must prove to you, my worth. If not to you, then to your people. After all, I am but a weak little human girl!" She added with smiling sarcasm, gaining even more laughter among the dwarves.

When the celebrations began that night, Horotu and his King, were still arguing whom would be Sheera's Holy Protector. She gave the general his first defeat, ever, along with the twenty other Dwarven warriors that took up the challenge. Massy, shaking her head, realizing, the girl was even smoother, quicker, and maybe better than Father JC, with this strange fighting style called "Kung Fu". She could only wonder how; Sheera would be if there was more strength to her hits and throws.

Kuan Yen looked on, in amazed wonderment, as she was the only one not drinking nor regaling in the celebration of the arrival of the Golden Dragon. Not understanding the Dwarven life style she sat watching, as even the High Priestess Sheera Lu Che had joined in on the celebrations.

But, now at least, Sheera would have her army!

"Fear not, Kuan Yen." Leaf sat down next to the priestess.

"This is just the dwarven way. They do accept her with open respect. Sheera has proven herself today to all the dwarfs. Possibly, to all the non-humans, as well. Today, this will go down into the history books."

"But this is not the way of peace, Leaf." Kuan Yen mumbled.

"She is The Golden Dragon. She is not here for peace. She is here for our salvation." the gnome answered downing what was left in his cup, standing to go for a refill.

The dimensional door opened almost unnoticed as the monsters spilled out into the great lab. Following the eight large creatures, two females stepped into the room just before the door way closed.

Purana, bent over her table, working as she most often was, sun up to sun down, noticed not at all. High Priest Torel and the High Priestess Binel both looked up, but, before they could yell out, they were flung back with a wave of one hand landing hard against the back wall. They both slumped to the floor, as Purana annoyed from the sound of their crash, looked up from her work.

"What in the name of the Creator, are you two doing?" The Chosen angrily yelled.

She turned to take in the horror, and faster than thought, two of the three largest devils exploded to a psychic blast unrivaled on any continent. She sent two more at others, but they were dispelled as quickly by the two females behind the monstrosities.

Purana teleported, using wizardry to the far end, behind the devils, wanting to save her lab table and the work she had been working on. Instead of following, though, the remaining thirteen and a half tall Pit Fiend walked towards it, as the other seven devils moved her way.

Purana reached out to the Fiend, with its gorilla like body, bat like wings ending in a hooked talon at the top of both. It's ogreish large head with two large tusks hanging from its large mouth, blazing red eyes shaped like pears and bat like ears on the sides just above tufts of long bluish hair.

The horns, almost bull like is too small for the head and are only noticeable because of the white coloration against the red leathery skin. In one hand was an anch-like weapon and the other a jagged toothed club. Her psychic crush was tossed aside, as the fiend had now placed a shield against mental attacks, but it was still staggered by the shear strength of it.

"You are a powerful one, Chosen." One of the female devils exclaimed. She was tall, standing over six feet six inches.

Almost as beautiful as Purana herself, with pale skin, long flowing reddish hair, the color of flames dancing through it; it seemed to be changing color in the lights, as she moved. Her eyes were black, with no visible pupils and the overly large roundness to them only added to the exotic look as her transparent wings, small hardly able to support her size, caught the light revealing the otherwise invisible appendages.

Her walk was smooth, a glide as she seemed not to be touching the floor, she was almost on Purana as the sorceress desperately tried to save her work from the Pit Fiend, now setting it aflame.

With each spell cast by the devil, Purana countered with one of her own. Fire begets water, air begets calm, ice begets heat. Each time, Purana also would send three or four spells into the remaining enemy as well.

The other female devil was surrounded by five Malebranche, or horned devils. Each over nine feet tall with yellowish scaly skin, and two large antler like horns extending high above their boorish faces. Their bat-like wings closed against their bodies as though armor.

The trident they carried was long and only two pronged instead of the normal three, but many barbs are clearly seen on the curved blades.

Zepar, the second female looked much like Bensozia, the first to attack Purana. She was much shorter, though, only about six feet eleven inches tall. She also had larger wings, that were not as invisible, and a tail that ended with barbed spikes that looked as though they could be used as weapons. The tail was swishing back and forth, and the devil was unmoving, allowing the larger female to enter the battle first.

Purana saw all her mental spells being tossed aside and decided she needed more room. Giving up on saving her work, she opened a gate to another room, the ball room in the palace, and backed through.

The devils all teleported in surrounding the woman, who was now not alone. There were twenty of her clergy in this room, all of whom were accomplished sorceresses. The priestesses all begin sending energy blasts into the Malebranche as

Purana created a fist shaped ball of air over the smaller of the females. Zepar, only just dodged the impact as it still crushed down on one of

her wings, mangling the appendage. The deviltress screamed and Bensozia sent a mind blast of her own that threatened to crush the protective shield of the sorceress before her.

The second crushing blow of the air made fist, larger than a horse, struck Zepar again, and Purana created a flaming sword to attack Bensozia. The two forms of attack used a lot of energy, but Purana kept it up as the smaller of the two was slowly succumbing to the crushing blows. Bensozia, unable to dispel the attacking magical apparition swinging in and out at her, creates one of her own to counter it. She was unable to attack with another spell, though, while holding off the mystical blade of Purana.

Purana, under no such restriction, cast another spell, this time four sparks of energy flying from her out stretched hand, hitting Zepar squarely on the chest as the crushing fist smashed down onto her for a solid blow to the head. The devil screamed a death wail as the first descended again and then again. The large mound of broken flesh and blood, began to smoke and the odor of Brimstone filled the hall.

Purana in a mental sword fight with Bensozia almost failed to see the Pit Fiend enter the room, and barely dove to the side, avoiding the large club descending on her. Her sorcery created sword almost wavered out, but she quickly regained control and re-enforced the battle with Bensozia, at the same time, she sent three bolts of acid into the Fiend's chest that staggered it backwards where one of the priestesses hit it with eight sparks of energy flying out from her two out stretched hands.

Purana turned back to the female devil and renewed her attack bringing the crushing fist into the battle. As Bensozia was struck with the air made fist, Purana's sword severed an arm, and then a leg on the cross swing. The devil's own sword blinked out, and with a final mental thrust on both apparitions, Purana crushed and stabbed with her magic, Bensozia fell to the ground in a heap. The body began as well to smoke, and Purana, tired, turned to see the Pit Fiend rip the priestess in two, as two of the Malebranche were just done killing the last of the remaining priestesses in the room.

With a psychic scream, delivered at a pitch higher than human ears could hear, Purana, crushed the minds of the horned devils, and caused the Pit fiend to drop its prey as well.

Staggered, the fiend tried to open a dimensional doorway, when it was hit with twenty-four sparks of energy, eight at a time in three consecutive volleys. As it staggered from the damage incurred, Purana lashed with a whip of electricity that wrapped around the fiend's neck and with a mental pull, tightened until the head was severed by the electrical garrote.

The room reeked of brimstone, as the gust of wind blew through dissipating the dust remains of the devils. Only three of the priestesses remained alive, and the Queen could only sit hard down on a step, her energies nearly depleted, sweat flowing down her face, she was exhausted.

Purana was sitting on the lowest step below her throne, when Torel and Binel finally walked in. Her head hanging with the fatigue making it difficult to move. She had not had to use that much effort in all her short life.

"They are all dead, my queen?" The high priest asked as the two arrivals moved to the prone priestesses checking, until only the three still alive were healed. One of the fallen priestesses did not survive the healing, and Purana only looked up to say,

"Eighteen are dead, and I could not heat water for tea at the moment. How did they get in through our protections so undetected?"

"We did detect them, Purana, but were not fast enough to react." Torel calmly exclaimed. He did not want to add that she should have been more aware.

"Well, I have need of my bed, now. Have the mess cleaned, and we will have to start anew on the morrow." She walked off, not allowing the horror to affect her, drawing on the coldness at the loss of her most powerful allies. She could not let it distract her.

Torel watched as the Queen exited, and began to shake his head. He heard a mumbling oath come from the priestess Binel, and moved to whisper in her ear. When she nodded, the two left, telling the only two priestesses, now sitting up, to have things done as the queen ordered.

"She has gone insane over creating a new magic, Torel." Binel started, quietly when they entered the women's room. Placing a dome of silence around themselves, Torel was sure that someone was trying to watch.

"The whole palace is wizard eyed, Binel. Hold me, to avoid suspicion." The woman and man embraced, as they whispered into each other's ear their plan to keep the empire alive.

Watching, Doreen Faulin, saw with disgust, the two High Clergy embrace. He was sure he was about to get something good that could be used against them.

"Those two are so caught up in their own plans that more often than not, they are working against each without knowing. It, of course, is making things easier for me!" Faulin smiled.

"The palace is destroyed and they go off to copulate. Holy Isis, why have you done this to me? How can I keep the girl alive, if you give me these people to work with?" His prayer goes unanswered, of course, but the man moves on, leaving the two "love birds" to their fun.

****

JC was staring at the statue rising over twenty-five feet above his head. Standing only five feet seven inches, shorter than the average human male in the North, he still made for a daunting figure to look at.

The wide shoulders, and overly developed forearms of someone use to swinging a hammer against heated steel on an anvil, he now spent most of the days swinging a long narrow curved steel like blade into Hell Spawn flesh.

His hair hanging loosely had grown to a length of just past his shoulder blades, the usual tie he wore to keep it back, hanging loosely around his neck. His light blue leather vest was unlaced and his linen shirt was open at the top two laces. The heat was unusually warm for this far north, and he was feeling even more heat, as the Order of Brigitte clergy were trying to convince him to join the Council of Nine.

C'renan, the elven priestess newly raised to the head position was attempting to enforce the oath he had made her a few weeks ago. JC, was feeling the heat of the entire clergy of priests and priestesses as the vote in favor of his taking the newly vacated spot was 186 to 0.

Unprecedented, for any, but even more unusual was the fact that he was a man. No man had ever been more than a minor high priest of this order of Selene's church, let alone a High Priest of any note. That JC was the promised prophet, *The Sword of Vengeance* of the Holy Goddess, went without question, now.

Even among those that were insulted in Alyndra, were even more emphatic about it than some of the others.

Dyanea watched him pace and stare at the statue for a few more minutes, before exclaiming.

"For the love of the Goddess, if looking at that statue, bothers you so much, then have one made that looks more like her!" The whole audience mumbled; the word that had spread fast that the three had been blessed by a meeting with the Goddess. Most of the Selene Temple, had also heard about that first day, when JC had insulted the looks of the Holy shrine here in the Temple. Now, it was actually being suggested that a new one be made!

JC stopped his pacing and looked at the Reverend Mother, and smiled.

"You are most wise, Reverend Mother. And, you are correct that looking at a pale resemblance of our Mother Goddess, in her greatest Temple should bother me. It should bother us all!"

JC drew a deep breath and brought the picture of Holy Selene into his head. Then concentrating on molding stone, he pushed out with his sorcery and slowly, starting at the head, he reformed the idol to match, exactly what he knew to be correct and to that of the woman, the two Council heads, C'renan and Dyanea had seen in the palace. After he was done, smiling, he turned to face the Hall.

"As I was saying. I will accept the appointment, because I really do not have a choice. That I am The High Priest of Mother Selene, as well as her Sword of Vengeance, is without question. That I am now, Selenian Order of Brigitte, and an accepted clergy of this order, well only you all can say.

"I am just saying that my next six plus years cannot and will not be tied up in political struggles with the church. I am going to unite all the factions of Holy Selene's clergy and I will have enough of politics with the royalty and with combating the Hell Spawn that have invaded our lands. I just want you all, my sisters and brothers, to be aware of my responsibilities.

"First and foremost, my number one priority is to the Goddess Gia, and her children, all of the Ancient Ones." The stirring in the room as he made his proclamation was unsettling. Many voices were raised in wonder that he did not say Holy Selene his first, but JC only locked eyes with Dyanea before turning to C'renan and winked.

"Of course, my second priority is more personal, one that was presented by my Mother Selene, and witnessed by our two most holy of Reverend Mothers."

Dyanea blushed as his eyes fell on her, once again, as he was speaking, she knew very well what he was referring to, as did C'renan and a couple of the others present in this room. When he was finished, speaking, Reverend Mother C'renan stepped forward.

"Then, since it is agreed in a unanimous vote, JC d'Badger, will hence be known from this day forward as Reverend Father JC, within the circles of the Selenian Temple and to those that address him in the capacity of the Selenian Priesthood. Reverend Father, you will now recite the vow."

JC completed the ceremony, accepting the blessing and the silk light blue robe, with dark blue trim, of the Council of Nine. His status was unsure, as he was in reality forty-nine years old, making him the fifth oldest in the council, but he was untrained in the verses, and therefore sat ninth. A position that most argued against, except for he himself.

Essmelda was the first to congratulate him, and Mythalla was heard to gasp as she stood staring at the three most powerful sorcerers in the room standing side by side. The only one besides JC that was trained to read the full threefold spectrum of auras, she suddenly noticed something odd about the three. She quickly left the Temple, without saying anything to anyone.

After several hours, JC managed to free himself. He was walking around the square returning from a visit to the smithy when a young priestess came running up.

"Reverend Father, you have a visitor at the Temple. A Father Meritt from Holy Phaleg, I believe he said his name, was? Quite adamant that he only speaks with you."

"Lead the way, he is a friend." JC answered.

Upon entering the Temple, the two High Priests greeted with formal soldier's shakes, and JC asked if the father would like to go to the Inn for some refreshment.

"I cannot stay, Father, not this time. Perhaps on my next visit!" he smiled. "I only came to give a gift, from Lord Quen. He was quite insisting that you be given it immediately."

Raising his eyebrows, JC crossed his arms and indicated the father go on.

"Please, worry not at the number of people, we had a rather special meeting today. Please, Sir, go ahead." Seeing the concern in Meritt's face at the crowd in the sanctuary.

Nodding, Meritt turned to the large bundle, floating on a disk of air, next to him, and pulled out four brand new blades, not yet placed on hilts. Handing one to JC, he also uncovered 150 kilograms of pure raw mythral.

The crowd of priestesses moved to watch, some with disdain on their eyes seeing weapons so casually handled in the Temple.

Dyanea took a place beside JC, placing a hand on his shoulder. She was staring not at the blades, but the raw ore, a smile lighting her pale face.

"A prayer answered." she said aloud as she squeezed JC's shoulder.

JC took the blade, and delving with his sorcery, began to shake his head.

"There is very fine workmanship here, my compliments to your smiths. Dwarven, if I don't miss my guess. These won't, though, survive a battle against a true devil lord. They will help against any of the lesser demons and devils, certainly, but not enough heat for a lord."

"That is why I came to you, my lord JC." The emphasis on I, not lost on JC. Meritt continued. "I knew that the first attempt would require a little smoothing, as they say, and, insisted that I be the one to present these to you. Your friend, my own Lord Quen, agreed.

"These are the first ones made, and we hope that you will accept them, even flawed as they are, as well as this small number of ore, as a small gift in return for the great service you gave my master.

"He was most insistent that you know he would also trade with you for future mythral you might need. We did not think you had access to any, and do not mean it as an insult." Meritt added seeing the priest stiffen at his first words.

"No insult was taken, Meritt. I only react from joy at the wealth of such a gift. Mine to him, to you, was small in comparison, and Quen's show of charity has touched me more than you can know." JC's face relaxed, and he showed the priest what was done wrong, adding that the metals had to be heated with sorcery, not just add heat to it.

"Meld them together with electrical heat, my friend. Then will the three metals become one new one! As far as my cost for casting the spells, hmm, how about a good dinner, and a good workout with your emperor, he tests me better than I can get anywhere. I had rather hoped, my slight at his abilities would have caused him to at least attempt the spells. He is strong enough to do these three that were changed. He only chooses to believe he is not. You tell him, I continue to believe that, Father Meritt."

The two spoke for a little while longer, and as the High Priest of Phaleg turned to open a gateway he bowed to JC, exclaiming that he did not think Lord Quen would accept any payment for the mythral other than their need for silver, but he would be sure to make JC's counter feelings known.

"And, if I may, My Lord JC? I would request that someday; I be allowed to come and watch you make a blade. A nice beautiful bastard sword for my liege, comes to mind. The thought of seeing one fashioned by your own hands, that of a Chosen One's, I would find most insightful. And, my lord Quen often speaks of wanting a bastard sword instead of the long sword he carries."

JC nodded and agreed, keeping his emotions in check, he watched the man leave. Dyanea embraced him, a tear of joy forming in her eye.
"It is a prayer answered, my Lu…, um, Reverend Father." She quickly regained her composure, remembering where they were. "Holy Selene has answered our prayers!"

Smiling, JC, held the Reverend Mother, and shook his head.

"Yes, so it would seem. As well, another prayer answered to me. Quen is becoming a friend!" Dyanea did not understand, but she only could think of the aid, her priest and love, would be able to finally have others that could fight with him, as well.

****

Meritt, had noticed the looks a couple of the priestesses gave seeing the ore.

"They do care for the man. And, that tall one, with the elven blood in her, was actually crying over the ore. He did not have any ore, we were correct." He thought, as he moved to the smithy, with the corrections.

"So simple, and he gave so freely. What power the man commands, though! I could feel it just standing there. My Lord must watch himself, around that man. Father JC, must have some ulterior motive for all this. Dinner and practice with the blades, indeed? No one is so free with his power. What is it, you really want, Father JC? HMMM?"

Meritt, cast the simple correction spells, melding the three metals together, using the electrical heat he was commanded, and the dwarves went to work.They commented on already being able to feel the difference, in the beginning stages. Meritt smiled, when he left them to their work.

****

High Priest Torel teleported to Bornesta. The cellar in the inn, was often empty, and rarely ever used. He knew, from his days of visiting a very lovely young lady that he had met when he was but a man of twenty years. He had been sent as an emissary, here, and would often come just to visit her. He still found it amusing that none of those priestesses to Holy Selene could teleport. Of course, none of the priestesses to the Goddess were wizards, as far as he knew.

Teleporting for some strange reason could not be duplicated with sorcery. The differences in the magiks involved, seemed to stop psychic ability from moving matter instantaneously. Wizardry was more than adequate to instant movement, but most of the other spells were just too slow, and too cumbersome. Although, even Torel had to admit, Purana seemed quite able to mix and match her spells, easily casting one or the other types quickly and smoothly.

355

Torel listened at the door, before sneaking up and out the back of the Golden Hand Inn. Moving invisibly, another wizard spell, that sorcery could not quite duplicate, he traveled easily, unnoticed, across the town's square and into the Temple of the Order of Brigitte.

No one seemed to notice the opening of the doors, and Torel immediately came to a halt, staring at the statue, that was still radiating freshly used sorcery. Stunned, the idol he looked at, was not the one he saw all those years ago. He listens as a couple of priestesses are talking, only fifteen feet away.

"I still can't believe the power he displayed. I get the strangest feeling every time I look at that thing, Berga. It's almost like the statue is alive, and looking back upon us!" One elderly priestess exclaimed.

"I know what you mean, Zaina. Can you imagine how much power it took to do that? I don't think, even Dyanea could have molded stone like that, and he did it without even a strain, in a matter of seconds! Not to mention the added Bless that he placed on it!" The woman in her mid to late fifties, answered.

Torel listened, stunned. Could this man, be the same one he was looking for? Purana had said he was weak, and she always would go on about how inadequate he was. But stone shaping was very difficult through wizardry, let alone sorcery.

"She really is insane!" Torel thought.

Just then, the two women stopped their conversations and turned looking right at him.

"Whose there?" The older of the two, asked. Torel could feel her enter his awareness, and immediately teleported to the square outside. Knowing, he was more powerful than the elder priestess, he could have fought her dispel of his invisibility. But then she would have known he was there. But, the two of them together would be too much to fight.

"Let them think on that for a while. I need to find out where this High Priest is, first." He thought to himself, as he headed up the stairs to the Temple.

Entering, he saw the women, still studying the area where he had been, only moments ago. Smiling, he bowed, and began.

"Reverend Mothers, I am High Priest Anu, of Holy Isis. I seek the one called High Priest JC d'Badger!" He lied about his name. Just in case, always be able to claim innocence.

"You mean the Reverend Father JC!" The one called Berga answered. "Or you can call him High Lord Father JC. He's the newly crowned Lord of the surrounding territories."

Torel could only raise an eyebrow, over that.

"Yes, he is a Council member, Father Anu. But he is not here. He is away. You can go to his castle, and see the priestesses there, if you like. They might be able to help you!" She finished.

"His castle? I was hoping to find the Chosen One of Holy Selene. Certainly, he could not have a castle. Maybe, I have the wrong name?"

"He was knighted, just a couple weeks ago and given the Queen's own keep, as a gift. Feel free to follow the road out of town about a mile, and take the road that branches off to the right. The castle is only four miles away." Zaina added.

Torel, looked at the two, and nodded.

"Thank you, Holy Priestesses. May the two Goddesses bless you, this day!" He turned to leave as both women greeted him back with similar farewells. Torel exited the Temple.

Not one to want to invade a keep, Torel walked outside of town and teleported home. He had found a little more information than he had.

"Father JC is much more than our empress has led us to believe. And remembering the man, facing Purana that day, ten days ago, he is not one to fear Purana, either. He is just as strong as her, or else, really as foolish as she says he is." Thinking about all he saw and heard.

"I would be willing to bet the former! Perhaps, I can use these people. Certainly, if this JC is weak willed enough to bow to a mortal Queen, instead of simply usurping her, then he can just as easily, be manipulated. After, allowing Purana to talk to him the way he just stood there, smiling at her tirade, he can't be that hard, if I go with diplomacy. Certainly, he will see that she is insane!"

357

****

The first invaders landed on the eastern shores, in the southernmost kingdom of Stidtorn, near the beaches of Worg. The ships landing, discharged ten thousand men in just a little over three hours, as the North West continent sat quiet, not ready for it.

The one that saw, stood stunned as he watched thousands of men, and monsters disembark killing the few fishermen unlucky enough to be close enough to be seen.

Turning his horse, he fled, knowing he had to reach the capital of Worg, where King Victorn d'Cloud could be told. The kingdom had been at peace for almost a generation, the army not nearly large enough to hold back this invasion, especially with all the ships he could see still coming in.

He road hard, urging his horse beyond normal endurance's, knowing he had to move faster. With each village he passed, he would trade horses, in the name of the King, he must not fail!

CHAPTER 14
Finding strength within

Fire rained down out of the sky, as the balls of flame landed on or near the ships and long boats littering the ocean around Atlantia. As the invaders disembarked onto longboats, heading to the shores of the small island continent, the wizards and sorcerers protecting the empire were busy fighting back.

Purana thought nothing of the battles, knowing that her Temple more than capable of holding back the nuisance.

She had much work to do, and couldn't be bothered by the annoyances of petty war with humans and monsters.

"Call me, only if Hell Spawn are attacking!" She ordered when told of the invaders. High Priest Torel walked away shaking his head, knowing that they were all doomed, if his queen did not learn to pay more attention. In only little more than a month, the sorceress more than proved a capable practitioner of magiks. Equally skilled in wizardry as any in the kingdom, she showed even greater imposing power in the use of sorcery. Nearly a goddess in strength, she seemed possessed in the study of whatever she was trying to create. Torel walked the hall heading to the tower, in order to issue more commandments.

He smiled only slightly, as he knew that he was the one, truly running the empire. But her power would be needed, and she had already cost him several of their most powerful sorceresses due to her stubborn inttentiveness.

He wondered if she were to die, if Isis would notice. But, who to replace her? Perhaps this father JC would send that young girl. She was amazing, more powerful than any he had seen before Purana.

Only a child, and already almost as powerful as any of the Immortal Chosen. Maybe more so, than the men. He only got a glimpse of her, while on one of his spying missions, but it was enough. Even that High Priestess would do. She seemed stronger than all of Atlantia, as well.

"Certainly, the father would not leave us to flounder without a way to protect ourselves. Weren't the ones of prophesy sent to protect all the world?" He thought. Torel, moved to the very top of the tower, and watched as the magic continued to paint the skies. The invaders kept coming, but at least their numbers were dwindling.

Then, the flash of a dimensional door opening caught his eye. And from that doorway, poured Hell Spawn by the hundreds. Fearful, he watched as his own wizards began to fall.

"Tell her majesty that Hell Spawn have arrived." He calmly ordered one of the priestesses standing near him. Leveling his arm at the doorway some two kilometers away, he gathered his will and began calling lightning from the sky. More and more bolts rained on the doorway, until finally it closed only after more than five thousand Hell Spawn had poured through. The battle raged on, magic against spawn, magic against the thousands of invaders, and magic against magic. That day would go down in history as the day that Atlantia would fall.

Purana gathered her will and sent out five bolts of acid. The five-spawn died where they were hit, partially blocking the door. She was gathering all her papers, not wanting to lose them like the last attack, and stuffed them into a sack.

Four more spawn entered and she eliminated them just as easily. Turning to leave, she saw the wave of demons behind the door, blocking her escape. Sighing, Purana, tosses the sack across her shoulder and reverting to wizardry, teleported from the room.

Appearing in her chambers, she quickly grabbed the sack containing the papers in a lock box behind boxes in the back of her closet. Then she turned to enter the halls outside her rooms. As she walked, demons by the score were seared, disintegrated, burned, and generally removed from existence. The sorceress-priestess, showed no mercy as any being, she did not recognize, was immediately slain. Be it demon, human, or monster, the creatures dying in her path begin to add up.

She saw at the far end of the gathering hall, as she entered via the south doors, Torel and his little whore, Binel, in a struggle with several spawn. With a wave, she sent six fireballs into the demon crowded room, and watched as the room was suddenly half emptied, engulfed in flames.

When the smoke cleared, she saw that there were at least a dozen non-Hell denizens amongst the demons. She only momentarily hoped none were hers.

Torel, knocked back by the blast, rose to see Binel swarmed under. As he cast his spells, the woman's screaming suddenly choked off. He teleported out, using wizardry. Purana, standing atop the stairs, at the south end, was surprised.

"I didn't know he even could use wizardry!" She thought to herself, as she sent six more fireballs into the remaining demons. After four more volleys of six, she realized that she would not be able to exit out the northern doors, as the spawn just kept coming.

When a dimensional doorway opened and pouring out was more demons, she began to realize the palace was lost, for the moment. She must get outside to rally what troops were remaining. She turned to see coming down the hall behind her a wave of spawn, and opened a gateway to the city below.

When she stepped out, she was only just able to create a wall of air and push back the devils that were moving towards her. Quickly she opened another gateway and stepped out into a building that should be abandoned, on the far side of the city.

As the day wore on, Purana, leaping about the country, saw nothing but makatiels, goblins, and Hell Spawn. When she faced a half-makatiel giant, Purana faced her first loss, and the biggest shock of her life. Her magic is useless! Barely escaping from certain death, she almost did not react soon enough.

When twenty different spells and psychic attacks all failed against Martinith, only the arrival of a few soldiers, allowed Purana to escape. Even so, she saw the giant, even bigger than Odyseus, waste the thirty soldiers as if they were children. Those few Atlantians, that were still alive, had been captured, and she began finally to realize that she no longer controlled the continent.

Finally, after four defeats, at the hands of three of the other Chosen, Martinith could smile. The hordes of Haden had won the day. Martinith's third life claimed victory over one of the Chosen, even if she did manage to escape.

Thinking only about how to free her people and get out, Purana began to plan. Not beaten, only slowed, she told herself.

"Odyseus can be convinced. He will send warriors to help. Maybe, even Quen will be convinced to help. Torel tried to tell me that I needed to build the non-magical portion of the army. Anu did, as well! Why didn't I pay more attention? I was

361

so sure that with the power of our magiks, we could not be conquered. How could I have been so wrong?"

Wondering where her head priests were, she cast an invisibility on herself, using wizardry, and began to make her way into the first camp of makatiels. There were seven prisoners, there, and she wanted to collect as many of her people as she could. She knew, the spawn would be able to detect her, under the invisibility, but, was sure the monsters would not.

When Purana finally headed into the mountains as the new day is dawning, she was leading only thirty-seven people, twenty-one humans, of which only three are magi, and sixteen elves, of which twelve have some type of magical abilities. Only four priests or priestesses of Isis had been found alive. No one said anything, as they moved in search of the Dwarven clans.

****

The battle had been going for hours as the hundreds of dwarves and gnomes were able to hold ground against the ten thousand makatiels and humans from the southern continent called Haden. The goblins fighting with the invaders were even easier to kill, but their numbers were many, over twenty thousand, and the five thousand men and women army of non-humans, only was supported by twenty-five hundreds of the Sho Guns' troops.

The one advantage the dwarves had was that they were aided by the most beautiful human any had ever met in this part of the world.

Sheera, friend of the non-humans, as she quickly was coming to be called, fighting side by side with the princess of the Selenian continent dwarves, Massy Thistle Thorn. As the two priestesses cast spells and swung weapons, the hoard of invaders seemed to be falling back.

Being sent back to the beaches where they came from, a dimensional doorway suddenly opened and out poured a wave of Hell Spawn. Led by what seemed to be a part human giant riding a jet-black horse that had cloven hooves aflame, and blood red glowing eyes. It rose into the air traveling ahead to the front of the nightmarish army suddenly attacking.

The horse's nostrils were exhaling black smoke, and the man on its back was seemingly part makatielish, though twice the size of any normal makatiel. The rider

362

was leading the new additions to the invaders against the dwarves, as the makatielian and human army turned all its attention to the gnomes.

Leaf suddenly appeared and started assisting the gnomes against the opposing forces, as Sheera released a gas cloud of acid, and pushed it forward with air, and added to her spell a hail of lightning bolts from the sky, directed at the demons and their makatielian leader.

The rider and horse rose above the gas cloud, and he turned his attention to the two priestesses at the rear of the Dwarven army. Massy called on the power of her goddess, Gia, and cast a spell of duplicity upon her hammer.

The sudden magical aura surrounding her hammer made of spirit, was thrown from her strong arm, as she watched it fly into the flying horse. At the same time as the hammer hit, a lightning bolt falling from the sky was deflected by the rider, and he was able to send it into the opposing army below. But he was not able to catch the four magical bolts of acid that Sheera's next wave of spells sent.

Martinith, screamed as he was unhorsed by the power of the bolts. The dwarves renewed their attack on the Hell Spawn and with the aid of the magical hammers being thrown into the fray, by all the Dwarven shamans, they quickly regained control of the ground. The three thousand minor Hell Spawn were being swarmed under by the superior fighting dwarves, and the devil horse, a Nightmare, was eliminated by Sheera's magic.

The result of the fallen leader was unknown, until a large path was being weeded out through the dwarves.

The man was immense, Sheera noticed. Standing taller even than Odyseus, easily over two hundred twenty-five centimeters tall, and broader than the large Chosen boy, as well. The Haden Chosen's sword was cleaving dwarves in half with a single swing, as his battle cries renewed the demon attacks.

He had dark skin, almost makatielish in color, but of a lighter tone of the gray green. His hair was brown and his plate mail armor was a ruddy rust colored. His sword was a bastard sword, but the man's great strength and size was easily handling the one- and one-half meter blade one handed.

Sheera cast a psychic crush on the man, but he shrugged it off as if not even noticing. Lucifer's champion seemed to be moving through the dwarves with so much disdain, as his target was becoming obvious, to be Sheera.

When the two met, the young woman quickly realized that this man was almost as quick as she was, and with his strength, her only advantage, was the years of training she possessed. But, as the battle wore on, it began to lean toward Martinith's advantage.

Massy, swung with her hammer joining in to help the Immortal, and was quickly cut down after delivering her blow. Martinith was not even staggered, being immune to the non-magical weapon, but even as he tripped from a kick by Sheera, his great sword cut through Massy's arm sinking deep into her chest.

Sheera swung with her small curved blade, and the wakisashi cut quickly on the large man, delivering three deep cuts, one in the monster's leg and two in the abdomen.

Martinith seemed to blur, and appeared twenty-five meters away, giving Sheera a chance to check on the fallen priestess. Massy's breath was labored and her heart was too slow, Sheera immediately realized that healing would kill her, except for one person she knew.

Martinith was in the process of healing himself, and Sheera seized the moment, as she grabbed her pendant and concentrated, "James Carl Tigara, I need you, now!" She said it loud, in an almost yell. It appeared to those around her, that she was summoning someone or something!

A half a world away, JC looked up with a start, in the smithy, he almost dropped the hammer he was using. Tossing the lump of metal, he had just heated, into the vat of water, he handed the hammer to one of the other startled armorers. Looking at him with curious faces, he said not a word as he picked up his katana leaning against the far wall, and exited the building.

Wearing only his pantaloins, and boots, he looked up into the sky noticing the time. It would be dark in Katiketa, he mumbled aloud to himself, as he concentrated five yards away from the origin of the name pounding in his head. The gateway began to open as Dyanea, Mythalla, Marcus, and Essmelda, as well as sixteen other clergy and soldiers came running up.

Having seen him react, in the smithy, Dyanea did not hesitate from where she had been watching him work. They all preceded him through his gateway, before he could tell them to wait. It closed behind him, as the Selenians all entered a war zone.

To his right JC saw the large half-makatiel, that he had fought just a few weeks ago, and to the left, Sheera, leaning over a large figure on the ground. It was a few seconds before he recognized the unmoving figure to be Massy.

Sheera looked up at the other Immortal with tears in her eyes, but before she could say anything, Martinith, the half-makatiel assassin created by Lucifer, began to move towards JC.

The High Priest only hesitated a moment, before stepping away from the twenty mortals that followed him.

"Mythalla take them over to Sheera, this one is mine." The mortals stared at JC, as the words poured from him.

So cold, so hate filled, almost evil looking, none had ever seen the absolute lack of emotion in his eyes. Even when angry, he had a softness to his visage, but not this time, and they did not hesitate to follow his instructions. They were witnessing the Sword of Vengeance side of the man, and the women all took note!

Martinith saw the man he hated most, the one he owed a debt of pain to, step from a gateway. The girl forgotten, he saw his new target and inwardly laughed.

"I will have two today. You will die, this day, Selenian!" He growled.

With the addition of three more sorceresses and soldiers with sorcery powered blades, the war took another turn, and the dwarves and gnomes claimed victory that day.

The two men, that met on the battle field alone, one short, powerful, steadfast, met the other, tall, gigantic, quick. Their blades touched and the sparks that flew lit up the night.

Lilith was behind a tree off to the side watching. She smiled, seeing once again, the target she intended to make hers one day. She eagerly watched the battle.

In the forest, just a few meters away from where the Dwarven priestess was laying. Sheera was unaware of the devil female that watched.

The invisibility was only good as long as she did not move, and Lilith feared she might have moved in too close. She had seen the woman call out for James Carl and within a few moments he had arrived.

Lilith had breathed hard seeing the man, shirtless, sweat stained chest, his arms showing signs of heavy straining.

"You have been in battle already, and still you come to the girl's aide, my love. Just as you should have done for me, back in the garden, all those millennium ago! You love her, just as you did me!" She thought to herself. She frowned seeing the women and men that came with him, though. Two were part angels themselves. One, was the same woman that had been seen near him, since his arrival.

The duel was fast, furious, and deadly to both combatants. No art in this duel, no style. JC was a machine, striking with all the skill of someone that had swung his blade daily for the past year. His great constitution allowing a man that did not seem to tire, no matter the hours he had already spent pounding metal in a smithy, that day.

His muscles already loosened, the sweat already prominent on his shirtless upper torso, he entered the combat with the precision style of reckless abandonment.

Martinith, having spent the day leading six armies, in a synchronized assault on the six continents, was feeling the wearing of the day. And, this being the first time this body had been hurt, the pain of being cut was somewhat slowing, to him.

Kutulu Lucifer had created a man with many powers, but not forcing him into training, Martinith was unused to skilled combat. Only his great strength and God like quickness was keeping him alive as JC's blade moved in and out, as though a serpent on the hunt.

Seemingly unconcerned by the damage he was taking from the big man's own blade, JC continued to push the duel backwards, until the larger man realized his death was eminent. As a swarm of minor demons moved in on JC, Martinith turned and ran.

The priest screamed as he eliminated the demons without seemingly a thought and yelled for the fleeing man, as he tossed four bolts of acid arrows into the half-makatiel's back. Sheera had already thrown four of her own sorcery made acid arrows into Martinith, as well.

The magical protection around Martinith suddenly was dispelled, by some unseen force, and the arrows all found their target, as he fell through a dimensional door. Lilith laughed, as her magic dispel worked, just as JC and Sheera released their spells. She heard the smaller human's cry as Martinith already dead, was falling through his doorway.

"Remember this day, Hell Spawn! Run back to your master and tell him, his end is coming as well." Still swinging the blade as the Hell Spawn around him, once again moved in, the victory this day, for the Continent of Katiketa was heard.

When the invaders were pushed back into the sea, only twelve hundred dwarves, nine hundred fifty gnomes, and three hundred ninety-five humans were still standing. The death of those fallen, had their names raised into the skies of glory, as the funeral fires burned brightly.

But, the miracle of life given this day was the news that traveled even faster, than anything else.

Once again, Lilith watched in amazement at the man's concern for his pets. She was even more stunned by what happened next, though. Something, even an Archangel would not try to do.

JC leaned over Massy Thistle Thorn, Princess and heir to the throne of the Dwarven clans. He found no heartbeat, and looked up with tear filled eyes. Placing his hand on her heart, he began to draw energy into himself, as he concentrated on life.

He heard Sheera, sounding so far away, yet he knew she was only to his left. Her pleas for him to stop what he was doing, and then there were others, equally sounding as far away, just as hard, trying to stop him.

He could not move, and the power he was drawing from came from the world, coming from Gia, or someone equally aware who had heard his prayer, filling him with more and more until he felt he was to explode with it.

367

Arms were trying to pull him from the dwarf on the ground, as he released the energies into the dwarf's still body, the prayers of life, issuing from the mumbled lips.

Her damaged body suddenly was renewed, and even her burn scars were wiped clean. Her hair was restored and even her beard was full, several inches as an adult female would appear.

Four sets of arms seemed to be on JC, pulling or pushing, but he would not be moved. Massy will live, Gia had granted his wish, he knew.

The power flowing from him was that of a God, he had never felt so much in touch with everything, yet, so alone, all at the same time. So small, and yet so large. So weak, yet so strong.

JC was no longer there, in spirit, as he flew the universe at the speed of light, faster than light, he was traveling faster than thought, it would seem. His spirit finally found Massy's and he pulled at it to come with him. It only fought the pull, briefly, following the pure love in the spirit tugging at her.

As the two spirits headed back to the waking world, another spirit appeared, that of a large beautiful woman, with dragon like transparent wings, long dark hair, and glowing black pupiless eyes. She hovered in front of the man and dwarf spirit, only briefly watching before stating.

"You should not be able to do this, James Carl Tigara. You should be dead, now, having tried. Fear not, I come not to hamper you, only to watch a god being born. Know that Lilith has put a claim on you, James, God of Vengeance! We shall meet again, soon!" She disappeared.

When they returned to the tiny world of Zindar, the two spirits slammed into their bodies. Massy's eyes popped open, and JC collapsed in on himself, sprawling across the priestess.

Massy, stirred and sat up as the priest released the energies he had been casting, and rolled off of her to lay in a trance, eyes still open. His face was a deathly pale, those standing around moved to him to insure he is breathing. His collapse looked that of a dead man, but for the haggard breath coming from his smiling lips.

The dwarf moved to stand and suddenly fell back to her seat, legs too weak to support her. She instead rolled over to the high priest and began to shake him.

"Wake up, you fool man! Do you know what you have done?" Massy screamed, as Dyanea tried to help her awaken the entranced priest. Tears flowing down both women's faces.

The others only crowded around in wonder, awe, and fear. Raising of the dead was something only a necromancer would do, and the evils of creating zombies was not what was done here. Only the gods could truly resurrect the dead. Sheera and Mythalla both delved Massy at the same time, insuring she was a woman, and not some undead creature.

But, Massy and Dyanea ignored them, continuing to shake and move the priest laying on the ground, until he finally snapped out of what ever had been holding him.

"I'm fine, people, I tell you, I'm no undead." Massy said to the others, when JC moved with a moan, the women's shakes on him relaxed.

"Gods, the power was so overwhelming. So beautiful, the universe is!" He mumbled, as he tried to sit up, failing he rolled onto his back.

"It would seem I forgot how hurt I was. All that pain when I was placed back in my body. The shock of it. Damn, it hurts, still! Can someone help me up?" He asked, matter of fact, calm to his tone.

The hand that took his, was small, soft, and familiar. It had been in his many times over the past few weeks. The strength she possessed in sorcery was unmatched in mortals, but her slight frame had strong arms, as well, and she pulled the man up into her arms.

Dyanea's hands held under his shoulders and the energy of a healing spell grabbed hold of him, as his wounds were closed and the pain from the legs and back and chest were erased. His knees buckled from the shock on his system, and he fell forward holding onto her legs.

Marcus moved behind him and helped the Priestess lift JC once again, back to his feet. Massy being helped to hers, the two stared at each other, before embracing.

"That was a wonderfully foolish thing to do, JC. Boy, don't you know you could have been killed, yourself. Only the gods can raise the dead. I don't know how you found my soul, but you are one lucky man."

Her tears fell, the Dwarven female not use to such emotion, was embarrassed by the show, and kept her head buried in his chest. JC cared not who saw his tears, as they flowed freely.

"Thank you, my friend. I can never repay this!" She finished.

"Gia granted my wish, my loyal loving princess. The Princess of the West, could not be allowed to die. I would not allow it!" The words came forth, and Dyanea, still holding onto JC's arm, placed a hand on Massy's head, as well. Sheera only watched, seeing more of the man, than she had ever thought possible from him.

"And, we are twins? Nay, Mother and Father, we are not twins. He is so much more." she whispered to herself.

His sword moved like nothing she had seen outside of Quen, and now, seeing the power in his sorcery, once again doing what he should not have been able.

"JC was holding back on all of us," she thought. Her smile was just as awe filled as the crowd watching.

"This day, is a day to celebrate." Dyanea started. A soft blue glow formed around her as she elevated her voice. Enhanced magically to carry to the whole army, she started.

"Sheera Lu Che, The Golden Dragon" has led a great battle and victory for her country and the man that only she could summon forth to aide in your war, the High Priest, Reverend Father JC d'Badger, of Holy Selene, has raised the dead; that, a feat only the gods can grant."

Dyanea's voice being raised with sorcery was heard throughout the army that was now crowding in around, to gain a closer look at this near-human speaker.

She began to move through the entire army, as she preached. Still with the sorcery induced voice and azure halo surrounding her. An angel giving a proclamation to the crowd.

Touching the people, healing them as she would pause in her sermon, all the people, dwarves, gnomes, and humans, listened, seemingly entranced by the sermon being given, by The Reverend Mother Dyanea.

All, heard her words that day, and the names were chronicled in history. She continued, praising Gia, Selene, Jeasuas, and all those that will come to fight the armies of Hell. The cheers from the warriors raised and lowered as Dyanea preached the victory and the miracle of life.

She carefully manipulated her words, ensuring that Sheera got the credit for the victory, that all knew, the power she commanded that she alone, could seemingly summon other Immortals, yet, she insured too, that all knew it was JC that performed the miracle of a god. When she was done, JC and Sheera stood together, the man between Massy, holding one arm, Sheera in the other, they all watched the Reverend Mother preach to the masses.

"She's so beautiful, Sheryl, and so angelic!" JC said without thinking. When he realized what he said, he turned to the woman on his side as she gripped his arm knowingly.

"She is an angel; I can see it. But she is only part, she isn't one of Gia's, is she?" Sheera shook her head in the negative and continued.: She is better at preaching than you are, James!" Sheera winked at him. "She's the one, isn't she?" Her soft elbow to the ribs caught him as she chuckled. Massy smiled at the young woman, and JC began to somehow, feel trapped.

Fully exhausted, as well as feeling thirsty and tired, when Dyanea finished her sermon, he made the introductions. Introducing them to each other as all the women that held his heart. The two embraced in a knowing hug and all of the women moved off to talk.

Leaving the tired man to fall back onto the ground chuckling at the feeling he was being trapped in a cage. He swore he could hear the door crash shut and a lock being set.

Marcus just stood guard over the priest, arms crossed, in the young man's eyes, a total reverence for the man on the ground. Leaf stood off to the side, carefully remaining from the man's sight, as Kuan Yen, eyed the man sitting.

"He has just proven himself a god, and yet, they ignore him like it was nothing?" She mumbled. She moved to JC, and bowed, her right hand cupped into the left under her chin. JC moved to stand, taking the hand offered by Marcus, and returned the bow, never lowering his eyes, much the same as Sheera would do.

"I am JC d'Badger, good priestess. May I know the name of she who honors me?" He asked.

"It is my honor, to meet the prophet of Holy Selene, Father JC d'Badger. I am called Kuan Yen, Priestess to Holy Jeasuas, and follower of the Golden Dragon. I apologize for my own Priestess' lack of respect at not offering you any comforts, after calling for your aid." She turned to accept a canteen and handed it out to the father.

Chuckling, JC looked at the meek priestess before him, with more power than anyone he had seen, other than his own Dyanea, and her apprentice, Essmelda. He saw in the woman's aura much confusion, and calmly responded.

"There are no apologies necessary, Kuan Yen. I am JC, not the deity you seem to think. The one you call the Golden Dragon, is a very much-loved daughter and sister prophet, and her summons will never go unanswered." he paused to take a drink. "I willingly serve those I call my friends and family, think not small of their actions. It is only as I would expect and command."

"You are as full of charity, as Sheera Lu Che has said, JC d'Badger. I am glad to have finally met you. My Golden Dragon, speaks well of you, and, often."

The three humans moved off, seeking food. After the healing that Dyanea performed on him, JC complained of thirst, and the two mortals took that as a command. Leaf followed, watching in amazement, at the calm, that JC seemed to radiate.

"Selene, you made a very interesting man! He instills into others that which your brother Jeasuas does. Such power, he can only be the champion we are waiting for!" Leaf thought to himself, continuing to remain out of sight.

****

The battle is brief, the two were almost late in coming, though. Over two hundred makatiels managed to make it to shore, before Hecate could sink the ships. Odyseus, using his two-handed fighting style waded into the one and a half meter tall

372

monsters, with human bodies, heads like that of a pig, and ears of a dog. The tusks were useless appendages, but fierce-some to look at.

When the battle was over, a small, stout woman stepped from behind a tree, watching the large man and small woman sink thirty ships, and kill over two hundred makatiels, without very much effort. She stood about one hundred meters back among the tree line, but still could see the immense size of the man, that was the promised prophet of Holy Minerva.

Only 100 cm tall, the gray haired and eyed woman with overly large bulbous nose, waddled down the beach towards the couple, on short legs. The gnome is smiling as the light breeze catches her long green dress, causing her to keep her hands down for modesty's sake.

"Good eve, to thee Chosen One of Holy Minerva. I am Circea, High Wizardress to Coeus Willow, King of the Willow Clans. I bid thee Welcome!" She said, with a voice that was high pitched and strong for a woman of her obvious elderly age.

"And, a fine welcome, it be, good lady! How be thee here, at this most fortuitous moment?" Odyseus smiled, holding his hand out to shake the woman's own. Instead, she took his hand, bowing she kisses it before letting go.

"I beg thee, *Spear of Reason*, please to come with me. Thee and thine most beautiful woman!" She waved back into the forest, behind, and after turning to look at Hecate, Odyseus responded.

"Lead on, good woman. We are at thy disposal for the moment!"

After more than an hour of walking, they entered a clearing, where a large gathering was taking place. There are over fifty elves, about as many gnomes and even three humans, in the dark gray markings of Holy Minerva. When Circea led the couple out of the forest, the talking amongst them ceased, as all turned to witness the hulking man and tiny wizardress moving towards them. Two of the humans joined an elf and gnome, in walking to meet Odyseus part way.

When the seven met about twenty meters from the large gathering, Circea made introductions.

"Odyseus d'Brell, may I introduce the High Priest Dionys and High Priestess Appola." The two humans gave the man an arm shake. Dionys, stood about 194 cm, with arms the size of tree trunks, those accustomed to battle or athletic events. He had dark olive skin, black short hair, and light brown eyes. Appola was a tall almost 188 cm, with the build of an athlete. Her dark brown hair is wound tightly on her head, and the medium brown eyes seemed to take Odyseus in with a quick calm. Circea continued next to the elf.

"This is Antaeus ip Rille, High King of all Lemuria Elf Clans, the Seldarine. He is the direct descendant of the great Rillifane Rallathil, first elf created by Mother Gia's Archangel, Pynelthorella." Odyseus moved to shake the man's arm and saw the more than two-thousand-year-old venerable elf grab his with a strength that was that of a much younger man.

"And this is, my King and brother, Coeus Willow, High Father to the Holy Mother Gia." Odyseus dropped to one knee, bowing without lowering his eyes, and kissed the gnome's outstretched hand. When he rose, the elderly gnome likewise, dropped a knee and returned the kiss.

"Be now formalities do be out the way, to what honor to be I for thine beautiful messenger deliver this wonderful invitation?" Odyseus smiled and all seemed to relax.

"We had heard you to be one of the people, Great One!" Antaeus began. His voice the melodious singing of all elven speech. "Alas, we were not sure what to expect of the *Spear of Reason*, sent by the Holy Minerva in rescue of the demons that have plagued our world, of the sudden."

"Lead on, good woman. We are at thy disposal for the moment!"

After more than an hour of walking, they entered a clearing, where a large gathering was taking place. There are over fifty elves, about as many gnomes and even three humans, in the dark gray markings of Holy Minerva. When Circea led the couple out of the forest, the talking amongst them ceased, as all turned to witness the hulking man and tiny wizardress moving towards them. Two of the humans joined an elf and gnome, in walking to meet Odyseus part way.

When the seven met about twenty meters from the large gathering, Circea made introductions.

"Odyseus d'Brell, may I introduce the High Priest Dionys and High Priestess Appola." The two humans gave the man an arm shake. Dionys, stood about 194 cm, with arms the size of tree trunks, those accustomed to battle or athletic events. He had dark olive skin, black short hair, and light brown eyes. Appola was a tall almost 188 cm, with the build of an athlete. Her dark brown hair is wound tightly on her head, and the medium brown eyes seemed to take Odyseus in with a quick calm. Circea continued next to the elf.

"This is Antaeus ip Rille, High King of all Lemuria Elf Clans, the Seldarine. He is the direct descendant of the great Rillifane Rallathil, first elf created by Mother Gia's Archangel, Pynelthorella." Odyseus moved to shake the man's arm and saw the more than two-thousand-year-old venerable elf grab his with a strength that was that of a much younger man.

"And this is, my King and brother, Coeus Willow, High Father to the Holy Mother Gia." Odyseus dropped to one knee, bowing without lowering his eyes, and kissed the gnome's outstretched hand. When he rose, the elderly gnome likewise, dropped a knee and returned the kiss.

"Be now formalities do be out the way, to what honor to be I for thine beautiful messenger deliver this wonderful invitation?" Odyseus smiled and all seemed to relax.

"We had heard you to be one of the people, Great One!" Antaeus began. His voice the melodious singing of all elven speech. "Alas, we were not sure what to expect of the *Spear of Reason*, sent by the Holy Minerva in rescue of the demons that have plagued our world, of the sudden."

"It is nice to see and meet, a young human, with manners, that has been sent us." The beautiful singing voice from the crowd is familiar, and Hecate tightened when Bel ip Phon stepped from behind some men, to join the group of kings and clerics.

"Bel ip Phon, it be honor and pleasure to be seeing thee, once again!" Odyseus bowed, chuckling at Hecate's look, when he kissed the elf maiden's hand.

"I see you traded your grandmother in for one more suitable to your age, my young friend!" She turned to Hecate extending her hand to the young tiny human female standing next to Odyseus. "I am Bel ip Phon, protector dedicated to Holy Minerva. And you are?"

"I am Hecate, Bel ip Phon. I believe we have already met." Hecate took the maiden's offered hand, giving a thin smile.

"Of course! Ahem... it was after dark then, and I didn't get a good look, obviously." Bel ip Phon looked into the angel's eyes, only nodding slightly before releasing the hand.

The rest of the group joined and after long discussions, Odyseus was able to secure a pact from the two non-human groups. In exchange for the secret of making magical weapons, a promise of two hundred warrior-mages would be sent from the elves and one hundred from the gnomes.

The two High Priests of Minerva would send word to the Temples and soon, Odyseus should have an army of Minerva soldier-priests added to the cause.

After a week of celebrations, the couple, Odyseus and Hecate left, with an understanding that in less than a month, the army of three hundred would be fully equipped with sorcery made weapons and would meet their new leader back at this grove.

Odyseus was whistling, happily as they walked away, Hecate on his arm. Hecate sighed, just glad to be away from that

"Elf witch, Bel ip Phon!"

****

Samael looked at Martinith with as much disdain as the makatielian Immortal had ever seen. Martinith wanted very much to rise from his throne and eliminate the Archangel, but knew the commander general was too quick. The distance between them was over ten meters, and even Martinith was not fast enough to cover that distance.

"Your incompetence is getting my people killed, Martinith. Do you even think at what you are doing when you send people out? Are you that much an idiot?" Samael seethed.

"You tempt much, devil! I could kill you where you stand and no one would stop me. Be wary of your tone!"

"Your idle threats are meaningless, Chosen One. I fear you not. You have been defeated too many times for me to fear any reprisals. You cannot even defeat a little girl. And how many times has my daughter or Lilith taken you down? Hmm?"

When the half-makatiel teleported, Samael did likewise. They materialized even further apart from one another. Smiling, the ruler of Hell's ninth level nodded and disappeared.

"You will follow my orders, Samael. You will do as I say, or die by my own hands." Martinith whispered.

****

The small group of humans and the last of the elves, found alive in Atlantia, moved into the Fallen Fire Mountains. Home to the Fire Dwarves, Purana wondered at what she has been told. Anu was talking to her, but she only half heard.

"My Queen, they are even less inclined to react the way you would want, then those of us, did, when you first arrived. Please remember, Chief Danthedin will not like it if you try to command him!" High Priest Anu was the only one left that had any real power in psychic strength. There were a few others that were good wizards, but most of the sorcerers had refused to believe that anyone could be immune to their magiks.

When Anu first saw large half-makatiel, riding on the back of a nightmare, a demonic horse, with flaming cloven hooves, and sulfur smelling smoke issuing from its nostrils. The red glowing eyes, and almost skeletal look, had caused fear in many of the young. It did not take long for him to realize a hasty retreat was in order.

After a few well-placed spells hit and bounced off, and the impenetrable mind shields the monster had, Anu, knew that it was time to go. Grabbing those he could, he opened a gateway and left those other poor fools, the soldiers to face the onslaught of the makatielian and goblin army.

Now, with his queen, they were seeking the last of the only Atlantians that would be able to stand up to the invaders. Except, he knew that diplomacy was not one of Purana's strong points.

"Perhaps, with my mood the way it is, Anu, you should do the talking?" She absently stated. "If they are so behind in the times that they would not bow to their betters, then I really don't understand why we are even here!"

"The dwarves are almost as immune to sorcery and magic, as that half-makatielan devil was. The dwarves are our last hope for real soldiers, my Queen."

377

Anu was beginning to wonder if all that talk that Torel was always mumbling was true. Could all the power that Purana possesses, really be making her insane. He may be thinking it, but he would never say it aloud.

"You must hold on, young lady! There has to be a way, for you to find a heart."

"High Father Anu, you are much too secretive, of late." Purana softly said. "You would not be planning anything behind my back, would you? Torel was, but at least I knew he was up to something. You, I have never been able to read!"

"My loyalty is beyond question, my Queen! Why are you even suspecting such a thing? You knew that Torel was not as loyal and yet, you allowed him to be raised above us all, while still, you treat all of us that are loyal as lower class." Anu had finally had enough.

Stopping, he ordered the others to move ahead and behind a few meters. Looking at Purana, he waited for a space to clear, then he looked up into her eyes.

She was calmly allowing him to direct the people and when he put a dome of silence around them, she only nodded.

"It is about time you and I had a talk, young lady!" Anu began. Purana tightened at the term being used. She only smiled when he continued. "You seem so intent on the fact that your power makes you a goddess to all of us lesser humans, that you forget, an army of even lesser monsters just ran over all of your country. Even your great power could not stop them." He stopped and took a deep breath, before continuing.

"We are grateful for your rescue, Purana. But, remember this. These people that you may have rescued, are all very much thankful, for it, but they follow me. Only I follow you! Try and remember, that you have much to learn about life. You blew up at, and, threatened the one person I believe could help us, and you refuse to even allow his name mentioned. I have been to speak with all the Temples, and do you even care to hear what the other continents are saying? What are you up to, Purana? And, what are you intending?"

"Anu, you dare much. I could lay you to the ground now, and you think any of these people would raise a hand to stop me? You are an old man, a semblance of strength in you, so I allow you your words. But, remember, I was sent

378

by Holy Isis to face a foe that threatens the universe, not some minor country that is filled with such weak humans and elves, that they were so easily routed.

"I don't have time for your whining. I will be victorious, yet!" She was calm, and emotionless. Anu only stared; he was shocked.

"Torel was correct, Purana. You are insane with your power. Holy Isis, I pray that you find yourself, someday. And, the sooner the better!" He continued, "Fine, my Queen! You have it your way, and let us find out if you can beat down the dwarves into following your commands. Remember, I follow the *Songs of Sorcery*. I will still be here, when you finally return to sanity! If you ever do!" He turned, tensing, waiting for the blast, he knew was coming. When he dropped the shield and made it to the waiting others, he was mildly surprised no reprisals came. Instead, Purana walked along side of him, and the group continued on in silence, for the search of the Dwarven clans.

****

As their gateway closed, JC handed the sleeping body of Essmelda over to Marcus, asking the man to take her to her rooms. Dyanea turned to follow after smiling at the high priest, placing her hand in his for a soft squeeze. Mythalla went to leave, but JC brought her up short.

The frowning face, she was making and had been making every time he was around Dyanea or Essmelda, had not gone unnoticed.

"Mythalla, you have been in a bit of a sniff ever since I was raised to the Council. You have a problem, child that you wish to get opened up?"

"No, Father." She stopped, but did not turn to face the man. Her head lowered, he could see the consternation in her features, as he walked up to her.

"Child, you are my most trusted apprentice. You are as a daughter to me. You have been taught ways that no other sorceress in our Temple know, to include any on the Council. I love you like you were my daughter. If you cannot trust me enough to tell me what is bothering you, how am I to trust teaching you even more of our ways?"

"Father, please don't make me tell you! It has nothing to do with you being made Council member. I am overjoyed by your raising and to be your apprentice, as

379

well. I just don't understand what I am seeing and feel afraid of your reaction if I tell you. Please, Reverend Father, please!"

"Mythalla," he said as he placed a finger under her chin, lifting the young woman's face to look him in the eye. "Mythalla, I can command you to tell me, but I won't. I am asking you to tell me, because we need to air this out. It hurts me more that you are so sad, than it would if you were to stick a knife in me."

At the accusation the priestess brought herself up, with a start. Her eyes took on a spark of anger at being the cause of any pain to the man she openly worshiped.

With a deep intake of breath, she looked around to make sure no one was in ear shot and nodded her head.

"All right, Father, if you insist. I think that Essmelda is your child." As JC smiled, she continued, placing her hand over his mouth to forestall any comment he was about to make.

"Either you all have been lying to me, or the impossible is proven. And, after the one miracle you performed today, who's to say there are not others within you?"

JC looked at the young priestess and only nodded. Turning, he took her hand to his arm and led them both into the keep.

"She may be my child, but I don't know how. But I agree something is strange about our connection. I have only been on this world a few months. You know that much. To the best of my knowledge, I have never been anywhere near Dyanea before that first day, that I entered Bornesta. Except as a dream I had sixteen years ago. Whatever you have seen in her and I, must only be that of coincidence or the Angel that made Dyanea's parentage maybe is the same that made Essmelda mine."

"But, Father, your auras are nearly as identical as hers and the Reverend Mother's. She has never denied being Essmelda's mother, but she has never fully admitted it, either. And, you are the father, no matter what you say!" They were entering the doors, when Dyanea stepped from the cloak room beside them.

"It is probably true, my love. No matter how impossible it may seem." The Reverend Mother stated. With a jump, Mythalla fell to her knees, whispering apologies for the betrayal.

"Mythalla, get up, child." JC pulled on the young woman's shoulders. "You have betrayed no one."

"He is correct, High Priestess." Dyanea said calmly as she knelt to the front of Mythalla. "That you are so loyal to the father, has been proven too many times. That you have always been loyal to me, is also without question. When JC and I are married, Mythalla, you will become the Castle's High Priestess. You should know everything about your lieges. Now, I think, is the time for us to talk." Dyanea rose pulling the younger woman up with her.

"Let us go find someplace more private and get something to drink. And eat!" She finished looking at Father JC, she winked. His stomach's growls telling him that was a very good idea.

Even as he wondered on Dyanea's last statements.

JC and Dyanea sat staring at each other. Mythalla, sitting in a chair between, just watched. Nothing more could be said. That JC could not see his own aura, and Dyanea had not learned to see auras, yet, they had to take the young woman's word for what she saw.

JC had touched inside Essmelda's mind and knew the connection between him was more than coincidence, but since he could not explain it, he had kept it to himself.

JC knew that Mythalla was getting good at auras, and she never made mistakes anymore, when she could see them. Now, she had sent them to wonder.

Dyanea took a deep breath and started.

"My husband to be, you claim I was a dream you once had but you never told me fully what your dream was. Well, let me tell you the facts of how your face and name came to be oh too real for me." she sighed before she sat up and took a deep breath. "A little more than sixteen years ago, I was out wandering the forest because I was in upset that most men were too fearful of being with someone that was so powerful. That is why most priestesses are without mates.

381

"Well, I was being childish and prayed that Holy Selene would send me a real man that would not be turned away. I know childish, but even us older women are put to it at times." she smiled before continuing. "Well, my power has never been really reliable when it comes to animals, probably because I love them more than people at times."

"I often had said the same." JC interrupted.

"Yes, well... While wandering the mountain forest I was beset by a mountain lion. I threw trees in its path I threw rocks at it, but it kept coming and I soon thought myself dead. Then suddenly floating down a cliff I was backed against, a hermit looking man in strange clothes, fell from the sky. Floating down directly in front of the lion between the cat and me.

"No weapons, just his big strong arms and torn shirt, pants with tears, soon to be even worse off, you were that man. You wrestled with the lion until it ran off. Somehow, you had nothing more than scratches!"

"You, my love, introduced yourself as James Tiger."

"Tigara, most likely." once again, he added.

"Possibly, I wasn't really listening after you looked at me with those beautiful brown eyes and said only that you could fall in love with staring at my violet eyes.

"Well, we spent several months wandering the forests and mountains, walking by day, and making love at night." she shivered before moving on after taking another drink of water.

"Then one day, we were attacked by a badger of all things, and I watched you die fighting once again to save me. I put you to the fire sending you off to Holy Selene and only thought about I would never find another man like you.

"Six months later, way too early really, Essie forced her way out of me, rather than being born, exclaiming to the world that here I am. She was already showing the angelic powers she claims and it took a lot of my own powers not to lose myself in the birth."

He knew that he and Dyanea both thought they had met. Dyanea told him that for the aging in his face and the few streaks of gray in his hair, that he was the spitting image of the man that was Essmelda's father.

Now, stunned into silence, he had to admit to her his real full name. Mythalla had heard it a couple times, but she did not know that would be how JC would have changed it, had he not wanted to forget his past, all together. Finally, he started.

"Dyanea and Mythalla, my real name is James Carl Tigara. In my language, that last could be Tiger. This is just too unreal to imagine." He began and finished with his whole life story, to include the month of being in a coma after the accident.

"Mother Selene, what have you done to me?" He finished.

"Why, I have done nothing, but give you the family you deserve, my son!" The answer came from nowhere, as the Ancient One slowly materialized between the couple opposite Mythalla. Both women, dropped to the floor, bowing to their Goddess. JC simply stood.

"How is it possible?" He excitedly stated. The thought that he might actually be Essmelda's father, was suddenly very appealing to him.

"You survived being born in a snowstorm on the side of the road, to a dead woman; you survived falling down a mountain in a train accident with only a broken leg, which healed in less than half the normal time; and, you walked out of the hospital just two days, after receiving a wound that should have killed you, and yet, you were in a coma for over three weeks with a minor head injury? Think, my son, don't you think that a little peculiar?"

"Are you saying that while in the coma, I was actually here on Zindar for several months? Why?"

"Marduk was answering Dyanea's prayer. She wanted a real man and he acted without my permission. Something he is prone to do. I allowed it to see what would happen. I was wrong, as incredible as that may seem, but true. You were not ready, and the last sixteen years proved it." Selene looked at Dyanea and sighed putting a finger under her chin as the High Priestess rose.

"How have I not seen this, child. Who is your maternal grandparent, do you even know?"

Dyanea shook her head before responding. "My grandfather was never told a name; he only knew it to be an angel. He thought it was one of Gia's, since it was a female with male characteristics. It was in the form of an elf, but I have always been drawn to you, Holy mother! Could it have been one of yours?" There was fear in her, as she stared at the Goddess, and the tremor was in her voice when she answered.

JC only stared at Selene, wondering if he should laugh or cry. Mythalla was still kneeling, but now only watching the exchange between Goddess and priestess. After a few moments, JC broke the silence with a sigh.

"I thank you, my mother. I cannot think what else to say! Nor can I imagine a greater gift. A daughter that is really mine?" Her arms opened feeling the man's need and the two embraced. That did not stop her from making a last sarcastic comment before she faded away.

"Now, that is a first, James Carl! You, my son, not knowing what to say? Hehe" she chuckled as she disappeared.

"Mother is Pynora one of Gia's as Hecate is?" JC asked before she was fully invisible.

She did not answer, only adding.

"Children, your marriage is already blessed, as are you, my dear little Mythalla!" The words came from open air, the Goddess already gone.

****

Returning from the invasion, Burlga's first response was to check on her cousin. He had been put to bed by Belusa, his personal maid, after he was bathed and fed. Satisfied, she moved to the wizard's wing to get some more reports about the problems within the continent. Having spent the past week gating between kingdoms, she had brought two of the four kings into her fold. Her own king, Ulfa, would have to be handled sooner or later, but she had time. Right now, the most important ones were those that have lands that are open to invasion from the southern continent, Haden. More than thirty thousand makatiels, goblins, and

384

human scum had been wasted by Martinith. There had to be another reason for it. Where were the Hell Spawn?

Burlga advised the Merylon wizards and priests to start sending men to all the kingdoms with sorcery made weapons.

"Have the Generals give them out to their best warriors. They would certainly kill spawn, but they would also cut through even the toughest armor. And tell those Temples and guild halls that they better start supporting the armies. There is no reason those ships can't be sunk before any of those creatures can make landfall." Burlga was no military leader, why she was suddenly expected to be the expert, she had no idea. Only that for some reason, the kings seemed to think they could put off any plans onto her. And, the way that the guilds were acting, one would think they all could just ride above everything.

"The fool kings think that you are not really the prophet, come to Brautania. They wait for you to fall, so to speak, so they can be vindicated. I really believe those that sit high in the guilds think only that they can rise above it all." Marut calmly said.

"I am here to fight Kutulu Lucifer and his flaming ilk. You had all bloody well better start working to protect your lands, or I'll just pack it all in, and move to the flaming North. At least there, they are not so stubborn about things. The Chosen One, up there is not having to fight his own temple, you flaming idiots!" She screamed at them, before realizing her temper.

Calming herself, she took the next note, and after reading it, crumbled it up and tossed it in the fire, burning in the hearth.

"What is this supposed to mean? Dragons? There are no flaming dragons, and haven't been for over ten centuries! What kind of damnable idiot would be spreading these kinds of rumors?"

"But, Mistress Burlga, there has been confirmed complaints about dragons all over your lands. The people of two villages all say the same thing. One a very large blue skinned dragon and the other a smaller white skinned one. They attack together, and leave nothing standing. They are devouring people while still alive, according to some reports." One of the wizards stated quickly, thinking she would interrupt.

"And, how many of you blasted wizards or sorcerers have you sent to investigate?" She stated with a little sarcastic edge to her tone. She already knew the forthcoming answer. After getting the confirmed, none, from the abashed guild members, she took a deep calming breath and grabbing the nearest man to her, by the collar of his robe, she pulled him so that his face was just centimeters from hers.

Marut had wisely moved to the far end of the hall. He knew what was going to happen after hearing the useless news from these incompetents.

"More incompetence from you people is going to result in some very dangerous repercussions delivered by me! Do I make myself clear? You are going to begin acting like a part of this world, or else," Burlga held the man while she only hesitated finishing her comment, "next time some demon lord arrives, I will simply leave it to you!" Releasing the man, she stormed out of the room, exclaiming that she had had a long day and was going to bed.

CHAPTER 15
When a Queen begs!

Quen was cleaning his blade, just having led an army against the invaders. A few thousand makatiels and goblins were no match for his fifty thousand that walked through several gateways created by his twelve most powerful priests. Those monsters that managed to get to shore found themselves badly outnumbered and out classed. Looking like demons to most of his men, the young ones having never seen the monsters.

Goblins, an average one and a half meters tall, yellowish to orange skin, with brick red to orange colored hair. Their eyes were yellow to red in color, and they dressed in crude skins and metal links. They used shields and short swords with slings and spears for their launching type weapons.

The armory was rusted and dirty, and their clothing a dingy gray to brown in colors, equally filthy. The dog to ape shaped faces, with high pointed ears, gave them a truly demonic look when charging forward in mass.

The makatiels, were pig headed humanoids, with the massive bodies of a warrior born. The snouts all had rings of silver or gold through them, and the over one and a half meter tall creatures with brownish to bluish green skin, were wearing plate and chain mail type armors. The tufted prickly hair was green to dark blue, and their red eyes highlight the pinkish snout and ears in the piggish faces. They most often used long pole arm type weapons, with some archers and sword users as well. They were not very organized, and fought the goblins as much as the humans they were attacking.

When the dimensional doors opened and out poured several thousand Hell Spawn, those monsters still alive began to cheer. Quen's army, though, had several hundred specialists, all trained in combating the spawn and all with blades made from mythral and sorcery empowered.

The sorcerers all linked to close the doorway, and succeeded before more than five thousand of the minor spawn could come through. The battle was over quickly.

He was moving his army away from the beaches when the tidal waves started that sank the fifty ships anchored some hundred meters from shore. Those still aboard, died as the fury of the sorcery made storm, pounded down on the hapless monsters.

The cheers rose from the successful army and Quen, turned to walk away. Where would the next attack be, he wondered? He was more than a little anxious to get after that. Time was on their side, they knew it, but he was getting tired of the minor skirmishes he had been subject to.

His strength lay in duels and individual combat, and sometimes, Quen forgot the agonizing boredom of a long-standing war. The world was at war, and he was just a minor pawn in it. That was something he had a hard time accepting.

A gateway opened a couple hundred meters away, and out stepped a small army of forty soldiers, with a few priests and priestesses, all baring the colors of Isis. The female that followed, was Purana, and the word was sent to Quen, immediately.

The woman, was visibly upset, by the time Quen arrived, having an entire squadron of soldiers and sorcerers surround her small attachment. She forgot, for the moment where she was, and began to order the mortals into submission. Not knowing the woman, Quen's disciplined army did not budge.

"So, Purana, you do yet live! We had heard about your little problem." Quen calmly stated as he made his way through his battle-ready soldiers.

"And, not only that, I can see that you even come with the same attitude, you have always possessed. I would have thought, having your whole continent usurped by lowly makatiels, would have taught you a little humility."

"Your soldiers threaten me, Quen? Have you not taught them the circumstances surrounding the threatening of one of the Chosen?" She arrogantly questions. "My people would never treat you this way, had you come to visit!"

"That is probably because you have beaten or killed all you're really good ones. Mine are all well trained, not the useless children you have pretending to protect you. I respect my people, and they respect me. Not fear me! That is why my continent is still standing, and yours, well, is not yours anymore!" Quen's sarcasm was biting, and Purana began to wonder if this had been the best place to come. She visibly fought herself for self-control before speaking.

"I have come to propose an alliance, Quen. Not argue over who is right or wrong in how the mortals are treated. You are beginning to sound an awful lot like the old man. What happened to the emperor's son, I came to know and love?"

"Love has never been a part of your character, Purana. Funny, considering you allegedly worship the Goddess of Love." He smiled, "Though, I would believe you to not actually worship anyone, other than yourself.

"And, Purana, what kind of an alliance could you possibly want that would interest me? We are already supposed to be aligned, or have you already forgotten our teachings?" Quen had yet to order his soldier's down, and his sarcastic quips with the sorceress, had her small contingency about on edge.

"Quen, can you call off your dogs, and let us retire to talk in private?" She asked, the effort of controlling her voice, did not go unnoticed by the other Immortal.

"My dogs, woman, as you call them, have just won a great victory over the hoard of Haden. You will treat them with the respect they are due, or I shall let them at you. You are not their queen on these lands. A good thing, too! I would suggest that if Isis had mistakenly sent you here, instead of Atlantia, an assassin's arrow would have found you long since." Quen, wondered the breaking point of his fellow Immortal.

She blew up at JC for a lot less than the insults, she was putting up with now.

"Well?" Quen added, waiting for an answer from the sorceress.

With a deep breath, Purana finally exhaled,

"Very well, I am sorry for my wanting attitude. We have been on the run for a few weeks, now, and are all tired. That half-makatiel that leads the Hadenites seems immune to sorcery, and he is very good with the blade. He almost singles handily brought my empire to its knees."

Quen looked over the female, and then walked to stand in front of her. Her people were about to stop him, until he looked one in the eye who, without a word backed off.

With a nod to Meritt, the high priest stood the army to at ease, and all of Purana's people visibly relaxed, as well. Purana almost fell into Quen's arms. She did not cry, but the embrace was tight, and the little shakes, reminded him of someone sobbing. When she looked up, she had regained her composure.

"This Martinith seems possessed, Quen. I am not sure even you will be able to stop him."

"Well, JC, Sheera, and Odyseus all have. If they can, I'm better than all of them with my sword. We shall have to see, if he ever gets the nerve to face me."

The High Priestess of Isis stiffened at the names, Quen so easily sounded. Purana shook her head, at the thought that those three proved victorious where she failed. As incredible as that sounded, she could not believe it.

"Certainly, they were mistaken? No way the three weakest among us did what I could not. They must have faced him all together, then."

Quen just shook his head, laughing boisterously at her. His own people looked at him never having heard him anywhere near this jovial.

"You never did listen to anything anyone else said, did you, Purana? There are no weak links amongst us. Did you not even listen to your own Goddess? We all have our strengths, and we all have our weaknesses. You seem to speak with hatred, even though JC is not around, yet, it is so obvious that you care for our old man, as much as the rest of us, do. He fought Martinith twice, alone, and almost killed him, both times. JC is not the weak link you make him out to be. Do not underestimate his importance amongst us.

"It is because of him; my army has blades that can hit the Hell Spawn. It is because of him, that we all know of your country's falling. It is because of him, that we are a team!"

Their talk continued, as Quen walked her to where a tent had been erected. The two were at odds, as she did not understand the other's insistence for including all six Chosen in any discussion at getting her kingdom back. The talks ended after midnight, and Quen begged off to bed, leaving Purana in the war room tent, standing alone, she began to think! She really began to have the feeling of loneliness.

"He will not help." She mumbled as he walked away. After three weeks of running, the dwarves, that low born chief thinking he could command her, would only help if she could get the other Chosen to vouch for her.

"Chief Danthedin actually accused me of killing all the elves!" She thought! As she moved to the bedrolls set up in the tent, she was appalled by the idea having to sleep with the others. Quen only offered her one tent, and then dismissed her like some commoner.

"What will we do, now, my Queen?" Anu asked. He watched for her reaction.

"This man seems to command an army that truly respects him, and he certainly respects them, far better than our own queen does." He thinks to himself. "At least he treats them far better."

"Perhaps, I can talk to that High Priest? Meritt, I think his name was! He seems to carry some small weight with his King!" Anu spoke aloud.

"We shall talk, once again, tomorrow, Anu. I am tired, and I could tell Quen was, as well. Things have to go better, after a good night's rest!" She bedded down, and quickly fell asleep.

"She really is insane, isn't she?" Quen spoke with Meritt, as the two walked out of the tent they shared in the morning.

"Or very afraid, my lord!" Meritt answered. "I would say that the Lady Purana is afraid right now, and you are the only one she considers her equal. Her reaction when you mentioned our Lord JC, was most interesting."

"Yes, I thought she was going to have a seizure right then and there." The tightness to his lips, told Meritt the Emperor found it amusing.

As the two men were talking, a dimensional door opened only 15 meters away. Out flowed thirty boned devils, three-meter-tall skeletons with scorpion like tails, all holding a long hook like snaring device made from bone. They were followed by a large five-meter-tall human with large bat-like wings. The psychic crush was almost immediate and Meritt collapsed as well as all the soldiers close by.

Quen was barely able to get his own psychic shield up. He moved gracefully through the smaller devils, his long sword flowing as though alive. Quen saw a long lightning bolt hit one devil and branch out to strike another, continuing until all the devils had been hit. It could only be Purana's power that launched that bolt, and he

391

began to make his way for the larger of the devils, leaving the smaller ones to the sorceress.

Smiling because he finally got to face a devil lord, having felt left out at being the only one not to have beaten one, yet, Quen moved straight for the tall human like devil.

When Sallos' large Hell made two handed sword met Quen's sorcery empowered long sword, sparks of red and blue lit the area. The clang of hell forged steel on Ancient One made steel was loud and the two master duelists went into a dance.

The twenty-two remaining bone devils were eliminated by Purana and her fellow priestesses, and Quen enjoyed the duel without being bothered by the lesser creatures. The duel was short, but exhausting, not having much talent in attacking spells with sorcery, Quen's one major talent was that of protective shielding. When he got a shield in place around him, he is able to hold off all but the strongest of mental attacks.

Sallos, on the other hand, was not only an accomplished duelist, he was also very good at psychic attacks, and continued to blast away at the Immortal's shield.

After less than three minutes, both combatants were nicked and bruised, the bigger creature looking steadier than the smaller human. Quen's psychic block was finally blasted away and he felt the pain eking into his mind, as he tried a last resort suicide move.

Diving into the devil, Quen managed a thrust with his sword into and through the devil's lower chest. As he did, he twisted causing Sallos' sword to miss the smaller man's chest, but instead took out a large chunk of meat out of Quen's right shoulder.

Screaming at the pain, both duelists fall back, Quen having his grip ripped free of his hand. But at least the psychic attack ceased with the great injury done to the devil.

With the blood flowing from the shoulder injury, and the pain beginning to add dizziness to the nausea within the Immortal, Quen knew his time was limited in this battle. As he stumbled to his feet, realizing he no longer had his own sword, which was still sticking out from above the devil's abdomen, Quen picked up Meritt's weapon, a long stiletto dagger, the length of a short sword, made during some of the earliest pieces. Only able to swing with his left arm, now, Quen moved in to renew his attack.

Sallos finally was able to get Quen's own blade free, but he was hamstrung from a slice by Quen, and as he fell, the Immortal sliced across the other leg.

When Sallos rolled to avoid a third swing, his back felt a sharp pain as Quen severed the upper spine, below the neck. A fourth and fifth swing removed the devil's head, just as the dizziness overcame the Immortal. Quen fell to the ground, and found himself staring at the sky, just before losing consciousness.

When Purana moved to Quen, she saw he was still breathing, the odor of brimstone permeating the air. She ordered her priestesses to heal him, since she never learned to heal, even though she was begged to.

Let the lesser sorcerers heal, she was going to fight in the last battle not heal the lesser's. Now, she wished she had paid more attention.

Her own country taken over by non-human monsters, and her attempt at allying the only other person she considered her equal, not only in the Chosen, but also in blood as well. Quen was an emperor's son. He was true nobility, and a king even here, in this world. He should have helped her, but instead, wanted her to seek out a man that not only had never been noble, still refused to rule his continent, like he should, with his power. And, then to top it off, the man was not even the equal of that other Terran. Why did Quen think that JC could help her?

She watched as the fallen Immortal awoke with a start, the healing sending a shock through his body. When he relaxed, Quen sat up, and shook his head, he walked over to pick up his blade and then moved to check on Meritt, who was still unconscious from the psychic crush delivered by the devil. Only then, did he acknowledge Purana.

"Thank you for the timely aid, Your Majesty." was all Quen said. Purana only stared at him, mouth half opened, as the man turned to lift his High Priest from the ground.

"That is all you have to say?" She asked, finally after snapping out of her momentary stun.

"Umm, what else would you like me to say, your highness? That is what we are here for, is it not? Killing devils!"

"We are here to rule and to subjugate the mortals, preparing them for the war against Hell. That is what we are here for!" Her answer was harsh, and Quen only shook his head.

"I really wish I would have read your Goddess' prophesies. Mine say nothing about ruling or subjugating. Only leading the war and fighting the spawns of Hell. Your Goddess promised you much! Too bad, you could not keep it." Quen's sarcasm was still very evident, and he walked away, leaving the sorceress to wonder once again his motives. She called her people together, and as Quen disappeared into the tent that was the make shift war room, she opened a gateway leaving Funtaland, the South East Continent.

"Odyseus will give us a better reception, for sure! At least in him, I can manipulate his actions!" She thought aloud.

Anu could only look at his Queen in wonder. Shaking hishead, he refrained from comment.

****

The second meeting went smoothly, only because Sheera, Burlga, and Quen were the only ones to make it. JC had sent Mythalla to advise that he was sorry, but he was too involved in trying to gain support for the war. Dyanea went with her, as well as Gulnara and Randall, another of JC's apprentices. Dyanea strangely, kept quiet, only talking with Sheera and Quen, after Burlga left.

Mythalla was overjoyed to see Meritt, with Quen, but when she tried to talk to the Immortal, he seemed distant, and not at all like he was when JC was present. But the elder priest was happy to converse with her, and with the Reverend Mother Dyanea, even Emperor Quen seemed captivated by the High Priestess' presence.

"Would you be one of Gia's angels that we were told JC had none of?" Burlga accused before shaking her head. "No, you would be better at controlling your aura's if you were."

"I am an assimar, Chosen, but not an Archangel as Hecartae the dryad is." Dyanea responded with an almost icy frost to her tone.

Mythalla had been told to keep any mention of a relationship between JC and the woman quiet, and since Sheera never mentioned it, the subject never came up. The talk never got around to JC, and only Mythalla was asked about him, in any instance. With the power that Dyanea showed in her auras, and when she admitted that she had been told she was the most powerful of all the Selenian priestesses, she was welcomed into the discussions with the other Immortals as the meeting came to a close.

What seemed peculiar to Mythalla, though, was that Sheera acted like she did not know who Dyanea was, until after the Lady Burlga left. Then everyone seemed to relax. Massy, of course remained quiet and only observed as she had done the first time, three months earlier.

The Chosen of Merylon, seemed the most upset by JC's absence, and made no remark at all about the missing Odyseus. Of course, with the things happening on Lemuria, no one seemed surprise by his absence.

As things wound down, After Burlga made an early exit, Quen approached Dyanea and bowed to the Reverend Mother.

"As the most accomplished sorcerer in your church, you may very well be the most powerful non chosen in the world, Reverend Mother." Quen started.

"I can only dream of doing things I have seen Sheera and JC do, your Highness." Dyanea responded.

When Sheera told Quen that this was the woman that would eventually marry their father JC, he came immediately erect and only stared at the Katiketain Chosen.

"Then you do know who The Lady Dyanea is, Sheera? That was wise keeping it from Burlga, though I am not so sure how long that subterfuge will last." Quen cracked a smile.

"Next meeting, we will let JC introduce them." Sheera answered.

"That will be an interesting day, Reverend Mother."he smiled then continued. "That you can even admit to loving the man, is a show of your strength. Your abilities, aside, I think for someone to want to spend their life with him, and his attitude about giving of himself so that others can be at ease, will test your own life and your patience. Good luck, if you decide to go through with it!" Quen stated.

"As long as he only gives himself, and not his life, I can live with it, your Majesty. I worry more about what it would do to you Chosen, if he was to die, saving one of you.

"Youth has many strange attitudes about someone having given up their life for them. I hope you all know; he really does love you as his own!" Dyanea responded.

Quen's nod and Sheera's fumbling with that strange pendant she wore, was all Dyanea received as an answer.

"My Lady is most wise, and I can already see why he would fall in love with you. I hope that you really do love him, as well, Reverend Mother! Make him forget about that silly curse he had mentioned." Quen answered.

Meritt, had been listening to the conversation, and did not notice that he had taken Mythalla's arm in his. She did not remove it, but instead laid her head on the man's upper arm, as she too watched the conversation. When Meritt looked down, and, noticed what he had done, he became a little startled, but decided he rather enjoyed the closeness of this young woman.

Massy stood off to the side and watched the whole affair with studying eyes. She smiled as she fumbled with her new hammer, that Mythalla had brought with her. Made out of a mixture of silver and steel, reinforced with sorcery, made by JC himself, the female could feel a strange power within it.

She was told that a sapphire of high quality was embedded within the hammer, and it would allow some protection. Although not able to stop the Hell Lords psychic blasts, it should allow her to aid Sheera and eventually JC himself when she returned to travel with him. She understood that it would not be able to hit the Archangels and some Greater, but should take care of anything else.

That he made it, only endeared the weapon more to the Dwarven Princess. She had to admit, she was almost as upset by the man's absence as The Chosen Burlga was. How to get JC some mythral.

****

Martinith arrived at his favorite place for contemplation. The stasis chamber that held the vats of his brothers, or more importantly the vats, containing his next bodies for use after he dies. Three of the vats were now empty.

With each awakening he had subtle changes to him. He knew everything of his former life, but too, the new body had spirit as well. Each had its own personality.

Lilith watched, hidden from sight, as the newest form exited the chamber. She wondered what this one was really like. After the defeat to James Carl Tigara, for the second time in less than a month, he was less inclined to go after the Immortals.

Choosing to lead the battle as most Generals do, from the rear. He had spent the last seven weeks directing the attacks on the six continents, as well as running the cleanup of the Atlantian Continent. The people of that country that had managed to escape, were held up in the mountains, and even his makatiels and goblins seemed to be having trouble with those.

The giants and ogres were useless, as they were hard pressed to get to go through the dimensional doors or gateways. And, since both were deathly afraid of water, almost as much as dwarves are, they could not be coerced into following on ships. Even under the threat of death.

Lilith continued to watch as the man stared at himself into the mirror, talking as though he was actually having a conversation with the other submersed spirit inside his body.

"Three dead in less than six months. Too fast! I must need guide them, for my plans to succeed." She sighed, thinking about what it will mean having to be around this makatielian monstrosity.

Stepping out from the shadows she was watching from, she smiled at the half-makatiel Chosen of Holy Lucifer.

"Well, little brother, how do you feel, learning from that last mistake?" She asked.

"Tell me, Lilith. Why was I not talked about attempting to teleport into the Merylon's protective domes? I owe you a debt of death for that, demoness!" He seethed, without even turning from the mirror.

"Yes, Martinith, you do owe me. You would have died had I not pulled you back from the dome, as quickly as I did. You never asked, and all I did was save you. The death debt is yours, little brother, not mine! You are always so intent in tasting my charms, that you never want to learn from me, anything of importance. Are you ready to be wise, or do we continue to fight each other, Martinith?"

The half-makatiel studied her, in the reflection of the mirror, knowing this was the one devil he needed to really be wary of. His plans for Proserpine were already made, but what to do about Lilith?

"All the Archangels, those still alive anyway, fight amongst themselves. And, then there is you, Lilith! Possibly the most powerful of the Greater Angels, yet, you too, appear to be fighting our father's commands. Would it not be better if we were all to cooperate with each other? At the least until, this is over?"

"A show of wisdom, Martinith. Our latest commander is finally showing maturity! Come little brother, let us talk. I will show you how to win this war. I may, if you are a good boy and win, even allow you a taste, of that which you have been chasing after all these months. But only if you win!"

Her diabolic laugh stirred through the man, just enough. It was not this body, but the man still remembered that first day he met this devil. She had left a long dagger sword in his back, then! But now, his newest body was feeling the urges once again, watching what he thinks, the most beautiful of Lucifer's creations moving away.

Lilith was wearing a long clinging gown, as she always had, since that first day. She no longer talked to the man in her natural form. Of course, Martinith had no self-control, so why should she not be wary. Three times he had tried to force himself upon her, and, on each of those occasions, Lilith had been able to easily avoid him.

"I'll listen to you, this time, Lilith. Even if I must refrain from touching you. But, beware, I'm better with sorcery this incarnation. I will have you, yet! You will bare me offspring, woman!"

398

"So, you keep saying, Martinith! So, you keep saying."

Martinith followed the laughing devil, into the sitting room, where Lilith had prepared a meal.

****

Burlga was riding out to the next village seemingly to be attacked by "dragons", no matter how ridicules that sounded. Persides and Sorlons, followed quietly behind her, not sure what they were expected to do against dragons.

That their swords were made from adamemnite, a magical material that allowed them to hit most any demon, and even some of the devils, they still could not go up against the mythical dragons, with such small weapons.

Of course, they were not really expecting to find any dragons. They had been to several villages that had sighted or been destroyed by "dragons", and had yet, to find any.

She would be glad to see the others, in just two days, Burlga was thinking.

"I will have to watch my tongue, though. I've gotten too free with my swearing words, being away from the old man." It had been three months since the last meeting, and then, three of the Chosen did not make it to that one. This one was going to be at Quen's palace, again. To be wined and dined the way she thought they all deserved would be nice.

Besides, she would be interested to see how JC was adapting to being a noble.

"Smart move on that queen to do that to him. Ties him to her, and gives the man a title for the army to follow." She continued thinking aloud about the man that lately was even entering her dreams.

He will learn, she was sure, but right now, to the problem at hand. It was probably just minor demons that could fly, but she did not want to take a chance.

"That woman that came with his apprentice, last time is a bother, though. She's an elf, and of immortal blood, as well. I wonder where she got all that power. She's as strong as Quen or Odyseus, and she knows how to use it, unlike those two

399

idiots! She could easily gain JC's interest, if I don't work harder. I wonder, though." She continued to think, as she moved on at a nice leisurely pace.

"Could that woman have been one of Gia's angels? Hecate swore JC didn't have one, but she could easily have lied. It would not be the first time, I'm sure!"

The invading army from Haden had her nerves on end. She had been casting a lot of spells to turn back minor armies that could easily be handled by a large opposing force, but the kings were all being slow to react.

And here and now was a real problem that she was actually looking forward to facing. That she was only accompanied by her two faithful body guards, was another thing that bothered her.

That all the wizards were gone, didn't surprise her. They left one lone sorcerer, too weak in strength to matter, to face her wrath. Of course, there was none, when Marut told her they had done what she told them to do, and left for the other kingdoms.

As she neared a farm, her horse suddenly became nervous and increasingly hard to control. Then Burlga saw why. Out of the forest sped several hundred Hell Spawn. Concentrating on three fireballs, they all exploded twenty, thirty, and forty yards away. Another similar volley, followed another.

After scores of the demons fell to the fire, she changed her spells to lightning. Calling it from the clear sky, three bolts hit into the spawn and then three more, and then four. The first or second most powerful sorceress the world had ever seen, Burlga hammered the spawn with three to four spells at a time, continuing the barrage of fire and lightning as she continued to attempt to make her horse respond to her physical commands.

Persides and Sorlons had tied their horses to a tree, and were standing in front of hers, easily taking out the few that would manage to break free of the damaging sorcery.

The Hell Spawn continued to come and she was still having little luck with her horse, when she decided to levitate herself away from the rush. Over one thousand spawns lay dead or burned, but she could see easily as many still closing behind those as she floated into the sky.

"You two get back to your horses and ride out of here. Take mine with you." She called down to the men.

Burlga heard it before seeing the beast, and was hit with a series of lightning bolts from behind that would have certainly killed her had she not had a protective shield around her.

As it was, she took a lot of damage, the power of the dragon's breath getting partially through even her massive shields. The pain was such that she almost lost the concentration of her levitating.

She turned in time to drop a few yards avoiding the dragon's charge. As it soared past her, missing with its great maw, and she quickly resumed her position in the sky, watching as the blue dragon, easily two hundred fifty feet long, began to climb into a long turn. She rose another fifty yards skyward and at the edge of her vision saw a white dragon flying into view.

Almost looking like a fast-moving cloud, the monster came on fast and let loose a breath of pure white ice cycles at the floating sorceress.

Sending out four bolts of acid into the blue one, Burlga quickly raised a shield to protect her from the cold blast of ice. All four bolts hit their intended target and blue dragon screeched releasing its lightning breath wildly missing the floating woman.

The white coming hard, was met with pain as Burlga sent a fireball after the smaller one hundred fifty-foot-long dragon, and two more bolts of the acid after the blue. The dual attack on either side of her was cut short by the sorcery as both spells hit effectively.

The blue was taken in one of the wings, and fell quickly hitting the ground in a loud crash below in the forest.

Screaming from the damage it had taken from the fireball, the white dragon slowly transformed into a human like female with clear white nearly transparent dragon like wings on its back. It eyed the sorceress, and the psychic blast on Burlga's mind was barely deflected by her quickly raised shield.

"My mate will be avenged magi!" It screeched. "Your final day is my pleasure!" It finished.

A second psychic blast rocked Burlga's shields, much too powerful to be just a simple devil, and she dropped from the sky, almost reaching the ground before regaining her senses.

She just caught herself, but with all her shields down, Burlga was unable to protect against the next attack, as she began to stop her fall.

The fire that enveloped her felt as though it went right through her. She screamed, and concentrating on the first person to enter her mind, she sent out the call for help. Screaming loud just before she passed out to the pain, her sorcery sent cry traveled faster than thought, across the lands until thousands of miles to the north, JC heard his name being screamed in pain.

Burlga finally succumbed to the pain and dropped the remaining five yards to the ground, to strike hard as she passed out. She did not even notice that her two sworn swordsmen were caught up in the heat of the fireball, and lay near, on the ground.

JC's gateway opened where she was, and was barely able to regain his balance as he dropped the five yards, to land beside Burlga. The oncoming hoard of spawn rushing to where the sorceress had fallen, were surprised when a katana wielding sorcerer dispatched them with a wave of air that sent the fifty demons flying back several hundred feet.

Turning to the body of the badly burned sorceress, lying face down, JC rolled her over, and, laid his hand to her heart and began to heal, sending a part of his energy into Burlga.

He stopped when she moved, not wanting to drain himself with so many Hells Spawn around. Looking up at the spawn regrouping, JC failed to remove his hand from the woman's chest and her hand grasped his.

"There is a time, good sir, when I would love your touching me so familiar. Now, is not the time, though!" Her joke was forced, and the pain she was still feeling from not being fully healed.

Bringing his hand to her blistered lips, she lightly kissed it, and began to sit up. JC helped her to her feet as he sent a cloud of gaseous acid towards the charging spawn. Burlga joined his spell with a similar form of her own and the hoard seemed finally to be dealt with.

"I can't believe those did this to you? What else are we missing?"

"Finish healing me the correct way, your luscious lug, and I'll tell you!"

The shock of having her own internal energies used to heal, sent her into a momentary collapse, as JC easily caught her under her arms. She held onto him a moment until she gained her breath, and finally spoke, enjoying the closeness, even though she knew it inappropriate timing.

"I thought it was dragons, but it was thedevil lords Malphas and Goap. At least I am sure of Goap. The big blue hit the ground hard without changing so I can only guess on the Malphas, thing." She explained quickly the whole situation and then the two moved out towards where she saw the blue dragon fall.

The ground was dented with a mold of where the dragon hit, but no dragon was found.

"Of course, a devil would leave no evidence of death behind!" Burlga said.

"Except the odor of brimstone would still be present." JC answered.

"And there is none!" They both said together, as they began looking around the area for the devil lords.

JC, suddenly felt the psychic blast hit against his shields. Looking up they saw the two lords of Hell, hovering above. JC sent four bolts of energy out of his outstretched hand, and Burlga sent three fireballs into the air, while screaming,

"Use fire on me, daughter of a dorcal, feel it in return!"

Sending forth four more blasts of energy, JC saw the male suddenly disappear. Without thought or even turning, he thrust his katana straight behind him, in an upward jab.

The scream and the impact, told him that he hit, and as the devil screeched in pain, it raked it's clawed fingers down JC's back. But they weakened as the sorcery infused katana sank deeper into its chest.

JC kicked backwards and rolled forward ripping his blade free with a twist. Rolling to his feet, JC turned to see Malphas staggering, but at the same time attempting to crush the Immortal's mind shield. JC quickly sent four energy blasts, little sparks leaving his out stretched fingers to hit the devil in both its eyes.

Malphas screamed again, lashing out blindly, but it's mind crush was released, along with the pain it had been causing!

Goap, seeing her mate in trouble avoided Burlga's last series of spells by teleporting behind where JC was standing. As the Immortal moved in on Malphas, he blocked the devil's wild swings. Goap raked into JC's back with her own taloned fingers.

JC reacting to the new pain at his back, barely avoided a swing from the still blinded Malphas, who reacted to the Immortal's yelp of pain.

Burlga moving in behind the female devil removed its head with a quick swing from her short sword, but as Goap fell, a last buffeting wave of its wings caught the sorceress, flinging her back to land heavily against a tree some twenty yards away. She slumped to the ground succumbing to unconsciousness.

Still swinging wildly, Malphas' vision began to clear and he began to fight with JC matching him swing for swing. Talons against blade, was no match however, and, JC first removed several fingers. Then when Malphas once again teleported, JC swung a wide arc that sliced through the right leg of the devil.

As it reacted to the loss of the limb, by attempting to fly, JC cut into its right wing. Reversing his cross swing, the katana sank deeply across the massive chest opening it up for an eighteen-inch-long gash, three inches deep. A second sweep cut across the chest downward for an even longer laceration and even deeper, cutting into the devil's black heart.

As JC quickly moved over to his fallen friend, the familiar odor of brimstone permeated his nostrils. Burlga smiled as her eyes opened, and she allowed the man to lift her as he carried her all the way to where her fallen horse and friends, lay half eaten. Opening a gateway, Burlga, still in his arms, was carried into her own sitting room, where JC lowered her into a chair.

"Now, that, my lord..." She winked at him, "is how a lady should be treated."

Chuckling, JC looked around at her room, and finding a pitcher and glasses, filled a couple with the citrus scented water turning to hand one to Burlga. Raising his into the air for a toast, he exclaimed,

"Burlga, if I were twenty years younger, I think I might have fallen for you. But, now, my dear child, you will have to settle for me just loving you." He drank deeply from his glass.

"Hmm, too bad, at that!" She only answered before drinking from her own glass.

As JC turned to open a gateway to his own keep, Burlga added,

"You had better bring your new lady love next week. I want to meet who it is that can make you resist me." The man laughed after he kissed the woman and then stepped through to home.

"You've already met her, my sister."

CHAPTER 16
Deadly Nights

After JC left, Burlga returned to the spot of her horses and fallen companions. Too, many deaths, too much destruction, she thought, as she retrieved one of the horses, still alive.

Loading the remains of the two men in bags, she buried them, in the forest, creating head stones, out of fallen timber. She marked the graves "With loving memories, we fell heroes beside The Chosen of Holy Merylon." She then inscribed their names.

Removing the saddle off her horse, and that off of Sorlons' dead animal, she loaded everything on Persides' mount. Walking away from the area, she created a gateway back to the castle. The groomsman, watched sorrowfully, as Burlga herself, handled the care of the horse.

Marut entered the stables, and watched his mistress care for the beast, talking out loud, as though to the stable keep, about the valiant battle the two men fought, and had she not been so arrogant, she would have taken more men with her.

"Would not that just have gotten more killed, my lady? From what you said, it was a fireball that killed them. No one, but you, could survive such a spell!"

"Don't try and make me feel any bloody better, Marut. I've lost my two most faithful warriors, and JC, all in one day! He didn't say so, but when I accused him of having a lady love interest, I could tell by his reaction, it was flaming true!"

"That just means, my beautiful lady that you only need try harder! He is not lost to you, yet!"

She turned to face the man, and saw a waver in his outer spectrum. The man was lying, but she could account that only that he was trying to make her feel better. She smiled.

"Marut, why are you lying, to me? What do you know about JC and his loves?"

"Why only what you tell me, M'lady!" He calmly stated, while inwardly cursing his carelessness at controlling his aura. "I only know that this Chosen of Holy Selene must be a very great man, to have you in the fits you are in!"

Seeing no changes this time, she realized, she talks too much about the man over three thousand leagues to the north. Shaking her head, the two headed into the castle.

****

Entering into his own castle from the smithy, JC had stopped to pick up and finish the dagger that he had been working on when he got the call from Burlga.

He had forgotten to ask her again, how she had done that. To call him like that from so far away, was something he would need to learn. He wondered if Dyanea could do it, or Essmelda or any of the others.

That certainly would make things easier on his worrying about the others when he was away. Especially while he was trying to entreat the other kings and queens into coming together against the invaders.

At least the Temple had made sure that sorceresses were in all the port towns to attack the invading armies while at sea, and could get word back to him, to come for aid. He had fought Martinith twice more these past couple weeks and each time the half-makatiel was seemingly getting tougher to beat.

As JC put the last finishing touches on the dagger's hilt, molding it to look like Selene's Holy Symbol, the hilt guard, in the shape of a balance, the coiled entwined snakes ending in a kiss, for the grip. He used sorcery to mold it to a more precise look that his tools could not make. He still was rusty, having been over a decade since he last worked a smithy, but it was coming back to him.

This was the third blade he had made, and it was his best. He thought as he dipped it back into the water to cool, before adding one last spell. A locator spell similar to the one that he had placed on the pendant for Sheera. Only in this hilt was a blue sapphire, that he had found in the city last time he had gone to see the queen. He hoped Dyanea would like this.

He was winding hemp cord around the snakes on the hilt as he entered the keep. He had forgotten about the wounds to his back and the shredded shirt when one of the maids shrieked,

"My lord, is injured!"

The call brought several guards and priestesses running, before JC could settle everyone down. One of those that entered the entry hall, was Dyanea, herself.

After allowing for explanations, everyone finally calmed, JC walked with his favorite High Priestess to her own sitting room, in the suite that she shared with Essmelda and Mythalla. It was a small suite, only having three rooms, but that was all the priestesses had wanted, and JC was glad that they at least had moved out to his new keep.

He was having enough trouble getting use to all the servants and guards, let alone if he would not have had his closest friends with him as well. And, with his three other guests, Gulnara and Marina, and the little Natylia, whom only wanted to live with the father, Dyanea was needed to help with her training, as well.

Although, JC was sure something was not quite right with her. Natylia would rarely if ever make a mistake but her auras would sparkle when they should not. JC kept an eye out, but likewise, kept it to himself. Both she and Pynora, he was sure seemed more than they pretended.

The four of the six that had first kneeled to him, now were all at the keep, and he still was only beginning to understand the title he had been given and the reactions of those others that were around him.

Finishing the tying off of the cord, he moved to stand in front of Dyanea, and focusing his sorcery into the sapphire encrusted hilt, he caused the end, that he had made of pure silver, to form into a small closed petal of a rose, above the snakes.

"Dyanea, I have nothing to give you, except the worry and danger, since you decided I might be worth spending a little time with." He took her hand in his and placed the dagger, made of sorcery infused mythral, silver, and iron. He concentrated once more and the hemp cord wrapping changed to a light blue, to match her Temple robes. The dark blue sapphire shined starkly against the silver rose at the end.

"I have created this with you in my heart, hoping that you would accept it as a token of my love for you. No matter where I am, how far apart we may be, the stone has a piece of me in it. Simply touch it and say my name, and I will hear and come."

Holding the dagger in her trembling hand, she looked at the rose, and a tear came to her eye. They embraced, and she moved to kiss him when the door to the suite opened. Essmelda walking in.

The two separated, as the tiny teenager, blushed, realizing what she interrupted.

"Reverend Mother, Reverend Father, I'm sorry. I'll just go."

"No child, don't. Hear, this is for you." JC too quickly said as he pulled a simple long dagger out of his belt, made from the same batch of mythral and sorcery made metal.

She took it, with a smile that touched all the way to her ears. Grabbing the father's hand, she kissed it, and ran to her room, exclaiming how she would make the best sheath anyone had ever seen. The two adults still recovering from their own embarrassment at the girl's entrance, just chuckled.

"She will love that more than you know, my love. As do I!"

"Just a small token, from a man that wishes to give you the world!"

Taking hand in hand, they moved to the door. JC stopped as he was about to exit, and lightly kissed Dyanea, who looked deeply into his eyes as he pulled away.

"I love you, my priest. And, I thank you." The tall pale woman quietly stated.

"Love you, too, my queen!" Was all he said as he turned and exited to his own rooms.

Entering into his own castle from the smithy, JC had stopped to pick up and finish the dagger he was working on when he got the call from Burlga. He had forgotten to ask her again, how she had done that. To call him like that from so far away, was something he would need to learn. He wondered if Dyanea could do it, or Essmelda or any of the others. That certainly would make things easier on his worrying about the others when he was away. Especially while he was trying to entreat the other kings and queens into coming together against the invaders.

At least the Temple had made sure that sorceresses were in all the port towns to attack them while at sea, and get word back to him, to come for aid. He had fought Martinith twice more these past couple weeks and each time the half-makatiel was getting tougher to beat.

As JC put the last finishing touches on the dagger's hilt, molding it to look like Selene's Holy Symbol, the hilt guard, in the shape of a balanced scale with a pole sticking up and the coiled enter twined snakes ending in a kiss, for the grip. He used sorcery to mold it to a more precise look that his tools could not make. He still was rusty, having been over a decade since he had last worked a smithy, but it was coming back to him these past few weeks.

This was the third blade he had made, and it was his best. He thought as he dipped it back into the water to cool, before adding one last spell. A locator spell similar to the one that he had placed on the pendant for Sheera.

Only in this hilt was a blue sapphire, that he had found in the city last time he had gone to see the queen. He hoped Dyanea would like this.

He was winding hemp cord around the snakes on the hilt as he entered the keep. He had forgotten about the wounds to his back and the shredded shirt when one of the maids shrieked,

"My lord, is injured!"

The call brought several guards and priestesses running, before JC could settle everyone down. One of those that entered the entry hall, was Dyanea, herself. After allowing for explanations, everyone finally calmed, JC walked with his favorite High Priestess to her own sitting room, in the suite that she shared with Essmelda and Mythalla. It was a small suite, only having three rooms, but that was all the priestesses had wanted, and JC was glad that they at least had moved in to his new keep.

He was having enough trouble getting use to all the servants and guards, let alone if he would not have had his closest friends with him as well. And, with his three other guests, Gulnara and Marina, and the little Natylia, whom only wanted to live with the father, Dyanea was needed to help with her training, as well.

"Now, I only need to get Pynora out here. I still think she is one of Gia's, but can't be sure.

410

Finishing the tying off of the cord, he moved to stand in front of Dyanea, and focusing his sorcery into the sapphire encrusted hilt, he caused the end, that he had made of pure silver, to form into a small closed petals rose, above the snakes.

"Dyanea, I have nothing to give you, except the worry, concern, and danger, of being with me. Since you decided I might be worth spending a little time with, we know the next six years are going to be trying, but I want to assure you that after this war, I will do whatever I can to make it up to you." He took her hand in his and placed the dagger, made of sorcery combined mythral, silver, and iron. He concentrated once more and the hemp cord wrapping changed to a light blue, to match her Temple robes. The dark blue sapphire shined starkly against the silver rose at the end.

"I have created this with you in my heart, hoping that you would accept it as a token of my love for you. No matter where I am, how far apart we may be, the stone has a piece of me in it. Simply touch it and say my name, and I will hear you and come."

Holding the dagger in her trembling hand, she looked at the rose, and a tear came to her eye. They embraced, and she moved to kiss him when the door to the suite opened. Essmelda walking in.

The two separate, as the tiny teenager, blushes, realizing what she interrupted.

"Reverend Mother, Reverend Father, I'm sorry. I'll just go."

"No child, don't. Hear, this is for you." JC too quickly said as he pulled a simple long dagger out of his belt, made from the same batch of mythral and sorcery made metal. She took it, with a smile that touched all the way to her ears.

Grabbing the father's hand, she kissed it, and ran to her room, exclaiming how she would make the best sheath anyone has ever seen. The two adults still recovering from their own embarrassment at the girl's entrance, just chuckled.

"She will love that more than you know, my love. As do I!"

"Just a small token, from a man that wishes to give you the world!"
Taking hand in hand, they moved to the door. JC stopped as he was about to exit, and lightly kissed Dyanea, who looked deeply into his eyes as he pulled away.

"I love you, my priest. And, I thank you." The tall pale woman quietly said.

"Love you, too, my queen!" Was all he said as he turned and exited to his own rooms.

****

For nearly nine months, now, Odyseus and Hecate had cleared the Lemurian villages of demons and other monsters of Hell Spawn. They had also combed the beaches sinking invaders before they were able to make land. Hecate's power was strong and her peculiar angelic magiks were no match from the lesser magicians among the Hadenites.

Avoiding the cities, Hecate explained, it was necessary for Odyseus to get the commoners support before the nobles.

"The senate is voted on by the nobles, the king by the people. The elections are won by people not by nobles, and the villages will make you a hero!" She would continue to say. Hecate was careful not to let him suspect her real motives behind keeping him out of the cities.

The cities were filled with fool nobles that would view him as a rival and hire assassins.

The devils and demons were bad enough, and the demon lords, he had faced, three of them were tremendous, but they were easily seen, assassins would be able to kill him before he or she could see them coming. It was working, though, her plan, and he was becoming more a hero and less the feared demigod that he had first been thought of.

The people were spreading the word of the large barbarian demon slayer and his beautiful young wizardress.

Of course, Odyseus knew she was really not a wizardress, her incantations were unnecessary for the casting. She only did that for show, to keep any from suspecting what she was.

She was behaving herself, and he felt more in control than ever, so he allowed her little guises. And, she no longer called him boy, and the nights were not nearly so cold, anymore, as well. He was enjoying life again, and thought it good.

412

Sitting in the Inn, the two were just finishing dinner, when the doors to the common room banged open, a very frightened half crazed middle aged man fell through. He was too far gone to be very coherent, but the mention of more have returned, had the big man moving to the door, without thought.

Running through the swinging door, Odyseus stopped short at the sight of nine Malebranche, horned devils and the largest devil he had ever seen. Just eighty meters down the street, walking the road, destroying with fire and lightning, the buildings and people they could see.

Placing a mental shield to protect himself from psychic attacks, he drew his long sword, made by the Holy Minerva with sorcery and mythral, his left hand clasped the hilt. His right, pulled the spiked club, equally strong in sorcery, made by the Goddess, as well.

Screaming a war cry, he threw himself towards the devils even before Hecate could call out to wait. As she cast her first spell, Odyseus had already eliminated two of the smaller two-meter-tall horned devils.

Azazel, the four-meter-tall gorilla with tusks and bat-like wings was casting fire at the wild barbarian, but his spells seemed to dispel just before hitting Odyseus.

Cursing at her big bear's impetuousness, Hecate could only run on her short legs and dispel each cast by the devils. She could only hope, she could continue to match the larger devil, spell for spell, as she realized he was as strong or stronger then even she was. This greater angel of Lucifer was very psychically powered. And the other lesser devils were also casting, the psychic battle was straining Hecate to her limits, something she had not faced before in her many millenniums of years of life.

Odyseus managed to kill five of the horned devils before taking a punishing blow from one of the two pronged tridents they carried. He staggered and his psychic shield folded in on him. Unprotected from the mind blasts, Hecate was too slow to stop all of the spells coming on him, and one got through, as Odyseus lowered his weapons, standing in stunned silence.

Hecate screamed to get all their attention, and her own mind scream inside Odyseus' head, snapped him out of the charm, even as she cast three lightning bolts into the remaining horned devils. All three bolts branched and all four smaller devils were eliminated by the powerful spells.

413

Odyseus just managed to raise his sword in time to parry away Azazel's club. The impact though, sent a sting all the way up his arm causing him to drop his own weapon. He swung immediately with his club, hitting the devil in the leg, just above the knee, causing it to bend inwards too far.

As Azazel was falling to the damaging blow on his now, broken leg, he teleported to the Archangel, reappearing behind Hecate who was standing just twenty meters away. Hecate was just finishing another spell of protection upon the big man, when she was knocked unconscious by a viscous blow to the back of her head. As the impact from Azazel's club sent the tiny form flying forward, she landed face down just two meters from Odyseus, who was bending down to retrieve his dropped sword. The blood oozing from the back of her lifeless head caught his eyes.

Odyseus lost all control as a rage within him welled up. Only once before, had he gone so utterly berserk, but seeing Hecate, the woman of his heart lying dead, face down, caused his mind to go blank. He charged the devil lord, swinging with both his weapons as the fury of a tornado.

Mixed with his gigantic god like strength, the mind blank on himself and the protective shield placed by Hecate, made it nearly impossible for Azazel to counter with any spells. Those that he did manage were shrugged off by the combination of shield and blinding rage.

The devil was being beaten down, barely countering with his own club, he was only managing to hit Odyseus once for every four or five blows he was receiving. Teleporting away became impossible due to the flurry of attacks by the barbarian, and Azazel could see his end coming.

One last attempt to teleport, Azazel was clubbed in the head and as he raised his weapon to knock Odyseus' club away, he took a stab to the chest. He screamed as the sorcery powered sword sunk deep, and doubled over when the Immortal's club smashed into the other leg.

As Azazel fell, no longer with any good leg to stand on, he tried flying up, but found his right wing sliced through and his left wing crushed by the warrior's club. The next two swings of the sword gutted the devil cleanly and another swing of the club caved in several ribs. Odyseus continued to pound the fallen angel even after it had dissipated and was blown away.

The fury of his blows on the now, bare ground, seemed to shake the village, as the few onlookers thought the man possessed. Slowly his fury was spent, and calm returned the berserker to a sense of sanity.

Odyseus turned and ran to the tiny form of Hecate scooping her up into his strong large arms. He saw that she was barely breathing, opening a gateway, he stepped into Bornesta, running for the Temple of Selene. The villagers moved out of the way of the running barbarian yelling at the top of his lungs, the loud deep baritone voice speaking over and over again the name of the one man he knew would save his angel. "B-A-D-G-E-R! J-C-D'-Bad-Ger!"

As Odyseus neared the great Temple of Selene, several priestesses come through the door, at the bellowing man. Standing over 210 cm, the seven-foot-tall human was even broader across the shoulders than their Reverend Father. And, this boy, only twenty years old, was crying for the father.

They led the Immortal up the stairs into the Temple and showed him to a room where the tiny woman in his arms could be laid down. When they tried to push him aside to inspect the woman, he would not budge.

"Please, you must let us work. Her breathing is labored and she must be taken care of, immediately. We have sent for the Reverend Father already! Please, good sir, move back and let us work!" Odyseus took one step back, hovering over the smaller priestesses as he watched them work. After less than an hour, Essmelda walked into the room, followed by Dyanea.

Odyseus, tears flowing down his face, he begged for the man's help, but Essmelda and Dyanea told him that JC was not home. They assured Odyseus, that JC would be here as soon as he was found. Essmelda, stepped forward, and excitedly claimed she could heal just like the father,

"I'm just like him, the only one, he claims." She proudly exclaimed.

Essmelda looked over the Angel, and after delving, looked back at Dyanea, a confused look on her brows, she exclaimed.

"Odyseus, she will be fine. She will wake up by morning, if not sooner. Did you know that she is not human? I don't know what she is, but whatever it is, she is immortal, and her body is healing itself. Much like the father's does, maybe even faster."

Odyseus' jaw dropped open before he quickly closed it, he began to chuckle.

"Yes, I guess I did forget. I be in a panic at my Hecate like that..." Odyseus told the story of what happened and then excused himself to a wash basin so he could clean his face.

Essmelda opened a gateway to the keep, and Odyseus carried his angel through, following Dyanea to a room, that was always prepared for any of the visiting Chosen. As she left the man, she shook her head.

"This is the boy that JC loves so much?" She mumbled to Mythalla. "He is the one that JC thinks to become the Chosen Champion?

"He must grow a whole lot more, if that is the case!" The younger priestess only shook her head in agreement.

****

That night, JC had finally returned home and after checking on the Lemurian guests he retired. He had spent a considerable amount of energy in the battles on that day, and he was both physically and mentally drained.

JC was lying in bed, not quite asleep, when he heard the gateway close and saw the shadow of the female standing at the foot of his bed.

Willing a small blue glow to appear at the ceiling, JC saw Dyanea, a look on her pale skinned face. A sultry look like he had not seen on her before. When he sat up, he asked,

"What is it?" Worriedly, but the woman only held a finger to her lips answering,

"SHH." As she walked slowly around the bed, while her hands untied her robe, letting it fall to the floor, revealing a nude body underneath.
So enraptured by the sight of the woman he loved nude bay his bed, he did not think about the fact that Dyanea did not know how to open a Gateway. Nor did he think about the fact that this woman was not radiating the angelic aura of an assimar.

Not wanting to question the priestess' actions, he instead, pulled his blankets down moving over to allow the woman to join him on the bed. He did not notice there was no aura, as if being concealed. Nor did he notice that her skin was even paler than normal, nor did he notice that Dyanea's ears were even more pointed than her normal subtle rounded point.

He also, failed to notice that the woman's eyes lacked the hint of violet, and that her breasts were too large and too high for the woman he had only seen nude once, in since the sixteen years earlier. And that once was nearly six months ago.

JC failed to notice all the subtle things wrong with the picture, only eagerly accepting into his bed, the woman that held his heart. He failed to notice all those things, until the woman's hand moved down his chest and stomach, reaching inside his loin cloth to grab at his groin. As her head moved to his in a passionate kiss that began to fog his mind, he suddenly opened his eyes.

JC knew something was wrong, his mind clearing, Dyanea would never be so foreword, he tried to push the woman away, but she was far too strong to be the priestess. Her legs quickly wrapped around his, her one arm holding him between the legs, the other behind his head at the neck. Her kiss was locked tight as he felt his life force beginning to be drained by the succubus.

Unable to simply push her away, JC bit down with all his great strength into the leather tough tongue of the female devil. At least he thought it a devil, now, though it still possessed the form of his beloved.

The woman moaned of pleasure at the pain, until his bite was able to sever the tongue. The moan, then, turned into a gurgled scream, as JC was able to get his hands around the woman's throat.

Still weak from the battle earlier that day, his energy field barely was able to wrap the hell Spawn in a holding spell. As she tried to dispel it, JC only hesitated a moment before clubbing Dyanea's face with his fist. Twice
His mind was turning, his heart knew this was not his lady, yet his eyes kept telling him she was and he held back on his hits. But, the first punch was enough, as the body fell limp atop him.

Grimacing as the woman went limp, the devil still did not reform into its true form, leaving JC holding the form of Dyanea's nude person in his arms. The twist in his stomach wrenched his nerves and he opened a gateway to Dyanea's room, jumping from the bed he quickly stepped through.

Dyanea was startled awake when the blue light appeared over the headboard of her bed. Sitting up quickly, she gathered her will to cast a spell till she saw it was JC near her door holding a nude woman, limply in his arms.

"What is it?" She hesitated, seeing the man, no clothes on except for a loin cloth, dangling from only one side being still tied, the scabs from his earlier wounds not yet healed, he swayed slightly staring at the woman in the bed, and unceremoniously dropped the one in his arms.

Dyanea stiffened, pains of jealousy hit her, until she suddenly saw the face of the one, he dropped, when the woman rolled towards the bed after hitting the floor. The High Priestess was stunned looking down at herself, a large bruise forming on the jaw just below the left cheek. The Reverend Mother slipped out of bed, moving hesitantly to the woman sprawled on the floor and leaned down next to her, in front of the man still standing dumbfounded mumbling, to himself.

"I am so sorry, Dyanea! Forgive me!" JC was saying. He repeated the same phrase over and over, as Dyanea inspected the woman. JC continued to stare straight at the bed, not hearing the questions Dyanea had, he only responded with his mumbled shock filled plea.

A knock on the door and outside it, a young girl's voice.

"Reverend Mother? Are you all, right?" Essmelda sleepily asked through the closed door.

"Yes, child, I'm fine. Go back to bed!" Dyanea answered, quickly retying JC's loin cloth into place. He did not seem to notice, in the state of shock that his mind appeared. She patted his cheek in a loving tap, shaking her head, and turned to look down at the woman, at herself, laying on the floor, once again.

As she moved, JC took one of her hands in his. Still in shock, the comfort of having the touch of his love's hand seemed to calm him. Dyanea stepped across the laying woman and leaned down, still holding JC's hand. The Immortal took an involuntary step forward and dropped hard to the floor landing on his knees.

418

As his right knee struck the ground just above the devil's head, his left knee landed hard on the woman's neck. The crushing sound of a wind pipe, the cracking of the neck bones, the neck snapped breaking, the polymorph spells the seductress was under, seemed to pop and with the broken spell, the body of the devil, was none other than the Greater Angel Eisheth Zenanim, as it began to smoke.

The impact of hitting the ground, alerted JC from his trance and seeing the woman he had just killed, he fell to his hands, retching.

Dyanea moved an arm around him, placing her head on his back, half laying across his still scarred shoulder blades, she held him like that till long after the predawn began, JC still shuddering, as he was with dry heaves, his stomach being long empty.

The next morning, when Hecate woke up from her forced sleep, they all laughed when JC made Odyseus tell her what happened after she was injured. Sitting on the big man's lap, Hecate patted him on the cheek, lovingly exclaiming,

"That's my boy!"

Hecate admitted to Essmelda and Dyanea her origins, and the near mortal women, acted surprised, even though they both had been told about Hecate and the possibility of other angels living among each of the Chosen.

Dyanea looked to JC, who was still unsettled from his own ordeal earlier that morning, she lifted his arm up around her shoulder.

"When we marry, my Lord, am I always going to be in the company of angels, demigods, and gods?" JC could only shrug, Odyseus laughed, seeing the man uncomfortable, for what was the first time since knowing him.

"You are part angel, yourself, Reverend Mother," Hecate smiled. "Should you be so surprised that it would take another one to make you happy? They all try to ignore it, but the Chosen are angels, after all. Your intended a natural born Archangel from Selene's own loins!"

****

Quen woke with a startle, as the woman crawled into his bed. Nude, Nileena was already stroking him, as she moved closer under his blankets. He had already sent her to sleep in her own tents, and had not expected this.

"Not tonight!" he mumbled.

But he did not send her out, as her hand reached down under his loin cloth.

The kiss, was what alerted, the man, that something was wrong. Reaching for the demoness' throat, he began to strangle, as his mind was blasted with a mind crush, and then with a mind blank.

His own shields in place the moment he awoke, the succubus, then tried charming.

Quen was finally able to break the kiss, as the succubus changed into her true form and began to rake him with her claw like finger nails. The clawed attack was weakening to him, as Quen still maintained his grip, attempting to kill the woman by strangulation.

Finally, after what seemed an eternity, the demon went limp, and he was able to remove her head.

Quen did not wait for the brimstone, as he was running through the camp to Nileena's tent. When he entered, he found the girl, face up, eyes open in a death stare, having had her life drained, most likely by the very same demon.

He did not cry, but felt the loss of his first apprentice, and occasional lover as he slowly returned to his own tent. Now, showing no signs of the struggle, with the exception of course, of the odor of brimstone.

Meritt watched the man work with the younger priests, the next morning. He worried, over the young Chosen that was becoming something close to a friend. Meritt wondered what would have happened to make a man so emotionless, when the other Immortal Chosen all seem so filled with it.

Even the man, that Quen so obviously admires, Father JC, openly acknowledges his care. Quen does not deny that he cared for the girl, but he shows no signs, outwardly, of any remorse at her being gone.

"All in the price of war, Father Meritt. We will all loose someone we care for, before this is finally over. Let's just hope it is not me, hmm?"

Meritt saw the joke in it, but did not laugh, this time.

****

The small army of elven archer-magi, and Minervian clerics were moving through the city when a large army of zombies, ghouls, and skeletons moved in to attack. Seeing food, they quickly swarmed over the humans and elves. Odyseus began to chop and smash the undead creatures while Hecate blasted them apart with spells of disintegration and psychic implosions. When the large baboon like demon appeared with over thirty minor demons, Odyseus moved away from his people and charged the monster. Standing over three and a half meters tall, the demon was very large, and very powerful, physically.

Purana, walked out of the gateway, behind her people into a war. She saw ahead just a few dozen meters, the man she was seeking, in a death grip with a large baboon like demon.

A tiny human female was wielding magic like no other mortal she had seen on this world. Easily as strong as Sheera, maybe even Burlga. The hundred elves and thirty humans fighting against the hundreds of undead that were surrounding the two did not go unnoticed as well. Purana's small army went to work joining in on the battle.

The additional help made the battle quick, and when Hecate turned to see who their benefactor was, she stood to her full height of 150 cm, and crossed her arms across her chest under her breasts.

The look directed at Purana was not one of friendliness. She did maintain the psychic mental shields on her loving bear, though. And the army of humans and elves following Odyseus, moved to protect their little human wizardress, seeing the look she gave the woman commanding the smaller army of Isis worshipers.

They are dressed in the colors of Atlantia and Isis, and most had heard what had happened in that southern continent.

421

Several of the elves began to move among the undead, pulling their arrows, attempting to save as many of the precious arrow points as possible. All were sorcery made mythral steel, and each elf only had forty to their quivers.

Odyseus wrestling with the demon twice his size, literally, Ogheil, demon prince of the undead, was almost four meters tall, gray skinned, with goat like hair, a long tail that was poison tipped, huge bat like wings and standing on goat legs, with human looking arms. His club was two meters long, and Odyseus avoided the swing of it, by grappling with the demon, which now seemed to be losing ground to the more powerful, if smaller human. When the big man, finally twisted the head off the huge body, he then dropped to the ground, the ferocity of the move gained Purana's army an unsettling feeling. The man walking towards them, in their sights, was massive.

"Now, now, my loving little angel. That be not a stance to take with a friend!" Odyseus said, as he calmly rested a hand on Hecate's shoulder, when he walked up to stand behind her.

"Thou hast come as a friend, Purana? I be not JC, and won't put up with thine yelling, like there did him!"

"He deserved it, my former lover. I see you have replaced me." Purana answered with some disdain in her tone.

"Nay, be not replaced if never had, Purana. Found much better! Hecate knows love to me, thou don't, anyone!"

Hecate was on the verge of casting, Odyseus could feel the tenseness in her shoulders. He knew the jealousy that ran in the little angel, and was not sure what would happen if Purana got to one of her moods. He decided to diffuse the situation before it went any farther.

"What dost thou, Purana? Word comes thine continent be faced more than just the few thousand makatiels the rest of us be facing. I heard Quen no be helping, whatist be thou wanting with me?"

"Does everyone know?" She returned.
"Pretty much, yes! JC's apprentices do be keeping good watch on things and we be getting messages, at least once a week. From them, if not JC in person."

At the mention of his name, Purana tensed. Odyseus, seeing the sudden change in her, raised an eye brow, as a smile came to his face. Hecate began to uncoil her arms, slowly, readying herself with a spell.

Odyseus felt himself surrounded with that familiar warmth that told him that a magic protective shield had been placed on them, by the angel's unique form of sorcery.

"Tell your little imp, there, that I am not going to attack. She looks ready to scream!" Purana almost purred. "And really, Odyseus, did you really think you would need a shield to protect you?"

"I did not, but my beautiful angel remembers Pan those months ago. You screamed at us for no reason."

"I screamed at the old man, not you. And, he called me child within thirty seconds of me arriving. I had reason to scream."

"He calls all of us his children. Thou are lost to think it an insult."

Odyseus had all but forgotten how really beautiful, the Immortal was, and began to chuckle feeling Hecate's reaction to the sorceress' words.

"I be not controlling my lady, Purana. So, beware thy words. This do be my continent! And Isis no be ruling in Lemuria!"

Purana, took a more at ease stance, a sultry look coming to her. She seemed tired, Odyseus noticed. And, maybe a little fear in her, as well. All her people certainly appeared to be afraid.

"Dost thou some wine and food? I be sure we at least, do have a civil talk whilst thou try to decide what be thy needs of me."

Hecate turned, holding her arms to be lifted. Odyseus had half expected it, and was already leaning down. As he straightened with the woman in his arm, she kissed him soundly and turned to make sure Purana had been watching. The big man chuckled, as he walked away through the streets of the town. He turned when he reached the Inn, to see that Purana had indeed followed. The elven and Minervian army falling in behind the Isis clergy and squad members.

Thinking that this was going to go no better than it did with Quen, Purana was about ready to leave, but her ragged army was tired and hungry, and she knew that at least for her part, she could use a bath and a night's rest in a real bed. She decided that she would accept the boy's hospitality, and see if there was a chance.

She had to try and find a way to get that little girl away from him. How did he ever find another immortal? Her aura was that of an angel, and by the power she was wielding, an Archangel at that!

"Who are you, angel? And, what about Gia's command that the angel's stay out of the war?" She asks when they were seated in the now, crowded common room. Purana handed the inn keeper three large sapphires and an even larger ruby, and the man began to fawn over the tall exceedingly beautiful noble and her retinue. When Odyseus announced her as the Empress Purana of Atlantia, the place was suddenly a bustle of food, wine, and even entertainment. The likes, the Blue Mermaid Inn had never before seen.

Hecate only shrugged. And Odyseus seemed amused by the two women, the two most beautiful women he had ever known, eyeing each other as if readying themselves for a match of wills.

"She is one of Gia's angels, no be of the Ancient One's, Purana. There be no commandment, with her. She does be here, because of love. And, I love her, thou will be nice. As I said, I do be not having the father's patience!" There was the mentioning of that man, again, and Purana finally gave in to her disgust.

"Are all of you under his spell? Why does everyone think he is the coming of God? Quen all but ordered me to go and see him. What has gotten into you all? Can't you see he has a spell of charming on him?"

"Oh, don't be ridicules, Chosen of Isis!" Hecate stated, almost laughing. "He is just a very nice man. A very nice and even more powerful man, that truly cares for all of you. There is no spell! Just unconditional love, even for you, Purana!"

"I tell you there is!" Purana hissed. "We all hated him, except for those two tarts, maybe. But we true nobles could see him for what he is. A nobody being risen above his station, with no talent and only a wasteful attitude towards himself. Why is it that even you angel, seem to see more in him than there is?"

424

Hecate was laughing now, and Odyseus as well. Which did nothing to calm the sorceress down. As the night went on, when they finally retired, Purana was still fuming, and had yet to get any real answer from Odyseus on whether he would help her or not. The couple simply stood to leave, and with a goodnight, Odyseus and Hecate walked up the stairs to their room.

Going unnoticed by the couple leaving, one of the priests with Purana, was Apshai, a High Priest of moderate strength. He moved to the table, closer to Purana, and whispered something in Anu's ear. At a nod from the higher-ranking priest, he disappeared.

"What now, my Queen? Once again, it would seem that these Chosen have decided you should seek another. I wonder what there is to the man, that you seem to fear and they seem to embrace?"

Anu spoke softly, not wanting their conversation to fall on too many ears. Purana started, momentarily, before calming.

"I fear nothing about him, Anu. Since that day, in the mountains, you have become increasingly insolent. Do you not fear my wrath, anymore? Am I becoming too soft, of late?"

"You are what you are, Purana. And, yes, you are correct, I do not fear, anymore. We are already dead, you move me forward that much sooner, I will not weep. Take heed, my Queen. Most of us feel that way!" He excused himself and gained a room. Purana could only watch as the last of those she thought truly loyal to her, disappeared up the stairs.

Apshai, knocked on the door to the couple's room. When Hecate answered, he was staring in disbelief, shaking his head. She stepped out into the hall.

"What are you doing, telling him?" The priest of Isis asked.

"He or should I say, JC found me out. Actually, it was one of the Chosen's lower priestesses. Be wary, JC teaches his people all the craft. I know that at least one of them can transfer energy, and many of his priestesses are quite powerful.

He is the one chosen champion that will face the final battle, Apshai. We thought that Jeasuas and Selene were up to something with their creations, and we

425

were correct. Don't make my mistake! Or do, perhaps we should aide these young people? Lucifer cheats, why should we all die, without at least fighting?"

"Mother will not be happy, Hecartae. She will punish us, if she finds out."

"I care not, any longer, Apshailith! I have found what these humans call love. I have found my destiny. I will not return to the Garden, not as long as this man lives. Mother will not keep me away from this! She can't!"

Apshai only nodded, and moved down to the room he was sharing with Anu. Hecate returned back into hers. Odyseus, only raised his head questioningly, when told,

"Never you mind, my big bear! Just move over and give me a kiss!"

The next morning, Odyseus gave Purana the dreaded command.

"You do need seek JC for help. The Father has already said he could probably spare thee a small army to invade Atlantia. One that can fight with both magic and arms. The elves of Selenia be thy savior, now, Purana! He is the one that faced Martinith the most. And, dost send him running every time. Besides, JC do be with the most sorceresses of true power, Purana. And his clergy all know how to heal, be even some, his way!"

Shaking her head, Purana thanked the big man for his hospitality and she rose to leave. There is always, Burlga, she decided. Maybe she can be convinced. Especially if the old man really is planning a wedding, Burlga's jealousy might be able to be used.

CHAPTER 17
The golden dragon

It will come to pass that the devil's seed will reawaken.
The Ancient One's blood will rise again, for 2000 days
Until one stands alone.
                          From the Order of Brigitte

From the beginning, the Chosen planned for the devil's own.
They did not think about the wars fought around them. But,
those that are mortals, depended on their help and
their leadership.
Only One seemed to the task.

        From the journals of Massy Thorn, High priestess of Gia

When Lantor Stone, the King of the Tor Lang Gnomes, entered the camp with over five thousand warrior-illusionists as escort, he was first stopped by Dormathin.

The two traded punches to the arms, and then wrestled for a few moments, falling to the ground laughing, when the much larger dwarf landed atop the smaller gnome.

Both were of an age that such childish actions should long have been left behind, but neither were injured, and instead, moved to hug each other, as the old friends that have not seen each other in years, that they were.

"Lantor, you flea bitten excuse of a mutt, you have finally come to witness the Golden Dragon?" Dormathin exclaimed.

"Actually, you over sized cess pool, I've come to see that pretty little princess that all your soldiers seem so interested in. I hear, that she doesn't have much of a beard. That should at least make her passable, if only she had a proper amount of fur to her chest."

Moving up to the men, Massy and Sheera came to a stop. Both women were grinning, and Massy finally interrupted.

"If it is fur you want, your highness, I can always wear the skin of some porcupine, for your enjoyment!"

The two men, still sitting on the ground, both erupted in laughter, as they moved to rise.

"Sheera Lu Che, Massy Thistle Thorn, I am Lantor Stone, the meager King of the Tor Lang. Forgive me, not coming when I first sent to you, the few men, those months ago." The middle-aged gnome, standing only 115 cm tall, was slightly overweight, with a very large oversized horn for a nose. His puffed cheeks were glowing, and he was with a smile that showed most of his white teeth. Sheera bowed, and Massy nodded at the Gnomish monarch.

"But I see I waited too long, your beard has grown out to almost natural length, your highness."

"A byproduct of the Chosen's healings on me." was all Massy answered with.

"I am glad you have finally come, your highness. I have been looking forward to being joined by someone with a little more manner than our loving king over there. I hope you have brought someone!" Sheera sarcastically added, having spent so much time with the dwarves, she was picking up their off-colored humor, and the dwarves all chuckled at her attempt at a joke. The gnome, on the other hand, slapped his leg, laughing overly loud, tears seeming to come to his eyes.

"Dormathin, you are corrupting the most awaited human in history. She comes and you are turning her into one of your own people? You are a cad of a dwarf!"

"Not I, Lantor, she learns on her own. Still too nice, but we will make a proper dwarf out of her, yet. If we can only figure out how to get her somehow, grow a beard!" The two chuckled and Sheera smiled.

They all moved to the main war tent, and over drinks, began comparing notes. With the addition of over one hundred Gnomish armorers, to aid the one hundred Dwarven, as soon as the mines could produce the mythral, Sheera's army should all have weapons soon.

428

The fifty swords from JC and the one hundred from Burlga had more than helped her cause, but her own people looked forward to when they could make their own. She was eager for everyone to have what was needed.

When they moved to retire for the night, Sheera was happy, drunk, and in need of a little help, as Leaf guided her to her tent, the gnomes and dwarves all laughing, at the weak human priestess and her non tolerance for the Dwarven ale. Morning came way too early, for Sheera's pounding head.

"I think that I am ready to go home, Sheera. You have your army now, and even have a much better set of protections than I can give you."

"You miss him almost as much as I do, don't you, Massy?"

The dwarf princess only nodded before regaining her dwarven calm.

"Yes, I suppose I do. Something happened when he brought me back from death. I almost sense him, now."

"It's like you are connected, because you are. You have become a sibling of sorts when your two spirits intertwined. You are as much a twin to him as I am, now." Sheera sighed. "I know because I feel you, as well, Massy. You and I are connected like sisters. I'll take you to the meeting in a couple weeks and then I will cry seeing you gone."

"Not gone, my sister, just at a distance. Maybe you can make me one of those baubles you carry around your neck and then you and I can feel each other, as well."

Sheera smiled and gave the dwarf a hug before they exited out the tent they shared. Kuan Yen followed as she smiled at her High Priestess, The Golden Dragon.

****

Of all things to argue about, the third meeting of The Chosen, was turned into a battle of wills between Sheera and JC. The two resumed arguing over something there were no words for in Zindarian, nor the other planets of the Immortals. The three others stood asking questions only when they thought they understood that the weapon the other two were arguing about.

"I tell you Sheera, I do not want to think about bringing a gun to Zindar. The Ancient Ones have forbidden it. And, I cannot make it!"

"You are a chemist, correct? You are a blacksmith? Why else would Selene have gone and made such a combination. I know enough about it to know that we have the stuff to make it. I have sulfur, saltpeter, and charcoal. You can figure it out, you are a scientist, after all. And besides, Gabriel, one of the Archangels of Jeasuas is the one that came and told me. It can't be forbidden!"

"What is this "gun" you two keep talking about?" Quen asked

"The fires of Hell!" JC stubbornly answered interrupting Sheera before she could explain.

"It is a weapon of such force that it could send a sling bullet over several hundred meters and still have the force to go through a wall. It is a controlled explosion that could win this war, for us with very little loss. Maybe even kill Lucifer, with it as well!"

"I said NO!" JC insisted. He walked away, shaking his head, the young lady not understanding his insistence against the deadly advantage.

"I will not bring that technology to this world, even if I could make such a weapon, which, by the way, I am not sure I can! Making a gun, is not so easy as you think. And, one other thing, you are a lover of peace, how can you even think like this? What kind of demon is this Gabriel that has been putting words into your ears?"

"Because, I have watched too many dies, needlessly. Because, Reverend Father JC d'Badger, I am not as good as you are in taking the world upon my shoulders! I am not the near god that you becoming!" Sheera's tears fell as the elder man stood stunned.

Burlga watched the reaction of the two, and moved to comfort her friend. Sheera, laid her head on the taller woman's shoulder, and continued to sob. Burlga watched JC, seeing within him a change from only a few days ago. He seemed not to be as relaxed, nor was he as compassionate towards them, as he had been, during that whole time in training.

He would never allow Sheera to cry like this, and he would not have been so cold in his answers. Knowing something had happened, between then and now, just a few days, she turned to look at Dyanea. Sitting, calmly, and knitting.

"Knitting? What does the bloody woman think she is doing?" Burlga thought to herself. "That is good, though, at least, JC has not been turned away because of a prejudice towards the mixed racial bloods, like Quen is."

Burlga had wondered about if that might be a reason for his resisting her advances, just like Quen always did. Dyanea's aura, was what Burlga found the most fascinating. Having only briefly seen it once before, she had left the meeting three months ago, in a rush, so now, she studied it.

Dyanea's inner spectrum was a mixture. Not a pure silver of human, nor was it the gray of non-humans. It had a tinge of gold to it, indicating her parentage was more than just human and elf. She already knew that much and even Dyanea had admitted to being an assimar.

She appeared quarter or half-elf, but with that gold tinge, to the inner spectrum, she would have to have been at least part Greater Angel. Burlga thought that last time she had met this woman, she was the one. But, to know for sure, now, was not a comforting thought.

The inner spectrum, though, would explain the incredible middle spectrum. The blue, was a pure azure blue, and almost solid. Very little transparency. One would almost believe, the woman to belong to the Chosen, rather than sitting with the other mortal visitors. Dyanea's absolute lack of any black in the aura showed a very pious woman.

"No wonder, JC is taken with this woman." Burlga thought. "Hells, I want this woman!" Burlga chuckled inwardly.

"JC, if that is all this "gun" is used for is projecting metal balls, why is it so wrong. We could do that with our sorcery, after all? If it would help the mortals to fight?" Burlga stated, attempting to sway the man.

The meeting was interrupted by a disheveled priestess of Isis, falling to the floor behind, the servant that was leading the way.

"It has fallen," the priestess was whispering. Quen moved from the table and following JC to the woman, the older man lifted the woman to a chair, where she was handed something to drink and could tell them what had happened.

"She is captured, the queen is captured, and all of Atlantia belongs to Haden, now!" The young woman finally finished. "All our magiks could not stop the hundreds of thousands of the monsters that just kept coming. They just kept coming!" She choked out between sobs as she grabbed JC's arms.

"OK, child, your safe now. Calm thy self, you will be safe."

"But the queen has been taken!" She nearly screeched. "One of the Chosen has been taken."

"She is still alive! And not captured." Quen added. "She has already been here and Lemuria as well. Calm yourself, priestess. The matter is already being considered.

"Why is it that we have only been harassed with a few thousand at a time, and maybe some spawn with them, and they send an entire army into Atlantia?" Burlga asked.

"Martinith sends Hell Lords to us or comes himself, while keeping our armies busy with fodder." Sheera answered.

"Keeps us busy, and it do keep us from sending forces south to protect or rescue Atlantia. It is the second smallest of nations, least likely to have real soldiers, and the closest to Haden. It's easy see, to be choice for first conquest. That Purana was unable to stop it, well, that do mean that the numbers be great, or, Martinith do be involved." Odyseus explained.

"Who, besides Sheera, Odyseus, and I have faced Martinith?" JC asked, but the other two just shook their heads.

"That's because we are deemed the ones with the most weaknesses to exploit! Burlga, you are at least as powerful as Purana in magic, knowing several different kinds, and you can fight with the sword, as well.

"Quen, you are nearly immune to psychic attacks, yet, possess the skill with a blade that Martinith would not be able to withstand. Besides being as strong as

432

Odyseus, Martinith is also, almost as fast as Sheera, and as strong against spells as you are, Quen. He is quite the intimidating foe." The other two to have faced him, shook their heads, in agreement.

"A bullet to the brain would stop him!" Sheera added in, only to get a stern look of disgust from the older man.

She stuck her tongue out at him, like a child, and pouted, still holding onto Burlga.

As the meeting was coming to a close, the night was late, and all were tired. Quen ordered rooms for the group, the mortals and immortals alike. He was the last to leave, standing with JC and Burlga looking at the world map, brought in sometime earlier.

"It would seem, Burlga that your continent might be next." JC pointed to the map. If he truly has control of the Atlantian Kingdom, he won't wait long. He is striking fast, and the use of makatiels and goblins has some of the mortals' thinking demons, anyway. At least on my continent. They have never seen the creature, before."

"Bloody Hell, my continent thinks dwarves a myth out of children's stories." Burlga commented.

Then apologized for her language when she saw the look JC gave her. As she turned to leave, she touched JC's arm. He was startled, still on edge from the ordeal of two days ago, with Eisheth Zenanim. She looked at him with concern, squeezing his arm, and moved out of the room shaking her head.

Quen left the older man as well, thinking JC looked paler than normal, he was not sleeping, the King could tell. As the two Immortals exited, they were stopped by Dyanea in the hall outside the great dining room, where JC was still standing over the map, alone.

"What is wrong with him, my lady?" Quen asked.

"He killed a woman devil, Eisheth Zenanim, I think he called it, she had taken on my appearance." She answered and then through tear filled eyes, briefly told them what happened. Burlga reacted with inhaled breath, and Quen only nodded.

433

"You should go to him, then." Burlga softly choked. Regretting her next comment, she knew it for the man's best, though. "I would, but he avoids me, now. I saw it a little, the other day, and tonight is even worse, as well.

He belongs to you, and I fear, out of my reach." A little envy entered her tone as she looked at the near immortal standing before her.

Shorter, older, not as attractive, but beautiful still. Burlga seemed to weigh the woman standing there, no apparent awe, at facing two immortals, as most humans seemed to act. Burlga finally sighed.

"Yes, I can see why he loves you. I can't have him, so you might as well. At least, you are an elf. I can be thankful for that!" She almost said it to herself.

Dyanea straightened, but still did not back away. Quen placed a hand on the High Priestess' arm, and lightly squeezed. Concern edging the normal emotionless tones to his voice.

"Go to him, Reverend Mother, please! Get him to sleep, somehow. Make wild love to him. Whatever it takes. We will have need of him in this war. I will have need of him in the end, when I face Lucifer's champion! He moved off, with Burlga softly arguing with him on who would be the one to face the Ancient One in the end.

Sheera stopped the couple in the hall, when Dyanea finally convinced the JC to come to bed. She saw something in the man's eyes that have never been, in the past year and nine months she had known him.

"James, Reverend Mother, I overheard your talking with Burlga and Quen. I know what that must have done to you. Please, let me know of anything I can do. I still have need of you, whole, my bro... Father!" Sheera took Dyanea's hand, and the JC's as well.

"I will be fine, Sheera. I just need to get over this feeling of letting my lady down. It was what I almost did, that bothers me most, not the slaying of the devil." Dyanea took a scornful look to her, as she turned to JC.

"You did not let me down! How many times do I have to say it?"

The next day before the Immortals left to their respective homes, an unexpected visitor arrived. The priestess that stepped through a gateway, was JC's apprentice, Gulnara. She quickly moved to Dyanea and when the Reverend Mother nodded after whispering a command, the woman turned to face the others.

"A call for the Kings has been made, Father. Queen Alyndria has ordered your presence, and that as well of the Princess Massy. She intends to install you as the Lord Marshal of all the continent's armies. The Temple has been asked to provide transportation. Also, the King of the elves and the reigning Chief of the gnomes will be there, as well."

JC only nodded, saying that he had been expecting it. He turned to Dyanea, and something passed between them before she nodded.

"I also, want to announce that we have set a date for our wedding, kids. You all are expected to be there, I hope, you know?" He only barely makes it sound, not like a command. Then with a chuckle, added. "That is, I would really appreciate it if you would all consider coming." He adjusted to a softer tone.

The smiles and handshakes and hugs were passed and when Odyseus lifted Dyanea into his arms, the look on her face was one of bemusement.

"That do mean we start calling thee, Mother!" As he soundly kissed her on the cheek. When he sat her back to the ground, she was a little uneasy on her feet as she smoothed her robes.

"Odyseus, if you can convince that old man to love you, then I can accept you calling me anything you want." She wryly answered. Shaking her head, she smiled up at the man, and pinched his cheek.

Quen maneuvered the priestess away from the rest, a little way and whispered to her,

"Is he going to be all right, Reverend Mother?" At her nod, he gave a tight small smile, "I welcome you into our little family, and will enjoy having a mother's point of view. Someone that can finally argue against him, maybe?" His amused manner, Dyanea patted the young man's cheek.

435

"What is the matter, young man? Feeling too overwhelmed, having both JC and Meritt to give you parental wisdom?" She only half joked. Quen uncharacteristically, chuckled.

"Yes, I can see the woman he needs, in you! I can see how you won his heart, my lady! And, I, for one, will always thank you for it!" He bowed to the woman.

Sheera agreed immediately when asked to attend Dyanea. Having an elven wedding should be interesting, but she only knew that having been asked, that will keep her in the couple's life. Something she did not intend to lose.

Sheera genuinely liked the two times she had spent around the older priestess, and could easily see the attraction Dyanea would command on JC.

"Besides, he never would have seen me as anything other than his daughter. This way I shall have a mother, as well." She sadly reminded herself.

When they all left, Sheera gave Massy a tight hug.

"I think I will miss you even more than I always do James. Take care of him, Massy! He is more fragile than he pretends, at times.

"You both are so much more than you think you are, Sheera. You are a child of an Ancient One, after all. I will see you soon. Make sure Dormathin takes a bath at least once a month. Even if you have to dump a lake on top of him." She said it loud enough that the King who was standing near waiting for his hug, could hear.

When Sheera let go of Massy, she turned to the large dwarf and gave an all-tooth grin.

"Your beard is almost that length of an adult, cousin. Finally, you begin to look like a queen." he sarcastically stated, even though his awe in her was still there.

"Your old flea-bitten carcass, you best take care our girl makes it where she needs to be. I will tear you apart if he," she pointed over to JC, "leaves anything left of you if you fail." No one was sure if she said it as a joke or if she really meant it, but the King only nodded.

"I will see you in a few months, Massy Thistle Thorn, Queen of Selenia, Princess of Katiketa, Priestess of Gia." The titles were said with honor, and Massy only nodded.

"Yes, my cousin, you will. I will look forward to being able to properly gift you, when next we spar." The two locked arm, their hands squeezing the other's forearm.

The Chosen agreed to another meeting that would be called for later. Next one to be at JC's.

"Burlga, you be sure and keep us all appraised at what is going on with any changes in the size of attacks. If it does happen it could be sudden! I will come, if needed. But, of course, you already know that, kiddo!" JC said. Odyseus, only nodded, and gave the woman a hug.

"Beware, Purana do be coming to the next. I heard her saying to her people before she left."

"She will probably like my welcoming even less!" Burlga said, upset over something, but refused to admit it, when Odyseus tried to push. With a shrug, he kissed Burlga on the cheek and said simply,

"See thee at the fathers in three months, then, if thy call for me do not be earlier. See thee, then, Burlga."

Burlga watched as JC moved to leave with Dyanea and his three apprentices. The men with them never said a thing, seemingly watching the one woman. She had wondered about that, and the fact that Marina had evil in her aura, was also disturbing. But it was less than that first time all those months ago.

"It would be, like him to think he could "turn" someone away from following evil. He really has no idea just what he is, and yet, continues to do instinctively what only an Archangel or demi-god would do." She thought to herself. She was startled out of her thoughts, when Dyanea tapped her arm.

"Lady Burlga, I wish to come and visit with you if I may?" Dyanea asked, looking very serious.

The spread of her outer aura told Burlga that the woman was somewhat jealous or envious of someone. "Could it be?" She thought before responding to the woman.

"Reverend Mother Dyanea, you can always come, or if it would be easier, I would be willing to come to you."

"Perhaps, I really do not have good control of these gateways you all seem to work. I know I have to learn, but..."

"It is not natural for an elf, to walk through a rip in space! Yes, priestess, I agree. I had trouble learning myself!" The two smiled at each other, knowingly, it seemed.

"When do you want me? I assume when JC is not around!" The woman's nod, answered the question. "Would tomorrow morning do? I bet; he still works his "kata" first thing every day. We could talk then!"

Dyanea smiled, as the envy in her aura got stronger. Burlga smiled knowing this woman was actually fearful of her. "Good!" She thought, "she should be!"

"You really do know my mate, well, Lady Burlga! I'll see you tomorrow, then! He also spends time in the smithy, every day afterward." She left with JC, answering his question with,

"Never you mind, girl talk!" Burlga still felt the burning of envy within her, but she knew, this was a woman,

"I could actually relate to, and probably will even like!"

Quen over heard the exchange between Dyanea and Burlga. "This cannot be good!" He thought. JC had been pursued by the half-elf, for almost two years, since that first day. Now, another part elf, has caught his attention. Older and wiser, Dyanea, was almost as powerful as Sheera, who no longer seemed as strong as JC.

But, Dyanea, was very powerful, in her aura, and is, after all, not entirely mortal.

"Meritt, tomorrow would be a good time to take some mythral to the fathers. You did want to watch him in the smithy, I believe?"

"Yes, I did. But what is the real reason, Quen?" The lack of title, indicated that Meritt was seeing through the man. Quen inwardly smiled.

Meritt was more than an aid. Dyanea had it right, Meritt was becoming the other parent in the young man's life.

"The Reverend Mother and Burlga are getting together, tomorrow morning, I heard them mention. Keep an eye or rather an ear out. JC will not be so observant, I think."

The nod from Meritt, indicating his understanding. They were interrupted by the swaying motion of Burlga as she came walking over to the two, having given the others a sendoff.

"What is it that JC won't be observant of, Quen?" She asked.

Quen looked at the pretty woman, wishing inside that she was not of elven blood. He could see the charms in the woman, and she would definitely make life interesting.

"Uh, only the changes in his personality. And, that he seems to becoming more, than he was." He finally answered.

"He is just becoming what he always has been. When are you going to?" She kissed the man on his cheek, giving him a pat to his buttocks.

"What do you mean, Burlga? I am what I always have been!" Quen stepped back away from the woman.

"Bloody Hell, if you are! We are all the same, Quen. Yet, you still insist you are less in sorcery. Open your mind, lover! Open your fool bloody mind." With a wink at the elderly priest standing next to Quen, she opened a gateway back to her castle. Laughing as she seductively stepped, lifting her short skirt slightly, exposing even more of her beautiful long pale leg, as it lifted through the space.

Meritt watched as the elf maiden stepped through, and turned to the young man beside him.

"She is the most interesting of you Chosen!' the matter of fact stated.

"She is something!" Quen dryly stated, as he walked away.

****

Meritt watched the man as JC pounded on the metal. He was hitting with a strength, none of his Dwarven smiths were able to match, let alone the gnomes or human ones. He then lightened the strikes upon the flattened metal, and alternated between solid strong raps to more subtle ones, without even changing the stroke. The artist in the Lord of the keep kept the pace up for what seemed hours.

What amazed the elder priest more, was the ability that JC had to talk and instruct while even casting his spells, at the same time as he pounded away with the solid iron hammer.

Even including the more powerful spells, that he had first suggested he might be too weak to cast. When Father JC looked up, after finishing the first round of shaping, he offered to allow the man to finish.

Meritt eagerly agreed, and taking up the tools, was amazed by the ease of which JC had at teaching his art.

"I wonder, Father JC, if you are this good at teaching other skills, as well?" Meritt asked.

"I would like to think, I was a good instructor, once upon a time, Father Meritt." After pausing a moment, he added. "Meritt, if we are going to become friends, or at least partners in taking care of Quen, is there any chance, I could convince you to drop the title and simply call me JC? At the least when we are not in public?" Meritt heard the chuckles from the other smiths present, and holding his next swing, he looked to Father JC and nodded.

"You seem to be rather at ease, around your people, um JC, at first, I thought it strange. But I can see that you are one that commands by your actions, and not through titles. I think, good sir, that we can become more than the partners you mention." He resumed his striking, and added a minor spell, before saying,

"The young man, does need guidance, and I think, your Reverend Mother Dyanea, is just the one to teach him. I have seen the boy around her. She would be a good influence. If that is, Lady Burlga does not get to him first. She is quite... exuberant, at times."

440

"That is just her way, Meritt. She has a big heart, and a refreshing attitude at life. Worry not for the Chosen of Merylon. She is easily the most powerful among us, I would think, and when she finally grows into her body's age, she will be quite the woman, as well. I would think, she would be a good choice for our dear Quen. If he was not so prejudice against mixing races!"

"She says the same about you, Father! Being the most powerful, that is!" Meritt mumbled, as he resumed his work.

The blade was not as good as any of the others, but when Meritt finished it, late that afternoon, he felt a sense of accomplishment, and even some small pride when JC told him, a fine first attempt.

"Practice makes perfect, Meritt. Take this one with you, as a tool for learning with. You will do fine, with and if you practice. It's been a pleasure, but I think that I had better get back to my little war. I should have left several hours ago." Turning to the others, he called out.

"Gregorin, take over. There should be enough for a few days, at least. Make sure Father Meritt gets his silver, will you?"

With a grunt and a nod, the Dwarven smith laid his hammer down and the sword he had been working on into the water.

"Come with me, High Priest Meritt. You got a valuable lesson in life, today, did you not?" The dwarf moved to a locked room.

"He is a rather intimidating man, yet, an easy one to be around, isn't he?" Meritt said to the nodding man.

"On both accounts. I myself am glad Mother Gia sent him to our side of the world." The dwarf evenly said without any hint of humor to his comment.

Moving the many kilograms of silver to an area where he could open a gateway, Meritt held it open while several Phaleg priests transferred the metal between continents. He then saluted the Dwarven smith, exclaiming,

"See you next week, Gregorin Thorn."

"Yes, Father Meritt. You will! Don't forget Emperor Quen's Bastard sword!"

The priest turned and stepped back through the gateway grabbing the cloth wrapped sword that he had cleaned up against the wall. With another salute, he backed through the hole in space and allowed it to close.

****

Lilith had watched as JC had taken Martinith apart, that first time. She saw the second time, the Selenian had killed the Haden Chosen, as well. Even with the injuries JC took in the battles, he still defeated the half-makatiel rather easily.

She watched as the makatiel dropped to the Jeasuas Chosen, as well. That girl was amazing, her balance and quickness, was much more than even the devil thought it was.

Not Evelith, she thought at first, that she might be. Something more, and now, acting like a true Archangel.

"Even more a daughter to you, than I was, father!" Lilith thought aloud. "And, she can summon James Carl at will, it would seem." She smiled at the thought of him raising the Dwarven priestess from the dead. Such power, such compassion.

"With that kind of passion and strength added to mine, there would be nothing, we could not accomplish!"

Lilith had also seen, Martinith battle the Lemurian Chosen.

"What are you up to, Hecartae? Is Gia even aware? Or is she hedging the war, like Kutulu does?"

When Martinith finally won a victory, it was over the Atlantian. Lilith was correct; she was sure Purana would be the only one not able to stand up to the Chosen of Haden.

Over a hundred lives would unhinge anyone, and Purana certainly fit the diagnosis of insanity.

"Isis you never were one to believe the stories, Merylon would give. Now, your own Chosen will fall!"

She turned from the magical font she had been watching in. JC was preparing for his wedding. Lilith's envy and anger would not allow her the concentration to hold the font steady.

"Marduk's granddaughter will need be dealt with. Perhaps, Martinith can handle that! Perhaps, Proserpine will get lucky and after Mammon and her fall, James Carl will go off on a vengeance spree killing all of Hell's Angels?"

Lilith smiled at the thoughts of her consoling the Selenian Chosen, for the loss of his new mate. She fantasized his touch on her, creating children of unparalleled power, created in lustful love.

Not the ugliness of those born from her unions with Lucifer. There was never any love there. But, with James Carl, Lilith would create new life out of love! She knew he was her Adamunith reborn. She was sure of it.

"Too much power, not to be!" Lilith continued to smile. Feeling her own urges raised by the fantasies of her only true love, she went off in search.

Seeking a man to sate her lustful thoughts, Lilith finally found one on Funtaland. A tall Nubian that she could easily drain the soul from.

But not before he pleasured her, tasted her charms, felt her own lust driven passions!

****

Purana had been running for most of the year. Well, not running exactly. Yet, she had been making the circuit of the Chosen, asking for help in getting her country back.

"And, those two ungrateful louts, have said to go to JC!" She mumbled aloud. "How can they all turn on me, this way? I offer them power, and they say to go to the old man!"

"Perhaps, my queen, he is not so weak as when you knew him?" The priestess hinted with her head bowed, knowing the temperament of her queen, these days.

443

Purana, traveling with twenty-six clerics, twenty-three of them priestesses of moderate power, the other three males of slightly above that. She still had not been able to understand why the men were the more powerful in sorcery. Certainly, a joke being played on her by Isis.

The thirty-four soldiers, remaining with her, were almost useless, but they had managed to save her group here and there, this past year. Purana looked down at the bowing, woman, and patted her on the head.

"Borella, I cannot imagine, this father JC, being anything, but what he is. A commoner, with no urgency to rule, no ambition beyond collecting a few followers to aid him in his one-man battle. He will certainly be the first of us to fall, regardless of the comments you have heard from the other Chosen.

"They are not telling the truth, no way has he killed so many devil lords in less than a year." She shook her head in disbelief.

Purana knew now, that the others would not react without the old man's say so. He had successfully gathered them to his way of thinking. Except for Quen, that is.

"I think that with time, I could convince Quen to help us, but he is so intent on keeping Martinith out of his continent, he won't spare any people for an invasion of his own."

"It seemed to me, my queen, that if he did, we might have as hard a time getting our lands back from him, as we are the monsters!" The priestess said.

"Yes, there is that. Gods, but I wish Doreen was still alive." Purana said for not the first time, in the past months of their exile.

****

Arriving in the early morning, to the spot she saw in JC's gateway, Burlga was met, by a late middle-aged woman, in the livery of the castle servants followed by four guards.

"I am the Lady Burlga d'Venta, I believe I should be expected!" Burlga immediately announced.

444

"Of course, M'lady! My Lady Dyanea advised me to expect you." Curtsying, as was proper, Burlga looked at the woman, with some psychic strength, but unused! When she asked her name, the head maid, answered, "I am Nevahlina, the charge house maid for the d'Badgers, M'lady. As a friend of the family, you may call me Neva."

"Well, Neva, shall we not keep the Reverend Mother waiting. She had something very important she wanted to talk to me about."

When she was escorted to the dining hall, Dyanea was already setting tea and cakes out on the table. Shooing the staff away, she asked Neva to be sure to close the doors and not to allow any to interrupt. The charge maid, only nodded as she closed the doors.

"I know you are probably use to that, but it still is like I'm dealing with apprentices that cannot use spells. I am not as bad as JC, though!"

"Yes, I can imagine he tries to befriend all the staff. Probably embarrasses them to no ends, Reverend Mother."

"Lady Burlga, can we just dispense with the formal names? I hope that we can become friends, if not for ourselves, for JC's sake. He needs you, and he loves you all, therefore, I need you, as well. And, I want to learn to love you, too!"

Burlga was startled by the comment, and looked at the woman sitting across from her. Pouring tea and offering and pouring for the elder woman, Burlga sat the pot back to its place before speaking.

"Dyanea," she started with an inhaled breath, "I would like that we could become friends, as well. Though, I am sure, if you have spent any time talking with Sheera or the others, they have told you that for the past year and a half, I have been pursuing the man with my own intentions."

Dyanea nodded, and added,

"Well, some of the words, the others used were not as nice as your pursuing, but I like the sound of your way better. Yes, Burlga, I have heard." Her smile, hinted at what she was not saying that the others had mentioned, and Burlga could well imagine, the unspoken thoughts.

The women talked, and even laughed. When after two hours had passed, Burlga agreed to the woman's request.

"Dyanea, I would be honored to stand with you in your wedding. It will form a bond between us that should only strengthen our friendship; that if I can read things, will be for a very very long time. How is it that you have immortal blood in you?"

The question caught Dyanea off guard, and she looked down before lifting her head, her face still slightly red from blushing.

"I thought everyone suspected! My mother was half-elf, half angel, Burlga. But it is not common knowledge the pure elven part! Even JC does not know that part. I don't think! My father is a descendant of the Queen's grandfather's brother. We are cousins. I'm really not sure how much JC knows or doesn't know. He knows I might be noble by birth, but he has never asked and I have never said. No one else needs to know!"

"You have my word on it, elf to elf, Dyanea. I won't spread any of this around. That explains the power in you, and also explains how an eighty plus year old woman can look to be in her late twenties!" Dyanea nodded, and grabbed the Immortal's hands.

"You do know, that after a few hundred years, he might become a little suspicious, though!" Burlga added, with a mischievous smile.

"Hells, young lady, he will probably figure it out a whole lot sooner than that! If he doesn't already suspect. He's quite intuitive, you know!"

"Yes, Dyanea, that I do know! Except when it comes to bloody women!" She added.

"He knows about your advances, child. He really does! And, truth be told, he enjoys them. He really does love you all the more, for those advances, I think!" The envy in her aura momentarily returned.

"JC is not the only one that is intuitive, Reverend Mother!" Burlga stated.

****

When she arrived to face, her sister sorceress, Purana was not met with any better reception than she had gotten from the two men. If anything, Burlga was even more distasteful.

"Purana, you never even bothered to listen, to any of the teachings. You forced us to tolerate you for that year, your high-born attitude. Well, hear these words, Empress!" Burlga's sarcasm at the title, garnered fear from her own people, and a stir among Purana's. Purana only stood watching, the woman, somehow, even more powerful than before.

"You do not cause me any worry. I am your equal in psychic strength, your equal in wizardry, and I know how to use my sword. You do not even carry yours properly." She smiled before continuing. "It was JC, showed me how to carry it without gaining bruises when walking!" Emphasizing the name, she knew caused Purana fits, she calmly uncrossed her arms, lowering her hand to rest on the hilt of her sword.

Purana was seething, and Burlga appeared to be enjoying it.

Although, more powerful, Purana thought, she knew her people were outnumbered here, by magic as well as sword strength.

"Burlga, you seem very sure of yourself, comparing your meager strengths to mine. You actually think, you could equal me in a psychic duel? I would very much be interested in that challenge, if it were not forbidden."

"You stand behind that, even though, you do not follow the one command of your Goddess that matters most? You have no love within you, Purana, and yet you cower before me, now, with false pride!

"I am not like the others, Chosen of Isis! I see what is in the man, you refuse to enlist. He will be the one to face off in the end. He has the power; you seem to think is nonexistent. He has been holding back on us all, Purana. And, I think it simply wonderful!"

"You would, you tart. You have chased him like some small-town whore, and now, you even seem willing to forgive him his marriage!" Seeing the eyes open a little wider on Burlga, Purana smiled.

"Yes, I have heard. I would think you would have gone and eliminated your competition, by now. It figures he would marry a mortal. Only thing that is below him, in stature."

Burlga was laughing at the comment when Purana frowned. She did not understand the humor, and thought simply that Burlga had lost her mind.

"Dyanea is no low born mortal, as you said. Do not underestimate the High Priestess, Purana. Dyanea is a very formidable woman,

and like me, she is of elven heritage. Very powerful, possibly the most powerful non-Chosen alive. Even more so than Quen or Odyseus.

"And, Empress of Nothing, I am to be one of her attendants. She even is more of a mother to us, than JC is a father. Be very careful, what you say, when you finally get the nerve to face the man."

"I will never go to him for help. I loath to go to the other commoner, but at least she has power."

"You do know he is knighted by the Queen of his kingdom. He even is the Lord of the lands surrounding his Temple. He is no commoner, and is even more a Lord right know than you are an Empress.

"You still don't understand! The Father not only has power, he is power. I have fought beside him, I have seen him, when he did not think I or anybody else, noticed. He has been holding back on us, Purana. He's better than you think!

"Now, excuse me, but I have a war to direct. Will you see him before or after, Sheera?" Burlga turned to leave, laughing at the woman, she knew was just starting.

Her soldiers did not, turn their backs, though, still holding that threatening stance.

Purana, with a sigh, finally turned to open a gateway, when she realized she had no way of knowing how, since she had never been there, she redirected her spell.

Instead, she opened a dimensional doorway into the Astral plane and thought Katiketa, when she saw Sheera, she opened the door back to the prime material plane, several hundred yards away from the Chosen's camp.

CHAPTER 18 Blessings

Quen was preparing final plans before heading to JCs for his wedding, when the dimensional door opened and out spilled thirty bone devils followed by the tall half-makatiel assassin, that he had been waiting for. Quen smiled!

Martinith was the one person, Quen would face knowing that he and only he, could do what the others claimed not to have been able. Quen would kill the man.

The duel is over quickly, as Lalia and Meritt closed the dimensional door, and continued to cast lightning and fire into the hoard of devils.

Quen moved in on the man, he knew was as strong as Odyseus and as quick as Sheera. But, if JC can out duel the man, then so could Quen.

The devils that attempted to get in his way, fell quickly and easily, to his blade, a true bastard sword of perfect balance. As Martinith moved with equal disdain through Quen's *Blades Elite*, all attacking the devils with swords that were sorcery made of the new "God Stone."

When the two leaders met, Quen was shaken by the power of the half-makatiel's swings, but he managed to avoid all the jabs and stabs, slicing through the makatielian leader's legs, and removing his arm in a cross swing. When Martinith attempted to teleport, Quen's cross cut, caught the man's upper shoulder, cutting into the throat, and down across the chest.

Martinith fell back, and Quen quickly moved in to remove the man's head. The body smoldered and dissipated like that of the Hell Spawn, as Quen turned to join his Blades in eliminating the rest of the filth.

He smiled, knowing that the devil's Chosen was finally down, and wondered at the dizziness he was feeling just before passing out. Quen was not aware of the cut he had taken that opened an artery, causing him to lose so much blood.

When he awakened later that day, he was still smiling, knowing that Martinith was finally out of the picture.

"This news will be welcomed tomorrow, by the other Chosen!" He was sure!

****

Martinith summoned Samael, immediately upon exiting the stasis chambers. He was in his latest body and the spirit in this one, was even weaker willed than the first three. His own mind melded with it in a much quicker time frame, and the man was already thinking on his next move.

"What is it you want now, Martinith?" The commanding General of all of Hell's armies sighed. Teleporting in. Martinith smiled seeing the disgusted expression Samael gave the half-makatiel. It was one of complete disdain, and Martinith took note.

"You will send an Archangel and several score of accompanying lesser's to interrupt the Selenian's wedding." Martinith smiled. He and Lilith had worked this up, and decided that Proserpine's punishment should be retribution.

The half-makatiel was sure Proserpine would survive, but by sending Mammon to do the dirty work, the deviltress would lose her mate, and then Martinith could lay claim to her. At least that was the plan that Martinith had.

Lilith was hoping that both Mammon and her chief rival, Samael's daughter would die. She was sure that JC would survive, having so many of his pets to protect, his godhood would come out, and besides, what no one seemed to realize, was that all the Chosen would be there, as well.

"I want the Selenian and his sorceress witch dead by nightfall. You hear me, Samael? You will not disobey me this time!" He smiled at the devil's reaction.

"So, Martinith, you are too much a coward to do it yourself, who do you think to send on this suicide mission, then? You do know that the Selenian has trained many people in his command as well as equipped them with the ability to kill our kind, as well as you?"

"That is why it should be someone of proper power. He will be an Archangel, so it will be one of the best. If you are too afraid, Samael, then send Mammon. He owes the Chosen a debt for the elimination of his chief lieutenant, in any case. I would think Mammon would jump at the chance for retribution!"

Samael nodded, giving the man a look of suspicion.

451

"What are you at, Martinith? Why this sudden interest in the Selenian's destruction? Are you finally going after him, for the two times he has managed to kill you?"

"I want him dead, and I plan on taking out the Phaleg follower myself. But I need the Selenian busy, while I do it. Just follow my commands, devil, and I won't have to replace you as the commander general. You are dismissed!" Martinith watched as the devil lord turned to leave.

"You do know that all the Chosen will most likely be there. It should be fun watching you die, again!"

Samael laughed before disappearing. The concerned look on his expression had the half-makatiel smiling even through the insult.

****

Kuan Yen woke up to find Sheera outside the tent, that they shared. The girl was working at her forms, and the mid-thirties priestess moved to do her own form of Tai Chi. She watched the girl dance with her short-curved blade, that she called a wakisashi and shivered. Use of a weapon of any kind seemed so foreign to the peaceful training of the Church.

Sheera, noticing the dwarf King was watching them, stopped and walked over to him.

"Are you missing your home, my friend?" The Immortal asked as she was wiping the sweat from her face.

"I have been out of the clans for almost three months, now. I do miss my family, but such is the problems of war. I am sure that the queen, really has things all right, and I have only lost half my authority."

"Dormathin, I'm sorry. You should have said something I would have gotten you back long before now." Sheera exclaimed with an apology in her voice. "I can take you home anytime you want, you know?"

"Child, truth be told, I have enjoyed myself a lot, these past months. You Immortals are not nearly so frightening as the prophesies make you out to be." He looked into the Chosen's eyes and smiled.

452

"At least your younger ones! As a matter of fact, young lady! I think that in a lot of ways, you people are more fun to be around than us mortals are, of any race. So much power in one little body, and yet, all the five of you that I have spent time with, anywise, have even less confidence than a lot of so-called kings and queens do. Of course, if you had a beard, I might have had to make you my second wife." he laughed at her punch.

"I wonder what would have happened last night if Purana had attempted to follow through on any of her threats, old man?" She changed the subject.

"I would have been forced to bring the entire power of the mountain on top of her. I'm a lot more afraid of what Massy would do to me if I allowed you to stub your foot, Dragon!" he answered.

Sheera laughed and patted the King on his cheek.

"Well, your highness, I guess we will have to make sure I don't break a nail or stub a toe on any rocks from here on out, won't we?" she joked back.

"Of course, your father JC could just raise you, like he did Massy. That still has most of us afraid to cross him."

Sheera only shook her head and resumed her forms.

After she had finished and returned to bath in her tents, she dressed in a formal gown heavily beaded, that Kuan Yen had gotten for her. She felt somewhat uncomfortable, but it would be worth it to impress everyone at the wedding. It was going to be filled with many nobles, she had to keep telling herself.

Sheera opened a gateway, and followed a retinue of ten dwarven soldiers as she stepped through, with Kuan Yen by her side and King Dormathin following with General Horotu, his brother. The large room they stepped into was a roped off area in JC's keep, used for gating.

They were almost immediately met by a servant, who sent another to tell the Reverend Mother that guests had arrived. Sheera was well known to most of the keep, and the entire group were escorted to a sitting room where refreshments would be offered.

"The lord and lady will be available shortly, please make yourselves comfortable." The maid told them, as drinks were served to the group.

"May we be allowed to join the soldiers outside? We hear the clanging of metal and would like to join in the exercises." Horotu asked.

"Of course. Just don't hurt any of them, old man." Sheera warned as they all moved out.

****

"High Priest Torel, you wish to talk to one of the Chosen, you will have to talk to us all. We hide nothing from each other, in my keep!" JC said, taking the offered cup with a thank you from his chamberlain.

He did not like this man, and the oily feeling he was getting was just heightened by the man's aura. There were so many black spots throughout, that even the women he had taken from Morella, all those months ago, seemed clean in comparison.

Sheera had just come into the room, and with Massy, Dyanea, Essmelda, Sir Marcus, as well as several other guards and servants, the High Priest of Isis was feeling uncomfortable facing so many all within hearing distance. He stared at the largest dwarf he had ever seen, as the man kept playing with his hammer as if a threat.

"Dormathin," Sheera whispered, "You can relax, this one is not going to be able to do anything." But the King was having bad feelings about the priest of Isis standing and looking at all of those in the room.

Torel's eyes kept moving to each.

"This man seems to have no mistrust, and that could be his downfall. He could be easily betrayed, or even more easily assassinated." Torel was thinking.

"My Lord JC," the man began again. "I have been following my queen for more than eight months. I seem to keep missing her, where ever she goes. I know that she will come here, next. She must! You are the only remaining one."
"You could not be trying too hard." Burlga interjected. She saw the absolute evil in the man, and the lie, he had just told.

454

JC watching the man, watching his aura's change, he thought Torel, was either very nervous at what he wanted to say, or was just plain lying. He was not able to say which, and Burlga, the best among them at reading the colors was not indicating which way the man was leaning.

JC would look at her, yet, she maintained the straight almost unreadable face of someone playing poker.

Burlga, sat watching the man from Atlantia. His aura was bouncing between betrayal, fear, lying, and murder. If she was to say anything, and she knew by the way, JC kept looking to her, that is what he wanted, but if she did say what she saw, the priest of Isis, would be dead, before they could learn anything. Especially with the way, Odyseus would react! She kept silent, sitting with as straight a face as possible. Her anger swelling inside the more she watched this man.

JC, could see the anger in Burlga and Sheera and knew something was up. Finally, he sighed, and decided a warning was needed.

"Torel, all present in this room, are family. Whatever you say to me will get to them, anyway. You might as well say it now, and just get it over with. If you continue to dance around the truth making your request, I may just have to interpret the lies of your request my way, and then you shall be forcibly expelled, if not more! Do you understand my meaning?"

JC bored into the man's eyes, and Torel found himself flinching. His mental shields were buckling under the weight of JC's probe, and he knew that the man was not even trying, yet! This man was not at all, the weak man that Purana had made him out to be.

He had been watching on several occasions, and had seen the man in the presence of kings and queens. He could intimidate as well as any of the Chosen, but often would use simple tact and diplomacy as well as any diplomat, Torel had ever seen.

But, in the end, he was obviously one of the Chosen, and was not to be easily manipulated.
"This Immortal, could very well be useful," Torel thought to himself, already changing his mind from his earlier thoughts.

"There are those that say you are willing to help any that come to you, with righteous need. What I need is to have someone of power placed on the throne of Atlantia that is not filled with so much," he hesitated as though looking for a word, "confusion, as that of our present queen." Torel finished.

"You mean insanity?" Quen interjected, to see the high priest flinch.

"Well, as you just said, the queen has been rather uptight of late. But I would never say she is that!" The High Priest of Isis, lied.

"Of course, you wouldn't. She'd have your head, wouldn't she?" Burlga smiled a very hateful smile. "And, just how do you know how she is, of late?"

"So, you want me to send one of us, to usurp that which the Holy Isis has commanded? Is that what you are asking us to do?" JC asked incredulously. "Of course, that is after we get you your continent back!"

"Certainly, the Goddess is aware of what has happened to Purana, and that is why she allowed this to happen to Atlantia. I know you to have at least three lesser women of great power, my lord. Equal to even some of your Chosen, so I've heard. I'm not asking you to abandon your own continents, just send with me, someone you can do without, someone, unnecessary to your own needs, that I can use to get mine back!

"Certainly, you can spare one of your lesser unneeded mortal priestesses, to sit the throne? Someone so minor, you would not miss them, in the battles!" The smile that Torel attempted was quickly replaced with fear, as he noticed the looks all of those, in the room, turned toward him.

JC leaned from his chair and looking into the priest's eyes, holding him with complete disdain. Torel flinched as his mind was suddenly drained of most of its psychic power. He dropped to his knees the pain was more than he could handle and when his mental shield folded in on itself, with so much ease, the man suddenly felt all his powers closed off.

Quen grabbed Meritt's arm and shook his head slightly, when he saw the man move forward. He watched Dyanea and Essmelda to see Dyanea grab the young teenager's shoulders. The Reverend Mother's expression, though, had Quen the most worried.

She looked ready to strike out, herself, as well as did Sheera and Burlga. JC, seemed to be the worst, his face did not change, but his aura changed quickly, all the seven colors of his outer taking on a dark deep semblance of hatred and violence.

Quen readied himself for whatever came next.

"My Chosen? Do you not mean, the Gods' Chosen, worm?" JC seethed. Not one to normally insult another, JC seemed to have no problems debasing the man before him.

Torel saw absolute hatred in Selene's Chosen's eyes, even if the face maintained a calm outlook. As he attempted to stop the man from draining his power, he felt his mind being probed.

"This cannot be happening." He thought, softly aloud, just before he reached for the edge of unconsciousness. Laying on the ground, Torel felt the pain suddenly stop.

"Yes, Torel, it can be happening! You underestimate me, threatening my family!" JC told him, telepathically, as the man, writhing on the ground, felt the words rather than hearing them.

Burlga and Sheera stared at JC, stunned in disbelief at what he had just done. They were not even aware something like that could be done! Not by any of them, anyway!

"My wife and my daughter, go nowhere, Torel. Certainly not to be placed in danger from a manipulative man that would have them killed just as quickly as you are planning with Purana. You dare come to me, with murderous plans, insulting those under my protection? You are a mad fool, to have come here, thus. Even more so, than you claim, Purana!" JC paused, to gain better control, having the evil energy within him, he felt the strain on his own sensibilities.

"Only, my daughter's presence, stops me from slaying you, right now, priest. I have half a mind to imprison you until Purana does come. At least she should be the one to pass judgment on you, not I.

"Perhaps, your insignificant piece of trash, I shall just hand you over to Holy Isis, herself!" So casually said, the tone of the statement had the man falling back to the floor, face down, begging forgiveness.

457

The other Chosen sat or stood watching the man, so far beneath any in this room, mortals as well, that they were hoping JC would do just what he threatened. Sheera was the first to break the silence.

"Father, perhaps Isis should be the one to look after this, man." She paused before finishing. "IT, is her priest, after all. Or was, before you just did that!" The others quickly agreed, and the man, now prone on the floor, was groveling in a manner that none of JC's followers had seen before.

JC would not let any take a knee to him, let alone act the slave, yet he said nothing while the man gesticulated and begged. Dyanea had seen enough! Not one to usually interrupt when the five Chosen were together, she could not let this continue. JC did not need this, at this time, to be threatening the evil, she could see in his aura. She had to do something, quickly!

"Reverend Father, this has gone on far enough! Are we to arrest him for treason or slay him for it? I care not which, but I will not have a man, even a despicable one as this, act the animal in my living room!" The emphasis on "my" was not lost on those present, and JC visibly relaxed and smiled. The female Chosen began to chuckle, and even Odyseus laughed.

"Me thinks, my Lord Father, that thine wife do be running this family!" Odyseus chuckled.

"Mother," Sheera toned, "forgive us for allowing this defiling of your carpets. We were only reacting to the sin against one of our companions."

"Be that as it may, daughter, either take this man to the dungeons, or to Holy Isis, or send him to the Hell, he so surely deserves. I tire of having such evil trash in my sitting room, and have much to do before tomorrow! I certainly do not need to have to clean my rugs, of this offal!" She rose, and left the room.

Stormed out was the more proper word. Followed by most of the mortals. Mythalla, the only to remain with Meritt and Hecate, of course, watching the man on the floor, no longer groveling, but still eyeing the Immortals through fear filled eyes.

"She has a point, JC." Quen coldly spoke. "He is acting the dorcal, a rabid dorcal, at that. And, you have never allowed that from even a thief! If he is a rabid dorcal, then he should be put out of our misery!"

Looking at Mythalla, JC, smiled.

"Well, I would say that I am too involved, having my loved ones so threatened, has me beside myself, and, hence, I cannot make an impartial decision. Therefore, I turn this over to the Keep's High Priestess for judgment. Mythalla, what say you? Yours is the proper word in this matter. You heard Dyanea's proclamation, which is to be the command?"

Mythalla, stood, and after a moment, turned to whisper something with Meritt, who nodded. When she turned back to the kneeling man, she spoke.

"Since the man is obviously in the robes, no matter how defiled and disheveled they may be, of the Holy Isis, it should be noted that he is of her following, not ours. Since, the Holy Selene speaks of forgiveness, we would hold him to our own teachings. Something, I cannot do, at the moment, Father. Therefore, I say turn him over to his Goddess, if you can, and let her decide the man's fate!" She eyed her mentor with a questioning expression, but held firm to her decision. JC, smiled and nodded, even as the other Immortals agreed.

"So be it. I will call on Isis after, my wedding!" JC finally said, as he wrapped the man in an air made force field, expelling the taken energy he had drained from Torel. Tightening the field around the man, so he could not move nor speak, JC ordered the guards to take him to the Temple room. With Torel removed, JC then turned to the others.

Whispering to Quen, Burlga turned to face the elder Chosen.

"JC, only the gods can do what you just did. No one can drain another of psychic energy and hold onto it like that. Certainly not with the same control you used!"

Smiling, JC calmly stated.

"If I can do it, child, certainly you can. You need only, but have faith!" He shrugged his shoulders, before changing the subject.

"Well, I guess we wait and see what happens, if Purana will come to me. She does not know that Martinith is dead, does she? I wonder what her reaction will be when she finds out, and if she will even have need of us to get her country back, with him momentarily, out of the way."

"That woust be a fine battle to see, Quen. Woust I coud have been there to see it!" Odyseus said. "He fights all the rest to a stalemate, good on thee, man!"

The Immortals all exited, their meeting decidedly at an end. Mythalla, Sheera, and Burlga all going to Dyanea's rooms to discuss the wedding tomorrow. Burlga still watching the man calmly sitting in his chair, like nothing spectacular had happened.

"I tell you Sheera, no one can do that, except a god." Burlga said as they were walking up the stairs.

"Well, that is what they say about raising the dead. And, I watched him do that, as well!"

"Chosen Ones, could he not be truly, the son of Selene? I have heard the Goddess, herself, calling him that, and he does not worship any of the gods, as all the rest of us do!" Mythalla inquired.

"He's not a god. Not, as we know it, any ways." Sheera said. The three continued to discuss as they headed into the room.

Meritt was visibly shaken by what he heard Burlga say.

"Did he really drain the psychic energy out of the dorcal?"

"Yes, he did. I don't know how, so don't ask me. Burlga says it cannot be done. I wonder what else, the man can do, that supposedly cannot be done. Raising the dead, draining energy, using it to tie the man up, who knows what else the one we call Father can do, Meritt?"

Hecate rushed Odyseus into their assigned room. Closing the door, after she dismissed the servant that had been assigned to them.

"Did you see what he did?" She rounded on the big man. Odyseus only looked at her, shaking his head that he had missed, whatever she was talking about.
"What do be thee referring? JC do be showing more restraint, not to kill the dorcal. I be wanting the man dead, he threatens thee, like that!"

"Not that, boy. I'm talking about taking the man's psychic power away. JC did something, I am not sure I could do!" Hecate shook her head. "It is easy to freely

460

give your power away, even to completely drain the power of a lesser, but to take it only partially away, against someone's will, is only done by higher powers, boy! Your precious JC is not what he seems!"

"Of course, there be right! The old man hast always held back to make us feel more special. I saw that during our training. I do believe him to be the strongest amongst us all!"

Hecate starred at her lover, before beginning to laugh, softly, the young man smiling at her.

"You never cease to amaze me with your insight, boy. You may be innocent in many ways, but wisdom is not one of your weak points. Guess, that is why I love you!"

****

Early morning, predawn, JC was pounding on metal out in the smithy. Alone, he enjoyed the time when he could contemplate on things while keeping himself physically busy.

He did not sleep much the previous night, and therefore finding himself in his favorite room of the keep, he was working on something, when the Priestess Essmelda entered in and took up a stool.

She always enjoyed watching him pound the metal especially watching a block of metal turned into a tool or weapon.

When he pulled a small hammer off the wall, and offered it to her, she jumped out of the stool she had been sitting, and eagerly took it.

Showing her what to do, he backed away and watched the girl swing for the few minutes, until her arms grew too tired. She had barely made a dent on the hot red metal, but JC still praised her for the work on her first day. She tiredly laughed at his praise.

"Father, why does it hurt so much?" When JC hesitated a moment before answering, Essmelda quickly added, "I'm sorry, Reverend Father. I should have not gotten so familiar."

"Essie, if you ever call me reverend again, I will put you over my knee. I don't care how old you are. Do you understand me?" She nodded and gave a tight smile.

"Now, to answer your question. It hurts because...." JC spent the next hour talking to the girl.

Years of experiences with teenagers as an instructor, and councilor, did little to prepare him for acting like a true father. But, the girl relaxed, and when she told him that she did not mind that he would announce her his daughter, JC gave her a hug, and the two reentered the castle, walking side by side, the man's arm around the girl's shoulder. Hers, holding his waist. The Keep's staff, only looked briefly before resuming their duties.

Late morning, a gateway was opened into the Temple of Selene in the capital city of Alyndra. The large entourage that entered, was only briefly bothered, when the clergy saw all nine members of the Council exit the gateway, as well.

****

Staring at the woman, getting dressed, Burlga sighed.

"Well, girl, this is it. He will truly be out of your hands, after today!" She thought to herself. "Dyanea, really is an attractive woman, and her whole attitude is one of absolute devotion to the man. He will be getting a truly good woman. I hope he realizes what kind of gem; he is getting!"

When the bells rang out, the women all left the room they were in, and began moving to the great hall.

Alyndria d'Dragoran had held her ground. When the retinues of the Kings and Queens all began arriving the week before, she had insisted then that the "small" gathering would be only what was proper for the wedding of the Lord Marshal to all the Continent of Selenia's armies. She had won the argument, simply by not arguing.

That the wedding was to be at the palace, was merely a commandment given to the Lord of the Badger Forest. That the Reverend Father and Reverend Mother had agreed was a testament to the strength of the friendship the Queen had garnered over the past year.

C'renan ip Breylan, High Reverend Mother of the Selenian Temple, and considered the most politically powerful elven priestess of any religion, in all the world, was to preside, and all took their places in the palace's great hall. The over five hundred people present made JC's stomach quiver, as much as the fact that Essmelda had been acting like a pouting teenager all day, causing much stress to Dyanea.

That their wedding was not what either of the clerics had originally discussed, caused enough nervous energy, but then to have his wife so sad on their wedding day, was more than he could stand.

Pacing in the room with his men at arms, Gen. Hanlon d'Boar, a man that had become as close a friend as any JC had, Odyseus and Quen, two of the Chosen, prophesied saviors of the world. The three men watched the man and openly chuckled. None had seen the father nervous about anything, before, and to see him thus, caused by something so simple as getting married, had their mirth up.

"Certainly, you are not afraid of this, are you, JC?" Quen asked, with his usual calm. "Of course, being afraid of Dyanea, is not so foolish a thing." He added with a little sarcasm and tight up turn of his lips.

"That all of us are to be in one room together, of course, I'm concerned. It would be really easy for a trap to be laid." JC stopped and looked at the men, sitting in the room. He almost missed Quen's joke, but managed a smile for the man.

"My Lord JC," Hanlon, intoned. "You can actually believe that our Queen would allow anything to interfere with this day?"

"Not by mortal means, no. But I'm talking an attack. It has been several weeks since any of the higher angels of Hell have appeared. And then there is the problem of the still missing Purana, and the whole Atlantia mess we still have not fixed. Not to mention that Martinith was only momentarily being dealt with.

"Though, I do not believe him to still be dead. Not for long, in any instant. I am a little concerned, yes, but mostly I want Dyanea to be happy, and fear that maybe we should have waited until after this whole thing with Hell is over with!

"And, there is also the curse on me, of any whom I love and love me in return!" JC finally blurted out what had been bothering him the most. "Hell, yes, I'm concerned!"

"That the mother has so captured thine heart be a testament to her own great love, my father." Odyseus started with unusually proper grammar, "and thy thoughts of trying to protect her, only be consistent with everything thou hast always done, with all of us.

"Alas, there could no longer keep her from this day, then thou could stop the world from turning." Odyseus looked to Quen then added, "There no be stopping our world's turning, can thee, Father?"

And, the men all burst out laughing. JC only looked to the big man stunned, until he too smiled.

"No, my young barbarian son, I am not that good, yet! Maybe you need to ask your little angel if she could, you want it stopped so bad!" The jokes began to fly, as the banter between the men seemed to relax the atmosphere.

After a couple hours a single knock on the door and Massy entered dressed in what looked to be ceremonial steel chest plate over highly shined chain-mail and blue painted leather bindings. Her pantaloins were of a black leather padded for battle, but polished to show an obvious new design.

Although void of any weapons, she still looked very much the soldier, and all the men complimented her as she entered.

"Your highness honors me with your attendance!" JC commented.

"What did you make this out of, JC? This plate is as light as leather and yet seems stronger than steel." she answered with a smile.

"My body guard is now protected by an armor made of the same material as your hammer, m'lady. With a couple added protections I could think of. I hope it fits you well. The chain is dwarven, of course, but your chest plate is all Terran!"

"These fits surprisingly well. One would think you have been studying my body overly much to make this, young man." she joked.

They all laughed, and the banter continued between Massy and JC.

She sighed then gave a soldier's salute to the other three men, and accepted one back from each.

464

"My friend, you are only feeling what we all feel on their wedding days. You need to stop feeling like you are cursed. You are blessed beyond measure, as are all of us that know you." Massy finally interjected. "I love Sheera very much, but am so glad to been back home to help keep you alive, again."

"We have never really talked, Princess Massy." Quen stated. I believe you to be cousins with my own King of the mountains and I find him to be very relaxing to be around. I know JC must feel the same way when you are near."

"I'm not sure about him feeling relaxed with me by his side, but I do allow him to say things he would not say around anyone else." she winked at JC and he only smiled.

At noon, the bells from the tower began to ring, and the men all dressed in royal silk with blue mantels, and wide shiny black belts, followed an escort with Massy walking beside JC at the end of the line.

Their hose was a lighter shade of cloud blue, under the white silk shirts, and all four men wore their swords at their sides in new shined sheaths that appeared to have been gem encrusted for the occasion. Massy grabbed her hammer and tucked it in an equally shined black belt as the group made quite the entrance.

The Queen had gone all out for the occasion, and it seemed to JC that his soon to be wife, had enjoyed it all too much. Pulling out the ring, he had made himself, with sorcery, from the tiny box on the table, he handed it over to Massy. The sapphire set in-between two small rubies, laid in silver and gold, shined with a life of its own.

That it was infused with some of JC's spirit, only added to the glow that it put off. The ring would grant its wearer a protection against most psychic attacks, as well as even some physical.

As the group entered the great hall, JC felt overwhelmed by the crowd, seeing all the nobles and royalty present, those that were not on the war's front leading the armies, that is, made him feel lucky, for some reason. That they would want to be here, he still could not fathom.

Not, the simple upbringing he had been raised with. King Morenz d'Maren Vist Lyeen of the Lion Kingdom, King Vyctorn d'Cloud of the northern Worg Kingdom,

465

King Bisbain d'Maren, of the Maren kingdom and uncle to Morenz, and Queen Aykallia d'Ferret of the small Fenel kingdom.

All were present with their own small retinue of retainers. As well as every one of the thirty-six high noble families of the Dragoran kingdom had sent a representative, if not the high seats themselves.

As nervous as JC was about something happening, that could ruin it, the wedding went well. When Dyanea walked in behind her escorts. Sheera leading, Burlga, and then Mythalla, all wearing gowns of expensive light cloud blue silks, they all looked radiant, and even more beautiful than normal.

When the bride walked the hall, Essmelda holding her arm wearing a matching gown as the other attendants, Dyanea dressed in her high necked deep blue silk gown, with the trailing train of white lace, her head adorned with the crown of twisted vines and lilies, JC's breath stopped.

The whole audience saw the blue aura, a nimbus glow surrounding the female and the dwarves, gnomes, and elves in the audience, reverently cheered the presence of Holy Selene, whom so obviously was blessing this union.

Dyanea's pale skin was shining, her dark violet eyes radiating, and her dark brown, almost black hair hung back, flowing down beyond her shoulders to rest at the base of her spine, under the blooming flowered crown. She looked regal as she stately appeared to be gliding down the aisle.

She looked more beautiful than ever JC could remember any woman looking, and the love that was radiating from this woman, made him forget all the worries he was having. When the ring was placed on her finger, and C'renan announced them husband and wife, the crowd cheered as they kissed.

The elven style wedding was a change from what the humans were use too, but JC had said that it most closely resembled the services of his home world, and Dyanea was more than happy to acknowledge her own elven heritage, being more than a quarter of the elven blood.

The only slight to the afternoon was at the celebration party, when JC announced that not only did, he gain the most beautiful of wives, this day, but also a most lovely daughter, some of the crowd was stunned by the news that Dyanea's apprentice was in reality her child as well.

466

The pouting girl had not seemed very happy the whole day, but with the announcement, she suddenly smiled. As the evening lengthened, the nobles and royalty retired, and the immortals left, claiming the need to get back to their own fronts in the war. They had been gone for a few days, now, and needed to see how things were doing.

Burlga turned to the couple, hugging Dyanea, and giving JC a tight hug, with a single kiss to his cheek. She had tears in her eyes, and could only hold onto the man, though he did not push her away.

"I hope you know how lucky you are, JC? She is too good for you! I suppose, this means that I shall have to refrain from anymore inappropriate comments, from now on?"

"Oh, I don't know about that, child. I did rather enjoy them!" He softly whispered. Dyanea punched his arm, and then stated, equally quiet.

"Burlga, as long as you remember who he comes home to, you are welcome to give him as hard a time, as he deserves." She winked.

And, JC could only stare at the two women, knowing something had passed between them, back at Quen's those few months ago.

When she left, JC and Dyanea, wished her luck, insuring she would visit more often, then just the meetings of the Chosen.

Quen kissed the bride, and uncharacteristically added,

"You are truly the most beautiful bride I have ever seen, My Queen. I hope someday I can find someone that makes me feel even half what you do, to the father. I welcome you into our little family. As I told you before, I welcome a mother's touch to us all!"

Taken back by the most words used, any had ever heard Quen put together, the couple watched the man. JC saw a tiny bit of emotion in the man's eyes, and smiled up at Quen.

"Your Majesty is too kind." Dyanea answered. "I trust that fate has someone you will latch onto, someday, Quen. Your hold on your emotions is admirable, but when they finally are released, the woman had better be strong enough to hold onto, the rushing out of them." Quen nodded, giving a genuine smile at the Reverend Mother.

"As you say, my most Revered of Mothers."

Meritt gave JC a wink, as he followed the emperor through their gateway.

Sheera was openly tearing up, and Dyanea held her in a tight embrace.

"Anytime, you have need of a mother, young lady, you come and see me. I know about that necklace our priest gave to you, and know you can get him anytime. But you and I are now, just as connected. I don't want you to stay away, just because you think I might not understand." The Reverend Mother whispered. Sheera shook her head, whispering back.

"Thank you, mother. I will remember, and I will come and see you. I love you both, and know that you both love me. Thank you and good luck!"

Kuan Yen bid the newly married couple a good night, adding,

"I am happy to know you, both. That one of the Chosen can marry one of non-Chosen blood, and to even have it blessed by the Gods, gives me new perspective. I still have a hard time believing in your modesty, JC d'Badger. You are more than you seem, even if you claim not to be! Have a happy and long life, together, JC and Dyanea d'Badger."

"Kuan Yen, thank you, for coming. You take care of our daughter, Sheera. We shall see you, again!" Dyanea said. JC smiled and echoed the thank you.

Sheera opened a gateway to her home, and stepped through, after hugging Massy farewell.

"Dormathin, remember, I have no problems you sending your smiths here. The new modifications without mythral will help with the army and still be able to hit most Hell Spawn. Only the Lords of Hell will require Sheera or your weapons. I will try to somehow get more to you, when I can." JC held the large dwarf King's arm.

"You are as much a friend to the dwarves as is the Golden Dragon, Lord Father. The Golden Dragon's Sword of Vengeance is always welcome in the Shang Dragons caverns."

Sheera cringed at the words but JC smiled.

"I like that. I'll remember that phrase!" JC stated.

Massy grabbed the King's arm and pulled him into a hug.

"She stubs a toe; cousin and you won't have to worry about him coming at you." she pointed over to JC. Her smile was deadly and evil. But Horotu had a big grin on his face. Dormathin just looked at Massy with wide eyes.

"Damn, she talks to you like this, JC?" the King asked.

"All the time, your Highness." both men laughed as the Katiketain party all disappeared through the gateway.

All that remained at the reception were a few elves, a couple human nobles, three of the Council, C'renan, Berga, and Mya, and about three dozen dwarves, that were not about to let Massy get out of their sight.

Alyndria and Hanlon were about to leave, when the dimensional doorway opened expelling over one hundred Hell spawn followed by two Hell Lords, Mammon and Proserpine.

Standing fifteen feet tall, the red-gold skinned monster, with scales that shined and similar scaled wings gleaming like rubies. The devil's Archangel appeared fat and bloated, but moved with the grace of something quite powerful.

A round face, large mouth with fangs and tusks sticking out, long pointed ears extending above the head and two large straight horns above the narrow long white glowing eyes.

Mammon was carrying a weapon that was three yards long, on one end a shape like a falchiard sword the other end a three-pronged tip of a battle fork.

The other lord, Proserpine, one of the most beautiful of all the female devils, and one of the most powerful. The daughter of Samael, she stood almost ten feet tall, with copper colored skin and slanted black pupiless eyes. Only the height, tiny bat-like wings, and forked tail and small horns give her diabolic origins away. She was carrying a short sword with a poisoned tip.

The human and Dwarven soldiers, all with sorcery made swords and hammers, moved into action. Badly outnumbered, all still felt confident, because they knew who was in the room with them. JC had never been defeated by the Hell Spawn, and with his wife, the most powerful sorceress in all the Selenian Temple, they were confident that they would win this day, as well.

Massy moved over to Hanlon and the Queen to aid the general in protecting the royal, and Dyanea moved to stand by Essmelda, who was already casting spells at the spawn. JC and Marcus began cutting a path through the spawn to get to the large lords in the back of the room.

Mammon and Proserpine teleported out of sight, and spinning around, JC saw Mammon appear to the side crushing the soldiers to his right about thirty yards away.

Proserpine appeared in front of Dyanea to slap the woman with the strength of a devil born lord, sending his wife backwards to fall crumbled to the floor some five yards away, against the wall.

Essmelda sent eight sparks of energy as the magical missiles flew out of her extended fingers of both hands all landing into the devil, even before JC could react. Yelping in pain, Proserpine teleported away to reappear beside her consort.

JC cast a searing tower of flames on the large devil's head, and Mammon was momentarily stopped from the attack on the humans. The pain rushing through him, as his shields were eliminated, had the devil howling. Moving towards his wife, laying sprawled on the floor, JC saw the two devil's attempting to dispel the flaming strike.

Essmelda was holding Dyanea's head in her arms as she looked up at JC through tear filled eyes.

"Forgive me mother, forgive me father. For acting like a child, this day!"

Delving into the woman, JC found her heart beating strong, and no real injuries, only unconscious due to a psychic mind crush, that her ring, did indeed protect her from the worst.

He stood to see his flames finally dispelled and cast another to see it only hold for a few seconds, before it was dissipated by Proserpine. JC then dispelled Proserpine's shields, and sent a tower of flames on both devils, once again.

"She'll be all right, chi... daughter." JC said as calmly as he could make. "Right now, though I need you! I need you to watch over your mother and protect her!" The girl nodded, standing up as she pulled her long dagger that JC had made for her a couple months earlier.

The Immortal began to make his way through the battling hoard towards Mammon and Proserpine, yelling to get their attention. The devils that came near him, in his controlled anger, died, to sorcery or his katana.

The air became thick, as a cloud of poison moved through the room. Devils and humans alike began to succumb to the gaseous slumber caused by the sleep poison. Even the elves, immune to most sleep spells, seemed affected.

The dwarves, though slowed, still seemed to be remaining awake, as Essmelda, fighting off the affects created a small tornado of air above her mother, which seemed to clear the air in that area. JC concentrated to dispel the cloud, but failed to be able to overcome the power of Proserpine's spell. He was, though, able to fight off the effects of it on him.

As Essmelda forced her tornado to begin to move through the room, JC gained his equilibrium, and only his instinct enabled him to avoid being sliced through by Mammon's attack.

Teleporting to the Immortal, Mammon swung down with the sword side of his staff, and just giving way, JC sliced through the devil's leg with his swinging katana. With a spinning sweep, the Chosen's blade cut through the other leg, and as the devil fell, a third two handed sweep sank deep into the chest, cutting a path across the massive front, twenty inches deep, through ribs, flesh and finally cutting the black heart of the devil into two.

The blade flashed free as JC stood from his spin. There was no scream as the death was instant, but when JC turned, he was knocked down by a slap to the jaw, delivered by the devil Proserpine.

Entering into the palace, Purana was asked to leave her soldiers in the waiting room. When she was led to the Grand Hall of the Dragoran Palace, she heard a battle going on. Her priests and priestesses that followed, become fearful.

Too many times, they had walked right into a battle with Hell Spawn. And, here, where she was welcomed, and told she was expected, she was about to go into another. At least now, she would get to see the power of the man that everyone had said he possessed. Purana pulled the doors open.

He gathered his will to strike out, but when he looked into Proserpine's eyes, he let his spell disassemble and suddenly felt the protective shields begin to yield to her superior psychic strength.

The pain began to grow in his mind, but he could not bring himself to strike out at the female. Instead, he hardened his shield.

"You are so strong, human, yet so weak." She laughed. "You had me caught off guard with that spell, and would not cast it. You are not a man, human, you are a mouse. You will die, knowing a woman killed you because you would not fight back!"

The long dagger point that suddenly poked through the devil's chest between her breasts, brought the female devil's speech up short. The tiny voice that began a whisper ended with as much force as the dagger did.

"My father may have trouble, devil, only because he is a caring real man. But he needs not kill women when his daughter can easily do it!"

Essmelda began to apply a psychic crush to the devil's mind, as she twisted the foot and a half long blade empowered by sorcery, back and forth, until it sliced into the devil's own heart.

Proserpine screamed as her own protective shields dropped and the force of Essmelda's will and determination caused the Greater Angel's head to finally explode, internally as well as externally.

Essmelda dropped to the floor as the headless body she had been holding on to, fell. The long dagger still poked through in the back, dropped with it. Never having been blooded, the first time she had caused a death by close contact, the girl dropped into her father's arms, sobbing.

Tears fell on the man's face as well, as he realized he was not able to keep his daughter from feeling the sense of wrongness at taking a life, no matter how deserved. JC began to cast lightning, while still holding his daughter, and watched as it branched out to encompass all the remaining devils.

The room was filling with the odor of brimstone, as a flash of lightning from the great hall's door, brought death to all the remaining devils. Purana sent out several more spells as she walked down the stairs towards JC still holding the tiny girl to him.

"Thank you, Purana, and nice to see you. Nice that you finally arrive for my wedding day. I truly had hoped you would have come earlier." JC calmly stated, with no hint of sarcasm to his voice. He lifted the girl and moved to carry her over to where Dyanea still laid on the floor.

Hanlon helping his queen to her feet, as most of those that were placed in a slumber by Proserpine's gaseous cloud, began to stir.

Purana looking at the disarray followed in silence to where the man laid the girl to hold onto her mother.

"Thank you for the help in finishing off the spawn." He said as he turned to the woman. "I was wondering when you would be coming here, since all the others had received a visit from you. What took you so long? You missed the wedding."

"Are you never wrong? You always act so self-assured, old man." The sorceress almost pleaded. "Gods, but why is it that I feel so small when I'm around you?"
JC looked at the woman, and frowned.

"Small? You have possibly the most potential, among us. Yet, you act that of a younger sister who has all the strength, yet lacks the wisdom on its use.

"You feel the way you do because you fight against what we were brought here to do. You fight against what you are!

"We are siblings in this war, yet you refuse to accept that you may need help as much as the rest of us do!" As the tears came to her eyes, JC calmed himself before continuing.

473

"Purana, you ask if I am ever wrong, well look around. I was wrong today. My wife lays unconscious, who knows how long before she recovers from the psychic attack on her. Because I failed to protect her!

I almost died, if not for my daughter, because I was wrong to feel so against harming a woman. Am I wrong? Of course, I'm not always right. I was wrong to be allowed a false sense of security on what should have been my happiest of days and look what it has cost me.

How many of my friends are dead, and how many injured? Because, I was wrong! And, child, I was wrong because I didn't make you understand me, like I should have! I allowed you to go your own way, when I should have reigned you in, somehow! Of course, I am wrong, child!"

Purana, regained her composure, as the Queen and her general walked forward with Massy and Marcus. C'renan, Berga, and Mya had already moved to stand over Dyanea and Essmelda. Worried over the raised voice of JC's they got within a few feet before the Immortal realized he had been nearly shouting.

"Purana, I am sorry. I did not mean to yell at you. I'm just frustrated." Looking at his queen, he nodded a short bow of his head and placing a hand on Purana's shoulder gently turned her towards the group.

"Purana, may I introduce you to Her Majesty the Queen Alyndria d'Dragoran, ruler of Dragoran Kingdom and her General, Hanlon d'Boar, my war leader over all the armies of the North.

"Your majesty, this is The Empress Purana bin Gage, High Priestess to Holy Isis, and the ruler of all of Atlantia, Chosen sorceress and my sister in the battle against the evils of Kutulu Lucifer."

With the introductions made, JC lifted Dyanea into his arms, and with Essmelda holding tightly onto him, he begged leave, saying only;

"Purana we shall talk in the morning, if you do not mind. I am tired, and need to get my wife and daughter to bed. Perhaps, rooms are available here at the palace for you to stay. If not, I know I can find you some at the Queen's Inn."

"Of course, we have room, JC." Alyndria exclaimed and they all exited the hall.

Taken aback by JC's outburst, Purana felt none of the effects on her mind, like she thought she remembered. But the pull was still there. She still felt small while standing over the man. A full hand taller than he, and yet, she still felt as though she was just a child, as he had called her.

Somehow, after all these months of running around from continent to continent, she finally understood why the others had told her to come here. JC, was indeed, changed. Lord JC d'Badger had not been simply given a title, he had earned it.

CHAPTER 19
Coming to an understanding

Sheera sighed as she walked towards her rooms in the Shang Dragon mountains. She turned to dismiss all those that followed her and smiled when she saw Leaf come walking towards the group.

"I trust the wedding went off without a hitch." The gnome asked as the party dispersed.

"Why didn't you go? I would have like to introduce you to my brother. Or father, or whatever he is supposed to be to me." she chuckled.

"I had things I had to get done. It was a little unfortunate that I could not go." Leaf attempted to skirt the truth.

"Lephorisal Prignome, you will either come clean right now or I will call on one of the higher powers. Maybe even say a little prayer to G..."

"Don't say that name!" Leaf interrupted.

"Why, Leaf? If I get her attention, you will be found out?" Sheera began to push on his shields and was met with an equal force to that of Quen's or Martinith's.

"Please, Sheera, you don't really want to do this, do you?"

Sheera shrugged.

"I do not want to be forced into this, Leaf. I don't want to hurt you like what we did to Hecartae Dryad. I never want to do anything like that again. Especially to a friend!"

Leaf was strong, but he could feel her mind and knew that the only way he would be able to stop her was to harm her. He contemplated his next move and stared.

"Sheryl Ling Mattingly of Seoul province, South Vietnam, born on Christmas evening, December twenty fifth, in the year of Terra, nineteen hundred sixty-four. I have actually watched you since your days in Israel, some two thousand years ago.

476

Please don't do this! You already know, or at least suspected, why do you need to hear me say it?"

"Because, you are the only one that it could be and James Carl advised me that one of those close to me is a sibling to Hecate. That is all he would say, he didn't even tell me who his two are. But he found the two that are following him and now claims to know all of our shadows. I want to hear you tell me in your own words why you have been lying to me this past year?"

"I have been an angel on your shoulder for most of your two thousand years of life, young lady. I have seen or been a part of each of your thirty previous lives, as well as, been with you for most of this life. In various forms." the gnome sighed. "Damn, you are strong, Sheera. I do believe you could have eventually defeated my shields."

"Just like my twin did to one of his angels! He got all the way into her mind, before she finally admitted it. Of course, reading a mind is not a nice thing to do, and I did not want to do that."

"What now, Sheera? Am I to be sent away?" he almost looked down, no longer holding eye contact.

"You are my best friend, Leaf. Why would I send you away? I want you to be around more often. Now, I know I can almost coerce you." she winked and grinned.

"Yes, you can do that, if you are inclined. But, understand, you go throwing a certain name about and if she looks this way and sees me, I shudder to think what will happen, then."

They walked into her rooms, and when only Kwon Yen remained, she made Leaf show his true form.

"Show me the two-meter-tall gnome of he that was the father of all your race. I want to see what Garl Glittergold saw when you made him."

Shimmering into a new form, Lephorisal stood and his head almost touched the ceiling. After Sheera thanked him, he returned to the form of Leaf and smiled.

"This is so nice, my friend. I can't wait to really exploit you, now." Sheera smiled as she changed into her night clothes and crawled into bed.

****

The Queen of Dragoran Kingdom and the Empress of Atlantia, spoke long into the night. Purana learned much about the man; she would be talking with in the morning. And, she learned much about the Reverend Mother that he had married.

"You spent a year with him, and yet, do not understand him? I find that incredible, to say the least, Purana. I find the man actually quite charming, in his own way. A little arrogant at times, so sure of himself, when he needs to lean on others, more. But his stubbornness is all a part of the charm, and I think, his wife will finally be able to break that out of him. Hopefully!" Alyndria spoke.

"The JC I knew, was not so full of himself, as he is now. Always, stubborn, yes, but he always deferred to allowing us to make our own mistakes and accomplishments. Everyone seems to think he has all the answers, of a sudden."

"He is the High Priest of Holy Selene, Purana. Here, any ways, most people think he is a demigod, or near to it, in the least. Especially they will, after tonight!"

"What happened in there? I saw Proserpine and several devils, but the stink of brimstone, before I arrived, tells me there were far more. A whole lot more!"

"Over one hundred of the smaller ones, you saw, and two devil lords, Proserpine and Mammon, I believe is the name I heard." She spoke as if it were a natural thing, and added the presence of Selene at the wedding earlier. Purana listened, and when asked about any other things that JC had allegedly done, the Queen just laughed.

"The day I met him, he exorcised a demon lord out of me. Cerodagon had my body, and Graz'zt was also in my town. In less than the time of two days, my city was cleaned, two demon lords of great power were slain, and I even had been healed. He also had arrested the culprit for bringing the demons amongst us, and made sure she could not get at anyone else. Also, Empress, he did this with only the aid of a small young lady, not even a full priestess, at the time.

"I can assure you, Chosen of Isis, that any stories you have heard, are probably not exaggerations, but may even be less than reality. JC is constantly trying to defuse the hero accusations, and a lot of the stories I have heard, are somewhat less than what I know to be the truth."

478

"This is not the man, I knew, Your Majesty. Not, at all!"

When Purana was shown to her rooms, she was very much deep in thought. Apshai and Anu watched her, with a little bit of wonderment to their expressions. More relaxed, not as filled with anger, queenlier!

"Your talk with Queen Alyndria, went well, Your Majesty?" The High Priest asked.

"Yes, it did, Anu. Did you know that somehow, everyone thinks these stories about some of his accomplishments, are real? The Queen even swears they may be less than the truth!"

"According to one priestess, I spoke with, he has managed to raise the dead, without the use of necromancy." Apshai announced!

"That has to be an exaggeration. He heals differently, is all. Can heal those that normal healing would kill. Probably just brought someone back from near death, is all." Purana absently commented.

"This was not the word of a lesser priestess, your Majesty. One of the High Priestesses told me this. She seemed quite shaken by the act. Even the gods do not do this so lightly!" He insisted.

"As I said, Apshai, I do not believe that one. But we shall have a talk with the man, tomorrow. I am going to retire, gentlemen. Good night!" They both looked at each other stunned for a moment, as the Empress walked to the door of her room.

When they finally rose and bowed, they both shook their heads, not understanding the changes in her, but happy to see the almost smile on her face.

****

Laying Dyanea into his bed, JC only nodded when Essmelda crawled in beside her. Covering the two with a blanket, he took one of the chairs and sat, watching as they slept.

Sometime the next morning, he felt a hand touch his brow and started awake, to see Dyanea standing over him. The morning light shined through the windows, as JC rose to embrace her. Holding her hand over his mouth, she led him from the room, closing the door quietly behind, after taking one last look at the sleeping girl in their bed.

"Why is she in our bed, instead of you, husband?" She asked once out in the sitting room. JC's noncommittal shrug was his only answer given.

"What happened after I was subdued, that she felt the need to stop our first night together, and you to allow it?"

JC briefly explained the end of the battle, and the arrival of Purana. His own explanation on what his inabilities have caused the girl to endure, left a sour taste in his mouth. Dyanea only nodded, and embraced him once again. They kissed and then got dressed to go and meet the day.

****

"So, this is the woman that taught our JC how to love again?" Purana purred after meeting Dyanea. "Lady, you have no idea how many are envious of you! Or do you?"

"I have met the others, yes, your highness. I am just glad that they are not as beautiful as you, or maybe he would not have been available for me. I was told how powerful you are, but no one ever mentioned your other qualities!" She gave JC a look, but saw him only staring at his juice glass.

As the talks moved into the reason for her visit, JC told Purana about the death of Martinith. He also told her about a certain prisoner that was to be turned over to the Isis temple. She was very surprised by the discussion, and most amused by Dyanea's reaction to the whole part of Torel prostrating himself to the man.

They spent the rest of the week, studying the prophesies and then headed down to Bornesta, where the Queen of Atlantia could begin to plan her reclamation of her country. When Purana moved to leave, she had regained all the arrogance as before, but showed no more animosity towards JC, and even gave Dyanea a hug, and well wishes.

"Well, that was a most fruitful visit." JC said as the sorceress' gateway closed. Shaking his head, he followed his wife back into the main of the keep, where a visitor was awaiting.

EPILOGUE

JC was just finishing the one-yard-long piece of wood he had been working on. He sanded the pole he had created out of the magically imbued remnant from the Tree of Life.

The most holy tree to the elves, it was a gift given to JC from the King.

A gift to JC for the many weapons given to the elves made by the man himself and his dwarven smiths. JC knew immediately all those weeks ago what he would do with it and now the weapon was finally going to be complete.

The pole was to be a handle for a hammer that JC had been making to give as a gift for the coronation of Massy Thistle Thorn as she ascended the throne of the Dwarves. She had fought the assention for many years, but now was being forced into accepting it.

JC needed to hurry if he was going to complete the hammer in time!
Placing the five stones, highly polished with sorcery, they radiated magic as much as did the wood. Each stone had a protection spell cast upon them. The red ruby, protection from fire; Yellow Topaz, protection from lightning; the black lava was imbued with a protection from all earth-based attacks; the green emerald, granted regeneration to the holder of this weapon; and the blue sapphire granted a protection from magic.

When JC placed each in the small notches, he had made for them on the handle, they seemed to embed themselves magically as JC gave a part of himself energizing the rod. The handle itself would make for a formidable weapon, let alone when he placed the hammer head to it.

When he placed the mythral, silver, and cold iron mix now named the "God's Stone", onto the handle, the hammer began to glow.

JC looked at the weapon smiling as he continued to pour his sorcery into the mix and suddenly when the glow subsided, a piece of art was being held in his hand that he was sure would be more than a damaging weapon.

The dwarven smiths looked on admiringly and when JC swung down with a force full strike upon the anvil, it was the anvil itself that shattered.

"This will be a great weapon, Lord JC." Gregorin commented. "You trying to become a proper man?" he insulted with a dry humor that JC chuckled to.

"This is a gift for your queen, Gregorin. This is art and no man should have need of it. It can only be properly swung by a real woman." he winked at the smith who only nodded.

"Massy Thistle Thorn will like this very much. You continue to honor us, the people of the mountains."

"Gregorin, I often feel your people honor me more than my own do."

"We don't allow you to become too full of yourself, is all, High Priest JC. That you are the Sword of Vengeance as well as the Chosen of Gia, means little if your head was to become too big to get through your shirt." he chuckled.

Handing the weapon to the smith, JC rinsed himself off as the smith was etching dwarven runes into the top of the handle, next to the head. To those that could read the dwarven it said simply, "Companion".

The gateway opened before the caves in the northwestern summit of the Dragon Back Mountains and the party of Gregorin and the two dozen dwarven smiths was followed by several humans and a single half elf.

The guards that exited the caves were at the ready until they recognized the head smith, and the man and woman trailing the gateway just before it closed.

They crossed their hammers to their chests in a salute to the Chosen and bowed to Dyanea as the leader spoke up.

"Massy awaits your arrival with great anticipation, Chosen One. Lady Sheera and her company is already here. She will also be happy to see so many of her friends coming for the coronation as well."

"We would not miss this, Captain. I would not miss this even if I were in the middle of battle!" JC replied.

The ceremony was easy and quick, the dwarves not being much on elaborate ceremonies, but the celebration was boisterous and filled with many jokes and insults.

When JC finally stepped forward to the new queen, they hugged and he dropped to a knee, causing all in the room to suddenly go silent.

"Massy Thistle Thorn, greatest of priestesses to the Goddess Gia, Sworn Protector and friend to me, a simple human with a small piece of business to take care of, I present myself to you with an equal promise you once gave me.

"You, Massy, are friend of the Chosen. First friend under Gia's arm as I had entered into the war of the gods, this I swear to you what you once swore to me.

"I will always be there to protect your back, never shall I waver, this do I swear in Gia's name and that of my mother, Holy Selene!"

When he finished, JC took the wrapped package that he had been holding all afternoon and held it out to Massy who took it as the man rose and took a step back.

The power of the hammer could be felt even through the cloth wrapping and when she unwrapped it, she smiled as a glow took hold of her, briefly as the hammer mated itself to her, and suddenly all knew that no other person would be able to swing the weapon.

When the rainbow aura subsided, she swung the hammer a couple of times before bringing it down upon a large boulder that had been being used as a chair. The rumble in the earth as the chair crumbled, becoming dust to the hammer's might.

"This is a..." a single tear fell down her cheek. "Ahem, this is a great gift, my friend. Is it named, yet?"

"I call it companion, but it has yet to be named by its owner. When a small bit of your blood is absorbed into the handle, you will be able to call the hammer to you, no matter where you are in the world." JC only shook his head and exclaimed, "You should be the one to name it, at that point."

"I shall call you Massy's Arm. What can she do, m'lord?" Massy asked.

JC chuckled before responding.

"In my world, there is a legend about a hammer that was made for the son of one of the human gods by the clan of dwarves. So great a weapon that the son together using the hammer became known as a thunder god. I don't remember the name of the hammer, but the God of Thunder, known as Thor Odinson, was a man of great strength and could slay the giants with one swing of his hammer.

"He owed the dwarves much, so the legends say and they became friends. I am not nearly as good as the dwarves, as you all know, but I attempted to make you a hammer that would be above all others.

"The wood is from the elves Tree of Life; it will never break. The hammer is as you can imagine made from the God's Stone, and can smash rock with as much ease as it can bone. It of course can hit anything, even me, if you should choose it." he laughed and all the dwarves chuckled.

"I may ask to borrow it on occasion, Dyanea joked causing all in the great cavern to openly laugh. Massy responded with a promise to hold the Chosen down while Dyanea used it, should the time come.

"It will also, return to you just by concentrating should you throw it or set it down, once you mix your blessed blood with the handle."

She pulled out her knife, a previous gift from JC, one made by Selene, and cut across her palm. Gripping the handle, she felt the Tree of life soak in mixing with her blood as her palm quickly closed, the regeneration starting immediately.

Massy without warning, suddenly threw the hammer high into the air as it swung wide throughout the hall, a trail of blue fire seemingly trailing behind it as it turned like a boomerang, to fly safely back to her hand. The crowd watched in amazement, as it flew and the wide-eyed dwarf queen was all smiles.

"A blue flame, JC? Are you trying to turn me to your lessor Goddess' fold away from the Mother Gia?" she insulted with a joke.

"One can only try, my friend." he laughed.

She hugged the man and pulled him down to her giving him a kiss.

"I accept your gift, my friend, and your oath. It is with love that I renew mine, so that all would know that The High Priestess Massy and the High Priest JC be as one wall against the darkness of Hell. We are the lantern that lights the way into the future."

As they once again embraced, all in the room cheered and the party really did become a dwarven celebration.

JC assured the protections and could see the power that now radiated from the Queen, as Massy was becoming one with the hammer, acting the child with a new toy.

The celebration lasted long and by the time that JC was taking his lady home, Massy was being called The Thunder Queen.

"I will be there in a couple days, my friend. I need to set up a regent, and ensure that everything is set before I join you. The problem is the most logical regent is my husband's brother but you have him tied up making weapons." When JC's eyes raised, Massy laughed.

"Gregorin Thistle is the Old King's baby brother." Gregorin rolled his eyes mumbling something about the thunder coming from the backside of the queen instead of her mouth and all those that heard that were half in drink fell to laughing at the joke.

"Take your time, Massy. You are in my heart and should you need, just touch yours and I will come." JC responded, placing his hand over his heart

She smiled and tapped her heart before turning back to the party.

Printed in the USA
CPSIA information can be obtained
at www.ICGtesting.com
LVHW091546110624
782912LV00001B/12

9 798869 293046